PRAISE FOR JOSH LANYON

"Josh Lanyon doesn't just top the A-List – he IS the A-List when it comes to blending wit, suspense and romance."

Lily for Romance Junkies Reviews - A Blue Ribbon Rating

"Josh Lanyon has penned another wonderful novel that completely engrossed me in from the first page. Fabulous world building coupled with deep, rich history and a great lead character had me glued to my eReader for much of our very rainy Easter Sunday. Lanyon is such a skilled writer, so talented that I wonder if there isn't a genre where he wouldn't excel."

Lynn for Reviews by Jessewave

"Nuances of gestures and dialogue are two things Josh Lanyon does as well or better than anyone. He builds the characters in a way that keeps us from being sure what direction he'll take us. If his books had a soundtrack behind it we'd be sitting waiting for that noise that indicates bad things are coming. There's great eroticism blended well into any Josh Lanyon book. This one is no exception as dreams lead into some powerful and intense sexual activity. Lanyon remains at the top of my list for great storytelling with a thrilling finale."

The Romance Studio

"Josh Lanyon is one of those authors who, regardless of the story, always tells a captivating tale that draws the reader right in."

Kathy K., Reviews at Ebook Addict

Sunshine or in Shadow Collected Short Stories: Volume I

Copyright (c) 2013 by Josh Lanyon

Cover design by Kevin Burton Smith
Cover photos by Fotosearch

ISBN: 978-1-937909-47-5
Printed in the United States of America

Just Joshin'
53 Rancho Vista Blvd.
Suite 116
Palmdale, CA 93551
www.joshlanyon.com

This is a work of fiction. Any resemblance to persons living or dead is entirely coincidental.

IN SUNSHINE OR IN SHADOW
COLLECTED SHORT STORIES: VOLUME I

JOSH LANYON

TABLE OF CONTENTS
SHORT STORIES 2007 – 2013

The sparrow, flying in at one door and immediately out at another, whilst he is within, is safe from the wintry tempest, but after a short space of fair weather, he immediately vanishes out of your sight, passing from winter to winter again. So this life of man appears for a little while, but of what is to follow or what went before we know nothing at all.

– St. Bede

PERFECT DAY

*This story simmered in the back of my mind for several years. I got
the idea from an essay by Elizabeth Choi. I think the theme of commitment,
of learning to let go and depend on another person, is dear to my heart —
orat least recurs a lot in my work — because I, too, was kind of
a slow learner in that department.*

"About last night," I began awkwardly.

Graham handed me the red plastic coffee cup. Steam rose from the fragrant liquid.

"Yeah," he said. No particular inflection, but I knew my worst fears were confirmed.

I sipped the hot coffee and stared past the blue tent at the meadow's edge, at the fields of goldenrod that in the early morning mist looked like a distant golden lake.

Stupid. Stupid. Stupid.

From the beginning — practically the beginning — from the third night I'd spent in the little cloistered house on Startouch Drive, Graham had said he didn't want anything serious. Not looking for anything serious. Not looking for a relationship.

It didn't get much clearer than that.

The problem was Graham was everything I wanted.

He was thirty-seven and a geologist. All right, geology wasn't part of the dream-man job description. In fact, I'd always pictured my dream man more *GQ* than *Field and Stream*, but Graham with his slow grin and gray eyes — gray, not blue or green — and that little touch of silver in the dark hair at his temples, and his wide shoulders and narrow hips, and his confident straight stance like an old-time explorer surveying the vistas — with his easy laugh and his maps and compasses and soft flannel shirts.

Short story long, I guess. I fell in love.

Despite my best intentions. Despite his warnings.

I fell in love.

And last night in the tumble of sleeping bags and inflatable mattresses, I'd been stupid enough to say so.

Not once. Which would have been bad enough. Not whispered against his broad shoulder where we both could have pretended I hadn't said it... could have preserved the fiction a little longer.

No, carried away on the tide of rich, rolling orgasm I'd clutched him and cried out, "I love you. I love you. I love you *so much*, Graham."

No doubt scaring park animals and Graham alike. Not to mention myself.

Because I'd known even before the words finished spilling out, even before Graham stilled, that I'd done it. Wrecked everything.

He'd already been dropping little clues that things were maybe getting too intense. Retreating. Slowly. Almost imperceptibly. Sand whispering through my fingers and the harder I held, the faster it slipped away.

I knew it. *Knew* I had to pull back, play it cool, give him space. Yet the words had come pouring out like scalding water hitting ice, and I could practically hear the cracks.

Graham had covered my mouth with his own, and there it had ended.

Literally.

Because Graham still loved Jase.

And probably always would.

"There's breakfast," Graham said now, nodding at the campfire.

I nodded although the knots in my stomach left no room for food. There had been breakfast the first time too. I think that was the moment I fell in love.

We'd met at the Kendall Planetarium during an OMSI After Dark event. It was only the third time I'd made it to one of the Eugene Gay Men's Social Network outings. I'd been tired after a long day of crowd control, and I almost hadn't bothered going.

Beer in hand, Graham had been wandering the hands-on science exhibits. He looked handsome, uncomfortable, and, in jeans and tweed blazer, a little older than most of the "adult only" crowd. The theme that night was sex. When I'd finally cornered him, he was studying a display of condom lighting art. His expression seemed somber under the circumstances.

"Hi, I'm Wyatt," I'd introduced myself. And then, jokingly, "Do you come here often?"

His eyes, cool as starlight, had lit. He smiled. No, it was a grin. He knew I was making fun of myself and the situation, and he found it funny too. My heart skipped a beat. Yep, like in the romance novels.

"I used to," he said.

We made small talk, all the while exchanging those quick glances, locking gazes, looking away.

After the museum we'd gone out for coffee and dessert. "What do you do?" he'd asked over the cheesecake.

"I teach."

His eyes flickered. "What do you teach?"

"High school. Science. Health. Health and science."

He nodded.

I said, "I teach sex education to ninth graders."

He met my gaze and started to laugh. I laughed too.

We'd ended up at Graham's.

He also lived in Eugene and maybe that wasn't fate, but it sure was convenient. The house was in the hills, shrouded by trees. Inside it was very quiet. Very neat. The floors were wood, the appliances stainless steel, the counters granite. But the main feature was natural light. Windows. The back of the house was a wall of windows and there were skylights in several rooms. The stars glittered and glowed all around us when we walked in that night.

Better not to let myself think about that night now. The tentativeness, the uncertainty, the awkwardness that had resolved unexpectedly in easy smiles and hugs. We were both cold sober so I'm not sure how we managed so quickly to shed that easiness, that friendliness for something hot and hungry and close to frenzied.

We'd done it slammed up against the wall of windows that looked out over the moonlit treetops and the lights in the valley below. Naked, noisy, nasty.

Afterward it was refreshingly easy and friendly again, and Graham had invited me to spend the night. Sometimes you just know it's right. Sometimes everything clicks. That's how it was for me. I'd imagined it was the same for Graham. How was I to know?

In the morning we'd done it again — leisurely, affectionately — there in his Egyptian cotton sheets, bathed in the dappled sunlight from the skylight. Afterward we'd showered together and he'd put together breakfast for two out of the odds and ends in his fridge: a truffle, three eggs, a cold boiled potato, a piece of smoked chicken. A meal that would do the soldier in "Stone Soup" — or a survivalist — proud.

Today's breakfast was instant oatmeal mixed with peaches, and the sight of it made my stomach do an unpleasant flip.

"Pass."

"You better eat," Graham told me. "It's a long way back to the car park."

"Are we heading back?"

"Yeah." He nodded at the forbidding wall of black clouds over the distant mountains. "That's coming straight at us."

"Oh. Right." I knew that regardless of the weather we'd have been heading back this morning. I helped myself to breakfast. "Listen, Graham — "

He wasn't looking at me as he said, "Nah. Heat of the moment. I know."

He was giving me an out. Giving me a chance to save my pride and maybe even salvage something of our friendship.

I almost took it. I *wanted* to take it. But I didn't only want to be friends with Graham, and somehow to pretend that I hadn't meant it, that I didn't love him, seemed wrong. I couldn't see lying about it. Anyway, he knew the truth. And we both knew that I knew he knew. So in the end it wouldn't change anything. It would only prove I hadn't had the guts to say it in the cold light of day.

They're not easy words to say at any time. Not when you know you're on your own.

So I put down my coffee cup and said, "No. I meant it. I mean, true, I wouldn't have said it if it hadn't been the heat of the moment." I smiled. Graham did not smile back. "I know you don't feel the same way. But I love you."

He looked ... I'm not sure how to describe it. Stricken? Guilty maybe. Definitely unhappy.

"Wyatt."

That was it. My name. It had a regretful finality to it. *Stop.* That's what he meant. *Stop, Wyatt. Don't say it. It's no use. There's no point.*

"It doesn't seem like something to fake."

"No." Graham stared down at his own cup. He said finally, slowly, "Thank you. I-I'm ... I like being with you, Wyatt. I care about you. But I don't feel like you do. It's too soon for me."

"Three years." Three years since Jase had died. I wasn't arguing, just ... three years.

Graham's gray gaze held mine sternly. "I don't know if *ten* years will be enough. I still miss him. Every day. Every single goddamned day I want him back."

You can't start a stopwatch on grief. Or love for that matter.

"It's okay. I know. You told me how it was."

The tension left his shoulders, which had braced as though for battle. He hadn't expected my acceptance, I guess. Had been prepared for me to try and make my case. Well, cue Sam Harris. *I can't make you love me if you won't.* I never had someone to love or love me like Graham had Jase, but that much I did know. You can't debate someone into loving you.

He said with excruciating and uncharacteristic awkwardness, "If it was — if I was — it would be someone like you."

Someone like me. *But not me.* Obviously not me.

Funny that of all the things he said that morning, that hurt the most.

"Sure." I gave him a smile that was probably at best polite. I swallowed the final dregs of my coffee.

What was there to say after that?

We ate our breakfast and packed up our camp.

I liked camping. I didn't love it. I'd wanted to go camping that weekend because Graham was going, and I wanted to be with him. I preferred museums and art galleries and brunch at Metropol Bakery. Graham liked those things too, though not as much as he enjoyed hiking and camping and fishing. We traded off. One weekend doing what he liked. Then the next weekend it would be my turn to choose.

It had seemed to work for a time.

I could almost pinpoint the moment things had changed between us. We'd been seeing each other pretty regularly. Casually but regularly. And one Saturday afternoon we were barbecuing salmon steaks on his deck and I'd said, "Hey, did you want to go to Mount Pisgah Arboretum next Sunday? It's the wildflower and music festival."

Innocuous, you'd think, but the implication was that we'd be seeing each other the following weekend. Not unreasonable because we had been seeing each other most weekends, but I could see it brought Graham up short. Broke whatever pleasant spell had settled over him over the past two months.

He'd said politely, vaguely, "Maybe. I might have to work. I'll give you a call."

It turned out he did have to work that weekend. I'd said that was too bad and I'd go with friends. And I did. And as much as I'd missed Graham, I'd had the brains not to call him, to leave the next move to him. To my relief he had called later in the week and we'd made plans for the following weekend.

But it had never quite been the same. He'd begun pushing me back. In little ways. He was never unkind, but he didn't call as often, didn't have as much time to see me. He was busy. We both were. But I knew. The easy instant harmony we'd known from the first had faded. We still got along, still had plenty to talk about when we did get together, but it felt a little off. I could feel myself trying too hard to recapture what we'd had, and the harder I tried, the further Graham withdrew.

And I had never really understood why. I knew it had to do with my assumption that we were going to be seeing more of each other. But how was that a wrong assumption?

No, maybe it was more to do with making plans. Making plans together.

I didn't know. I would never know; that was the truth.

It had been good for those two months. That was what made it hard. It had felt right. I had been so sure that Graham was going to be the guy I fell in love with. Well, he was. The part I got wrong was thinking Graham was going to feel the same way.

A honey bee zoomed in for a closer look. I waved it away.

"You know about colony collapse disorder?" Graham said.

Preoccupied with my own troubles, it took me a second to figure out what he meant. It took me a second to figure out that we were making conversation. So this is what it had come down to? Trading *SciAm* articles?

"You're talking about the fact that billions of honey bees are disappearing from hives all across the country?"

"Country? Try globe. And they're not disappearing. They're dying. There are almost no feral honey bees left. A third of the world's bee population is already gone."

Yeah. Old news in my corner of the science department. Someone should have told the bees in the meadow we were hiking through. I waved away another dive bomber. "I thought one theory was parasites?"

"It's probably a combination of factors, but the pesticides are a major contributor to weakening the worker bees."

"Right. That makes sense."

Now that I had time to think I realized I probably wouldn't see Graham again. Not after the night before. This would be the final straw. This would confirm what he'd already been feeling: that I was getting too attached, too involved. He'd run a mile.

Graham must have been thinking along the same lines. He said, "Am I going to see you again?"

That he put it in the form of a question surprised me, though I tried not to let my surprise show. "Yes. Why not?" I knew why not, but it seemed a good idea to try for casualness.

"I thought you might figure you were wasting your time."

"I like being with you too. So how is that a waste of time?" Pride almost made me add something like *I wasn't in a hurry to settle down either*, but the fact was I'd have moved in with Graham in a heartbeat if he'd asked. Or asked him to live with me, if I'd thought there was a chance in hell of prying him out of his glass foxhole. I had been open about the fact that I was interested in something a little more meaningful, even settled.

I said instead, "If *I'm* not uncomfortable — "

He said immediately, "I'm not uncomfortable."

I thought we both sounded defiant.

"Okay. Great." I tried to picture us getting together again after we said our good-byes today. I couldn't see it — as much as I wanted to.

Did it look like I was clinging to the wreckage? That I couldn't let go? But that was true, right? I was feeling like any part of Graham was better than none. Where was my pride? Or was it unthinking pride that had answered for me? *Hey, no problem! You want to be pals. I can switch it on and off.*

Who was I kidding? Wasn't I making it worse for myself trying to hang on?

Of course.

A clean break would be best.

But the thought of not seeing him anymore… Never hearing his voice, his laugh. Never holding him again. Never being held by him again.

I wasn't ready to face it yet. Couldn't.

The goldenrod had given way and we were hiking through a meadow waist-high in black-eyed susan and jerusalem sunflowers.

No more looking forward to Friday nights — even with the worry that he might cancel, even with the worry that every date might be the last, the sinking awareness that we weren't growing closer.

He had a high-powered telescope on the deck of the house and sometimes we watched for shooting stars through it.

I loved the telescope. It reminded me of the night we'd met. Later, I realized the telescope had belonged to Jase.

I remember once I said to Graham, "Did you know you can buy a star? Well, have one named for that special someone anyway. It's about twenty bucks. You get your star's name registered in the Universal Star Catalog database."

He'd smiled. Well, it was more of a snort than a smile, but it was tolerant, amused. I knew that if Jase had still been alive they would have looked at each other and shared a private joke.

That was the first night I'd felt alone with Graham. Even in bed, the stars glittering through the windows while we fucked, I felt on my own.

"You seem distracted tonight," Graham had said at one point.

I reached for him, teasing, "Hey, we can't have that."

He was gentle and inventive in bed. Passionate, yes, but the only time he'd ever lost control had been that first night. That was fine by me. When you spend your day with hormone-infused adolescents, you don't mind a little restraint. Graham was maybe the gentlest guy I'd been with, which I hadn't expected given what an outdoorsman he was. Not exactly strong and silent, but… laconic. Reserved.

Not really my type, I would have said. Before I met him. Before I fell in love.

It's not like I had gone looking for this, wanted this, had opted for the pay-per-view gay soap opera with angst in hi def. All I'd wanted was an ordinary relationship with a nice guy. A guy I could share my life with. The good times. The bad times. Maybe even share my mortgage with. A guy who could get along with my friends — a guy who had his own friends. Maybe even a guy I could take home for the holidays. I don't know. Whatever I had been thinking, the pleasant fantasy was so far removed from the vibrant and painful reality of Graham.

And now that I had Graham — or didn't have him — all those soft-focus dreams felt like someone else's memories. The realization that Graham was not going to be part of my future, was already on his way out of my life, hurt so much it was hard to think past it.

The very thought of his soft sleepy mouth finding mine in the lambent light of morning made me want to drop my pack and crouch down, hugging myself against what felt like a body blow. A mortal blow.

How did people get over this?

They obviously did. Every day someone fell in love with the wrong person and had to pack up all their fragile, misguided hopes and unwanted affection, and move on to the next picnic table.

How many times had I had to gently — and not always so gently — redirect someone's interest from me?

Payback was a bitch.

Nah, no dramatics. Hearts got broken every day. Nobody died from that. But it did kind of fade the sunlight and drain the color from the days.

And the nights ... the nights would feel too long to live through.

The thought of those nights had me drawing a sudden sharp breath.

Graham looked back at me.

I gave him a thumb up. Maybe a little too vigorously.

He turned hastily forward again.

I turned inward. Sure, for a time the nights would be bad. But then I'd get over this and move on and maybe, finally, find someone who appreciated me for being me, who didn't wish every minute we were together that I was broader and blonder and rode a bike and listened to Bonnie Raitt and loved to camp as much as Graham.

The thought should have comforted me, but it didn't. It hurt worse. Made my heart feel shrunken and lost, a pebble bouncing and clacking its way down a deep, empty pothole.

Why did it have to be Graham? Why couldn't it have been a nice normal ordinary guy who was as tired as me of the clubs and the earnest, organized efforts of social networks and of fucking around? Why did it have to be Graham with his perfect house in the hills and his tragically dead soul mate?

Seriously.

And why had fucking Graham had to drag me into it?

Why couldn't he have kept his crippled heart safe at home in his house of many windows? Why pretend to be open to moving on, to falling in love again when he was still mourning his ghost? Still grieving at the shrine.

It wasn't fair. It wasn't right.

Or was it simply that Graham was ready but I wasn't the right guy? Yeah, more likely that. It would take someone a lot more ... whatever, to ease his grip on the past. Someone more like Jase. Or just not like me.

Graham stopped walking and uncapped his canteen. He offered me a swig, which was surely a peaceable gesture seeing that I had my own. But I took his and tilted my head back. The water was warm and sweet.

"You're quiet," he said.

I handed the canteen back. Wiped my mouth. "Thinking."

"Yeah."

Way with words, Graham.

I tried to keep my face blank but as I met his gaze, I could see the reflection of my bitterness in his eyes. Saw his expression alter. Saw that he had no idea what to do about any of this. That he was sorry.

My anger leeched away. Kind of too bad because it gave me energy and purpose, but the fact was, it wasn't Graham's fault he didn't fall in love with me. Any more than it was my fault that I had fallen in love with him.

I took a deep breath. "The thing is, you're right."

His eyes narrowed. "Am I? About?"

"Not about wasting my time, because I don't think being with you was a waste of time. I liked spending time with you. I enjoy your company. And I would like to be friends with you one of these days. But."

I managed a controlled stop rather than looking like I couldn't go on, but it was close.

"But?" he asked when I didn't continue.

"But it probably would be a good idea if I didn't see you for a while."

His fluctuating expression was a study of emotions. It looked like everything from anger to relief flicked past while he absorbed my words.

"If that's what you want."

I guess my emotional equilibrium was still off because something dangerous surged inside me. *If that's what I* want? *You know goddamned well what I* want! Reason prevailed — on Graham's end too. Before I swallowed the heated words, he said, "Sure, Wyatt. Of course."

He sounded subdued. He gave great attention to screwing the cap on his canteen. "It's just…"

I closed my eyes. *Don't say it.*

"I'm going to miss you."

I opened my eyes. "I'm going to miss you too." I waited for him to turn. When he didn't, I walked past him.

For a long time neither of us said anything else. The only sounds were the even thud of our boots on the crumbly soil, the hum of pollen-drunk bees, the faraway boom of thunder. The clouds were rolling in, the temperature dropping, but we were still well ahead of the storm. We'd be back at the car before the rain started.

"It doesn't feel like three years," Graham said suddenly from behind me. "Since Jase."

"No. I guess not."

"Other times it feels like he's been gone forever. Like it all happened to someone else. Like our life happened to someone else."

"I'm sorry." Not the first time I'd said it, but what else was there to say? I thought I understood about as well as anyone on the outside could.

"You don't have to be sorry, Wyatt. I know I haven't been fair to you."

Since that was exactly what I'd been telling myself, I'm not sure why I felt a little ashamed to hear him acknowledge it.

"You were honest. And I thought maybe ..."

"I was angry for so long. Mad at Jase. Mad at ... life. Why give people that much happiness if you're going to take it away?"

"I don't know."

"I don't believe in God anymore. And if he — it — does exist, I *hate* it."

He did. I could hear the undertone of rage still vibrating in his voice. I began to understand exactly how much control he had.

I stopped walking, turned to face him. "I know it doesn't help, but some people never have that. What you had with Jase. Never have it at all. They look all their lives and don't find it."

Graham's look was fierce and bright. "You're right, Wyatt. It doesn't help."

"Okay."

He took in my lopsided smile and sighed. Such a weary sound. "No. That's not true. I know how lucky I was, and sometimes I can even remember it and be glad without getting angry." He added honestly, "More often lately. I think that's because of you."

It meant a lot to hear it. "That's the nicest thing you've ever said to me."

We stared at each other.

"It's true." Graham's gaze shifted to the mountains, his tone changed. "Maybe if the fucking killer had ever been caught..."

Killer? Maybe not in the eyes of the law, but didn't it amount to the same thing? It did for Graham.

"If there had been some justice. Something. Some ... closure."

How many times could you say you were sorry? I shook my head.

"It didn't have to happen. It *shouldn't* have happened. He shouldn't have ... ended like that. It's so goddamn fucking pointless." Graham's face twisted and then, shockingly, he was crying. His face screwed up, turned ugly as he fought it. But a sob tore out of him. A winded, broken sound. And then another.

My own eyes stung. I couldn't bear for him to hurt so much. I wanted to put my arms around him, protect him. I didn't think he'd welcome it, so I didn't move.

Why did we all crave love so badly when half the time it left us annihilated?

Graham choked out, "I think of him lying there. Not a mile from the house. I was *home*. I could have ..."

He'd never talked about it before. Not to me. Not really. I knew the bare facts. I'd got most of them off the Internet. Jason Edward Kane, 38, a professor of astronomy at the University of Oregon had been killed while out biking one early Saturday morning. It was a hit-and-run accident. The driver was never caught.

I knew more about Jase's death than I knew about his life.

Having been in that quiet, peaceful house on a Saturday morning … been there with the satiny light filtering through the trees and pouring through all those sparkling windows, the songs of birds outside, the smell of coffee brewing. The perfect start to another perfect day. A false start, as it turned out. A faulty reading on the barometer because despite indicators reading all being right with the world, in fact the world was seconds from being rocked off its axis by an asteroid.

Hard to not feel betrayed by the very cosmos. Hard to ever believe again in a beneficent fate.

Another sob ripped from Graham. He sounded like someone took a knife to his chest and carved the sound out. "If you'd known him …"

I hugged him.

Last time, I thought. *One last time.* And I held him tighter. For an instant he hugged me back. Held me like I was a drifting spar and he was a shipwrecked sailor lost on the dark and rolling sea. On this vast golden windblown empty ocean where we stood together — and alone. Then he freed himself, embarrassed, of course, and angry with himself for breaking down — and with me for witnessing it.

"I'm sorry," I said. "I wish I had the power to bring him back to you."

He drew another shuddering breath and then fell silent, his expression … odd.

We stared at each other. The moment stretched. For the space of a couple of heartbeats it felt like we were on the verge of some revelation.

I felt a burning sensation near my inner elbow. I jumped, looked down and saw a honey bee stinging me for all she was worth. I slapped my arm. "*Damn.* It stung me."

How the hell could something so little pack such a wallop? It was like it had punched a burning cigarette into my skin.

"Is the stinger still in?"

"Is it? I can't tell."

We both peered at my tanned forearm. There was a red patch about the size of a quarter near my elbow. Graham shook his head. "No. Little bastard lives to fight again." He absently wiped at his wet eyes.

"Good news for the collapsing bee colonies."

He grinned. "You're not allergic or anything, are you?"

"No."

"We're not far from the car park now. Maybe ten minutes? I'll get the antiseptic out of the first aid kit and fix you up when we get there."

"Sure."

The sky was getting darker. Graham was right. We needed to keep moving. We started walking again. My arm hurt like hell. I'd forgotten how much bee stings hurt. I tried to remember what we'd been talking about before I'd been stung. Of course. Jase. What else? But this had been different. For the first time Graham had loosened that tight control. He'd finally opened up to me. More than opened up. He'd cried in my arms.

It felt unreal now.

As a matter of fact, everything was starting to feel unreal. Everything but my arm which had stopped tingling and now throbbed with a dull, insistent pain. I glanced down and saw a large raised blister where I'd been stung. Worse, much worse, was the fact that my entire arm was swollen. My fingers looked like purple sausages. I rocked to a stop. "Oh *shit*."

An allergic reaction. *Anaphylaxis.* That's the word for when the immune system releases a rush of chemicals in response to allergens like insect venom or shellfish. Overkill, in other words — with the key word being *kill.* You can die from anaphylactic shock. You can die in a matter of minutes. That flood of chemicals released by your immune system sends your blood pressure plummeting, your heart rate skyrocketing, and your entire body crashing in shock. Signs and symptoms included a rapid and weak pulse, hives, lightheadedness, and feelings of anxiety.

I had them all. Especially the anxiety. That was increasing exponentially with each passing second.

How far were we from the car park? Far enough that it was still out of sight.

"Graham — "

He was way ahead me, shouldering out of his pack, dumping it to the ground and yanking it open. "You said you weren't allergic!"

"I didn't think I was ..."

Graham had the small first aid kit out. The white and blue metal tin looked like an antique. He popped it open to reveal a neatly stocked interior. Or at least neatly stocked until he began rifling through it. "Have you been stung before?"

"I think so. I'm pretty sure. Yeah." I held my misshapen arm up, examining the ugly welt. My arm looked like a prop in a horror movie. "Here I thought the day couldn't get any better."

"When?"

Oh fuck. Was it getting harder to swallow? Harder to breathe? Or was that simple fear closing my throat, shutting off my airways? My heart pounded all the faster in fright. What would happen next? Would I stop breathing? Would I lose consciousness? Would I die? I realized Graham had asked me something. I'd forgotten the question. "What?"

"Wyatt, when was the last time you were stung?"

I gulped out, "High school? It was a while ago."

"*Shit.*" He threw me a murderous look. His eyes looked black in his white face. "You can develop an allergy anytime."

I wheezed, "Well, how the hell would anyone know if they're allergic then?"

He made a sound of impatience, but I heard the worry. He wasn't alone with that. I was scared to death. I hadn't realized how much I wanted to live — even if Graham wasn't going to be part of my life — until my future was in question.

How long did I have? People died within minutes from allergic reactions. We were more than minutes away from help. Even if we could get to the jeep, we'd never get to the hospital in time. Which hospital? Where was there a hospital? I couldn't think of one. I felt faint, or maybe tired and faint. I didn't remember dropping my pack but all at once I was sitting on the ground leaning against it, watching Graham from what felt like a distance.

I'd never seen him look like that. I wouldn't have thought he *could* look like that. Scared.

"What do you need?" My voice sounded thick, slurred.

"Antihistamines. I used to keep a bottle in here. Oh goddamn it." His voice shook. "It's not here."

"I've got a bottle in my pack." That's what I meant to say but it came out sounding more like, "Ow… gow… boobie… ih… mah… pah." I was surprised I had the air left for that. It was getting harder and harder to form words. My mouth felt numb. My whole face felt numb. Even my ears felt numb.

I was even more surprised that Graham translated my words. But he did. He jumped up, brushing past me, and tore into my pack. I slumped over, watching dizzily as my clothes went sailing into the sky above my head.

Oh man. I was losing it…

"*Got it.*"

Graham scooted around beside me. He held my bottle of antihistamine spray. "Okay, Wyatt. You're okay. Tip your head back, honey."

I wasn't okay. I gurgled in alarm as he leaned over me. He ignored my panicked protest, stuck the small bottle up my nostril and squeezed.

If it did any good, I couldn't tell. I was dimly aware he repeated the procedure in my other nostril. The clouds must have been over us now, casting long, deep shadows dark as night. It was colder too. Much colder.

Graham was talking to me from outer space.

"Don't do this, Wyatt," he said desperately. "God. Not now."

Poor Graham. Some guys have all the luck.

∎　∎　∎　∎　∎

The next time I opened my eyes I was in a hospital cubicle. There were the usual hospital smells and sounds. There was a fire sprinkler positioned directly over my bed and a blue curtain separating me from the activity in the hallway. There was all the usual medical paraphernalia, but I didn't seem to be hooked up to any of it. Which was a big relief.

In fact, I felt… fine.

I turned my head. Graham was sitting next to the bed, watching me. I widened my eyes, narrowed them, blinked a couple of times. He stayed right there, eyeing me with equal interest. He said conversationally, "You know, the odds of getting struck by lightning are better than the odds of going into anaphylactic shock."

"I'm buying a lottery ticket first thing."

"You're not kidding." His eyes were the gray of imminent rain.

I cleared my throat. "What happened? I thought I'd had it."

"We weren't that far from the campground. I threw you over my shoulder and carried you."

Carried? I wasn't the Incredible Hulk, but I wasn't child-size either.

Graham continued, "There was a paramedic truck parked next to my Jeep. They'd been called out for a heart attack that turned out to be a case of campfire indigestion. They gave you a shot of epinephrine and then we all hauled ass for the emergency room. When we arrived here they pumped you full of Benadryl and cortisone and oxygen and in a couple of hours you were back to normal."

I felt back to normal. Tired. But wired. Like I could sleep for a month, but eventually. Not in any immediate future.

The full significance of what had happened hit me. As close calls went, it didn't get much closer than this. I said huskily, "Thank you, Graham. You saved my life."

"Team effort. Anyway, you may not thank me when you hear I phoned your parents."

I groaned so loudly a nurse pulled back the curtain. I hastily waved the all clear to her.

"I didn't realize how fast you'd snap out of it." His face fell into grim lines. "I didn't think you'd snap out of it at all." He drew a breath. "Anyway, it's okay. They're not driving down."

"Thank God."

"Tonight."

I groaned again. He laughed. Quietly, but it was a genuine laugh.

"They're nice."

"I know they are. I picked them." That was the family joke. I was adopted when I was sixteen months old. The story is my birthmother finally decided on Bill and Dana Finley when I tried to chew up their résumé.

Graham said awkwardly, "They … knew all about me."

"You should have let me die out there on the prairie."

I was kidding, of course. Graham was not. "Don't."

"No." I sighed. "Anyway, yes, I did tell them about you. They keep hoping I'm going to settle down. Don't worry. You don't have to meet them. You've done more than enough."

"I want to meet them."

"Uh …"

"I want to meet them," Graham repeated. His gaze was steady even as he stumbled over the words. "I want to … I want us to … I want to keep seeing you."

My heart started to pound so hard I felt a little sick. "Listen, Graham. I don't think — that is, I think you're forgetting. You had a shock today too. And you're mistaking that for something else."

"No." He was definite. "I was trying to tell you before you were stung. It got lost in ..."

His overwhelming grief for Jase. I did understand that. Too well.

He expelled a long breath. "The words came out wrong. I'm not good at talking about this stuff."

Who is? But I didn't say that. I patted his hand, tried to assure him without having to dig up the words, that it was okay. I understood. *Say no more.*

Please, say no more.

But he did say more. In that choppy, uneven, occasionally cracked voice. Dry. Parched. Like he hadn't had a sip of water in decades.

"I knew when you said that... about giving Jase back to me if you had the power." His eyes never wavered from mine. "It was the truth. You meant it."

"I ..." I badly wanted to believe I'd meant it. I badly wanted to believe what he was telling me, what he seemed to be telling me.

"I've never been afraid like I was today. With Jase there wasn't time to be afraid. It was all over before I knew anything about it. With you there was time to think of what we could have had, what I'd let slip away, and I knew ..." his breath caught "I had made the biggest mistake of my life. Because I didn't have the guts to take another chance. Because it didn't seem right that I get to... go on. I get to fall in love again. Be happy. And... it's... so fucking unfair. I know that sounds... that it's liable to sound... But it's not you, Wyatt. Except that you're this great guy and sometimes I couldn't seem to get past that."

I didn't say a word. I was pretty sure he was trying to say that he couldn't help resenting that I was alive and Jase was not, and while maybe it was understandable he would feel that way, I knew I wouldn't be able to forgive him. Even if he had saved my life.

Graham kept stumbling along in that earnest, pained way. "It almost made it worse because I was so sure I couldn't care about anyone again, not like I felt about Jase, but then I met you. And it was so ... It happened so naturally. Like it was meant to happen. I knew I could let go. Move on. And it felt wrong."

"How could it be wrong?"

He countered, "How could I forget him so easily?"

"You haven't forgotten him." The intention was to say it gently, but it came out harsh. Hurt.

"But I could." His face worked and here came the part that killed him, that he was ashamed of. "Not forget him. But let go. I want to. I want to move on. I want to love you. I can't change anything that happened. I can't fix anything. I didn't get justice for Jase. But I still want to move on. I want *you*."

I tried to swallow the lump in my throat. "You have me."

"I know."

The honesty of that made me laugh. Graham laughed too, a little uncertainly, and reached for me at the same time I reached for him. In that antiseptic atmosphere he smelled alive and real: woodsmoke and sunscreen and sunflowers —

The curtain rings scraped. We both retreated from our near-embrace as the doctor strode into the cubicle. "Sounds like someone is feeling a lot better."

"Me? I'm fine." In fact, what I mostly felt was exasperation at the worst timing in the world.

"I'm Dr. Geary." Dr. Geary was short and boyish. He looked like he should have been sitting in a ninth grade biology class trying to drop frozen frogs down girls' blouses.

"Don't go anywhere," I told Graham when he stood up. To Geary, I said, "I'm sure I'm okay now. When can I go home?"

The doctor ignored this, going unhurriedly through the ritual of blood pressure and heart rate. Graham moved to where he could get a better view of the sprinkler overhead. He studied it like it was a rare geode. I studied Graham.

When he'd finished his examination, Dr. Geary announced, "Good news. Provided you can stay with someone for the next twenty-four hours — just in case of relapse — we can see about turning you loose now."

"He's staying with me," Graham spoke up.

"*Relapse?*" I echoed.

"It's rare but sometimes patients have what we call a biphasic reaction. I'm going to give you prescriptions for Benadryl, prednisone and an EpiPen. You'll want to carry that last one from now on." The doctor cheerfully rattled off the rest of his mildly alarming information and retreated once again behind the blue wall.

"Relapse," I repeated.

The curtain swung gently to a standstill. I looked at Graham. He solemnly looked back at me. "Are you sure about this?" I didn't mean having me as a houseguest for the next twenty-four hours. I couldn't help thinking one of us was probably making a big mistake. If he'd taken me into his arms — but, no, the moment seemed to be lost.

Instead he nodded. As declarations went, it left something to be desired. Of course I could make the next move. I'd made plenty of them before.

I started to sit up. The curtain rings slid again and the nurse was back with a sheaf of papers for me to sign. It was too late for either of us to back out. Assuming one of us wanted to.

The house on Startouch Drive felt warm and welcoming when we walked in. The sun was setting and the rooms were filled with amber light.

"Are you hungry?" Graham asked.

"Probably. It's hard to tell with all these antihistamines bouncing around my system. I'm mostly tired." Tired down to my DNA. But I didn't need sleep. And I didn't need food. I didn't even need to hear again that Graham wanted to give us another chance. Well, I did, but Graham wasn't much for words at the best of times. What I needed was Graham. Not even sex. Just his arms around me. Just the simple reassurance of a hug. I wanted him to hold me like he meant it.

I looked up and he was watching me in that steady, calm way. "Why don't you jump into bed, and I'll bring you something on a tray."

"Nah. I'm tired but I'm too pumped up to sleep."

"We don't have to sleep." Suddenly he was smiling, his face relaxed, looking younger than he'd looked in all the time I'd known him.

I found myself helplessly smiling back. When he looked at me like that, it was easy to believe that this was real, that it was going to work out.

I walked into the bedroom. The final crepuscular rays of sun lanced through the skylight and illuminated the bed. I pulled off my T-shirt, stepped out of my jeans. They'd cleaned me up in the emergency room, but I needed a shower. Maybe I was more tired than I'd realized though, because I thought *to hell with it*, crawled into bed and pulled up the covers. I stared up into the funnel of light, watching the dust motes dance in the air.

"You okay?" Graham asked from the doorway.

I sat up. "Yeah. Only I..."

"Me too." He left the doorway and sat down on the bed, and all at once it was easy again, natural to put my arms around him, feel his arms around me. He needed a shower too — and a shave. I was smiling as our mouths brushed gently. The smiles evaporated in hungry fervor. Unsteady mouths exploring flushed skin, trembling eyelashes, before latching on once more in shivery, sweet kisses. The familiar heat coiled inside me, tingling all the way from the soles of my feet to the ends of my hair.

I could feel Graham's heart pounding against my own, feel the unevenness of his breath and the tremor of his hands.

When we finally broke the kiss, his eyes glittered. "It's okay," I said. "It'll be okay. It's not as complicated as it seems."

"Does it seem complicated to you? It seems simple to me."

I reached out to brush the tears at the edge of his eyes. The wet glittered on my thumb tip. "Are you still scared?"

"No. Are you?"

"No." Maybe a little. I had something to lose again — and I didn't think I could survive losing it twice

He smiled his wry smile, the funny little grin I'd fallen in love with. "I'll fix us something to eat, and then we can talk."

"We don't have to talk."

"Not a long conversation," Graham agreed. "I want to say I love you. How's that?"

"Perfect."

I was still smiling as he kissed me a final time and headed back to the kitchen.

I stared up at the darkening skies. The stars would appear soon, first a faint and milky glow, then a hard, adamantine glitter, burning steadily through the night. It would be a good night. Maybe the first of many.

I could hear Graham in the other room, comfortable, familiar sounds of dishes and running water. I could hear the birds in the trees saying good-night to each other. And somewhere down the hillside I could hear the buzz of a motorcycle like an angry bee growing fainter and fainter with the miles.

A LIMITED ENGAGEMENT

This story was written in 2008 for a charity anthology in support of gay marriage. It's a noirish little tale about the desperate things love can drive you to — or maybe it's about doing the wrong things for the right reasons. A lot of readers have trouble with this one, but I like pushing some of those romance boundaries. What would love really be about, if not the ability to forgive?

I heard the key in the lock, switched on the porch light, and opened the door.

The rain poured off the roof of the cabin in a shining fall of silver needles, bouncing and splashing off the redwood deck. Ross stood there, blue eyes blacker than the night, the amber porch light giving his skin a jaundiced cast.

"You're here," he said in disbelief. The disbelief gave way instantly to the rage he'd been banking down for — well, probably since the newspapers came out that morning. Even in the unwholesome porch light I could see his face flush dark and his eyes change.

I stepped back — partly to let him in, because really what choice did I have? Even if I'd wanted to keep him out, it was his cabin. Partly because... it was Ross and I had no walls and no doors and no defenses against him.

He followed me inside, shaking his wet, black hair out of his eyes. He wasn't wearing gloves, and his hands were red from the cold. His Joseph Abboud overcoat dripped in a silent puddle around his expensively shod feet. "I am going to kill you," he said carefully and quietly, and he launched himself at me.

I jumped back, my foot slipped on the little oriental throw rug, and I went down, crashing into the walnut side table, knocking it — and the globe lamp atop it — over. The lamp smashed on the wooden floor, shards of painted flowers scattering down the hallway.

Ross's cold hands locked around my throat. Big hands, powerful hands — hands that could stroke and soothe and tease and tantalize — tightened, choking me. I clawed at his wrists, squirming, wriggling, trying to break his hold.

till death do you part ...

"R-R-ogh — " I tried to choke out his name as he squeezed.

The blood beat in my ears with the thunder of the rain on the roof. The lights swirled and dimmed, the black edges swept forward and washed me out with the drum of the rain on the roof.

■　■　■　■　■

I could hear the rain pounding down. I opened my eyes. I was lying on the floor in the entrance hall of the cabin, the rug scrunched beneath me. The lights were out but the flickering from the fireplace in the front room sent shadows dancing across the open beamed ceiling. I could make out broken glass winking and twinkling in the firelight like bits of broken stars fallen around me. My back hurt, my head buzzed, my throat throbbed.

There was no sign of Ross.

Levering myself up, I got to my feet, leaned dizzily against the wall while I found my bearings, then picked my way over the fallen table and through the broken glass into the front room.

Ross sat in front of the fireplace, head in his hands, unmoving.

I felt my way over to the sofa and sat down across from him.

He didn't look up. I could see that his hands were shaking a little.

Mine were shaking a lot.

I croaked, "Rawh." Tried again. "Ross … will you listen to me?" It came out in a hoarse boy demon voice.

I guess Demon Boy was about right. He looked at me then, and even in the uncertain lighting the pain in his eyes was almost more than I could take.

He said tonelessly, "Why did you do it?"

I had to struggle to get the words, and not just because of my bruised throat.

He said, "I did everything you wanted. I paid every penny of your goddamned blackmail. Why the hell did you do it?" I could tell he'd been asking himself this all the long drive, all the long day. Six hours from New York City to this little cabin in the Vermont woods. He must have left not long after the news broke.

"I — " my voice gave out on another squawk.

His eyes shone in the firelight as they turned my way. I shook my head.

"Do you have any idea what you've done to me?" he asked. "You've destroyed me. *Why?*"

I couldn't answer. The burn in the back of my throat moved to my eyes and dazzled me. I could just make him out in a kind of prism — as though he were trapped in crystal.

"You don't think you owe me that much?" He got up fast. I flinched. He stopped.

"I'm … sorry," I got out.

"Sorry?"

I nodded.

"You're … sorry?" The bewilderment was painful. "You outed me to the press. You've ruined my career, my marriage — "

"Engagement," I said quickly.

There was a little pause. Ross said, "You've ruined my life … and you're sorry?"

I said, "I'm sorry you're suffering. I'm not sorry I did it."

I thought he really would kill me then. Fists clenched, he took a step toward me, and I straightened, squaring my shoulders. For a long moment he stared down at me, then, sharply, he turned away. I could hear the harshness of his breathing as he fought for control.

"Ross — "

"Don't say anything, Adam." His voice was muffled. "Don't speak. I'm not — "

Neither of us said a word as the rain thundered down on the roof. I could see it glinting outside the windows like grains of polished rice — like a shower of rice outside a church. But they didn't throw rice at weddings anymore, did they?

Finally Ross gave a long sigh. His shoulders relaxed. He moved away to the liquor cart and poured two brandies. Brandy in the wrong glasses: he really was upset. Handing me a tumbler, he sat down on the other sofa, and said conversationally, "That's twice tonight I've almost killed you." He met my eyes. "You shouldn't have come here, Adam. I can't believe you did."

"I'm not running from you," I said.

He raised his brows. "You should be running from me. Because I'm going to return the favor and wreck your life."

"All right." I tossed my drink back and then stared down at the empty glass sparkling in the firelight.

He gave me that dark, unfathomable look. "You don't believe me?"

I managed a semblance of a smile. "I think I beat you to it, yeah?"

Yeah. Because of the two of us, my career was less likely to survive. Ross was a playwright. A brilliant, respected playwright, at that. I was an actor. A mostly out-of-work and previously not very well-known actor. Not many openly gay actors find leading man roles on or off Broadway. Especially the ones who indulge in kiss and tell with powerful playwrights and producers. I was going to be a pariah, the Anne Heche of the *theatah, dahling.*

That wasn't the life-wrecking part, though. There also was the fact that I loved Ross — as much as he now hated me. That was the bit I wasn't sure I would survive.

He swallowed a mouthful of brandy slowly, thoughtfully. "Not a smart move from a career standpoint," he agreed. "Either of your careers. You know, you're not going to get far as a blackmailer if you betray your paying customers."

"Why did you pay me?" I asked.

He said as though explaining the facts of life to a numbskull, "Because you threatened to out me to the press."

"You could have gone to the police."

"How the hell would that have helped? It would just have outed me faster."

"You preferred to keep sleeping with me even though I was blackmailing you."

"You're not hard to sleep with," he said dryly. "Far from it. And as we — and now everyone — know, I like to sleep with men. And I'm not that choosy."

I ignored that last comment, although it stung. I pointed out, "And then when I demanded money, you handed that over too."

"That's my point," Ross said. "I gave you what you wanted. Everything you wanted, you got."

I said bitterly, "Right."

"What the hell did you not get? You asked for a part in the new play, and I got that for you too. Jesus Christ. I did everything I could think of — "

"That's right," I said, and suddenly I was on my feet and furious. "You're so goddamned *afraid* that you let me blackmail you into a part in the new play. Was there anything you wouldn't have done to keep my mouth shut? To keep yourself — "

He was staring at me, mouth slightly parted — not a look I'd ever seen on Ross's face before. Ross Marlowe was the living personification of Man About Town. The suave sophisticate who knew what to do in every social situation. But I guess confronting your blackmailing ex-lover wasn't covered in *Debrett's Etiquette and Modern Manners.*

"What the hell are *you* crying about?" he asked.

I wiped my face on my sleeve. "Oh, go to hell," I said. "If you don't know by now, there's no point me spelling it out."

He was very still.

It took some effort, but I got myself under control while he stared at me with those midnight-blue eyes.

"Look," I said finally. "You asked why. So here's why. Part of why. All these plays you write about characters finding their true selves and owning up to who they really are, and making difficult choices and standing behind them — *two* plays about gay men being true to themselves against the odds — and all the time you're hiding behind this … façade of Ross Marlowe the brilliant heterosexual playwright." Tears and my injured vocal cords closed off my words.

He said slowly, "I see. This was for my own good?"

I nodded, not looking at him, mopping again at my runny nose, leaking eyes. "I don't expect you to understand," I got out.

"Lucky for both of us." Watching me, he shuddered and pulled out a pristine hanky — and who the hell carries hankies? Wasn't that proof to the entire civilized world right then and there that Ross was gay? He tossed it my way. "Jesus, mop your face."

I took it with muttered thanks.

"So basically," he said, watching me scrub my face, "You had some idealistic image of me and I disappointed you, and this is your revenge?"

Horrifically the tears started again. It took effort to stop them. I managed. "You never disappointed me."

"No." His gaze was intent. "What then?"

I said — and I tried to be matter of fact, "I don't believe you would have been happy like that, Ross. I don't believe you — "

"Christ, you're young," he said, but he sounded weary, not angry. He set down his glass, rose, and came over to me, taking me in his arms. "Okay, listen, Adam. You're twenty-three. I'm forty. I think I've got the edge in experience here. I believe in the things I write about, but I don't want to live my life as some kind of gay poster boy for the arts, all right? I like my privacy."

His arms felt very good around me, strong and kind and familiar. He smelled good too: a mix of rain and pipe tobacco and some overpriced, herbal aftershave you probably couldn't buy in Vermont. I put my head on his shoulder. I was very tired. I hadn't slept since I'd done the interview with the reporter from the *New York Times* Theater section.

Playing Desdemona to Ross's Othello hadn't helped much either.

"This isn't privacy," I said. "This is… a lie. You're marrying someone you don't love."

I felt the steady, even pulse in his throat against my face. He was past his anger now; Ross was the most civilized man I knew — and maybe that was part of the problem. He said levelly, "I like Anne. I do care about her, whether it meets your… naïve definition of love. It's a good, working partnership — or it would have been before you blasted it to Kingdom Come with your exclusive to the papers."

Well, Kingdom Come was where I reigned. I didn't think he'd find that funny though — I didn't — and instead I said, "Marriage should be about more than friend-ship and respect, Ross."

"Respect and friendship — companionship, shared interests — that's a good basis."

I shook my head. "It's not enough."

"You're the expert now?" His tone was dry. "What's the longest steady rela-tionship you've had?"

"We've been together one year, eight months and twenty-seven days," I said.

He didn't have an answer. After a moment he couldn't even meet my eyes.

I added, "Depending on how you use the word 'together.'" I pulled out of his arms.

After several minutes Ross said quite gently, "Did you feel I used you? Is that why?"

I shook my head.

I could feel his gaze on my profile. "It was never my intent. From the moment I saw you I ... wanted you," he said honestly.

Yeah. No question. I still remembered looking up from reading for the part of George Deever in *All My Sons* and meeting those smiling, blue eyes. Ross, who was good friends with the show's producer, had been sitting in on the auditions that day. Every time I'd glanced up from the script I'd seen him watching me from the almost empty sea of chairs.

I hadn't got the role. Apparently I didn't look like either a lawyer or a veteran. But as I'd left the audition, Ross had followed me out of the theater. He'd offered to buy me a drink. And, as consolation prizes went, I'd have taken a drink with Ross over eating for the next three months easy.

We had cocktails at the M Bar in the Mansfield Hotel. Mahogany bookshelves, and a domed skylight. It had been raining that night too, glittering down like a fake downpour on a stage set. We drank and talked and then he took me upstairs to a luxurious suite and fucked me in the clouds of down comforter and pillow-topped mattress. In the morning he fed me cappuccino and croissants and put me in a taxi. I never expected to see him again.

I figured he did that kind of thing all the time.

Two nights later he had called me, and after a painfully stilted and painfully brief conversation, he'd asked me out. We'd had dinner at 21, and he'd taken me back to the Mansfield. And in the morning Ross had let me fuck him.

After that I'd seen him a couple of days almost every week. Stolen hours. Borrowed time.

The best had been the week we'd spent here at his cabin in Vermont just on our own.

That had been four months ago — in the summer. We'd swum in the lake and fished and sunned ourselves. We'd barbecued the rainbow trout we caught and drank too much and watched the stars blazing overhead as it got later and later. We'd talked and laughed and fucked and laughed some more. He'd let me read his new play. I told him I'd been offered a job in Los Angeles, and he told me not to go.

That was the happiest I could ever remember being — because I'd been sure Ross was falling in love with me. But the next week he'd announced his engagement to Anne Cassidy. I read it in the Theater section of the New York Times. Anne was an entertainment columnist for the *Daily News*.

Ross apologized for that, and said he had planned to tell me himself, but Anne had got a little overexcited about the upcoming nuptials. I told Ross that if he broke it off with me I'd go to the papers too. He'd laughed, but he'd kept seeing me — though not as frequently.

Their formal engagement party, a month later, received quite a bit of coverage in the local papers. I was still reading about it when Ross called and asked if I was free for the evening. I told him I wasn't free, and that if he didn't want me to tell his fiancée he was queerer than a postmodern production of *Not about Nightingales*, he would have to pay me a hundred dollars a week. He had been less amused but he'd given the money and he'd kept sleeping with me, and the wedding plans sailed smoothly along.

A month ago I'd told Ross that if he didn't get me a part in his new play, *God's Geography*, I'd go to the papers. He'd given into that too — granted, a very minor role — although he didn't sleep with me for two weeks after that escalation of hostilities.

He'd finally called me late one night, sounding faintly sloshed. I'd insisted that he come to my place, for once, and he had. He'd shown up at my battered apartment door with a bottle of Napoleon brandy, and fucked me long and hard in my blue and white striped Sears sheets while we listened to my next-door neighbors quarrel with each other to the musical accompaniment of their kid wailing in the background.

"I even want you now," he'd said, when he had rolled off me. It wasn't a compliment.

So as I stared at him in the shadowy firelight, I said, "I know. You never made any secret about it."

He said — not looking at me, "I wasn't going to dump you. You must know that. I didn't intend to stop seeing you."

"Is that supposed to make it better?"

His eyes widened at my anger. "I didn't mean to ... tried not to ... take advantage of you. Of your ... youth, your generosity." The words seemed difficult for him. "Did you feel used? Is that why?"

The playwright always wanting the loose ends neatly tied up. Living in fear of the critics?

I said, "I don't think you used me. I think you fell in love with me."

He was silent for a long time. I thought my heart would shatter into pieces like an asteroid waiting for him to say something. In the end all he said was, "And for that — ?"

I stood up, hugging myself against the cold, although between the brandy and the fireplace, the room was warm enough. "And I fell in love with you," I said. I wanted to sound strong and convincing, but I just sounded pained. "The second morning at the Mansfield, the first time you let me fuck you. I made some stupid joke, and you laughed, and you kissed my nose. I've never wanted anyone or anything as much as I want you. I would give anything — "

He looked away at the fire and a muscle moved in his jaw.

"And I couldn't stand there and watch you marry Anne Cassidy. It's not right. It's not fair to any of us. Not even to her."

He said impatiently, "Anne knows exactly what she wants. And so do I."

"Then why are you settling for companionship and respect when you could have all that and love and passion as well?"

"Because you're twenty-three years old and queer — and what the hell does that make me?"

"Older and queer!"

He put his head in his hands.

I stared at him. "Well, that's that," I said. "Anyway, you'll be okay. It's New York. It'll be a nine days wonder and then no one will even remember."

He looked at me with something close to dislike. "You don't think so?"

"Hell, I don't know." I rubbed my face. "I'm sorry. Sorry to hurt you, but not sorry to have stopped it." I added, "If it is stopped."

"Oh, it's stopped." He sounded sour.

And that really was that. All at once I was out of ideas — and energy. I said, "I can't keep saying I'm sorry. I guess … you know where to find me."

I started for the door and he said harshly, "Adam, if you thought you were in love with me, why didn't you say so?"

At that, I had to smile. "I did Ross. I said it in every way I knew. If I'd said the words, you'd have broken it off. You didn't want to know."

"You think I do now?"

I shook my head. "No. You'd still prefer to think it was just sex."

Ross said slowly, "But you came here anyway. Drove all the way up here on the chance that this is where I would come."

"Yeah."

"Knowing how I would feel about you after this."

I admitted, "I couldn't stay away."

Neither of us said anything. The fire popped sending sparks showering.

His voice was very low as he said, "I could have hurt you very badly; you know that."

"You could have killed me," I said, "And it wouldn't have hurt as much as watching you marry someone you don't love just because it fits your image or whatever the hell it is with you."

It wouldn't hurt as much as watching him marry anyone who wasn't me.

"You're so sure it's you I love?"

"I am, yeah." I said it with a sturdy confidence I was a long way from feeling — but that's what acting is all about. "I think that's why you kept giving into my demands, because you didn't want to break it off either. I don't think you're that afraid of me."

"I wasn't, no." Astonishingly, there was a thread of humor in his voice. "But then I didn't fully grasp what you were capable of."

To my surprise he held out a hand. I took it, and he drew me down onto the sofa. For a moment he sat there, absently playing with the fingers of my ring hand. My fingers looked thin and brown and callused next to his own manicured ones. When I didn't have a paying acting gig — which was usually — I worked as a bicycle messenger for a courier service. Yeah, safe to say eHarmony probably wouldn't have set us up as the perfect match.

He said, "Has it occurred to you that if I did love you, you destroyed it with your actions?"

I swallowed painfully. Nodded.

"And you still don't regret it?"

"Maybe I will." I met his eyes and tried to smile. "Right now I'm sort of numb."

"That's two of us." He leaned forward, finding my mouth, kissing me. I slid back into the cushions, surrendering to whatever he wanted. He kissed me softly, and then harder. His mouth bruised mine, a punishing grind of lips and teeth, but I opened to it, opened to him, and almost immediately he gentled. His hands moved under my sweater, pushing it up.

His touch was warm and sent a tingle spreading beneath my skin. I murmured approval.

"I have never known anyone like you," he said.

"But that's good, right?"

He snorted and sat up, but his fingers went to the buttons of his tailored shirt.

I yanked my sweater up, banging my head on the arm of the sofa as I pulled it over my head, dropped it. I humped up, wriggling out of my jeans.

Ross was hurrying to undress too, and it was a relief to know that the desire between us remained intact. It was always like this, hungry and hurried — and then sweet and satisfied. It was ... nourishing.

Because, regardless of what Ross told himself, it wasn't just sex — and it hadn't been for a very long time.

I kicked my legs free, kicked my jeans away. Ross stood up, unzipped, and stepped out of his trousers. I brushed his long, lightly furred thigh with my hand.

Naked, he lowered himself to me and I ran my fingers through his hair that was drying in soft silky black strands smelling of rain and firelight. I pressed my face to his throat and licked him, licked at the little pulse beating there. He exhaled a long breath. Relief? Resignation?

I said, "It wasn't easy. Just so you know — it — "

He pulled back a little. "No. I know. When you opened the door you looked ..." He considered it and then said, "Terrified and sick and hopeful all at the same time."

"That pretty much sums it up." I wanted to make a joke of it, but it wasn't funny.

Everything that mattered to me was going to be settled in the next few hours. Maybe minutes. I didn't know if this was a hello fuck or a goodbye fuck. Maybe even Ross didn't know.

"I love you so much," I said, and my voice shook.

"I know." He sounded pained. So ... good-bye then?

I kissed the underside of his jaw, and he tipped his face to mine and found my mouth in hot, moist pressure. Something as sweet and simple as kissing: mouths moving against each other, opening to each other, the sweet exchange of breath.

His tongue slipped into my mouth, a teasing little thrust, and I sucked back. He tasted like Ross with a brandy chaser.

I kissed him, and he whispered, "You're fearless, aren't you? Going to the papers, coming here tonight, opening up to me now. I don't think I've ever known anyone as fearless as you."

I moved my head in denial. "I'm scared," I said. "All the time. I'm just stuck in drive. When it comes to you, I don't know how to stop or how to reverse."

He shook his head a little, his mouth found mine again, nibbling my lower lip, moving his mouth against mine in feathery, teasing brush. I nuzzled him back and his kiss deepened. I liked his weight lowering on me, warm and solid, I liked the roughness of his jaw against my own, I liked his taste and scent, and the feel of his fingers against my cheek — and the insistent prod of his cock in my belly.

I put my hands on either side of his face and said, "Can you just tell me if this is hello or good-bye? I just want to know, so I can stop ... hoping." The alcohol and exhaustion made it easy to be honest, to accept whatever the truth was going to be. If the answer was no, then in the morning I would deal with it but tonight we were going to make love.

A little grimly, he said, "What if it's good-bye? Are you planning to write a book about me next?"

I shook my head. "If it really is good-bye, I'm all out of ideas."

Ross raised one eyebrow. "No ideas at all?"

"Other than the obvious: make this a night you won't forget."

His face softened. He said, "There isn't one night with you that I've forgotten. Nor a single day. You must know that much."

"I know how it is for me."

And then we said nothing for a time, communicating by touch. I thought, *he does love me, he does — even if he hasn't realized it, hasn't accepted it — he does —* hissing a little breath of pleasured surprise as he pinched my nipples, making them stand up in tiny buds.

"You do like that," he whispered, his mouth tugging into another of those sexy little smiles.

"I like it when you lick them too," I whispered, tugging him closer, smoothing my hands over the hard flesh of his back and shoulders. Hard muscle and soft skin — the musculature of a normal healthy adult man, not a movie star, not an iron man. Our naked bodies rubbed against each other, starting to find that rhythm, my own cock rock hard and requiring attention, jutting up, nestling against his.

Ross groaned, and his mouth drifted down my throat and over my shoulder, stopping to lick and kiss, to bite and linger. I groaned and my throat protested squeakily, and he kissed me there too, tenderly.

"Thank God," he said. "Thank God, I didn't ..."

I stopped that with more kisses.

"I could make you happy," I told him. "I'd do everything in my power to make you happy."

He looked up, surprised. "You do make me happy."

"Sometimes."

He bent his head; his tongue lapped across one nipple, drawing it firm and upright instantly. I sucked in a sharp breath. Moaned. He liked that. I felt his smile as his mouth ghosted across my chest. I moaned again, and soon the rasp of his tongue wet my other nipple. I pushed against him, loving that feel, loving that lave of tongue on teat. My heart was pounding dizzily in my chest. I worked my hand down through the fissures between our bodies, slipping past his groin, cupping his balls in my palm.

He grunted, closed his eyes briefly. I caressed him languidly.

"What do you want?" he asked.

Something old, something new, something borrowed, something blue, something to have and to hold from this day forward. I got out, "Will you fuck me? I need it. Need to feel like I belong to you."

He bit his lip. "I don't know if I can walk."

I chuckled, squeezed his balls, lightly.

"Hold on," he jerked out.

I did, stroking myself leisurely until he was back. He knelt over me, his cock long and thick and beautiful as it rose out of the dark nest of his groin. He rested his hand against my cheek.

"You're beautiful, Adam."

"So are you."

I started to get up, but he pushed me back, smiling. I looked my inquiry and then whimpered as he knelt and took the head of my shaft into his mouth. Oh my God how I loved this. Was there anyone who didn't? But especially I loved it from Ross. *His* elegant, clever mouth doing those unspeakably erotic things to me: *his* wide and warm and wet hole for me to bury myself in. I began to jerk my hips in response to that slow slide. Sensation shivered through me, stripping my thoughts away, and the trembling started.

You lovely, lovely boy, Ross said, without saying a word. His tongue and lips said precious, loving things instead.

I arched my back, crying out.

He began to suck hard. I groped for him — needing something to ground me with pleasure taking me that high. My fingers dug into Ross's broad shoulders, watching through slitted eyes, watching how beautiful he was with his mouth wrapped around my dick. I wanted to tell him so, but the sounds coming out of me were not particularly intelligent. An electrical buzz seemed to crackle up my spine, bright lights flared behind my eyelids, I wondered if I might just short circuit entirely in a kind of sensory overload.

Ross let me feel his teeth and I whimpered, and then he was sucking again so very softly, sweetly. He varied the pressure, sucking me hard and long. My balls drew tight and I began to come in hot, wet spurts, crying out his name.

And Ross swallowed it. I felt tears start in my eyes, but I blinked them back. It was not like he had never done that before, it just … meant more tonight. He swallowed my cum and licked the head of my cock clean, while I lay there panting and trying not to embarrass myself.

When I finally lifted my lashes Ross was smiling. He bent his head to mine. His mouth brushed my mouth and I tasted myself on him — salty and sort of sweet.

He said, "You've gambled everything, haven't you? What are you hoping for?"

I answered with a question of my own. "Did you think I might be here when you decided to come to the cabin?"

A strange expression crossed his face. "It went through my mind. I … didn't think you really would. I didn't think you'd have the nerve."

It was hard to ask, but I made myself. "Did you … hope I would be here?"

He seemed to look inside himself. "I think I did." He added satirically, "But not necessarily for the reason you hope."

"But you did want me?"

"I always want you. That doesn't mean …"

"What?"

And he said, "It's easy to be brave when you're young."

"No, it's not."

Maybe he read something in my face because he seemed to draw on something within himself. "No. It's not always," he agreed. "And you want me to be as brave as you, don't you? Idealistic youth expects no less."

I nodded. "There is recompense, though." I slipped from the sofa and got on my hands and knees on the rug before the fireplace. I glanced back and he was already settling on his knees behind me.

"Recompense." He sounded amused. "That's a good old-fashioned word." I heard the unlovely sound of something squirting, followed by the delicate scent of oranges and honey.

"Orange blossom?" I suggested.

"Dear God," he said, and his laugh had a choky sound. Still, his eyes were smoky with desire as his thighs brushed mine, and his finger pushed against my body.

Always so cautious and careful with this, although we both knew I had three times his experience. One finger insinuating a long, slender length through that tiny, puckered mouth, soothing with oil and honeyed oranges, then two slick fingers.

"I love this part," I admitted, pushing back against his hand.

He pushed the third finger in. Always, always three fingers with Ross. Such a careful, circumspect man. I liked the little rituals. I reached out my hand and he squirted oil on my fingers, and I smeared the oil the full length of my cock, stroking myself, enjoying the pull while his silky fingers slid in and out, knowing exactly where and how to touch.

"Now," I managed. "Please."

"You do have nice manners," he admitted. "Usually."

He withdrew his fingers, positioning himself at the entrance of my body, nudging slowly, slowly inside. He pushed smoothly in past the ring of muscle, joining us, wedding us. I drew back on my knees, resting against Ross's broad chest and belly. I turned and kissed the side of his throat. He stroked his hand slowly down the length of my torso, stroking my belly.

I shifted in his lap, Ross's hips pushing against me. His voice was warm against my ear, "I'll give you this much, Adam. I do love you. Nothing changes that. Nothing could."

Tears blinded me for an instant as we rocked together in gentle, lullaby motion, that seesaw of give and take, the balancing act ... and that was love, right? That was marriage? For richer for poorer, for better for worse, in sickness and in health, push pull, an irresistible force meeting an immovable object ... and somehow finding a way to make it work?

The heat built like a fever, like joy ...

Ross's hand stroked my hip as he steadied into that rhythm, and then faster and sweeter, and I thrust back at him trying to take him deeper, further, gasping with each hard stroke, shivering with the sweetness of it, the cycle, the circle, the beginning and the end of us that was hopefully just another beginning.

I pressed my back and spine against Ross and his fingers laced within mine across my chest, and then he surged up into me and held very still and emptied out all the heat and hunger and heartache.

Then, another couple of tight jerks, and he was slumping forward and taking me with him in a heavy, boneless sprawl on the soft fur of the carpet.

We lay there panting for a long time, unmoving. Ross lifted my hand to his lips and kissed the palm.

When his cock finally slipped from my body, he rolled off me, and the loss felt too familiar — like it could get to be a habit. But he put his arm around me, pulling me close, and we lay for a time on the rug. The rain beat on the roof in soothing rhythm, and the fire crackled in counterpoint, and our breathing slowed and steadied and evened out.

After a time he said, "And you think love is enough?"

"Sex helps." He didn't laugh and I said, "I think love is the point. Because anything else is just a business contract."

He said wearily, "I had my life all planned out."

"I know."

"You're not a very good actor," he said. "I've known from the first that you were in love with me."

"You're not a very good actor, either," I said.

The firelight moved across the ceiling beams in lazy, flickering shadow.

He said, "There's a justice of the peace in Greensboro."

"Is there?"

He turned his head and pressed his face into my hair. I felt his lips move against my forehead as he said, "Do you have any idea of what I should do with an unused marriage license?"

"I do," I said.

IN SUNSHINE OR IN SHADOW

This is probably one of my personal favorite short stories
I remember I wrote it in a day. I'd been to Ireland the year before, and the
place that stayed with me the most was an island in the west called Inishbofin
or Island of the White Cow.

"It's a little awkward," Keiran said, and his gaze — a green that was almost gray — dropped suddenly to the little bowl of peanuts on the table between them. His blond eyebrows knitted together in a little scowl; very important to select exactly the right peanut.

Rick's mouth quirked indulgently. They'd been partnered in Homicide for nearly five years, and he could be forgiven for thinking he knew Keir pretty well by now. One of the things he knew was that Keir preferred whole peanuts; he had an annoying habit of cherry-picking the perfect peanuts out of any dish. Another thing Rick knew was that Keir had a tendency to over-think things. Not in the field, fortunately. Nothing wrong with Keir's instincts or reflexes, but get three beers in him and he started brooding, and next thing you knew, he was spouting stuff from some half-forgotten philosophy course he'd taken in college.

Five years was a long time. Rick knew plenty of marriages that hadn't lasted five years.

"So?" he raised his mug, swallowed, watching Keir over the rim.

Keir's mouth curled derisively, and he picked out a peanut and tossed it in his mouth, crunching irritably, like he'd caught the peanut in a moving violation.

"It's just that I've been thinking…"

"I warned you about that."

Keir's smile was mostly perfunctory twitch.

Rick drained his mug and rose. "Want another?" It was Friday night. After two brutal weeks, they finally had a weekend off, and they were on home turf — a cop bar in Van Nuys. Decent selection on tap, plenty of Stones on the jukebox, and the knowledge they could let down their guard because pretty much everyone in the place was law enforcement or ex-law enforcement. Home sweet home.

Keir was staring up at Rick with a strange, disconcerted expression. He shook his head, and Rick moved to the bar. The memory of Keir's expression stayed with him — like an irritating finger tapping his shoulder.

At the bar he ordered two Harps, chatted with Bill Suzuki, also from Homicide, and unobtrusively watched his partner.

"Good going with the collar on the Martinez case," Suzuki congratulated.

"Yeah. It's a pleasure putting that scumball, Olmos, behind bars."

"What's eating Quinn?"

"Nothing." Rick said it curtly, discouraging further discussion on the topic of his partner. He couldn't help glancing Keir's way again.

Keir was staring at nothing and chewing his bottom lip, a sure sign he was edgy. What now for chrissake? It had been a good week. For once the bad guys were not swaggering away untouched, and tomorrow Keir was starting two weeks of well-deserved vacation. So what was there to bug him? Rick sighed inwardly. He was undoubtedly going to hear all about it when he got back to the table.

If anyone should be feeling out of sorts it was him. This was the first vacation they'd taken apart in ... three years. Keir had just announced it the previous week — right out of the blue. No warning, no discussion. Not that he *had* to talk his vacation plans over with Rick, but ... they were best friends in addition to partners, and they usually did spend a portion of their off-time together — being the only two gay cops in Homicide gave them a natural bond.

He collected the sweating bottles and carried them back to the table, hooking the chair with his foot and sitting down. Keir jumped as though he'd been miles away, and Rick studied him before turning his attention to topping off Keir's half-empty mug.

"So you've been thinking," he prompted.

Keir stared at him blankly before registering Rick's reference to earlier. His expression changed — Rick couldn't read it at all, and that gave him an uneasy feeling. What the hell was going on?

Now that he thought about it, Keir had been acting weird for a couple of weeks. Since the Martinez case had been dropped in their laps. No wonder. Nobody enjoyed it when a kid was the victim. Even if the kid was a gang banger. Suspected gang banger. Gang bangers had parents too. Well, one usually. Some overworked, out-of-touch woman — but in this case, a nice woman. A woman who loved her kids even if she couldn't control them, didn't begin to understand them — these young, tough, tattooed strangers who lived in her house.

No. The trouble had started before that. Before the Martinez case. Keir had been short-tempered, distant, absent-minded — not at all like himself for nearly a month now. And then this sudden vacation.

Rick asked abruptly, "You okay, Quinn? You're not sick or something, are you?"

"Me? I'm fine."

The tone was reassuring enough, but now that Rick examined his partner, he wondered. Keir looked tired. More tired than a Friday night warranted. And he'd lost weight recently — even for his normal wiry self. There were shadows under his eyes and it seemed a long time since that full mouth had smiled.

Full mouth. Yeah. Keir had a very nice mouth. He tasted nice too. Funny how people had their own taste ...

And no way was Rick letting his thoughts stray in that direction. They'd already tried that and it had been a mutually agreed upon disaster.

"You'd tell me if something was wrong, right?"

Keir reached for his mug and said, "Right."

Rick picked his own mug up, tilted it, pouring beer against the side of the glass. He nearly dropped the bottle as Keir said, "I'm resigning."

"You're ..."

"Resigning. I *have* resigned, in fact."

"Why?"

Keir shook his head — like it was too complicated to explain?

Rick gave him an easier question. "When?"

"Last week."

"*Last week*? And you're telling me now?"

"I told Captain Friedman I'd think it over for a week."

Rick stared at him, then gave a disbelieving laugh. "You're kidding me, right?"

Stone-faced, Keir stared right back.

"What the hell's going on? You can't *quit*."

Unbelievably, Keir laughed. "Wanna bet?"

"You resign and then you go on vacation?" It felt safer to give way to indignation on this score; Rick was still trying to assimilate the other.

"Hey, I'm entitled to my vacation."

"I don't believe this."

"I'm sorry — "

"*Sorry?* You didn't even discuss it with me."

Keir was giving him a strange look. "It's my decision to make."

"You're going to pretend this doesn't affect me? We're partners. We were." Rick kept his voice low although — shock wearing off — he was getting angry.

"I know that. I'm telling you now. Before anyone else — "

"Gee, thanks! I feel better already."

Keir sighed. "Listen, I know you're pissed. When I get back I still have two weeks. We can talk then."

"Talk? I don't want to *talk*." *I want you to un-resign*, that's what Rick meant. But Keir was looking at him as though this just confirmed a much-contested point. What point? What the hell was going on?

"Then we won't talk," Keir said evenly. "Either way, I don't give a shit."

What. The. Hell?

And now Rick *was* angry. Hurt and angry. "What does that mean, you don't give a shit? What am I supposed to make of that? What the fuck's going on with you?"

But Keir glanced at his watch and was already on his feet. "I've got a plane to catch. I'll see you in two weeks."

He turned away, and Rick rose too and grabbed his arm. Keir stood perfectly still. They were the same height, but Rick was broader, bigger. He was by nature cool and low key, relying on his build and obvious strength to get his point across to perps. Keir relied on the force of his personality — which was considerable. Especially after five years of it.

Rick let go of Keir's arm. He said, surprised to hear how aggrieved he sounded, "A plane to where? Where the hell are you flying off to?"

"Ireland," Keir replied.

■ ■ ■ ■ ■

Rick was very drunk when he phoned.

He'd stayed at O'Mally's after Keir left, joining the crowd at the bar. After closing the place down, he'd had a couple more when he got home. Not the brightest idea he'd had recently. The bed didn't levitate, but it was spinning nicely, and — proof of how drunk he was — Rick decided the best way to get his mind off how really awful he was going to feel in the a.m., was to call Keir.

The phone rang once.

"Yep?" Keir sounded perfectly alert for three-thirty — like he was expecting Rick's call. Or maybe he was still packing for this mystery trip to Ireland. Maybe he was on his way out the door.

Ireland?

"Why Ireland?" Rick asked. The bedroom window was open and he could hear the chimes on the front porch tinkling eerily in the summer breeze, the rustle of the old elm tree, the far off roar of traffic on the 405. Even at three-thirty in the morning, the L.A. freeways were busy — people on their way to airports, no doubt.

Keir gave a husky little chuckle. "We talked about Ireland."

Astonishingly, given how much he'd had to drink, Rick's cock twitched into life. It was that throaty bedroom laugh that did it. Bringing back memories of things they'd agreed to forget.

His hand moved. He scratched his belly instead and said, "Two guys named Monaghan and Quinn, I guess that's no surprise."

"No. No surprises," Keir agreed.

"Tonight was a surprise."

Keir seemed to be thinking over Rick's objection. He said finally, "It shouldn't have been."

"What's that supposed to mean?" He could hear the sodden belligerence in his voice. Yeah, he'd had too much to drink, no doubt about it. He wasn't used to it. Didn't like to lose control — and he was losing control, that was obvious.

Keir said levelly — his voice already sounding far away, "It means if this is a surprise to you, you haven't been listening to me for the last three years."

"Come off it," Rick said uncomfortably. He had a sudden vision of Keir in this house... this bedroom... this bed. That lean, muscular, brown body leaning over him, the soft gilt fall of hair in those wide, green eyes. Smiling eyes. Irish eyes.

It occurred to him that Keir hadn't answered. He said, striving to move the conversation back into shallow and familiar waters, "I hear the Guinness is like creamy, black silk over there."

"I'll have a pint in your honor. Two pints."

"Cheap bastard. Look..." Rick was nonplussed to hear that tiny fissure of emotion in his voice. "You're not really going, are you?" And he was aware — and was sure that Keir was also aware — that he was no longer talking about unplanned vacations.

"I am, yeah," Keir said.

In the silence between them Rick could hear the hiss of static on the line, the music of the chimes. The lilt of bells sounded vaguely Celtic.

In a broad brogue, he said suddenly, briskly, "Two Oirish cops are walking the beat one night after stopping for a wee nip. A severed head comes rolling along the pavement toward them."

Keir snorted, but said nothing.

Rick said, "Monaghan picks it up, looks it in the eye, and says, *Jez, that looks like Murphy*. To which Quinn replies, *No, Murphy was taller than that!*"

"Say goodnight, Dick," Keir said.

"Goodnight, dick."

CHAPTER TWO

He'd had some bad ideas in his time, but this was probably the worst: a GLBT singles bus tour through Ireland. And yet it had seemed like such a great notion when he was booking his trip. No need to play down his sexuality, a selection of available men with at least one thing in common — two things, counting Ireland — and someone else to do the driving. But he'd have been happier with a rental car and a map.

To start with, the available men were either too old or too young. And it turned out *all* Keir had in common with them was the obvious; he'd been out of the civilized mainstream for too long. He didn't know how to talk to anyone who wasn't a cop.

That had been another mistake: revealing what he did for a living. He should have known better. He *did* know better in real life, but the artificial existence of life on a touring bus had lulled him into uncharacteristic candor. The second night out in Galway he'd confided to Terry Schweitzer over a couple of pints. Terry offered a glazed smile, excused himself early, and by morning it was common knowledge that back home in the good old US of A. Keir Quinn was Detective Keiran Quinn of L.A.P.D. He found himself spending a lot of time with two very nice lesbians from Milwaukee — ex-FBI agents who'd had the survival skills to keep mum about it.

He missed Rick.

He missed Rick even worse than he had imagined he would, and he'd known before he ever started this that it was going to hurt like hell.

He tried not to think about it. No point. Rick was very clear about what he wanted and what he didn't want. He wanted Keir for his work partner and best friend. He didn't want him for his lover or life partner. He didn't want to talk about it. He didn't want to listen to Keir talk about it. As far as Rick was concerned they had tried it and it hadn't worked.

That was the part Keir didn't understand. Because it *had* worked. They had been good together. It had been comfortable and easy — the sex had been terrific. God, it had been nice to be with someone who knew him as well as Rick did — and accepted him as was. *Liked* him as was.

But then there had been the thing with the Holland chick. They'd been investigating the supposed suicide of Deanna Holland's boyfriend. Third interview, Holland had freaked and pulled a gun. Keir had moved to disarm her and the gun had gone off leaving a hole in Deanna Holland's ceiling, powder burns and a wrecked relationship for Keir.

"I think we'd better cool it," Rick had said the morning after what turned out to be the best night they'd spent together yet. Nothing like a close call to give the fucking a certain intensity. Nothing too kinky, just ... well, a little emotional, maybe.

"Why?" Keir had asked.

"It's getting ... too heavy."

What the hell did *that* mean? Rick's hazel eyes met Keir's impassively.

"Okay," Keir said, shrugging. "Me first in the shower or you?"

He didn't think Rick meant it. Or at least ... he thought Rick just needed time to work through whatever was bothering him. But Rick had been serious. No more sleepovers. In fact, no more hanging out together at all for a time — until Rick had started seeing the twink flight attendant from Colorado. Then they'd slowly drifted back to spending off-duty time together.

Gradually it had sunk in on Keir that it really was over. Over for Rick, anyway.

Keir had tried, but for him it was like trying to stuff the genie back in the bottle. He couldn't go back — and he wasn't going to be allowed to move forward either. The practical thing, the *only* thing to do, seemed to be to disengage. That was easier said than done. It had taken him four months and Rick dating a handsome, well-to-do West Hollywood veterinarian to make up his mind for him.

Anyway, he didn't regret his decision, and Ireland was beautiful, it was just that he could have done without the group tour experience. Not that it wasn't sort of relaxing sitting there on the bus watching the green countryside flash by. Everywhere you looked were the ruins of castles and towers, grazing sheep, old graveyards. They'd yet to pass through a village that, no matter how small, didn't have at least two pubs, and even the ugly little industrial towns seemed quaint and exotic because it was Ireland.

He just wished Rick were there to share it with him.

He just wished he could stop thinking about Rick.

■ ■ ■ ■ ■

The phone rang and rang, and then Rick picked up. "Monaghan." He sounded curt.

"Top of the morning to you," Keir drawled. He was lying on the bed in his "posh" hotel room staring up at the pattern cast by moonlight through lace curtains. He wrapped one hand around his cock, stroking leisurely.

"Jeeesus," Rick said, but Keir could hear the smile in his voice all the way across the Atlantic. "It's about time you checked in, you asshole. Having fun, I take it?"

"You bet." Loose limbed, he half-closed his eyes, moving his hand. He imagined it was Rick's big hand on him … .

"What the hell time is it over there?"

Keir made an effort, glanced at the hotel clock. "Late." Like three a.m. late. Which put it about seven o'clock in the evening in Los Angeles. Rick was probably on his way out. Was he still seeing the veterinarian? Keir's hand tightened; he pumped himself a little harder, a little faster. Said breathlessly, "How's tricks?"

"Same old, same old." But Rick promptly launched into a description of his case load. Once it would have been *their* caseload, but Keir would only have two weeks on the job when he returned, and gradually that awareness tinged Rick's tone and slowed his words until he came to a full and awkward stop.

It was during that pause that sensation shivered through Keir. He bit his lip on the sound threatening to tear out of him, feeling the quicksilver release spill through his fingers, spatter belly and chest.

From a long way away Rick asked — changing the subject, "So how's the Guinness? Did it live up to expectation?"

His pulse was already slowing, his breath evening. Not like the earth had moved; just a little tremor. He got out, "Yep. It really *is* different over here."

"Going to a lot of pubs? Listening to a lot of music, I guess?"

"Yep. We've had a *seisiun* pretty much every night. It's great. You'd have loved it."

"Yeah. Well."

Keir opened his mouth but found nothing to say. No. Wrong. There was too much to say. And even if he knew where to start, what was the use? One thing about Rick: he knew his own mind.

Instead, he tried to move the conversation back to shop talk. Rick interrupted him to say, "Was it the Martinez case? Is that why you're resigning? I know you hate it when kids — teens — are involved."

He took the comfortable lie handed to him. "Partly, I guess."

"You didn't have to resign, though. You could have transferred to another division. You could have — "

He hadn't wanted to bring this up long distance, but he couldn't lie, either. "The thing is… I'm moving out of state."

The silence was so abrupt and so profound, Keir thought they'd been disconnected.

"Rick?"

"You're leaving the… state?" Rick sounded dazed.

"I am. Yeah."

"I don't understand."

It was difficult, but Keir said it. "Yes, you do."

Another trans-Atlantic silence stretched.

Finally, harshly, Rick said, "What? Is this like some kind of ultimatum?"

"Come on, Monaghan. You know me better than that."

"I don't know you at all."

Rick disconnected the call.

Half an hour to departure; he had just enough time to run downstairs and grab something for breakfast if he moved fast. A piece of smoked ham — the Irish version of bacon — or one of those funky "puddings." He put his suitcase in the hotel hallway so the bus driver could collect it with the others, and behind him the phone began to ring. Loud, insistent… American. Keir plunged back into the room and leaped across the bed to grab it.

"Yep?"

"Two Irish cops walk out of a pub," Rick's voice announced.

Keir gave a half-laugh.

"Hey! It could happen!"

Keir caught a glimpse of his expression in the mirror over the desk. His smile faded; that was just *sad*. "To what do I owe this honor?"

"I don't know. Look, we're friends, right? Whatever else happens?"

"Of course."

"Okay. Just wanted to make sure."

Now how weird was it to get choked up over this? Very. "We're good," Keir said.

"Good? We're the best." Rick added awkwardly, "I feel like I did all the talking last night."

Keir did laugh then. His gaze fell on the bedside clock. "Hey, I've got to go. We're catching a ferry to this island."

"What island?"

"Inishbofin. The Island of the White Cow. It's off the west coast of Galway."

"As in home of the Inishbofin Ceili Band?"

"Right." Irish music, mountain climbing, Truth, Justice and the American Way. Just a few of the things they'd had — still had — in common. Too bad it wasn't enough. Keir said, "I'll send you a postcard."

"I probably won't get it till you're back."

Hell, he probably wouldn't get it till after Keir was gone.

They both silently absorbed that. Keir said, "Well, it's not a secret. I wish you were here."

The pause that followed was excruciating. Finally, haltingly, Rick said, "Keir — "

It was just too hard to hear it.

"Later," Keir said, and put the receiver down.

CHAPTER THREE

Deanna Holland was a little woman with a big gun. Not that you'd know it to look at her. Polite, quiet, well-groomed. Even as they ran out of suspects in her boyfriend's homicide, they'd treated her politely and respectfully. They didn't meet a lot of Deanna Holland's in their business.

They didn't have enough to arrest her, but Deanna didn't know that, and the third time they'd interviewed her in her Sherman Oaks home, she'd freaked and pulled a Ruger Rimfire out of an expensive Chinese vase.

Keir had been faster, going for her before Rick was even on his feet. Rick heard the shot as Keir jerked. Rick's own heart seemed to stop — the world seemed to stop. It was like that scene in that Hitchcock film when the merry-go-round spins out of control and smashes apart. That's what it felt like. Like gravity had slipped and he'd just gone hurtling into black space, and the earth was a blasted, empty shell falling in pieces around him.

Game over. Everything over.

But then Keir had still been on his feet, and he had the gun, and Deanna was shrieking like a banshee, pouring out her rage and terror. Keir was unharmed beyond powder burns on his neck and sports jacket. He'd been mad as hell about that jacket, which had been new.

That night the sex was phenomenal. It was always good — they were getting to know each other very well that way by then. Knew exactly what turned the other one on, what felt great — well, what *didn't* feel great? And the funny thing was how new fucking seemed when they tried it together. Yeah, it was always good, but that night...

But later Rick had made a fool of himself. Said things he should never have said, wrapping Keir in his arms and spilling his guts. Luckily Keir had slept through most of it. Not much for afterplay, Keir. He lived on his nerves too much, and when he let go... but Rick sort of liked the fact that he was one of the few people Keir could let his guard down with.

By the time morning rolled around, though, Rick'd had plenty of time to reflect on what a bad idea it had been to get this involved. They were already about as close as two guys could be — sex was really just confusing things. Rick didn't want to feel any more than he did, and, God help him, he didn't ever want to feel what he'd felt when he heard Deanna Holland's gun go off.

So he'd told Keir — they were always honest with each other. Keir seemed to take it all right. Better than Rick expected. In fact, if Rick were completely honest, he'd been a little irritated at how well Keir had seemed to take it. Okay, granted it was a little... quiet between them for a time. Each of them trying not to set the other off or send the wrong message. But then it gradually fell back to the way it had been before. It was good. It was safe.

And then, out of the blue, Keir had sprung this resignation bullshit.

Rick stood in the shower the morning after his phone call to Ireland. He dealt efficiently with the hard-on he'd woken with — thanks to painfully vivid dreams about his partner. His soon to be ex-partner. Then he quickly soaped up and rinsed down.

It was weird how much he missed Keir already.

Why couldn't Keir at least have talked it over with him? Not that he'd have been able to convince him to change his mind — there was no more stubborn sonofabitch than Keiran Quinn once he made his mind up.

Rick toweled off rapidly. He was running late, having overslept when he did finally manage to drop off. The news that Keir was moving — leaving the state had shaken him badly. It just kept getting worse and worse. Every time he managed to convince himself that he could deal with one piece of the puzzle Keir had become — like staying friends even if Keir wasn't on the job with him — he spotted a new tidal wave-sized wrinkle headed his way.

The leaving the state thing... that was the worst so far.

There was no going back from that. It was possible Rick might never see Keir again.

He'd already had a week of what that tasted like, and rat poison would be sweet by comparison.

But what was the solution?

There wasn't one.

He looked at the clock in his bedroom and swore. If Keir had been here picking him up for work like the bastard was supposed to, Rick wouldn't be running late — for the first time in God knew when.

He buttoned his shirt, zipped his pants. He reached for his shoulder holster and was hit by the memory of the last time Keir had been in this room, stretched out long and brown and lazy in the sheets of the unmade bed. Keir grinning up at him, alive and in one piece. Keir reaching for him...

These were the memories he didn't want. But it was all tangled together now. The man who stood shoulder to shoulder with him on the job and the man who lay in his arms at night. When Keir went he would take both those men with him — he would take everything. And wasn't this exactly what Rick had been afraid of?

■　■　■　■　■

The island made up for the rest of the trip. Not that the trip had been bad, but... Inishbofin was the real deal. From the blow holes and sea stacks to the ruined pirate fort... there was plenty to see, plenty to explore. He could be by himself as much as he liked — and he liked. Keir hiked out to the seal colony, walked the beaches, climbed in the green hills. The water around the island was supposed to be some of the clearest in Ireland, and he could have gone swimming or diving if he'd felt more energetic. He slept well on the island. The best he'd slept in a long time. He ate well too — he liked seafood, and the Doonmore Hotel had a good chef.

On the third and last evening of the island stay, Keir sat on a rock overlooking a pasture with gentle-faced cows, and knew himself to be truly at peace for the first time in a very long time. For the first time he felt at peace with the decision he'd made to leave LAPD — and Rick.

It wasn't easy, it still hurt, but here on the island he had a sense of the... ebb and flow of all things. Sometimes you won, sometimes you lost, but life went on — and he would be happy again one day. He knew it for certain sitting under the setting Irish sun, listening to a corncrake tuning up for the evening's serenade.

When he finally walked back to the hotel it was nearly dark. Several guests from the tour were sitting on the green overlooking the ocean and listening to a local group of musicians. A brown-haired girl was singing "Danny Boy" while the others accompanied her on an assortment of guitars, fiddles, penny whistles. It had to be a request from the American tourists, but Keir thought he'd never heard a sweeter version.

The summer's gone, and all the flowers are dying
'Tis you, 'tis you must go and I must bide.
But come ye back when summer's in the meadow
Or when the valley's hushed and white with snow
'Tis I'll be here in sunshine or in shadow
Oh Danny boy, oh Danny boy, I love you so.

He'd always thought it a trite little song — fake Irish — but that evening with the rush of waves and cries of the seabirds for added accompaniment — his throat tightened at the simple sweetness of the melody and words. Nothing wrong with a little sincere sentiment, was there? He felt an unexpected sense of the merging past and the present... his own Irish roots and the adventuring spirit of his ancestors that had led them to strike out for a new land and leave this tough, enduring loveliness behind.

He was probably never going to hear "Danny Boy" again without getting choked up. Rick would laugh his ass off.

And he remembered that soon Rick would be a memory too... like this evening, like this island. Except that Rick would be the most important of all his memories.

Or maybe not. He might get over it one day. But right now it felt like a grief that would never heal. Even if the ending had been written at the outset. God knows he should have seen it coming. Should have guarded his heart. When had any of Rick's relationships lasted more than a few months? When had his?

He just... hadn't had a choice in it. He'd pretty much loved Rick from the start.

In sunshine or in shadow.

The music was breaking up, people wandering back to homes and hotels to get ready for the night's festivities. There was music on the island nearly every night during the summer.

Keir headed for his hotel.

■ ■ ■ ■ ■

After a very nice seafood dinner with the tour group — even the lobster tasted different in Ireland — there was an evening concert in the hotel rec room, and immediately following the traditional music concert, there was an informal *ceili* in the hotel pub. With the exception of the tour group, everyone in the place — which was packed — seemed to play an instrument or sing. There was a great deal of Emmy Lou Harris and country western in addition to traditional Irish fare.

Keir was at the bar getting another round for himself and the couple from Milwaukee — Ceil and Kris — when he caught the eye of the bartender.

As in ... a blip suddenly flashed on the old gaydar. Keir had already noticed the bartender — Seamus, they called him — a very nice-looking young guy with curly, reddish hair and brown eyes, an easy smile and a nice laugh. About as different from Rick's tall, dark and handsome good looks as it got.

"Another one for you?" Seamus asked. Somehow his accent made it sound especially charming.

Keir nodded, reaching for his wallet. When he glanced up, Seamus was eyeing him. Catching Keir's gaze, he grinned.

"You're the copper, are you?"

Keir winced and Seamus laughed.

"I asked about you," Seamus admitted. And Keir started paying closer attention. "What do you think of our island, then?"

"Beautiful." Keir was horrible at small talk, but he tried. "Have you lived here all your life?"

Seamus laughed. "I was a stockbroker in Dublin. Decided to leave the rat race and came here. Used to holiday here in the old days."

"Must be a change."

"Change would be a fine thing." Seamus counted out Keir's coins and winked.

Was that a pun or — ? Keir said slowly, "Isn't the saying, 'Chance would be a fine thing?'"

"Aye, but this ... *change* could happen." Seamus was still smiling, but his gaze met Keir's steadily, unmistakably.

Keir swallowed. "What time do you get off?"

Seamus's grin was wry. "Depends on the *seishun.*" He nodded at the packed house of musicians and singers and tourists. "This lot ... could be two or three in the morning." He added, "But your boat's not leaving until eleven-thirty tomorrow."

Bemused, Keir carried the drinks back to the little table where Ceil and Kris sat.

"Making friends?" Ceil asked, and Kris chuckled.

One of the tour group requested "Danny Boy," and the island musicians obligingly launched into a long instrumental version. The tour group began to sing — not very well.

"'Tis you, 'tis you must go and I must bide ... ."

Kris put her hands to her head in pain.

The pub door swung open on a newcomer. A gust of fresh, sea breeze wafted through the crush.

"But come ye baaaaaaaaack when summer's in the meadow ..." roared the singers.

It was like in a film where a long distance shot suddenly snapped into zoom focus. Rick — *Rick* — filled the doorway, the night breeze ruffling his dark hair, his eyes raking the crowded room.

"Wow," Kris said. "James Bond just arrived."

"I ... don't ... believe it," Keir said.

His friends glanced at him, then turned back to the newcomer. That was the last Keir noticed about the ladies from Milwaukee. He stood up. Rick's eyes met his.

It seemed to Keir that he waited a long time to see that particular expression on Rick's face. Maybe five years. Maybe his entire life.

Rick started to make his way through the gridlock of chairs and bodies and musical instruments. Keir moved to meet him. It felt like it took a long time, and then they were face to face, fingers brushing tentatively — and then locking on, gripping tightly.

"What are you doing here?" Keir asked.

Rick started to laugh. "I think that's my line."

"You couldn't have just arrived. When did you get to the island?"

"Three this afternoon. It took me awhile to track you down."

"Some detective."

"For your information, this island is five miles long, has five villages, five bed and breakfasts — and three hotels. Although if you blink, you're liable to miss any or all of them." Rick leaned forward and Keir realized they were about to share their first public kiss. That was his last clear thought for several long seconds.

Warm mouth and faded aftershave. Rick needed a shave and a shower, but to Keir he smelled like... bright sunshine and gun oil and L.A. rain and the wind blowing through the open car window and the glint of sunglasses and the flash of badge and too many burgers and too many beers and talking late into the night and sheepish grins in the morning... and being held tight and told you were the one thing that really mattered — the *only* thing that mattered — from the one person you felt the same way about.

When they broke apart there was clapping, some laughs and a couple of whoops. It was okay. They were among friends.

Rick was looking around the pub. Keir looked too — no sign of Seamus behind the bar. He felt a twinge of regret. Not for himself. For Seamus. It must get lonely for a gay man on a little island in the middle of nowhere.

Rick said, "Is there some place we can go and talk?"

"You want to talk?" Keir raised an eyebrow. "I never thought I'd see the day."

"Nah, I want to tell you this joke I heard."

Keir nodded, patient. "Shoot."

"Two Irish cops walk into a bar. The first cop says..." Rick's voice dropped. He said gruffly, "I love you. Come home."

Keir managed to keep his voice steady. "What's the other cop say?"

The sweetness of Rick's smile was like a kick in his chest. "That's what I'm here to find out, boyo."

THE FRENCH HAVE A WORD FOR IT

*I really enjoy the idea of exploring what happens after the curtain comes
down on a very dramatic story. For example, all those bodyguard romances.
What happens after the threat has been neutralized and there is no great,
sensational catalyst for keeping two very different people together? How
much of the attraction is just the aphrodisiac of danger?*

"Colin?"

Something about the deep voice was familiar. Colin Lambert looked up from
his sketch pad, squinting at the tall silhouette blocking the blanched Parisian sun. It
was a golden autumn afternoon and the last of the tourists were crowding the cafés
and narrow streets of the "village" of Montmartre. The background babble of French
voices, the comfortable scents of warm stone and auto exhaust and Gauloises and
something good cooking — always something good cooking in Paris — and the old
world colors: the reds of street signs and awnings and the greens of ivy and window
shutters and the yellow of the turning leaves and fruit in the grocer stands ... all of it
faded away as Colin gazed up, frowning a little.

"It is Colin, isn't it?"

Gradually the black bulk resolved itself into broad shoulders, lean hips, black
hair and gray eyes. Colin blinked but the mirage didn't vanish, in fact it smiled — an
easy, rueful flash of white. "You probably don't remember me."

"Thomas?"

Not remember Thomas Sullivan? Did anyone forget their first love?

Colin was on his feet, sketch pad tossed away, chair scraping back on cement.
He moved to hug Thomas and Thomas grabbed him back in a rough, brief hug,
laughing. They were both laughing — and then self-consciousness kicked in. Colin
recalled that he wasn't seventeen anymore, and that Thomas wasn't —

And never had been.

He stepped back, Thomas let him go, saying, "I can't believe how long it's
been. You look ..." Words seemed to fail him.

Colin knew how he looked. He looked grown up. Ten years was pretty much
a lifetime in puppy years, and he had been such a puppy back when Thomas knew
him.

Knew him? Back when Thomas had been his bodyguard.

"How are you? Are things going right for you?" There it was: The Look. That keen, searching gaze — wow, Thomas's eyes really were gray. Not just something Colin had imagined or remembered incorrectly.

Gray eyes. Like cobbled streets after rain or smoke or November skies.

And Thomas's smile conveyed a certain... er... *je ne sais quoi* as they said over here. A friendly understanding. Like Thomas had been there, done that, and made no judgments — but nothing surprised him anymore either. It was almost weird how little he'd changed. A few faint lines around his eyes, a little touch of silver at his temple. What was he now? Forty-something?

Every woman in the café was looking at him. A lot of *les hommes* as well.

"I'm good. I'm great," Colin answered.

"Yeah?"

And Thomas was still studying him. Measuring the boy against the man? Or just wondering about what scars the bad times had left?

Colin said firmly, "Yeah. I'm here painting."

"Painting?" Thomas looked down at the sketch pad as though he'd only noticed it.

"Well, sketching just now, but yeah. I'm painting. What are you doing here?"

"You're a student?"

"No. I'm a... doing this." He nodded at the sketch pad, then reached down to flap the cover over the rough sketch of a steep flight of steps. It still sounded so... not exactly pretentious — or not only pretentious — but unlucky to say *I'm a painter.*

Thomas's smile widened. "Good for you. And you're making a living at it? At your painting?"

"Er... define making a living." Colin laughed, and Thomas laughed too, but his gaze continued to assess and evaluate. Well, old habits probably died hard. Especially for a guy in Thomas's line of work.

"What are you doing in Paris?" Colin asked again.

"The usual. A job."

Well, whoever the client was, they were lucky to have Thomas on their side. Still, Colin preferred not to think about Thomas's job — preferred not to remember that time in his own life. "How long are you here for?"

"Tonight. Just tonight."

Colin was aware of an unexpectedly sharp jab of disappointment. "Oh. Right."

They continued to stare at each other and then Thomas looked around at the small, crowded tables. "Do you have time for a quick drink?"

"I'd like that, yes."

They had wine, of course. Beaujolais Nouveau. The waitress brought it out, chilled, with two fluted glasses, perfumed aromas of plums and blackberries wafting into the bright cold autumn air. And for the space of a glass of wine, they could have been alone in the world.

An occasional fat drop of rain splashed down; there were dark clouds rolling in from the distance, crimson and gold leaves scattered the sidewalk, bikes and motor bikes flashed past like giant insects. Neither man showed any inclination to hurry away.

"It's beautiful here. I see why you love it," Thomas remarked, leaning back and glancing around the crowded street as though only now recalling their surroundings.

"I do love it. You're right." Colin studied Thomas's ruggedly handsome features. It was not a face that gave a lot away. "Are you still... what are you doing these days?"

"Same thing."

Colin's memories veered sharply. Not a path he wished to travel. "So you never went back... to the FBI?"

"No. I stayed in the personal protection industry after I left your grandfather's employ." Thomas suddenly grinned. "I don't know if I ever told you, but I was always proud of you for choosing to go away to college on your own terms."

"Even if it did put you out of work?"

"Even so."

Colin's smile twisted. "You said you'd stay in touch."

Thomas's gaze dropped to the red-and-white-checked table cloth. "I shouldn't have. I was always a terrible letter writer."

That had hurt. Thomas had meant... a lot. Had probably even known how much he'd meant, so to just drop out of Colin's life? Not even the occasional Christmas card? Yeah, that had hurt. There had even — embarrassingly — been a few tears shed over that.

"It was kind of hard to say goodbye," Thomas admitted. "I guess I tried to make it easier on both of us."

"Sure."

Thomas seemed uncomfortable, so Colin changed the subject. He didn't want to scare Thomas off. They had little enough time as it was. "So what's the job? Can you talk about it?"

"Not really," Thomas said. "Routine stuff. No drama."

"Yeah," Colin said dryly. "That's what you probably said about my case to your buddies at the Bureau. It's plenty dramatic when you're on the other side."

"Your situation was different." For an instant there was a glimpse of the professional Thomas Sullivan. Despite the easy smile, the frank gaze, he could be brusque and hard as nails. He was the man who had — almost single-handedly — saved the life of the kidnapped fourteen-year-old grandson of one of the richest men in America. There had been a lot of media attention on Special Agent Sullivan after that daring rescue. It couldn't have been easy for someone who valued his privacy as much as Thomas.

Absently, Colin moved his glass inside and out of the ring of wet on the table cloth. He really didn't want to think about that. Didn't want to remember the ninety-six hours he'd been kidnapped and held for ransom by John Riedel, a disgruntled former security officer at one of Mason Lambert's bottling companies.

It wasn't a big trauma for him. Well, it probably was, , but it's not like it haunted his days and nights. He had got past it, had moved on, and had even managed to forget a lot of it. Learned to trust people again, and — even harder — learned to trust himself.

Watching him, Thomas said suddenly, "You sure everything is okay? You hugged me hello like I was the cavalry and you were down to your last bullet."

Colin chuckled, looking up. "I hugged you hello like you were the first familiar face I'd seen in nine weeks. I'm not quite as fluent as I thought I was. It gets lonely sometimes." He thought it over and admitted, "Or maybe I was just kind of thrilled to see you again. I'd sort of given up on that."

He didn't mean it to come out like an accusation, but Thomas must have heard something. He gave another of those lopsided smiles and said, "I guess you sort of had a case of hero worship back then."

"It wasn't that exactly. Well, I guess it was, but it wasn't only that." Colin took a deep breath. "Um. I'm not sure you ever noticed, but I'm ... gay."

Thomas let out a sudden, soft exhalation — as though he'd been holding his breath. "It ... crossed my mind a couple of times." His tone was grave enough but he was struggling to keep a straight face.

"That obvious, was it? At fourteen?"

"Not at fourteen, no. At sixteen, sort of. Seventeen, yes."

"Just another way I managed to disappoint Grandpappy."

The amusement faded. Thomas said vaguely, "It's probably not that bad."

"No. Probably not." Colin finished the last mouthful of his wine. He'd made it last as long as he could, knowing Thomas would be saying goodbye soon after that final swallow. He would have things to do and places to go. "I knew from the time I was little. And when I got older, I couldn't help but notice that I didn't find girls very interesting. Not the way my friends did. I was trying very hard to talk myself out of it. But then you came along. And I realized it wasn't something I was going to grow out of." He added quickly, "I hope you're not offended, me saying this to you."

Thomas's dark brows shot up. "Why would I be offended?"

"Well, I just mean ..."

Meeting Thomas's steady, smiling gaze, something clicked into place for Colin. Warmth flooded his face.

"*Oh.*"

Thomas's grin widened.

"I'm an idiot."

Thomas laughed. "No."

"Yeah. I am." Collin was shaking his head. "God. Now I really am embarrassed."

"Why? It's not like that was a conversation we were ever going to have."

"I don't know why not. We talked about everything else." Especially at first. Especially after he'd been dumped back into the nest: the fledgling the cat had chewed up. Colin had still been in shock and terrified. For a time it had been hard to let Thomas out of his sight. Thomas had represented safety, security and four-teen-year-old Colin had latched on tight. Thomas had accepted it with good grace.

Maybe he understood that being taken had done something to Colin. Shattered his belief in people, made him understand how thin the veneer of civilization was, how fragile its protections against what his grandfather only half-jokingly referred to as "the barbarians outside the gate."

You didn't get over that right away — but you did get over it. If you worked at it.

Colin pushed back in his chair. "It's too bad we didn't talk about it. It might have made things easier for me. Knowing an adult who was gay, who I could have asked — "

"There is no way we were ever going to have that discussion."

Colin was a little startled at his vehemence "Sorry?"

"Nothing." Thomas rose. "Do you have time for another drink?"

Colin nodded eagerly and Thomas disappeared inside the bistro. The wait-ress appeared shortly after with another round. So that was the good news. Thomas wasn't in a hurry to say goodbye.

He puzzled over Thomas's odd attitude about not discussing being gay with him, but then Thomas finally came back, took his seat. He smiled and Colin blinked in the brilliance of that smile.

"So, why France? Couldn't you paint in the good old U.S. of A.?"

"Sure. But Paris … well, Montmartre. Monet, Picasso, Van Gogh." Colin added prosaically, "Plus it's over three thousand miles between me and Grandpappy."

"Things not so good between you?"

Colin shrugged. "I just needed a little room."

"Three thousand miles ought to do it." Thomas sipped his wine. "What was the problem? He didn't want you to become an artist?"

"If only it was that simple. No. No. He was always supportive. Arranged for me to have tutors, picked the best art college he could find, and started to plan my first show."

Thomas said nothing.

Reluctantly, Colin said, "However I explain this I'm going to sound like an ungrateful shit."

"So?"

"I said I wanted to study in France. That I just wanted to … try and do it on my own. Without his money or the family name to pave the way. I wanted to do it for real."

Thomas nodded noncommittally.

"And that hurt him. I knew it would, no matter how I tried to say it. So then he brought up the kidnapping and said that it wasn't safe. That it would never be safe for me because I would always be a target now." He grimaced. "I got angry."

"I'm not surprised."

"And I said I'd take my chances. And then he got angry and said that since I wanted to do it all on my own, I could try supporting myself like everyone else had to who wasn't as lucky to be born into a family like mine."

"Oh boy," Thomas said. That was something Colin had forgotten until now. Thomas never swore. Never. Rarely even raised his voice. Not even when he was negotiating with a raving psychopath who kept threatening to blow a hole in a terrified little kid.

Colin smiled sheepishly as he said, "It sort of deteriorated from there. I said that suited me fine and he said we'd see if I lasted two weeks."

"And you've lasted nine and still counting. Have you called him since you got here?"

"Nope. And I don't plan on it."

"He's probably worried sick by now."

Colin smothered the flash of irritation. "I send him a postcard every week. Knowing Grandpappy, he's probably got the phone rigged to trace me if I do call. Which means he'd be here on the next flight trying to blackmail me into coming home."

"You send him a postcard every week?" Thomas sounded surprised.

"Yeah. Why?" Colin added, "I mail them from different parts of Paris."

Thomas's mouth twitched like he was trying to keep a straight face. "Tricky."

Colin laughed. "No. I know it wouldn't be hard to find me if he sent one of his henchmen after me. I'm not trying to hide from him, just give myself a little breathing room. I'm nearly thirty, you know?"

"You just turned twenty-seven."

"I'm flattered you remember." He was, too, which was surely a sign of what a goof he was. Well, once a goof, always a goof. He said earnestly, "God, I wish you were staying longer. It's so great to see you."

Of course that might be all on one side.

But Thomas was eyeing him in that steady, thoughtful way. He said slowly, "Do you have plans for tonight? Maybe we could have dinner?"

"No, I don't have plans. In fact, I could cook if you like." God knows what he would cook. He'd have to take the money he had put aside for art supplies to buy food fit for company, but it would be worth it to get Thomas back to his place because …

well, you never knew. Thomas had hung around chatting with him all afternoon and there was something in the way his gaze held Colin's just a few seconds too long every time their eyes met...

Colin wasn't seventeen now or a virgin, and Thomas Sullivan showing up in Paris for one night was like a fantasy come true.

But Thomas said, "How about I take you to dinner? You can pick the place — one of your favorites — and we'll make a regular evening of it."

"Seriously?"

Thomas nodded.

"I would — yeah! That would be great." Almost too good to believe.

"I've got some things to take care of. What's your address? I'll pick you up at seven."

Colin gave the address and Thomas jotted it down in a little notebook. Then he pushed back his chair, metal scraping cement, and rose. "I'm glad I found you, Col. I'll see you tonight."

Col. The old nickname. What a lot of memories that triggered — not all good. He didn't want Thomas confusing him with the kid he had been.

Colin wasn't even sure what he answered. He watched Thomas disappearing down the cobbled street, that easy, long-limbed stride, at home anywhere in the world.

When Thomas was out of sight, he gathered his things and walked in the other direction, up the hill.

■　■　■　■　■

Colin lived in a 19th century block of apartments and shops. His particular flat was above a boulangerie and every morning he woke hungry from the warm scent of rising bread and buttery croissants drifting through the floorboards. He was very happy if a little lonely. Sure, it was worrying to be poor, to be uncertain that he could make the rent and to have to choose between food and paint, but he was happy just the same. Happy in a way he had never been before.

It had something to do with pursuing his life's dream. It had something to do with finally being on his own — and surviving. And it had something to do with the way the morning light streamed through the old windows and the way the silver moon shone over the grey slate rooftops. It had to do with the rustling leaves of the chestnut trees, the old Parisian songs, and the muffled laughter from the cafés below.

It was all still new, still exciting and vibrant. Maybe that would change one day. Maybe the day would come when he didn't notice the light or the colors or the shapes and shades of this old and beautiful, foreign city. When he was tired of being hungry and being lonely. But for now every single day was an adventure.

And tonight felt like the greatest adventure of all. Thomas Sullivan was in Paris and tonight they would dine together. And, perhaps, if Colin was lucky...

He went through his meager wardrobe looking for something presentable to wear. Something that wasn't paint-stained or torn. Not a lot in the jeans, tees, and flannel shirts to choose from. He had not come to Paris to socialize. He found a clean pair of Levis and then he discovered a soft lambswool sweater in a lemony bisque color that he'd forgotten about. It looked nice with his blue eyes and dark hair. Speaking of which: he needed a shave and a haircut.

He couldn't do much about the hair; it was always a mop, but he shaved and studied himself narrowly. He looked presentable. More importantly, he looked his age. So hopefully there wouldn't be any problem there. Assuming Thomas's mind was running on the same lines as his own.

Thinking again of the way Thomas's gaze had held his, the way Thomas had watched him so closely, Colin was pretty sure he wasn't wrong in believing there was some interest there. He smiled at his reflection.

At seven o'clock, right on the button, Thomas knocked on his door and Colin's heart leaped in his throat with something very like stage fright.

He was smiling at the ridiculousness of that thought as he opened the door and Thomas smiled back.

"Hey." Thomas wore dark jeans, navy turtle neck and a leather jacket. He looked unreasonably sexy even in this city that prized elegance and sophistication so highly.

"Hello." Colin stepped back and Thomas walked into his small, tidy flat. "Did you have any trouble finding it?"

"Nope. I'm very good at finding things." Thomas answered absently, looking around, checking the flat out. There was not a lot to see. An "American kitchen" with a two-burner range, refrigerator, and toaster oven. A few essential pieces of furniture: a battered armoire, a small table and chairs, and lots and lots of canvasses and art paraphernalia. In the closet-sized bedroom was a brass bed — the sheets freshly laundered. "It's nice."

"Thanks. I like it."

"Smells good."

Colin nodded. "You should smell it in the morning."

And perhaps Thomas would, given the way he was smiling as their gazes locked yet again.

This was one of Colin's favorite times of day. The twilight turned a rich indigo and purple as the shadows lengthened on the winding streets below. The first stars twinkled over the rooftops. At this hour the 18th arrondissement looked much like it had in the paintings of Van Gogh.

It smelled just right too: a hint of woodsmoke, a trace of rain, turpentine and paint, all mixed with the heady scent of café crème drifting from downstairs.

Thomas's smile wasn't a promise, or at least not a promise to do more than consider the possibility. All he said was, "Quaint little neighborhood. I couldn't park anywhere near."

"No, it's a pedestrian square." Artsy and residential. There were several cafés and about a five minute walk to the Metro stop. A lot of old timers complained Montmartre had changed past all recognition, but in Colin's opinion it still had a small village feel to it. At least in the daylight hours. Very, very different from anywhere in the States. At night, Montmartre was a nightclub district, but Colin didn't do nightclubs.

Thomas walked over to one of the stacks of painted canvasses. "You've been busy."

"Yes. That's what I came for." His nerves tightened. He knew he wasn't bad. Maybe he was even better than average. He'd sold a few things — but everyone sold paintings in Paris — and it really mattered to him what Thomas thought of his work. Maybe that was silly because Thomas would probably be the first to admit he was no art expert.

He picked up a canvas; a small study of Cimetière Saint-Vincent.

When he didn't say a word, Colin said self-consciously, "I'm trying to do in oil and alkyds what Brassai did with his photographs. You know, capture that mood, that feeling, that emotional texture of Paris at night, the moonlight shining on the wet streets, the secret walkways and gardens, the shadows of iron railings against brick walls."

Thomas said slowly, "I don't know who Brassai is but this is excellent." He looked up, serious. "These are all really excellent."

Colin laughed, scratched his nose in a nervous gesture held over from boyhood. "Thanks. They're not, though. But I'm getting better."

"I've never seen anything like this. You only paint in black and white? What do you have against color?" Thomas was rallying him, his expression flatteringly impressed as he put the one canvas down and picked up another, this of the Place du Tertre

"Nothing. There's a lot of variation in black and white, you know. Besides, I use browns and grays and blues, too. I want to capture the way Paris tastes and smells, you know?"

"And you think it smells blue?" Thomas was examining the delicate lines and details of the staircase and funicular.

"In the winter. Brown in the autumn." Colin loved his browns: burnt umber, raw sienna, burnt sienna, cinnamon, nutmeg, chestnut, bister, fawn, russet…

"Green in the spring." Thomas looked up, his eyes quizzical.

"And summer." Sometimes — rarely — he used green in his work, very dark green shadings. The greens of moss growing at the base of cracked fountains, or overgrown ivy, or the deepest of forests.

Thomas had picked up another painting. He said slowly, "And black and white at night."

"Yes," Colin said, pleased — probably disproportionately so — that Thomas got that. Starlight and black water, empty streets and white tree trunks, old buildings and shadowy figures.

"Looks like a lot of isolated, dangerous places," Thomas observed.

Colin kept his expression neutral but it took effort — he had tensed instantly at the suggestion that he wasn't safe, needed to be more careful, couldn't afford to take chances. Like he didn't already know? Like he needed a reminder? But he was not — refused — to live his life in fear.

"I'm careful." His voice came out more flat than he'd intended.

Thomas said, "Good. I'm glad."

It had never occurred to Colin to wonder, if he and the adult Thomas were to meet, whether they might have nothing in common. Might not even get along. The idea saddened him.

Thomas's look grew inquiring. "Something wrong?"

Colin shook his head.

Thomas put the painting aside. "Are you hungry? Did you figure out where we're going for dinner?"

Colin shook off the strange flash of melancholy. "I did. Chez Eugene. It's close by the Basilica du Sacré Coeur."

"Near the place where all the artists hang out."

"Right."

"Place de Tertre."

"Place du Tertre, yes."

"I was there earlier today." Thomas seemed about to say more. He changed his mind. "Are we walking or driving?"

"Let me grab a jacket and we can walk. Unless you'd prefer someplace closer?"

"It's a good brisk night for a walk."

Colin grabbed his jacket and they went downstairs and stepped out into the cold November evening. The cobbled streets were shining in the lamplight. It had rained, but the shower had passed. There was not a cloud in the night sky. The stars sparkled overhead.

They walked and talked, continuing up the winding street to Rue Lepic then turning right towards the intersection of Rue des Saules and Rue St-Rustique. Colin pointed out various places of interest. Interesting to him, anyway. He hoped they were interesting to Thomas. If not, Thomas was good at hiding his boredom.

"The Auberge de la Bonne Franquette was the one of the favorite hang-outs of the Impressionists," Colin said, pointing out the white restaurant as they hiked past. "Toulouse-Lautrec, Utrillo, a lot of penniless artists lived and worked around here — there's a museum dedicated to Dali up there."

Thomas smiled, his face enigmatic planes and shadows in the lamplight. "I can see why this is Mecca for an artist."

"It has been for me."

"You do seem ..."

"What?"

"Happy."

"I am."

Thomas said quietly, "It's good to see."

And surprising? Probably.

They followed Rue Poulbot to Place du Calvaire, and at last, right round to Place du Tertre. The square was brightly lit and still crowded with artists and easels, the cafés were ablaze with music and lights.

They found Chez Eugene without trouble, the famous brasserie in the shadow of the magnificent Basilique du Sacré Coeur. Outside tables with red umbrellas were charmingly arranged between heaters and romantic globe lamps within a white picket fence.

Inside it was warm and crowded and cheerful. There was confetti on the floor and Chinese lanterns hung from the ceiling. There were painted wooden horses and a musical organ, the organ cranking out cheerful Parisian melodies. The waiters were dressed like street urchins from the last century, with caps, suspenders, and cravats.

"What do you think?" Colin asked.

He couldn't read Thomas's smile at all. It seemed almost ... affectionate. "I like it."

"Okay, yes, there are merry-go-round horses, but the food is great," Colin promised. "You'll see."

Thomas laughed, but the food *was* excellent — as was the wine — and the company was even better. Colin had the lobster ravioli and Thomas had the veal, and they sampled each other's meals and talked and drank more wine and smiled into each other's eyes.

Thomas teased Colin about being a starving artist and Colin teased Thomas about being a cowboy; Thomas was originally from Wyoming and the papers had made a big deal of his "western" background after the daring rescue of Mason Lambert's sole heir. The fact that Colin had reached the point where he could joke about even that much was probably a good sign, though hopefully Thomas didn't notice.

All too soon they were finishing their melon and sorbet, draining their glasses, and starting the long walk down the hillside steps.

The smoke of their breath hung in the night air. Thomas put his arm around Colin's shoulders and Colin's heart sped up with happy anticipation. He was pretty sure that he and Thomas were going to spend the night together; the very idea made his head lighter than the wine they'd consumed. He put his own arm around Thomas's waist — it felt a little daring — moved closer into the warm circle of Thomas's arm.

Back at Colin's the lack of furniture became apparent when they carried their espressos from the shop below and sat in the uncomfortable wooden chairs on either side of the little table. Colin didn't own a sofa and the kitchen nook wasn't designed for seduction, although he was game — and grateful that Thomas showed no sign of wanting to bail.

"Are you… seeing anyone?" Colin asked tentatively. In the old days he hadn't had a clue about Thomas's sexuality, but he had known Thomas was single. His eligible bachelor status was one reason Thomas had been so attractive to the media.

Thomas said in that measured way, "No. Not steadily. I was seeing someone for a while but it didn't work out. My job is tough on relationships."

"You just need to find somebody who understands."

Thomas smiled faintly. Sipped his espresso.

"I don't mean it that way," Colin said. "I mean, you need a guy who understands that having *you* on someone's side means the difference between… making it through. Alive. Or not."

Thomas put his cup down. "Colin. That's …" He looked startled, even moved.

"Yeah, I know. I have a unique perspective." Colin smiled, trying to make light of it, but in fact, he felt strongly about this. He did see Thomas's job differently than most people would. Anybody who was going to share Thomas's life needed to understand that Thomas had a vocation, and that vocation meant life or death to others.

There was a crash against the wall dividing his apartment from the one next door. He jumped. Even Thomas tensed, immediately ready for trouble.

"What was that?"

Muffled voices filtered through the wall. The words were French. The tone was the same in any language. There was another door slam. *Bonjour* not *au revoir,* unfortunately. The voices grew louder.

"Oh *no,*" Colin groaned.

"What?" Thomas stared at him and then at the wall, where one of Colin's framed prints swung back and forth in pendulum fashion.

"The Sackos are home."

"The what?"

"My neighbors."

"Are they throwing chairs at each other?"

"Chairs? That sounded like the kitchen table."

"That sounded like the kitchen sink."

They started to laugh, breaking off at the sound of smashing glass. Thomas's eyes went wide. "What the heck?"

His expression was classic. Colin laughed. "Er, I think maybe it's a French thing."

"Le Homicide?"

"They're not going to kill each other. At least, I don't think so. They never have yet. It's kind of like ... you know those beatnik skits of French guys in striped shirts and berets, cigarettes hanging out of their mouths? Slapping around some sleazy mademoiselle. Like in *Funny Face.*"

Thomas blinked. "I'm not following."

"*Funny Face.* It's a film with Audrey Hepburn. She comes to Paris — well, anyway. There's a scene where she does one of those French beatnik dances..."

Thomas looked bemused, but he was grinning. "I see. Your neighbors are on the colorful side."

"Er, yes."

More splintering wood. More shattering glass.

"They must be heck on dining ware."

Colin groaned and then started to laugh again.

Thomas asked mildly, "How long is this likely to last?"

"Hours," Colin admitted.

Now it was Thomas starting to laugh. "Yeah? Well, why don't we go to my hotel?"

Colin looked hopeful. "Yes?"

"Oh, yes."

Thomas did the drive in record time. He was staying at the Hotel Lutetia in the heart of one of Paris' most fashionable and arty districts, Saint-Germain-des-Prés. The hotel had Art Deco architecture, period furniture, crystal chandeliers, a Michelin-star chef, and the flirtatious notes of jazz music curling from drifting through from the highly popular bar — none of which was remotely of interest to Colin.

They were still undressing as they fell on the bed.

Colin used to have dreams like this, dreams of himself and Thomas. Sometimes the dreams had been prosaic, the simple sharing of an experience; after he'd left for college there had been a lot of first experiences he would have liked to have shared with Thomas. Sometimes the dreams had been less easily defined, like his passionate but confused response to the way art coalesced into beauty, urgency, significance — and his need to articulate that to someone, if only so he could understand it himself. And sometimes, a lot of times, the dreams had been about sex. Having sex with Thomas. He'd dreamed about sex with Thomas *a lot.*

They landed on the creamy bed linens, Colin laughing as he dragged Thomas down on top of him. The solid reality of Thomas, the landing of his muscular length, knocked the breath from Colin. Or maybe that was Thomas's kiss, which was also harder and more substantial than the dreams had been. Colin opened his mouth to Thomas, kissing him back with every bit of experience he'd accumulated through the years. Oh, that taste, that pressure, that sweet moist heat washing through...

He felt Thomas shudder. They broke for much needed oxygen.

"*Qu'est-ce que c'est?*" Colin teased at Thomas's expression.

Thomas's mouth was pink from Colin's kisses. "That was one heck of a kiss," he admitted.

Colin tangled his fingers in Thomas's soft, dark hair. He offered his most seductive look. "I've had a lot of experience."

Thomas raised his brows, clearly amused. "You're a flirt, Colin."

Colin shook his head. "Flirtatious. Not the same thing."

"No?"

"No." Colin raised his head, found Thomas's mouth once more, and tried to tell him without words why it wasn't at all the same thing...

"Colin. Col. Wake up. You're having a nightmare."

He jolted back to awareness. He was in a dark room — a strange room — and a strange bed, and he was not alone, but the voice was reassuring and familiar. And for once it had survived the end of the dream. The joy of that brought unexpected tears to his eyes, chasing away the last shadows of the nightmare.

"God," he jerked out. "Thomas?"

"Right here."

"Sorry."

"No need. You okay now?" Thomas's voice was soft and intimate.

"Yes. I don't know why that — it's been years since I've — "

"It's probably me," Thomas said grimly, sliding his arm beneath Colin's shoulders, pulling him close. "Stirring up a lot of subconscious memories, waking up things better left sleeping."

That was probably true, but not what Colin wanted to think. "Nah. It was probably the lobster ravioli." He settled his head on Thomas's shoulder, getting comfortable again. He smiled faintly. "I can't believe you're really here. You can't know..."

How often I dreamed this. He wasn't dumb enough to say that, though. Talk about scaring a guy off.

Thomas's breath was warm against Colin's face. He smelled warm and sleepy and of a vaguely familiar woodsy scent from Colin's boyhood. Thomas must still wear the same aftershave. His fingers absently threaded Colin's sweat-damp hair.

"Do you remember much about it?"

Colin had no doubt what Thomas was referring to.

He said unemotionally, "I remember everything about it. When I let myself. It's better not to think about it."

Or he'd be too terrified to leave the house — as he had been for three years.

He could feel Thomas thinking, considering and discarding comments. In the end he just kissed Colin's forehead, warm lips nuzzling. Colin found Thomas's mouth with his own.

When their lips parted, he whispered, "I wish you were staying longer."

Thomas said softly, "I wish I was too."

"Do you get to Paris very often?"

Thomas said slowly, "If you'd asked me that question twelve hours ago, I'd have said no.

Colin smiled into the darkness. That was so much more than he had hoped for. He didn't want to risk ruining it with questions. Instead he rested his head on Thomas's shoulder, and closed his eyes. Thomas gave him another of those nuzzling kisses.

For a few minutes they breathed in peaceful unison. "Thomas?"

Thomas said sleepily, "Mm?"

"Yesterday afternoon. When you said there was no way we were ever going to have that discussion? What did that mean?"

He could feel Thomas trying to focus. "What discussion?"

"About you being gay?"

"Oh." A thoughtful silence. Finally Thomas said, "Because at seventeen you were an engaging, attractive, and very young man and it might have been difficult to preserve a safe distance if you'd known ..."

Colin snickered. "I'd've sure done my best to bridge that distance."

Thomas laughed sleepily. "And I'm not sure I wouldn't have let you."

Colin woke to the sound of rain against the window and a raging thirst. Quietly, carefully, he slipped out of Thomas's warm embrace, edged out of the bed and padded into the bathroom.

A glance back at the bed showed Thomas still sleeping peacefully. They still had an hour before he had to get up and start getting ready for his flight. Colin wanted to make every minute of that hour count; Thomas could always sleep on the plane, and if all Colin was going to have were memories, he wanted as many as possible. But maybe now there would be more than memories.

In the bathroom, he relieved himself, flooded a glass with lukewarm tap water, gulped it down. Refilled the glass and guzzled that down too.

On his way back to bed he glanced at the phone on the night table. The red light was blinking to indicate Thomas had a message. His gaze focused on the pad of hotel stationary placed there for the convenience of the guests. There was a phone number written in Thomas's firm hand.

It was a number Colin knew very well. It had once been his own — or rather, his grandfather's. Mason Lambert's private phone number.

The strength seemed to leave his body. He put his hand on the nightstand to keep from sitting on the edge of the bed. He felt … like he'd been hit by a car. Weak, shaky, stunned.

Was there a reasonable explanation for Thomas to have that number?

All kinds of reasons. And none of them applied. Colin knew with absolute certainty that Thomas Sullivan had come hunting him.

And found him.

And fucked him.

The betrayal was so massive he couldn't seem to think beyond it for a few seconds. He remembered their conversation of the day before — the careful, assessing way Thomas had studied him.

So what's the job? Can you talk about it?

Not really. Routine stuff. No drama.

"You bastard," he breathed, raising his head to stare at the bed. Thomas continued to sleep, untroubled, unaware, a small, content smile on his firm mouth.

Colin straightened up. For one brief moment he considered waking Thomas to tell him what he thought of him. To tell him how he'd looked up to him all these years, admired him, worshipped him, maybe — loved him, certainly. A kid's love, true enough, a first infatuation. Not what it … might have been if they'd had time. If Thomas hadn't been lying to him the whole time.

But what was the point?

What could Thomas say that would change anything?

Nothing.

And the conversation was going to be even more humiliating than this — and this was humiliating enough. The fact that it had not occurred to Colin once, not even once, that the odds of meeting Thomas Sullivan in Paris after all these years were astronomical? Way beyond the possibility of romantic coincidence. It just went to show what a sap … what a … *quel imbécile stupide et crédule.* As they said over here. Or screamed as they threw chairs and dishes.

As silent as a cat burglar, Colin found his clothes and dressed, grabbed his trench coat. On the way out, though, a thought occurred to him.

He tiptoed back, picked up the pad and set it on the pillow beside Thomas.

Thomas might as well know his little ruse was over. He'd been found out — and Mason Lambert with him.

But oddly Colin felt very little anger at his grandfather. At least that betrayal had been motivated by love and concern. Aggravating, but genuine nonetheless. His grandfather couldn't believe that Colin was safe and healthy and happy without proof — and control. But that was more about not trusting the world than not trusting Colin.

So Colin placed the pad of hotel stationary with the telltale phone number in the still-warm pillow indentation, and then he let himself out of the hotel room, closing it carefully, soundlessly.

The rain was coming down in a silvery mist when he reached the pavement.

He began walking.

■ ■ ■ ■ ■

At eleven o'clock Colin was sketching in the Square Jehan-Rictus. His fierce concentration was disturbed momentarily by the vision of a distant silver jet tracing its way through the slate sky above the famous I Love You wall.

It was probably not Thomas's plane, although — he glanced at his watch — the time was about right.

The righteous anger that had fueled him all the way back to Montmartre and his apartment — and then out again to work in the tiny park behind the Place des Abbesses, drained away. He was suddenly conscious that he was cold, that it was starting to rain, and that he would never see Thomas Sullivan again.

He lowered his sketch pad and stared at the long rain-streaked rectangle of 612 navy blue tiles of enameled lava bearing the inscription I Love You in over three hundred languages.

Je t'aime. That's how the French said it. Plenty of ways to say it. Plenty of ways not to say it.

Belatedly, it occurred to Colin this had been a really bad choice of a place to work that day. It was not a good day for working outside, in any case. Maybe he would just go buy a bottle of mulled wine, head home, and get drunk.

Instead he continued to sit and stare blankly at the glistening wall. His face was wet, but that was surely the rain because he was far too young to sit crying on a park bench like one of the elderly refugees who came here to gaze at the message of hope, to reassure themselves the world really wasn't that bad a place.

At least he had the square to himself. Not many people visited the park in this kind of weather. It was not much of a park in November. Most of the trees had lost their leaves with the night's rainfall.

Winter was right around the corner.

He really needed to pull himself together enough to get home.

The scrape of shoe sole on pavement. Footsteps on sodden leaves behind him. Colin glanced around, instinctively — he never quite lost that uneasy awareness of who was around him — and stiffened.

Thomas, face flushed with cold and possibly something else, was coming down the walkway. His eyes were dark and unreadable. He hadn't been kidding about being good at finding things.

Colin jumped up. He told himself the excitement surging through him was anger and shock, but there was a portion of disbelieving joy in that riotous clamor of emotions.

Still a few feet away, Thomas bit out, "For someone who paints a lot of shadows, you sure see things in black and white."

"Are you going to tell me I'm wrong?"

Thomas seemed to hesitate. "It's not the way you think."

"*I'm* the job."

"Yes. But — "

Colin turned and started walking.

Thomas caught him up in two steps. "Will you just stop and listen a minute, Colin? Yes, you were the job, but the job was just to check up on you, make sure you were okay. I accomplished that before we finished our drinks yesterday afternoon."

"Bullshit. Your mission was to get close to me and make sure I stayed safe."

"My mission?" Thomas's eyebrows shot up. "That is some imagination you've got. My mission wasn't to sleep with you. What do you think I am? What do you think your grandfather is, for crying out loud?"

For crying out loud. If he hadn't been so angry, he'd have spared a grin for that. But he was angry. Angry and hurt because Thomas had violated the trust Colin had placed in him from the time he was a kid.

He struggled to get the words out without revealing that embarrassing naïveté. "I think my grandfather has a God complex. I have no idea what your deal is. And I don't care. I don't even know who you are. I don't *want* to know."

He didn't walk away. He should have been walking away by then. But hurt and angry though he was, he did notice that Thomas had missed his flight in order to find him and talk to him.

Instead it was Thomas who half turned, looking skyward in exasperation.

"You cut off all communication, Col. Mason was worried. You're all he has."

"I didn't cut off all communication. I — I tried to set some parameters. You know how he is."

"I know he's a frail and elderly man who loves you more than anything on the planet. And I know he's worried sick."

That took some of the wind out of his already luffing sails. Colin did worry about his grandfather, was unhappily conscious that he wasn't getting any younger.

He said, and he could hear the resistance warring with guilt in his tone. "Look, I love my grandfather, I even miss him sometimes, but I don't have any illusions about him — maybe you do, but then you don't know him that well. He doesn't ask and he doesn't listen. He uses money to control and manipulate. He always has, he always will.

"I know. I do realize that. I know him better than you think. But it doesn't change the fact that he loves you and is worried about you. I'm not saying you should go back, I'm just saying you shouldn't shut him out entirely."

That caught him utterly off guard. "You're not saying I should go back?"

Thomas shook his head. "I don't think you should go back until you're ready. But you do need to let him know where you are."

Colin swallowed hard, almost afraid to believe this. "You didn't tell him?"

Thomas gave another of those brisk head shakes. "I told him I found you, I'd seen where you lived and you were all right and that I'd talk to you. See if you were okay with letting him know where you were, but that I wasn't going to reveal that information if you didn't give permission."

Colin opened his mouth, but Thomas added, "And I'd told him that before I ever agreed to have a look for you. There was no way — assuming you were okay — that I was going to get in the middle of your private war."

"It's not a war."

"Sure it is," Thomas said easily. "It's your war for independence. And, believe it or not, I'm in favor of that."

"If that's true, then why didn't you just tell me yesterday?"

Thomas sighed.

Colin flinched inwardly, remembering. Remembering too much. "Everything that happened between us was a lie."

"*No.*"

"All those bullshit questions yesterday afternoon. You already knew the answers: that I was here painting, that I'd argued with — "

"That's all I knew. It took me two days to track you down."

"Fine. So it was a fact-finding mission. That doesn't make it better." He felt like such a *fool*. That's what really hurt. One of the things that really hurt.

Thomas was shaking his head. "Your feelings are wounded and your pride is injured. I understand. I apologize. You must know I wouldn't deliberately hurt you."

He did know that. It didn't change the fact that Thomas *had* hurt him. And not for the first time, either.

But seeing his hesitation, Thomas said, "Do you want to hear my side of this or do you just want to tell me the way it is?"

What was the point? Maybe Thomas's motives had been pure. It didn't change the fact that last night Thomas had been on the clock and Colin had been falling in love. Colin had made a fool of himself — again — and Thomas had encouraged him to do so. He said quietly, bitterly, "No, I don't want to hear your side of this. I already told you that." He bent, picked up his sketch pad, lunch bag.

Thomas's hand closed on his upper arm. "You're going to hear it anyway. You owe me that much."

"I owe *you*?" Colin straightened, glaring. "Well, this ought to be good. Go ahead."

"You think last night was just about you? You think I didn't have a stake in what happened between us? That I don't have feelings about what happened? Grow up!"

The unexpected heat in Thomas's face and voice startled Colin. He said stiffly, "Okay. Sorry. What did you want to say?"

"What I wanted to say was, yes, I came looking for you as a favor to Mason, but I was already in this country finishing up a job. That's the first thing I want you to understand."

Thomas took a deep, steadying breath and Colin realized that this mattered to him, that the words were not coming easily. "I didn't come hunting you. I was already here, and since I was already here and had a couple of days to kill, I agreed to have a look for you to put your grandfather's mind at ease. And because *I* cared whether you were alright or not."

"Yeah, you cared so much you never so much as sent me a postcard."

"Colin." Thomas raked a hand through his hair. "There's a considerable age difference between us. It might not mean a lot now, but it sure as hell meant a lot when you were seventeen. Or even when you were in college. You think I wasn't aware that I had an inside track to your... affections? I could have had you any time from the point you formed an attachment to me. I kept a distance for your sake as much as my own."

"Your own?"

Thomas responded to the wariness in Colin's voice with exasperation. "Yes, my own. If you haven't noticed that I've got feelings for you then all I can say is you're the first blind artist I've met."

Colin didn't know what to answer. Thomas said, "Okay. So mission accomplished by the time we finished our first glass of wine yesterday afternoon."

Colin thought back to the previous day. "You went inside the café and phoned my grandfather."

"Yes. And from that point on, I was on my own time."

Colin was still rattled from his emotional high dive. He'd been so sure of Thomas's betrayal, so convinced that he had made a fool of himself the night before — plunging from the giddy high of falling in love and believing it was even reciprocated, to splashing down into ice cold reality of Thomas's real agenda.

Thomas added, "Last night was about you and me, and nobody else."

Colin protested — and he could hear the childish, aggrieved note in his voice, "Then why didn't you tell me — why'd you go on letting me think your running into me was just chance?"

"I was going to this morning. And I'd have done that if you hadn't run out."

"Why didn't you tell me last night — before we slept together?"

"You want the truth? We had one night. I didn't want to spend it talking about your grandfather or the past — let alone risk you freaking out. I wanted to... explore the present with you. See if there was maybe a future."

Thomas held his gaze steadily until Colin had to look away. He stared moodily out at the gray green shrubs. Was he being unfair to Thomas? Being unfair to both of them maybe?

"I don't know if that was selfish or not," Thomas said, watching him. "I thought, I still think, that's what you wanted too."

If he was realistic, yes. He had wanted Thomas to stop viewing him from the perspective of the past, to see him as a desirable adult rather than the traumatized kid he'd been. Last night he had wanted to pretend — wanted Thomas to go along with the pretense — that they were meeting for the first time.

Thomas said almost gently, "It's not a black and white world, Colin."

Colin looked back at Thomas who was watching him steadily, gravely. "You missed your flight."

"This is more important."

That helped. If Thomas was willing to stay, to try and talk things out, then it wasn't just about the job.

Thomas added, "You're not the only one with insecurities, Col. There's a part of me that wonders if what you feel for me, or think you feel for me, isn't just leftover hero worship."

That startled Colin. The idea that Thomas might be uncertain too, vulnerable too? It hadn't occurred to him. "No. Give me a little credit."

"Sure. But that goes both ways." Thomas rested his warm hand against Colin's cold cheek. "I didn't plan last night. I didn't expect last night to turn out the way it did. I'm off balance here too."

Maybe it was the sincerity in his voice. Maybe it was the tenderness in his touch. Colin took a deep breath and exhaled, let go of the anger, the hurt, the disappointment, and, yes, the fear. He tried for a smile although he felt out of practice.

"Where do we go from here?"

Thomas said, "I spent the last two and half hours searching for you. Let's start with breakfast — or whatever they call it over here."

"Petit déjeuner."

"Right. Let's start there. Where's a good place to eat? Some place we can talk."

Colin thought it over. He said, "How does fruit, croissants and petit pains with cheese sound? Or jam, or honey, or maybe Nutella. Whatever you like. And good coffee?"

"I'm hungry," Thomas said evenly, "but it's not so much the food as the company I'm interested in."

"I was thinking I'd fix you breakfast."

Thomas relaxed a fraction. He smiled, his eyes tilting in the old warm way. "Oh. Okay. Breakfast at home is good. Let's start there."

"We just have to make one stop on the way."

Thomas raised his brows inquiringly.

Colin admitted, "I guess maybe I need to make a phone call."

IN A DARK WOOD

In a dark, dark wood there was a dark, dark house ... Years ago
I read on the Internet about this creepy old house in the eastern woods —
there were even photos — and then when the idea came to write this story
and I tried to find the page again, I couldn't. Which seemed appropriately
eerie. Anyway, Tim's problems came as a revelation to me. I kept trying to
write away from them, but they just wouldn't go away.

"We're lost."

Luke came up behind me. I pointed, hand shaking, at the cross carved into the white bark of the tree. "We're going in goddamned circles!"

He was silent. Beneath the drone of insects I could hear the even tenor of his breathing although we'd hiked a good nine miles already that autumn afternoon — and no end to it in sight. My head ached and I had a stitch in my side like someone was jabbing me with a hot poker.

I lowered my pack to the ground, lowered myself to a fallen tree — this time not bothering to check for ant nests or coiled rattlers — lowered my face in my hands and lost it. I mean, *lost it*. Tears ... oh, yeah. Shoulders shaking, shuddering sobs. I didn't even care anymore what he thought.

"Tim ..." He dropped his pack too, sat down next to me on the log. He sounded sort of at a loss. After a minute he patted my shoulder. Awkwardly.

I turned away from him and tried to wipe my face on my shirt sleeve.

Feeling him fumbling around with his pack, I watched him through wet lashes. He pulled out his canteen, unscrewed the top and offered it to me.

I took the canteen, swallowed the warm stale water, handed it back. Wiped my face again. Perfect. My nose was running. Not that it mattered. It wasn't like I had a shred of dignity left.

First dates. You've got to love 'em.

But I mean, what kind of fucking sadist chooses camping for a first date?

Fast forward to the end of this one: we'd shake hands at my brownstone door — assuming we got out of this field trip into Hell alive — and he'd promise to call, and with equal insincerity I'd say I looked forward to it.

I'd never see him again — and that was the only bright side to this whole — literally — walking nightmare.

Luke pulled a cloth out of his pack and wet it with the canteen. "Here, look at me."

I looked at him. He wiped my face with the wet cloth, shocking me into immobility. His own face was serious, his hazel eyes studied me. I closed my eyes and he gently swiped my eyelids, washing away the sweat and tears.

"Better?"

I lifted my lashes, got my lips steady enough to form words. "Oh, sure. Great."

"I thought you were a travel writer?"

"I'm not an explorer! I write about comfortable hotels with clean sheets and hot water. My idea of roughing it is a two-star restaurant!"

The corner of his mouth tugged as though, against his will, he found this just a little bit comical. What the hell could be funny about any of this?

"Listen, we're not lost."

I opened my mouth and he said, "I don't mean I know where we are. But I can get us out of here, if that's what you want. I've got a compass and we can start walking east and be back to civilization within a few hours."

I swallowed hard. First off, there was no place in New Jersey that even remotely qualified as "civilization," but that was beside the point.

Luke said, "And, for the record, we're not going in circles. Look again at that carving on the tree. It's not a fresh cut. Look at the edges. They curl, but they're worn. It's not your mark. At least, it's not the mark you made today."

I blinked at him stupidly.

He said, "I think it's your mark from twelve years ago."

▪ ▪ ▪ ▪ ▪

Flash back four days ago to a dinner party at my best friend Rob's place in Manhattan. Rob'd gone all out: Chinese lanterns hanging over the table, shadows bobbing against the wall, all of us fumbling around with chopsticks, and the Peking duck from Chef Ho's, exquisite. I'd had three cocktails too many and Rob was egging me on.

"Tim, tell the story about the skull house, come on!"

I laughed, shaking my head.

"Come on," Rob urged. "Luke wants to hear it. Luke! Tell Tim you want to hear about the skull house in New Jersey."

Across the table and two faces down there was this very attractive guy, a few years older than me, with dark hair and crinkly, hazel eyes. He gave me a rueful grin.

This was Luke, the cop who Rob kept trying to fix me up with. "A cop?" I always said doubtfully. "I don't know."

"He's a detective, not a beat cop," Rob always replied. "He doesn't give speeding tickets."

Speeding tickets being kind of a sore subject with me. "I'm not really into cops," I always said.

"You're not into anybody," was Rob's standard answer. "And nobody is into you, which is your problem. One of your problems."

And that's where the conversation ended, except that night Luke was present and could speak up for himself.

"Sure, Tim," he said. "I'd like to hear."

He had a nice voice, not at all the voice cops use when they're slapping a parking ticket on your windshield or asking you to pull out your vehicle registration. He had very white teeth and a very nice smile. Did he know Rob wanted to set us up? Er — fix us up, I mean. He probably did, and he'd probably been resisting just as hard as me. He'd certainly kept a polite distance all evening.

I gave Rob a look that promised all kinds of retribution that I wouldn't remember once I sobered up. He just laughed and poured me another scorpion.

"Come on, Tim," someone else urged.

Someone else I didn't know. Rob knew everybody and everybody knew Rob. Most of them didn't know Rob as long as I'd known him, which was since we were the two most unpopular guys in Trinity School.

I gave in to peer pressure — not for the first time — with a sigh.

"I was thirteen and I was staying with a friend in the Pine Barrens for a couple of weeks during the summer. There wasn't a lot to do. Mostly we went swimming in this little lake and we spent a lot of time prowling through woods."

I glanced over at Luke. He set his glass back down, but his lashes lifted and he caught my eye. I couldn't look away. He didn't look away either. It was like tractor beams locking on. People were going to notice. My face felt hot, but that was probably the spicy sea dragon bass.

Managing to tear my gaze away, I said, "Anyway, one day we wandered farther into the woods then we were supposed to go. We get really turned around. Totally lost. Oh wait, I'm forgetting. There was supposed to be this house, see, where — I don't remember what the exact story was now — the Boogey Man or somebody like that was supposed to live in the heart of the woods. And when hikers or nosey kids like us disappeared, The Forester was supposed to have grabbed them."

"The Forester?" Luke asked. Everyone else chuckled, reaching for glasses or forks. Only Luke was paying close attention.

I focused inward. "Uh, yeah. I think that's right." Weird. I'd forgotten that he was called the Forester.

"So, anyway, we wander around, lost. We're afraid we're going in circles, and it's getting dark. I start marking the trees, making a little cross with my penknife in the bark, which is all white and shimmery that time of evening."

My heart started to thud against my ribs as it came back to me: the deepening shadows, the ghostly trees, the creeping chill of the woods closing in on us. "And then all at once there's a house right in front of us. Two stories, really old, falling down. There's a tree growing out through a big hole in the roof."

I gestured with my hands trying to make them see this creepy old house being claimed by the woods. "It has an ornate portico thing and little gable windows. Some of the other windows are broken, some of them are still there. The front door is hanging off its hinges…"

I stopped. For a moment it was like I was back in the woods. The smell of moldering house and weird animal scents and… the woods. The hush of evening — even the crickets were silent.

Too silent.

Rob laughed. He'd heard the story before — always when I was drunk. I don't tell this story sober. I couldn't help stealing another look at Luke. He wasn't smiling anymore; his brows were drawn together like he was studying me from a distance and not sure about what he was seeing.

"I took a step forward and something crunched under my foot. When I looked down it was part of a skull."

Laughter, some expelled breaths. Luke still stared, still frowning. "Skull or a bone?"

"Skull."

"Human?" someone else asked.

"I don't know," I admitted. "At the time we thought so, but we kind of wanted to think so, you know? I don't think it was."

I did think it was human, , but I sure as hell didn't want to admit it.

"So what happened?" a woman asked. The light from the blue lanterns bounced off her glasses and made her look blind. A blind lady insect.

"Nothing. We freaked out and ran home." I laughed. It wasn't a convincing laugh, but everyone else laughed too.

Everyone but Luke. "Did you tell anyone?"

I shook my head. "We weren't supposed to be there. We were afraid…"

We were afraid all right, and getting into trouble was only a little part of it.

"Did you ever go back?" the woman asked again.

Even her voice had a kind of hire wire whine to it. It hurt my head. I reached for my glass. "No."

"Do you think you could find the house again?" Rob asked slyly, looking from Luke to me. "If you had to?"

"No."

Luke asked, with a funny smile, "Would you want to try?"

■　■　■　■　■

I should have known the weekend would be a disaster when Luke told me later that evening that he would pick me up Saturday at six a.m.

"Morning?" I said uncertainly, hoping against hope that he'd got the a.m. and p.m. thing mixed up.

"Well, yeah. We'll need to get an early start. There's a lot of ground to cover, especially if we don't know where we're going."

He was smiling. He had a great smile: his hazel eyes tilted at the corners and his mouth — he had a very sexy mouth — did this little quirky thing. I felt a powerful tug of attraction — something I hadn't felt in a long time.

Still, I knew myself pretty well by then, and I wasn't at my best and brightest before noon on the weekends. Or any day. "Uh ... I'm not much of a morning person."

"Mornings can be the best part of the day," Luke said softly, and it was clear he wasn't talking cornflakes. His gaze held mine; I literally couldn't look away. My heart did a little flip.

"Do you have a sleeping bag?" he added.

"A ... sleeping ... bag?"

"We'll be spending the night, right? Camping?"

"Uh ... probably. Yeah." Oh. My. God. Did he mean — ? Were we going to — ?

"Don't sweat it," he said. "I've got you covered." His eyes twinkled. A cop with twinkly eyes? How much had I had to drink? I checked my glass.

So, yeah, the upshot: I went to dinner at Rob's on Thursday night and somehow walked out with a date — my first in over a year — for the weekend.

"Isn't Luke *hot*?" Rob demanded, when he called on Friday afternoon.

"He's pretty cute," I admitted, massaging my throbbing temples. I tried to focus on the monitor screen.

"*Cute?*" Rob exclaimed. "That's like saying Tom Cruise has nice teeth. He's gorgeous! That grin. Those eyes. That ass."

"Enough with Tom Cruise."

"I'm talking about Luke!"

I rubbed my eyes. Tried to read back what I'd written. Garbage. I mean, really, who gave a flying fuck about Scenic Hudson?

"I didn't even catch his last name," I said.

"O'Brien."

"Swell. He probably comes from a long line of Irish cops."

"Sure, and don't you know the way of it, boyo," Rob returned in a tooth-peeling brogue.

"I don't think he's my type."

"What are you talking about? He's attractive, smart, funny — and he has a steady job."

"He carries a gun."

"He rarely shoots people on the first date."

"I may beg him to; he's taking me camping." Against my will, I was smiling.

"*Camping?*" Rob recovered quickly. "Camping is a great idea. You'll love camping. Fresh air, sunshine, exercise..."

"I hate fresh air, sunshine and exercise. I haven't been camping since I was thirteen."

Rob ignored this. He knows me pretty well. "Where are you going camping?"

"New Jersey."

"*Jersey?*"

"Yeah, we're staying with the Jersey Devil."

Rob snickered.

I added, a little uncomfortable because part of the evening — including the part where I'd agreed to go camping — was fuzzy, "I think he just wanted an excuse to get me to take him to the skull house."

"You're taking him to the skull house?"

My head was really pounding now. I was going to have to take more painkillers. A lot more painkillers. My poor liver. "I don't think I could find it if my life depended on it. But Luke seems to think it would be fun to try."

Luke. His name felt alien on my tongue. Like it was the first word I'd learned in a foreign language.

"Wow." Rob's single word seemed a little inadequate. I'd have phrased it more like... WTF? "Well, for the record," he said, "he wanted to meet you before he ever heard about the skull house. He loves that column you write for the New York Blade."

Against my will, I was flattered.

"And," Rob added, "He said you were really cute."

"*Cute?* That's like saying Marcelo Gomes has nice legs! I'm gorgeous!"

■　■　■　■　■

At five fifty-nine a.m. on Saturday morning, my doorbell rang. I stared blearily into the peephole. A tiny Luke stood at the end of what appeared to be an inverted telescope. As I studied him, he raked a self-conscious hand through his hair.

I stepped back, unlocked the slide and the three deadbolts, and opened the door.

"You're early," I said.

He laughed. He had a very nice laugh. I laughed too, although I was still convinced the weekend was a mistake. It sort of worried me that I was looking forward to it so much. Looking forward to seeing Luke again.

He really was good-looking: just over medium height, wide shoulders, narrow hips, long legs. He wore faded Levi's and a white tee-shirt that read, *OK, so I like donuts!!* The tee emphasized the rock-hard muscles in his arms.

"Ready to roll?"

"I guess."

His mouth twitched at the lack of enthusiasm in my voice. He nodded to my backpack. "That it?"

"Yeah." I gave him a doubtful look. "You said you'd bring the gear..."

He picked up my bag. "Yep. We're good."

Were we?

I followed him out, locked the door with shaking hands and tottered down the street to where he'd parked. He unlocked the passenger side and I crawled inside, slumping with relief in the front seat.

He stowed my gear in the back of the SUV, came around to his side. "Buckle up." He smiled, but he was obviously serious.

I fumbled with the seat belt.

He started the engine and Springsteen's *We Shall Overcome: The Seeger Sessions* picked up where it had left off on the CD player. I was a little surprised. I'm not sure what I was expecting. The Stones? *The Seeger Sessions* was a good sign; hours of "I Can't Get No Satisfaction" would have been daunting.

Somehow the close confines of the car heightened my awareness of him. He smelled like he had just stepped out of the shower. There was another smell too, straight from my idyllic childhood — Hoppes gun cleaner. And here I'd hoped I was kidding about his carrying.

I asked, "Can we stop and get coffee or something?"

He glanced at me. "Rough night?"

"Late night."

He nodded like that's what he'd thought. He found a Starbucks and we got coffee and pastries to go — which Luke insisted on paying for. I felt a little better after the coffee and sugar.

We started talking. It had been a long time since I had to make dating conversation. Maybe the effort showed.

Luke asked, "How's the hangover?"

I glanced at him. "Wow," I drawled, "you really are a detective."

He lifted a shoulder. "Hey."

Hey yourself, I thought irritably, but I let it go. He probably didn't miss a hell of a lot.

"How long have you been a detective?"

"Nine years. In New York, detectives are the equivalent rank of police officers." He added very casually, "I'm a Detective Second Grade now."

I gave him another look. He wasn't a lot older than me in years, but in experience … light-years. "What's that like: being a queer cop?"

"I don't think of myself as a *queer* cop. I think of myself as a cop."

"Sorry. You know what I mean, though. Is it tough? Or are you not out at work?"

"I'm out." He drove with one hand on the wheel, very relaxed, and one hand resting on the seat behind me. My skin felt alive to the possibility of the brush of his fingertips. If he flexed his fingers he could stroke my neck or touch my shoulder.

"But you're right. Law enforcement is a macho gig. I don't go out of my way to stress that I like to sleep with other guys."

"Have you ever shot anyone?"

He laughed. "Why does everyone ask that? You know how rare it is for a cop to shoot someone?"

"Have you ever *wanted* to shoot someone?"

"All the time!" We both laughed.

When we reached the Garden State Parkway I began to reluctantly dig through my mostly forgotten memories of that long ago summer. My friend, Ricky, had lived outside of Batsto, that much I remembered, but how far outside, I couldn't seem to recall. Nothing looked the same.

We stopped for a late breakfast — or early lunch — at a little pub called Lighthouse Tavern and had a couple of thick, juicy "Alpine" burgers and a couple of beers. By then we were getting along pretty well, having discovered that we had a few vital things in common, namely love of Cuban-Chinese food, Irish music, and really, really bad kung fu movies.

I mentioned digging the Springsteen track on Jesse Malin's new album, and he suggested — very off-hand — getting tickets for Malin's Bowery Ballroom concert if I was interested.

I said, equally off-hand, yeah, I was probably interested.

I ordered another beer. Luke again declined on the basis of driving. He seemed thoughtful as I finished my drink. "So what's the deal with you and cops?" he asked.

"Huh?"

"Rob said you had this thing about cops. You get nailed for a DUI or something?"

What the hell was *that* supposed to mean? I set my mug down and stared at him, instantly offended. But he just seemed curious. "Hey, for the record, just a couple of drinks can put you over the legal limit if you haven't eaten."

"Sure," he said peaceably. "So that's it then?"

"Not really." I gave him a sheepish grin. "I mean, I guess everyone is a little intimidated."

"Some people are turned on."

Our eyes met. I said casually, "That too."

He grinned.

■ ■ ■ ■ ■

Just outside of a little hamlet we stopped at the one-hundred-fifty-year-old general store and picked up German sausages, smoke-cured bacon and insect repellent. On our way out of the market I noticed a glass-fronted bulletin board. Tacked on top of the faded flyers and browned cards was a recent poster of a smiling girl: Elizabeth Ann Chattam. Twenty-one years old, freckles, brown hair clipped in big daisy barrettes, blue eyes, last seen hiking in Wharton State Forest.

"Something wrong?" Luke asked.

I shook my head.

Historic villages and blueberry farms gave way to cranberry bogs and cemeteries and ghost towns as we wound through the deep oak-pine forest of the Pinelands National Reserve.

We left the SUV at Parkdale, an old ghost town with only a rusty railroad bridge and a couple of stone foundations to show civilization had ever made it that far. We loaded our gear onto our backs. Luke checked his cell phone. His mouth did that little pensive quirk.

"No reception?"

"I didn't really think there would be." He put his phone away. Pulled out a compass and then checked the sun. "We've got plenty of time before it gets dark. Any idea which direction we should head?"

I had exhausted my small store of memory getting us this far. I shrugged on my pack, shook my head. "Even if I — " I realized what I was saying, and shut up.

"Even if you ... wanted to?"

"Hey, this was your idea. I'm just along for the ride." I caught his expression, played my comment back in my head, and felt myself reddening.

He grinned that devilish grin.

We hiked the sugar sand road for a couple of miles, then moved off onto one of the narrower trails.

I knew Luke was hoping that something would trigger my memories, but Ricky and I had been lost for hours when we stumbled on the house. It could have been just a mile or so in, or it could have been a day's walk — we had *spent* a day walking, but that was as likely due to having lost our sense of direction as necessity.

"Let me know if anything looks familiar," he requested when we paused to drink from our canteens.

I gave him an sardonic look, and he grinned back. *When Irish eyes are smiling,* I thought. I still couldn't believe I'd let him talk me into this.

We kept up a brisk pace until it started to get dark. Then Luke set about finding a good spot to camp. I left it up to him. I was out of shape and feeling it. My feet ached, my calf muscles ached, my back ached. I was just glad I'd done enough walking tours in my time to know how to avoid blisters and heat rash.

I looked forward to sitting down and having a drink. I wished we could have just... gone away for the weekend; I knew a wonderful little historic bed and breakfast in Crown Point. But I didn't kid myself after miles of splashing through creeks and climbing over logs; the main attraction for Luke was not me; it really was the skull house.

That was okay. We could still have some fun. I just hoped the ground wasn't too hard and the night wasn't too cold. Or wet.

Luke found a nice little clearing that already had a campfire ring. I was glad to see the campfire ring, glad to have proof we hadn't traveled too far off the map. It was weird how a few miles could take you so far from civilization. It was like another world out here. He made up a campfire and we spread our bags out. He unwrapped the brats we'd bought at the little market.

I made my own preparations. "Cocktails, anyone?" I pulled the carefully-wrapped bottle of Bushmills out of my pack.

Luke raised his eyebrows. "So that's what was sloshing around. I thought you'd brought an awful lot of mouthwash for the weekend."

■　■　■　■　■

We dined *al fresco* on barbecued brats wrapped in toasted French rolls, washed down by beer and a whisky chaser. I'm not big on picnics or barbecues, but even I had no complaints that night, not once I'd had a chance to catch my breath.

"What's for dessert?" I asked, kidding.

Luke wiggled his eyebrows suggestively. I laughed and raised the bottle, offering it to him.

He took it, drank, handed it back. He was still smiling at me. Nodding to our sleeping bags lying a friendly distance from each other, he said, "It's going to be cold tonight. Should I zip our bags together?"

It took me a second to get it. I felt my face warm, but I tried to sound indifferent. "Oh. I guess so. Yeah."

He zipped the bags, turning them into one giant bag, and before long we were stretched out on our sides, not touching, but within arm's reach. "Where do you come up with the ideas for the stuff you write?"

"Things I see. Things I hear." I shrugged. "Stuff strikes me funny, and I write about it."

"I laugh my ass off reading that column you do for the Blade. It's such a kick the way your mind works."

I was insanely flattered, although I tried to hide it. I watched him under my lashes to see if he was serious.

"And you've written books?"

"Two." I lifted a negligent shoulder. "Travel books, that's all."

"That's all? That's amazing." His smile was genuinely admiring. "Travel books about where?"

"Italy. France." I stopped myself from shrugging again. It wasn't like I was being unduly modest, I just didn't think it was a big deal. I hadn't written the Great American Novel or anything. Not yet. Probably not ever, if I wanted to be realistic — which I rarely did.

It didn't matter. The alcohol was singing in my bloodstream, and I was the life of the party. And it was a lovely party: firelight and starlight and the wine-crisp night air, the smell of pines and woodsmoke and lube and latex.

We were lying next to each other on our doublewide sleeping bag, feet brushing, knees brushing, arms brushing. Gradually we shed our clothes as we passed the bottle back and forth. More back than forth, but then I was more nervous than Luke. He was smiling and relaxed, reaching over to brush the hair out of my eyes as I talked.

I totally forgot what I was saying. Luke prompted me by asking about the trip to France, and I answered that it would have been better with someone with me — and maybe he should come next time.

"Oh, yeah? Where are you going next time?"

"Ireland." I said at random, guessing that with a name like O'Brien, he might like to go to Ireland.

He was amused. His eyes sparkled. "When are you going?" He licked his thumb and reached out to circle my left nipple. I caught my breath, tried to catch his hand and press it to my chest. "I might like to come."

"You can come," I promised, leaning over him.

I ran my hands over the broad expanse of his chest, the wide shoulders ... communing. I could feel the warm flush beneath my fingertips, the damp of perspiration. I loved the language of his bare skin, the delicate punctuation of freckles and a tiny velvety mole on his rib cage.

I liked the contrast of bristly face and hard jaw with the softness of lips and flickery eyelashes. I scooted closer still, savoring the solid rub of our erections.

"Are you an innie or an outie?" he inquired huskily, his hand resting on the small of my back, pressing me closer.

I glanced down at my flat belly, and then chuckled, meeting his eyes. I'd never heard it called that. "I want you to fuck me," I told him. "I *need* you to fuck me."

"Happy to oblige."

He was in great shape, and I liked that too. Rock hard pecs, balls of muscles in his arms; what would it be like to be in that kind of shape? There was a lot of strength, a lot of power there. Big hard hands rested on my hips as he helped me ease onto that straight, rigid cock.

I cried out and I could see he liked it. He liked it vocal. Oh, he was truly Irish with his love of the blarney.

"Oh, fuck, you feel so good. You're so big," I told him, throatily.

"You *beauty*," he whispered.

That's not something you hear everyday. I chuckled again. Settled more fully on him, adjusting to his size and length. It had been a good long while since I'd had a real live partner and not a silicone rubber substitute.

He raised his head and kissed my breastbone, and I bent forward latching onto his mouth.

All this and kisses too? I kissed him until I thought I'd pass out from lack of oxygen, and his mouth parted reluctantly from mine. I liked his reluctance. The wet smack of his lips letting me go. I liked the taste of alcohol in his mouth.

"God, that's sweet," he muttered.

I rocked back and forth... gently... rising up and scrape-sliding down. The smooth swooping glide of a merry-go-round, that's what it reminded me of, and the merry-go-round pole driving up my hot little hole. We were just playing, but I started to feel that urgent aching need.

I planted my hand in the cushion of solid pecs and I worked my hips more frantically. Luke matched my rhythm easily, bucking up against my ass, thrusting deeply. His grunts excited me even more. I arched my back, went wild, begged him to fuck me hard, harder, *harder.*

I needed so much. There was such a big gaping emptiness in me. I needed him to fill it with heat and hungry demands; I wanted his need to overwhelm my own. I almost sobbed as he reached up and took my solid erection into his fist. He pumped me. Sweat broke out across my back. I was on fire.

I looked up and the sky was spinning, the stars rolling across the night, trying to drop into the little pockets. A dizzy swirl of stars and tree tops and the sliding moon, faster and faster and faster... .

Luke shouted and I felt that funny squish inside the condom, the rush of hot release. My hole pulsed in response to his orgasm, like a pink mouth trying to find the words. There were no words for this. I reached for the low-hanging stars and yelled right out loud as my own release shivered through me.

Like the cork popping on champagne, spumes of white shot out. Emptied, I slumped forward on Luke's sweaty chest. Closed my eyes. His arms fastened around me. The sparse hair tickled my nose pleasantly. His heart was thumping from a million miles out... echoing across the universe...

"Christ Almighty," he moaned. "Please tell me you're just the same sober."

The merry-go-round slowed... slowed... glided gradually to a stop. It was nice to lie there like that, skin on skin, listening to the faraway chirp of crickets and frogs.

His words finally registered. I laughed and lifted my head. "It's moot. I'm never sober."

His mouth was a kiss away. He said wryly, "You think you're joking."

That startled me. "I *am* joking." I shook my hair out of my eyes. "Listen, I like to drink, but I do *not* have a problem with alcohol."

"Okay, okay," he said, in the tone of someone who doesn't want to get into an argument.

It was like he dumped a bucket of ice water over me. I felt bewildered. Hurt. I pulled out of his arms and sat up. "Maybe you should work on your after-play technique."

"Sorry." He tugged me back down. "That really *was* amazing."

I didn't have an answer for him. He'd spoiled it for me. I lay there, head on his chest, more hurt than angry — but a bit of both. He stroked my hair. His touch was light, almost tender. I couldn't think of the last time someone was tender with me.

"Tim," he said quietly. That was all. I raised my head and he kissed me, his mouth warm and surprisingly sweet.

And we did it all again, only slowly, lingeringly.

■　■　■　■　■

The house loomed before me. Ten stories tall. The windows flashed red in the setting sun. The hinges of the broken front door shrieked as the door swung open...

I jerked awake. It was freezing. My head throbbed. My mouth tasted horrible. I needed a piss.

"Bad dream?" Luke asked softly.

Confused, I realized that we were somehow in the same sleeping bag, and I was lying plastered on top of him, my sweaty head resting in the curve of his shoulder. He was dressed again; we both were, although I didn't remember pulling my clothes back on, didn't remember zipping ourselves into the bag.

"I... No. I... don't remember." I answered in a whisper, responding to his own hushed tone, even as I wondered why we were whispering.

Somewhere to the left, a twig snapped. I shivered.

He pulled the sleeping bag — wet with dew — over my shoulders, and slipped one arm around me again. It felt very good to be held. Even like this, in jeans and flannel shirts, I could feel and was comforted by the heat of his body. His hand slipped under my shirt, absently smoothing up and down my spine.

Despite the soothing touch, I heard the steady, swift thump of his heart beneath my ear.

His other arm, I slowly realized, rested on top of the sleeping bag — and he was holding a gun.

"Is something wrong?"

"Not sure. I think someone might be out there."

I sucked in a sharp breath, starting to pull away. He held me still. His put his mouth against my forehead. "Shhh. Don't let on."

I made myself lie still. Stared at what I could see of his profile in the dark. "What do we do?"

"Wait."

Wait?

For someone to pick us off as we lay by the cooling embers of our campfire? And I thought I had to pee *before?* My own heart was ricocheting around my ribcage. I felt for the zip of the sleeping bag, gently pulled it down. Luke nodded infinitesimal approval, continued to stroke my back in that automatic way, his eyes watching the line of trees surrounding the clearing.

We lay there not moving for what felt like an hour. Then I heard an owl call: not the drowsy nocturnal hoot, but the screech they make when they hunt.

A dank, damp breeze scented with the tangled undergrowth washed over my perspiring face. And all at once the night was alive with sound. From silence to deafening racket; I could practically hear ants marching up and down the grass blades, the dew drops crashing from the leaves overhead. Even the stars overhead seemed to crackle brightly in the black and bottomless sky. Too bright for my eyes…

■　■　■　■　■

I woke up sick and shaky, head pounding, my ass feeling thoroughly kicked.

"Morning, sunshine," Luke remarked in answer to my groan. He squatted next to the smoky campfire and held up a sauce pan. "Coffee?"

I muttered assent, crawled carefully out of the bag. Everything was wet, as though it had rained during the night. The smell of frying bacon made me want to puke. I staggered into the bushes and relieved myself.

As I wove my weary way back into camp the empty Bushmills bottle caught my eye. It lay near the ring of campfire stones, a tablespoon of amber glistening in its belly. Why the hell had we finished the entire bottle? Now there was nothing left for today.

My gut tightened remembering Luke's comments. Well, fuck him.

Oh yeah. I already did.

I took the lightweight aluminum cup he offered, picked up the bottle and tilted the dregs into my coffee. He watched in silence. "Hair of the dog." Against my will, I heard myself making an excuse. "Sometimes it helps a bad hangover if you have a little drink."

He eyed me for a long moment, then rose and went to the sleeping bags, unzipping them. He re-zipped his own bag and proceeded to roll it into a tight neat bundle.

I drank my coffee and tried to stop shaking.

He tied his bag with a couple of quick yanks, and said flatly, "My old man was a drunk."

It was like getting punched in the chest. I couldn't get my breath. *He can't really think … .*

"He was what you'd call a functioning alcoholic," he added.

Maybe he's not talking about me. Maybe he's just … lousy at making morning after conversation. I said, "I … thought he was a cop?"

"He was. For thirty years. He drank and he did his job and he came home and drank some more. He was a decent cop and he tried to be a decent husband and a decent father, but he basically lived his entire adult life in a bottle. There's not a lot of room for other people in a bottle."

"I'm not… I don't have a drinking problem."

Luke didn't say anything.

"Look, I admit that I've gotten in the habit of drinking too much sometimes, but I'm not… I'm not an alcoholic." I offer him a twitchy smile. "Really. I'm not."

"I'm not judging you, Tim. It's an illness. It's like heart disease or HIV."

"The hell you're not judging," I said. "Not that I give a damn what you think. I just hope you're a better detective than you are … whatever this was supposed to be."

I threw out the rest of my coffee and went to tie up my own sleeping bag.

■ ■ ■ ■ ■

Which leads us to current events.

I stared at the ragged cross in the pale bark, my chest rising and falling.

"You couldn't be happy with dinner and a movie, could you?" I ask bitterly. "This is really all you dragged me out here for, to find this goddamned house. Why did you pretend it was anything else?"

"Look, I didn't kidnap you. You agreed to come. I assumed you wanted to."

"I wanted to see you again." It sounded pathetic, but I was so far beyond pride at this point, what did it matter?

His eyes flickered. "I wanted to see you too."

"Oh, please." Now it was my turn to be disgusted. "You were never interested in me. You're just looking to solve some big imaginary cold case. You're just… bucking for *Detective First Grade*." I mimicked the quiet pride in his voice when he'd told me his rank.

He flushed. "That's bullshit. I wanted to ask you out before I ever heard about this skull house of yours. Rob said you weren't interested."

"I wasn't. I'm not." Now I was just being childish, but I didn't care. I hated him for dragging me out here, for seeing me break down sobbing, for making me face things I didn't want to face.

His mouth tightened. He said, "All right. That story about The Forester? That happens to be an urban legend that every cop in the northeast is familiar with."

"I didn't make it up!"

"I know." He was cool again. "The night of the party… I watched your eyes when you were talking. You weren't making it up."

What the hell had he seen? I had no idea. I stared sullenly at the carvings in the tree trunk.

"Whatever you saw all those years ago… it still scares you. And I thought if I offered you a chance to face whatever that was, you'd… take it."

"In other words, this is just a job opportunity for you."

"I already told you…" He stopped. Shrugged. "I thought maybe we'd have a few laughs while we were at it."

"A few laughs? It's Lost Weekend. In every *fucking* sense of the word."

"Hey — " But he didn't finish it, which was probably just as well. Instead he said, "It's your call. You want to turn back or you want to see what's ahead?"

I wanted to start back, no question about it. I looked at him. He met my eyes. I knew what he was thinking. I knew what he wanted. We'd come this far. I stared again at that little cross in the tree.

"After you, Jungle Jim," I said bitterly.

We continued walking.

And walking.

And walking.

The markings on the tree were mine, but now Luke led the way like he knew where we were going. It was all I could do to put one stumbling foot in front of the other. Maybe there was a path, but to me it seemed like an obstacle course of poison oak and sharp stones and snake holes and bug-infested logs and things that slithered and skittered reluctantly out of our way.

Miles of it in the humid, autumn heat. My head pounded nauseatingly with each step; I felt my heart hammering in my side. I took one step and then another, and I stopped, slid off my backpack. My head swam. I was coated in cold sweat, dizzy…

I dropped down on my knees, fell forward onto my hands. I was trying to decide if I would feel better or worse if I let myself throw up. I probably couldn't afford to get any more dehydrated than I already was.

Luke squatted down beside me. "You okay?"

I raised my head with an effort. "Of all the stupid questions…" I didn't have the energy to finish it. "I'm sick," I whispered.

"I know."

He opened his pack and pulled out a silver flask. "Medicinal purposes," he commented, measuring out a stingy little dose. "I think this qualifies."

I eased the rest of the way down and rested my head on my knees. I wanted to tell him to shove his little silver cup up his tight ass. There was no way that I could.

"Here." I looked up and he handed the cup to me, steadying my hand with his own.

I was a caricature, a movie drunk. I could hardly manage to get the cup to my mouth.

"Jesus," he said softly.

I drank. Put my hand still holding the flask cap over my eyes. Like the magic potion in a fairytale, I felt it begin to work, burning through my system, snapping on the lights, warming, calming, illuminating… . Maybe it would make me invisible to Luke; I didn't want him to keep looking at me like that. I wiped my face on my sleeve. "I'm okay."

Oh, yeah. Superb. Sick and shaking — but for God's sake: I was exhausted and sleep-deprived and out of shape; it wasn't all withdrawal. I didn't bother telling that to Luke, though. I'd already told him three times that weekend — possibly more — that I didn't have a drinking problem, so there was no point telling him again.

Even I knew by then that I was lying.

Follow the signs to journey's end: I couldn't get through a single day without a drink. I was an alcoholic. A drunk.

"You can have another shot," Luke said. "But you may need it more later."

"I can wait." I didn't even know if that was true or not.

I didn't look into his eyes because I couldn't bear to see the reflection of what I already heard in his voice: attraction and liking replaced by pity — and distaste.

I heard myself say, "I've tried to stop. I can't." I listened in shock to the echo of those words.

Silence.

He said finally, "Have you ever thought about getting help?"

"You mean like ... AA?"

"There are other organizations, but yeah, like AA"

"I ... can't."

"You can't what?"

I swallowed hard. "I can't go and talk to a bunch of people about my ... problems."

I couldn't believe I was talking to *him.* Just imagining standing up in a room full of strangers made me feel light-headed: *Hi, I'm Timothy ...*

I looked at him shame-faced and said, "Besides, I don't ... think it would work for me. I don't think I can stop. I have tried." I dropped my head on my folded arms.

Why was I *telling* him?

And yet, as humiliating and painful as this was, there was a terrible relief in just ... saying it. Admitting it once and for all.

Luke rested his broad, warm hand on my back. "What about getting medical treatment?"

"You mean a hospital?"

"Rehab, yeah."

Voice hushed, I admitted the real truth. "I'm afraid."

"Of rehab?"

I moved my shoulders. "Of giving up control of my life."

He said gently, "Tim, you already gave up control."

∎ ∎ ∎ ∎ ∎

The house leaned crookedly behind a wall of forbidding trees. I didn't remember the gingerbread trim. Those frivolous curlicues sweeping up and down the edge of the roof above the wall of trees seemed incongruous with the house of my memory. The vines and tree branches seemed to be all that were holding it rooted into place; I heard the old boards groaning like the building was ready to topple over any moment.

One or two of the upper story windows still had glass panes. The others gaped blackly or had been boarded up. The double wide front entrance was also boarded up. I couldn't remember if there had been a door before; I didn't remember the baby blue posts holding up the sagging portico. There was no giant tree growing out through the peeling roof; my imagination must have supplied that.

But there was no question it was the same house.

"There must have been a raised porch that ran the length of the house," Luke said, studying the high windows.

If there had been stairs they had disappeared with the long-ago porch, and the windows were too high to climb through unless one of us boosted the other.

The building creaked ominously in the breeze, like the laughter of some demented old crone. The sound snapped me out of my trance. "We have to get out of here."

I tried to brush past Luke. He said something, and reached for me, and I struck at his hand, ducking back when he lunged for me again. He swore. His foot caught on a tree root and he went down on one knee. I slipped out of my pack and ran like a deer.

Only it wasn't running so much as trying to plough through the brush and bushes and trees. I didn't get more than a few yards when Luke caught me up. He grabbed my shoulder, and I turned around and swung at him.

He blocked me without particular trouble, not letting go of the steely grip he had on my shoulder.

I tried to slide out from under this hand, and when that didn't work I tried to slug him. He grasped my fist, yanked me forward, throwing me off balance, and I crashed against him. He still had hold of my arm and he twisted it behind me, turning me away from him.

The pain was instant and startling. I cried out.

"Don't struggle," he said, breathing fast. "I don't want to hurt you."

"You're fucking breaking my arm!"

"Then hold still, damn it." His other arm locked across my shoulders in a restraining hold that stopped just short of choking me. "Tim — stop."

I stopped. My arm felt wrenched out of my shoulder socket. I clenched my jaw against the pain, and nodded. After a moment he let go of the arm twisted behind my back; it dropped limply to my side. I tried to move my other arm to rub my shoulder, but he kept me pinned against him.

"You *asshole.*" I hated him like I'd never hated anyone in my life.

Luke ignored my trembling rage. "What happened here, Tim?" His breath was warm against my ear. "Something happened twelve years ago. What was it?"

I shook my head. "*Nothing.*" I made another half-hearted attempt to wrest free. "Look, this was a bad idea. We need to get out of here."

His arms tightened. "Talk to me. What happened the first time you found this place?"

"I don't know. Please. Let me go."

I started shivering from head to foot — and the weirdest part was, I wasn't even sure why. I thought my heart was going to tear out of my chest. Maybe Luke felt it banging against his arm, because his grip changed, turning to support, comfort if I wanted it. I resisted it. I couldn't trust him anymore. This was all his fault.

"Where would you go, Tim? Think for a minute. You can't go barging through the bushes. If you go tearing out of here you'll just get lost or injured."

"I'll take my chances."

"I can't let you take that chance."

"Jesus, who died and made you John Wayne?"

He didn't bother to answer.

I thought how strange it was that at this time the night before we'd been settling down to sex and maybe the start of something. In twenty-four hours everything had changed.

I sagged against him. "Luke... I don't remember."

"The hell you don't."

I shook my head hopelessly. He just waited — like we had all the time in the world.

I said, finally, so quietly that he had to duck his head to hear, "There were pieces of bone all over the ground... like peanut shells or sea shells. Like gravel. Broken animal skulls and... human. I know they were..."

Luke's arms tightened. "You're okay. Go on."

"I picked up a little piece of a jaw. I could see where the... teeth were supposed to go." I swallowed dryly. "Ricky wanted to see if we could climb inside through one of the broken windows. We snuck up to the side of the house." I took a deep breath, trying to get control. "We got to one of the windows, looked up, and — and suddenly there was a man standing there."

"Inside the house?"

I nodded. "He just... stared at us. Straight at us. And we stared back. Frozen. Like a pair of rabbits. And then he raised his hand like he was waving hello." My voice broke. "It looked black. He pressed it against the window... and it left a bloody handprint."

My voice gave out as though I had run out of oxygen, which is how I felt. I stared up at Luke, stricken.

"What did you do?" he asked after a moment. His voice sounded thick.

"He turned away from the window ... and we ran."

The dark woods of my memory opened up and swallowed me. That terrified scramble through briars, crawling and wriggling under when we couldn't push through, running blind as the night settled on the roof of treetops — and always the knowledge that *he* was behind us ... .

Luke said so calmly it was like a slap, "What happened when you got home?"

My mouth worked but I couldn't remember the words.

"You made it home safely," Luke said. "What happened then?"

"Nothing."

He let me go. "You didn't tell anyone?"

I shook my head, massaging my twisted shoulder. I could see the lack of comprehension on his face. "We were afraid. He saw us. We thought he would come after us."

"Then why the hell wouldn't you tell your parents?"

"Ricky — we weren't supposed to go into the woods. His dad said he would get the belt if he went back in there. We couldn't decide. We thought no one would believe us. And it's not like we could lead them back. We got lost so many times that day. I don't know how the hell we did finally get out."

Luck. And the fact that we were small enough to wriggle through places our pursuer couldn't. Mostly luck.

"But — "

"And my parents came the next day. I went home and it ... all seemed like a dream. I told myself we imagined it."

Luke didn't say anything; I read condemnation in his silence.

"We left him free to keep killing, didn't we?" I said dully. "Everyone who disappeared after that ... it's our fault."

"Let's get one thing straight," Luke said. "Nothing this sick fucker did is your fault. You were thirteen-years-old. And teenage boys don't have the greatest judgment in the world."

"I just ... forgot about it," I whispered. "I let myself forget."

He said dryly, "Yeah, well, maybe you tried. I don't know how successful you were."

"That girl on the poster in the store ..."

"Let it go, Tim. You have no idea what happened to her." He reached inside his shirt. He was wearing a shoulder holster. I already knew that. I'd felt it when I was leaning against him. He pulled out his gun, checked the chamber.

"Do you know how to handle a gun?"

I nodded wearily. My assent seemed to catch him by surprise.

"You do?"

"Yeah. My dad is ex-army. I know how to shoot. I grew up shooting." I understood his hesitation. In his shoes I wouldn't give me a gun either.

He knelt, opened his pack, pulled out a tightly-wrapped triangle, which, when unwrapped, turned out to be .38 revolver. He offered it to me.

I stepped back. "Don't. I'm not going back there. I'm not going with you."

His dark brows drew together. He continued to hold the gun out to me. "I can't. I can't. You *can't* ask this of me," I said.

"I *am* asking you."

"Luke … you of anybody knows that there's a limit to what you can … expect from me."

"I'm not asking anything more than you're capable of."

I gaped. "Are you … you can't be serious. Were you *here* five minutes ago?"

His hazel eyes met my own. "Tim, it's one thing to run away when you're thirteen. No one can blame you for that. But you're a man now. You have to stop running."

I blinked a couple of times, trying to focus on this idea. "But there's no need for us to go back. The Forester's dead by now." I rushed along, trying to convince him, convince myself. "The guy's dead. He has to be. He's not even there anymore. He can't be. We could just … call the cops."

"I *am* a cop. I have to check this out before I call anyone else in. Anyway, you don't believe that or you wouldn't be this frightened."

"Yes, I would! I am." I gulped. "If you want to go back … that's up to you. I'll … wait for you. I'll try to. But I can't …"

He just kept staring at me. *This is the face he wears when people try to talk him out of arresting them.*

"You have to. I can't leave you."

"Yes, you can, because I'm not going with you."

"Tim, for your own sake — you've got to face this before it destroys you."

"Jesus Christ. Stop it! You don't know me. You don't know what you're talking about."

"I know you this well. I need your help."

I couldn't look away from those hazel eyes. Finally, hand shaking, I took the gun, checked to make sure it was loaded, shoved it into my back waistband under my flannel shirt. I said unsteadily, "What the hell is this supposed to be? Intervention by serial killer?"

To my astonished rage, his mouth twitched like he found that funny.

I practically stuttered, "You laugh at me now, O'Brien, and I swear to Christ I'll deck you."

"You just keep channeling that anger and we'll be fine." His eyes assessed me. "Do you need a drink?"

"Is that a trick question?"

"If it'll help you hold together …"

I couldn't hold his gaze. I looked away and nodded, and he got out the flask he'd brought for medicinal purposes and handed it to me.

I didn't bother with the little cup this time; I just tilted the flask.

■　■　■　■　■

From the cover of a thicket of berry bushes we studied the row of boarded windows. "Let's try the other side," Luke said, his voice low.

"If he was watching us last night, he could still be watching us. He could be following us and waiting for dark."

Luke glanced up at the fading sunlight. He nodded. "Stay frosty."

Stay frosty? Was he for real?

"Frosty the Snowman, that's me," I muttered. I moved around him, kneeling to pick up something white in the weeds. I handed it to Luke.

He studied the bone. "Animal. Not human."

I nodded, but I wasn't reassured.

Luke started toward the front of the house, skirting the bushes. I followed closely, watching the boarded face of the house. It didn't look like anyone had been there for years, and yet... it didn't quite feel dead, either.

If anyone lived in that wreck, he wasn't coming and going through the front entrance, which had been secured with thick planks. We picked our way around broken boards and tree roots, ducking under the sagging portico. I saw a snake slither into the underbrush a few feet ahead.

The first-story windows were boarded on the other side of the house as well, but the trees grew closer to the foundation, and I saw that it would be possible to climb up and get in through one of the open second-story windows. I kept this thought to myself. I was still hoping Luke might give up and decide we were wasting our time.

"Let's try the back," Luke said.

"Let's not and say we did."

He threw me a brief grin.

We scooted around the corner of the house and paused in the deep shade. Something crunched behind us. I froze, staring at the moving wall of bushes a few feet away. Was it only the breeze stirring the leaves?

"Do you have your cell phone?" I whispered to Luke.

He didn't bother to turn. "It's back with my pack. There's no signal out here."

Maybe not, but I'd have been willing to try. My phone, unfortunately, was in Luke's car.

"The back door's not boarded up," Luke said. He started forward across the carpet of autumn leaves.

I hesitated, still watching the bushes. The dusty, purple berries hung in heavy clusters. I looked skyward. The sun looked distorted through the ragged tree-tops, splintered light glanced off the dark foliage and flaking paint of the house. White flakes in the weeds, too. I stooped. Picked up a sliver of white. Not paint. A bone chip. Bone chips dusting the grass. I swallowed hard, straightened.

We didn't have a lot of daylight left, and I didn't want to try and find our way out of the woods by flashlight. And I sure as hell didn't want to spend another night here.

"Tim."

I glanced back. Luke was at the rear door of the house. He gestured with his chin.

I threw one last uneasy look at the bushes and moved out from the shadow of the house. Blood red autumn leaves blanketed the ground, crackling underfoot.

Just like that, the ground gave beneath me with the shriek of rotten wood and corroded hinges. I crashed down through a pair of crumbling cellar doors and slammed into the hard-packed dirt floor.

Stunned, I lay on my side for a few seconds trying to process what had happened while dry leaves floated gently down around me.

In a dark, dark wood ... The words from the old children's song ran through my mind in dazed refrain. *There was a dark, dark house ...*

My ankle hurt. My knee hurt. My hip hurt. My wrist felt broken. Somehow I'd managed to protect my head, but that had been hurting before I ever fell through the broken doors — and this wasn't helping.

Thank God I hadn't fallen on my back and shot myself.

And in that dark, dark house ...

Light from the hole in the doors above me illuminated burnt and jagged timber — thank God I hadn't landed on any of that — wooden shelves with dusty jars and dusty cans, some broken furniture. A kerosene lantern swung precariously over my head, creaking on its rusty hook.

"Tim, can you hear me?"

I realized Luke was calling to me, that he had been calling for some time now.

"Tim? Can you answer me?"

"I'm okay." That was a slight overstatement.

"Tim!"

"I'm okay," I called more loudly. Gingerly, I made an effort to push up. My muscles screeched protest. Maybe my wrist was sprained, not broken. I cradled it against my chest, tried flexing the fingers.

"Jesus Christ," Luke's voice echoed with relief. "I thought ... look, don't move. I'm coming down."

Don't move. Right ...

I stared up. It was about a twelve-foot drop. Several steps led up to the broken doors, but they were blocked off by the broken timbers. The room itself was twenty feet long. Another set of stairs, probably leading up to the kitchen, vanished into the shadows.

Luke's head withdrew from the broken opening in the cellar doors. A moment later a shadow flashed across, and then was gone.

What ... ? Was that a bird?

I heard a thud. Swift, hard. And then another.

Hair prickled on the back of my neck. I yelled, "Luke?"

Nothing. No answer.

I listened tautly. Listened ... and heard something like ... a sodden dragging sound.

I opened my mouth to shout for Luke again, but something held me silent. I swallowed hard, and crawled out from under the opening in the cellar doors.

Grabbing onto one of the broken timbers, I painfully pulled myself upright. Okay, I was still in one working piece. Now I needed to focus on getting out of here. I could try climbing through the debris blocking the cellar doors and breaking out that way, but that might be what someone was expecting.

I picked my way across the junk-strewn floor and hesitated at the foot of the stairs. *And in that dark, dark house ...*

Maybe I was ... confused. Maybe everything was fine topside, and I needed to wait for Luke just like he told me to. The inner door was probably locked anyway.

Luke was pretty damned tough and pretty damned experienced. Nothing was going to happen to Luke that he couldn't handle. Me, on the other hand ...

My gaze fell on the shelf of dusty mason jars next to me. I stared. Picked up one of the jars. Wiped the grimy front on my shirt, studying the murky contents. Not peaches. Not tomatoes. I shook the jar gently and something small and round and unmistakable floated next to the glass, staring back at me.

I dropped the jar. It smashed on the floor, liquid mush spilling out.

"Oh, sweet Jesus ..."

I reached out to steady myself on the shelf, and pain from my sprained wrist twisted through my nerves and muscles, snapping me back to awareness. I fumbled under my shirttail for the comforting weight of Luke's .38.

I went up the short flight of stairs and tried the door. It creaked open onto a short dim hallway. Faded wallpaper and moldering carpet gave way to an old-fashioned kitchen.

A sweetish sickly pall seemed to hang in the dead air. It was hard to see. The only light came from the small window in the door that led out to the clearing behind the house. I could just make out dingy wallpaper, a grimy wall thermometer in the shape of a fish, and some filthy decorative plates on the wall — all in shocking contrast to piles of empty jars, broken dishes and bones.

A meat cleaver lay on the counter. A butcher's knife lay on the floor. There were bones of all different sizes and shapes: like a macabre soup kitchen. Giant kettles sat on the cold stove and in the sinks and on tables.

There was a table in the center of the room. Feeling like I was sleepwalking, I moved over to it. The wooden top looked ink-stained. There were sheets and sheets of butcher paper covered with the crayon scrawls of a berserk child. Pictures of somber and serrated woods, tormented figures, and fire — fire or fountains of blood?

I crept over to the back door and peered out the grimy window. It would be dark soon. The clearing behind the house looked empty. No sign of Luke. No sign of anyone. But a shovel lay in plain sight on the bed of red and gold leaves. A shovel where there had been no shovel before.

I tried to hear over the thunder of my own heartbeat.

Evening sounds. Crickets. Birds. Frogs.

What the hell was I supposed to do? I had no idea. Even if it were possible for me to escape into the woods, I couldn't leave Luke. Not until I knew … for sure.

I looked across the kitchen, across the boiled bare carcasses and glass lanterns and knives, to another doorway leading into another dark room.

Would he have had time to drag Luke inside the house? Or was he butchering him out in the woods right now?

Or was he hunting for me?

I glanced back at the cellar door. It gaped blackly.

I picked up one of the candles from the table, scrabbled around till I found matches, and stepped inside the adjoining room. Leaves and branches were strewn over the wooden floor, but otherwise the room looked startlingly normal: old-fashioned moth-eaten furniture, tattered draperies, china. There was a fireplace with the burnt remains of clothing and a shoe. Over the fireplace hung a large, framed photo of a WWI soldier.

At the far end of the room stood another doorway and a staircase beyond. The upstairs windows were not boarded. I'd have a better chance of spotting Luke and his assailant from the second floor.

Glancing down at a little pie-shaped table my attention was caught by the small pile of odds and ends: coins, hair barrettes — *large daisy barrettes*. I stared and stared at them. No worse than any of the rest of it, right? If I was responsible for this, I was responsible for all of it. All of it. All of these things had belonged to someone: buttons, keys, a silver pen … and one boy's bone-handled penknife.

I reached out automatically. I recognized that knife. I'd lost it twelve years ago in these woods.

Picking it up, I was surprised to see that my hand was steady. Nothing like the anesthesia of total shock. I slipped it into my pocket, started warily up the stairs, gun at the ready like I'd seen in a million TV shows. For all I knew there was a whole house full of these murdering freaks.

Halfway up the staircase I heard the kitchen door bang. I heard voices. An unfamiliar mumble and a groan that sounded like Luke.

He was alive.

My heart sped up with a hope I hadn't dared entertain until then. I snuck back down the squeaking staircase and darted over to the kitchen doorway. I had a quick glimpse of long, gray hair, a massive back, giant hands the color of mahogany. He was dragging Luke by his hair and collar across the floor. I could tell Luke was only partially conscious; he struggled feebly, kicking out like he was trying to get to his feet. His hands struck ineffectively at the powerful arms hauling him towards the cellar.

The Forester slid him like a sack of potatoes across the floor.

Luke groped blindly, and his hand found the butcher's knife on the floor, closed on it.

The Forester, still muttering that incoherent litany, kicked the knife out of his hand, and then reached for the meat cleaver on the counter.

I stepped into the kitchen, thumb-cocked Luke's revolver. "Stop," I said breathlessly.

He tossed Luke back down, and turned, cleaver in hand. His face was seamed with scars and grime, tanned like old leather. There were leaves and twigs in his hair. His eyes were muddy and lifeless. I saw that there was not going to be any reasoning with him, but I said, "Don't do it."

He stepped toward me, and I instinctively stepped back, which I knew was a mistake. There was no way I was walking out of here while he was still standing. He lumbered toward me, and Luke grabbed for his ankle. The Forester slashed down at him with the cleaver — like you would swat at a mosquito.

I fired.

Saw the muzzle flash in the dim light, felt the gun kick in my hand. The bullet hit him in the shoulder. I'd been aiming for dead center, so that wasn't so good. But I'd been distracted by my abject relief that he hadn't cut Luke's head in two, the cleaver crunching into the table leg, and missing Luke by inches.

The bullet didn't seem to faze The Forester. He yanked the cleaver free and flew at me. I clamped down on the trigger and emptied the remaining five bullets into his chest. He piled right into me, heavy and hot and stinking like a bear, and I banged into the door frame and then crash-landed on the floor — with him on top.

The coppery smell of blood was in my nostrils; it was too dark to see him clearly anymore, just a black bulk crushing me. Wet warmth soaking into my jeans and shirt. I felt his teeth snapping against my throat, as I wriggled and kicked frantically to try and get free. Every second I expected to feel the meat cleaver chop into my bones. I swore and prayed and fought for my life.

I managed to get out from under him; he didn't come after me. I backed up along the floor. He just lay there twitching and shuddering, his breath rattling in his throat.

Blood drenched my clothes, but I was pretty sure none of it was mine.

"Tim?" Luke reeled into the doorway.

"Hi," I said faintly.

He staggered forward, nearly fell over the Forester's body, and then dropped down beside me, feeling me over blindly. "Are you okay? Did he get you?"

"No. I mean, yes, I'm okay. He didn't get me." I put my arms around him. I needed contact with someone alive and warm and reasonably sane. I needed to reassure myself that Luke really was alive.

He hugged me back. Hard. "You're *covered* in blood. Are you sure … ?"

"I'm sure."

And then neither of us said anything. After a time the thing on the floor stopped moving. Stopped breathing. I wondered if I should be feeling guilty about that too.

Head buried in Luke's shoulder I thought that somehow we were going to have to get back to Luke's car, drive to where we could call for help, lead the police back here, spend the rest of the night giving our statements. I would probably be arrested, self-defense or not. Not held for long, hopefully, and I was pretty sure Luke would help me every way he could, and if I was lucky it wouldn't even come to trial …

"You're sure you're okay?" he said, and his hands felt kind and familiar, once again running over my arms and back, checking for injuries because what other explanation could there be for the way I was clinging to him.

I didn't misread him. He felt guilty as hell that he'd nearly got me killed, and grateful that I'd saved his life, and worried about what this was going to do to me, seeing that I wasn't exactly the Rock of Gibraltar. I wondered if killing monsters was a strong enough foundation for building a friendship. We could be friends, right? Because friends were good, too.

"Timmy?" The gentleness in his voice got me. I had to blink back the sting in my eyes.

"Yeah. I'm fine," I said, voice smothered in his shoulder. "I just … picked a really bad day to stop drinking."

■ ■ ■ ■ ■

I was dreaming that Luke was kissing me. His lips, a little chapped, pressed warmly, sweetly against my own. My mouth quivered. I wanted to kiss him back, but already he was withdrawing.

"Tim?"

I opened my eyes. Luke leaned over me.

"Hey," I mumbled, sitting up. I had been sleeping against his shoulder, which was more than a little embarrassing. It was late afternoon, and we were sitting in Luke's car on the street outside my brownstone. The sun shone brightly. The street was full of traffic, the sidewalk crowded with pedestrians. For a moment, I wondered if I'd dreamed the entire thing.

I glanced at Luke, who looked as battered as I felt. He had a funny look on his face. "How are you feeling?"

"Oh, you know. High on life." My neck felt broken and every muscle in my body felt bruised. I had a sprained wrist and a wrenched knee. I felt groggy, disoriented — and as always — thirsty. But... ... it did feel very good to be alive. "Sorry for flaking out on you."

Luke said seriously, "Hey, you were there when I needed you."

I gave him a tired smile.

I realized he was waiting for me to say good-bye and get out of his car. I said, "Thanks for convincing the troopers not to arrest me."

"Nobody wanted to arrest you. It's a clear case of self-defense. I don't think it's even going to come to trial. Although there will probably be a hell of a lot of press."

"Yeah. Well." I reached in the backseat for my blood-stiff clothes. I wasn't sure why I'd brought them home; I was never going to wear them again. I stared at the gore-streaked bundle and hazily remembered stopping at a campsite with Luke, and showering, and changing into our spare clothes. After that... a comfortable gray blank. I didn't even remember climbing back into the car.

"Um ..."

I glanced back at him.

"I can't promise that every time we go out we'll have this much fun, but... I'd really like to see you again."

I peered more closely at him.

"I mean," he said awkwardly, "If you're not too fed up about, er, everything."

"Are you serious?"

"Hell, yeah." He gave me that heart-stopping grin, but there was just a trace of uncertainty in his eyes. "Maybe next time we could just... I don't know ... go to dinner."

I stared at him. He *was* serious.

I still had a chance with him. He knew I was a drunk and he still wanted to see me. He had seen me at my absolute worst and he was still interested. Still attracted. He knew what to expect, and he was still willing to give it a try.

I so did not want to blow this second chance.

But I didn't want to be the guy responsible for taking the twinkle out of those eyes. I didn't want to see the affection and attraction die out — to be replaced with weariness and disgust when I slipped up and fell off the wagon — and there were going to be a lot of slips and falls ahead of me. As much as I wanted to believe I'd never let him down, I knew I was going to let us both down before I got better. If I got better. If I was strong enough.

It wasn't easy, but I said, "I'd like that too. But I... probably shouldn't answer till I'm... sober."

His gaze held mine and there was no disappointment, no impatience. In fact, his smile grew a little warmer, a little more confident. "Okay. I can respect that."

I realized I wanted his respect — among other things — almost as desperately as I wanted my own. All at once it was hard to control my face. I turned towards the door, and he put a hand on my arm.

"Listen, Tim. Sometimes it helps if a friend goes with you the first couple of times."

Oh. He meant to AA or wherever. I already knew I was going to need more help than that. "I don't need someone to go with me, but it would help to know I had a friend... waiting."

"You have a friend waiting." He leaned forward and kissed me, his mouth warm and insistent. His eyes met mine. "And just so you know, that's hello."

UNTIL WE MEET ONCE MORE

It ain't over till it's over. This story, written in 2009, was another contribution to a charity anthology. It combines some of my favorite elements: action and adventure and sifting through the wreckage of old relationships.

Anchors Aweigh, my boys,
Anchors Aweigh.
Farewell to foreign shores,
We sail at break of day-ay-ay-ay.
Through our last night ashore,
Drink to the foam,
Until we meet once more.
Here's wishing you a happy voyage home
  – "Anchors Aweigh" - Lt. Charles A. Zimmerman

Present day, 0001, Bagram Air Base, Afghanistan

"What we don't want," Lt. Colonel Marsden said, "is another Roberts' Ridge."

"Understood, sir."

Army Ranger Captain Vic Black was thirty-two, a tall, broad-shouldered man with dark hair prematurely silver at the temples, and eyes a color a former lover had once referred to as "jungle green." Those light green eyes studied his commanding officer as Marsden, his face lined with weariness, looked instinctively at the silent phone on his desk.

Vic understood only too well what Marsden was thinking. The parallels between this rescue operation and the disastrous Battle of Takur Gar — commonly known as Roberts' Ridge — were painfully clear. In the Battle of Takur Gar the rescue of a Navy SEAL had resulted in two helicopters getting shot down and the deaths of seven U.S. soldiers — including the Navy SEAL, Petty Officer First Class Neil C. Roberts. Yeah, the last thing anyone wanted was another Roberts' Ridge.

Marsden admitted, "I know what you're thinking, but we're in better position to get their man out even if they didn't have their hands full with Akhtar Shah Omar on the other side of the valley."

"That's what we're here for," Vic said woodenly. Well, it was one of the things the rangers were there for. Rapid response. Rescue. Whatever was needed. Like the SEALs, the Rangers were an elite special operations force, highly trained and able to handle a variety of conventional and special op missions — everything from air assault to recovery of personnel or special equipment. This missing Navy SEAL seemed to qualify as both of the latter.

"No QRF. No TACP. No USAF. Just a three-man rescue team carried in by a MH-47 Chinook and inserted at 0200 hours 1000 meters on the Arma mountain range." Marsden pointed to a place on the map.

"Has there been any further communication from the surviving SEAL?" Vic asked, scrutinizing the map. Those impenetrable mountains were riddled with Taliban and al Qaeda fighters. Another enemy was the weather — it was winter now — and the brutal terrain. The Shah-i-Kot valley and surrounding mountains provided natural protection. For the last 2,000 years Afghan fighters had successfully resisted everyone from Alexander the Great in 330 B.C., to the British Army in the 1800's to the Soviets in 1980.

"No," Marsden replied. "But this is a valuable man with valuable intel. They — we — need him back."

"That's what rangers do. Kick down the doors, take care of business, and bring the good guys home safe and sound."

Marsden met Vic's gaze — reading him correctly — and grimaced. "I know, Vic. I know. He may be dead. But his IR strobe is still active and a Predator drone live video feed showed him on his feet and making for the landing zone as of two hours ago."

"Good enough," Vic said. And he did mean that. If there was a chance of getting that poor bastard off that fucking mountain in one piece, he was willing to try.

"If we're all very, very lucky, you'll be in and out before the enemy ever knows you dropped by."

Vic nodded curtly. They would all certainly be very lucky if it went down like that. If he developed that kind of luck, he might take up betting on the ponies full-time when he got back to the States next month. "Does this frogman have a name?" he inquired.

"Lt. Commander Sean Kennedy."

The wallop was like ... looking both ways only to get hit by a passing freight train.

"*Sean Kennedy?*" Vic repeated faintly.

"You know him?"

Marsden was staring at him, and no wonder. Vic's nickname wasn't "Stoney" for nothing. He managed to say evenly, "If it's the same man. Yeah. I knew him. A long time ago."

"Sean Kennedy is a common enough name." Marsden was still eyeing Vic curiously. "Well, it's a small world, and that's a fact. Good friend, was Kennedy?"

"Yes."

The best.

And more.

"Funny how things work out," Marsden said, seeming to be in one of his philosophical moods. "Well, whether this Kennedy is your Kennedy or not, it looks like it's your job to bring him home. You deploy at oh one hundred hours."

Twelve years ago, 0005, Beneath the chapel of the U.S. Naval Academy, Annapolis, Maryland

Eerie blue light bathed the marble sarcophagus of John Paul Jones.

"Jee-zus, you're one crazy sonofabitch," Midshipman Second Class Sean Kennedy said admiringly — though this was very much the pot calling the kettle black. "Remind me not to gamble with you again." He looked around the chamber with awe.

"Yeah, yeah. Pay up."

"You want a blowjob in a crypt?"

Hell, provided Sean Kennedy was the guy at the other end of his dick, Vic would have welcomed a blowjob inside the sarcophagus.

"Are you chickening out?" Vic asked in a hard voice because if Sean was, Vic was liable to strangle him out of sheer frustration and murderous disappointment.

Ever since he'd seen fellow plebe Kennedy laughing down at him from the top of Herndon Monument — sunlight gilding his chestnut hair and honey-colored skin, turning his hazel eyes gold — he'd wanted him. Wanted him so bad it kept him up at nights. And it hadn't helped when they'd become friends. Or roommates. And if it hadn't been for the presence of their other bunkmate, Midshipman "Specs" Davis…

But then Vic had known he had a problem from the time he was fifteen. He was eighteen now. Oh, he liked girls okay. But not the way his friends did. In fact, he felt a little queasy listening to the stuff his friends talked about wanting to do to chicks. Vic liked to jack off in front of the mirror in his bedroom at home — position himself so he couldn't see his face, just watch his hand moving on his dick, watch his dick thicken and lengthen, and pretend it was someone else's hand and someone else's dick.

And then he'd met Midshipman Fourth Class Sean Kennedy and figured out whose hand he wanted — and whose dick. Because it turned out that Kennedy had the same problem.

"I'm not chickening out," Sean said evenly. "You won your bet."

Yep. He'd won his bet — and if they got caught, they were both out. Finished. Washed up. And goddamn if it didn't feel worth the risk standing there in the creepy darkness of the crypt beneath the chapel, Sean's eyes gleaming as they watched him. Not trusting himself to speak, hands shaking a little, Vic unzipped his uniform trousers.

Sean's shadowy figure dropped to its knees before him and Sean's mouth — lips so soft and tongue so hot and wet — closed around Vic's cock.

Vic groaned. He couldn't help it. But the sound reverberated off the marble floors and stone walls like old John Paul Jones had just noticed what was going on.

Sean disgorged him, spat out, "*Shut the fuck up!*"

"Sorry."

"I'm not bilging out two years from graduation. Copy that?"

"Copy that. Shut up and suck me."

He felt the huff of Sean's laugh against his groin. "Bastard."

And then, to his abject relief, that marvel of a mouth closed around him again. Vic closed his eyes and concentrated on that wondrous wet tongue licking and lapping at the head of his dick. Vic shifted, stepped further apart to give Sean better access. Sean's mouth closed around him and he began to suck in earnest. So good. So humblingly good, that fierce draw following the slow, reluctant repel, hard and soft, wet and hot.

Vic opened his eyes. It gave him a sense of power too; staring down at Sean's bent head, the dull gleam of his chestnut hair, the dark crescents of his eye lashes, and his mouth…

Oh, that mouth.

His gaze fell on one of the four giant bronze dolphins that braced the marble sarcophagus. The dolphin seemed to be sticking its tongue out at him. In the eerie blue light from above Vic could just make out the name "Ranger" carved in the marble floor above the "John" in *John Paul Jones*. All seven of the ships Jones had commanded were listed there.

Two things eventually occurred to Vic: never again was he going to be satisfied with a girl blowing him — and Sean had done this before.

In fact, Sean gave head like a he did it for a living. Like a professional whore. It made Vic angry and it made him crazy for more because it was so good. 'Good' being a feeble word for the best goddamned thing in the world.

That beautiful sucking pull, that wet slide… a sweet tension was building, building with every synchronized pulse of heart and dick, building… .

Oh yeah, and there it was, rolling through his nerves and muscles… bones and blood and every cell in his body… picking up weight and energy like a tidal wave surging up and then crashing down in wave after wave of shuddering sensation that sent sparks shooting behind his eyes.

Vic slumped against the black and white marble column. His legs were shaking so hard he wasn't sure he could stay on his feet. "Christ." His whisper seemed to echo in every corner of the crypt.

Sean was kneeling at his feet, breathing hard like he'd run a marathon, and Vic suddenly wanted to do it to him. Not just to taste him — although he did, to his shame, want to taste Sean's cock — but to give him that. That… rush.

But that hadn't been the bargain.

Anyway, Sean was pushing to his feet. Vic straightened, groped for his handkerchief and wiped himself off. He was astonished to see Sean unzip his pants and mop his own groin and genitals.

"You came *watching* me?"

Sean laughed a little unsteadily, nodded.

And because he was weirdly moved and excited by that, Vic said arrogantly, "Yeah, I have that affect on a lot of people."

"Making plebes pee their pants isn't the same thing, asshole." But Sean was chuckling, and something about him, about that husky laugh in the intimate gloom and the scent of him — sex and soap and an aftershave that was too old for him — Vic grabbed him, nearly knocking him down, and kissed him.

Caught off guard, Sean's mouth opened right up. Probably intending to protest, but Vic's mouth covered his. Sean's lips were warm and tasted of salty-sweet. A taste that was just a little too close to tears. Vic kissed him harder and kept kissing him until he recollected that officers and gentlemen did not kiss other officers and gentlemen.

At the same time, Sean pushed him away. "Down boy."

"You know you like it," Vic said aggressively.

And to his astonishment, Sean flicked him a funny look. "Yeah. I do."

When they finally went up through the chapel Sean pointed at one of the stained glass windows facing the altar. Sir Galahad with his sword raised. "Hey," he whispered. "Notice a resemblance around the jaw?"

To put him in his place, Vic said, "No way. You've got a mouth like a girl."

This seemed to hit Sean's funny bone — he always had a weird sense of humor. "Not me, asshole. I was kind of thinking he looks like you."

Present day, 0100, Bagram Air Base, Afghanistan

Afghanistan in November was a cold day in hell.

At one o'clock in the morning the Chinook was spinning up on the tarmac, the craft shaking like a giant, living, breathing bird. Warm exhaust gusted into Vic's face as he climbed aboard after combat controller Tech Sergeant Bill O'Riley and Specialist Paul Matturo.

This was Vic's handpicked rescue team. In addition to his mini quick reaction force, the Chinook helicopter was manned by five crew members including the pilot Major Kate Cheyney. Everyone on this mission—codename operation Blue Dolphin—was a combat-seasoned veteran.

They buckled in and the chopper rose, whirling them off toward the snow-capped mountains.

They had a hundred and fifty mile flight to the rendezvous point. Everyone had their job and settled down to it, planning what to do when they hit the ground. The basic plan was to land, set up a perimeter, extract the Navy SEAL, and bug out.

Vic put on headphones and listened in on the radio chatter between Bagram and the battle zone. Well-armed, well-outfitted al Qaeda mountain fighters were well-entrenched around their target. In other words, business as usual.

"So what the hell is this SEAL doing out here on his lonesome?" O'Riley asked, when Vic finally put the headphones aside.

"He was part of a recon team looking for Akhtar Shah Omar."

Akhtar Shah Omar was a Taliban leader in the Kunar province whose so-called Mountain Devil fighters had been delivering heavy casualties to the marines operating in eastern Afghanistan.

"Someone should have told them that Omar's on the other side of the valley."

Vic nodded curtly. It was obvious they didn't have the full story yet, but that was par for the course. What he had been able to learn was that Sean had been leading a four-man team. The three other SEALs had been killed after an extended firefight when their position had been discovered by mujahadeen militia. Sean had managed to survive and keep moving and was now within range of the landing zone, although there was no telling what kind of shape he was in.

"By now everybody in the fucking province, including Osama Bin Laden, will be looking for him. And they're going to be waiting for us," O'Riley said.

Vic looked from his weathered face to the dark, intense face of Matturo. "Yep. The Taliban know we always come back for our own. If they can, they'll lay a trap for us, but we're coming in fast and we've still got the advantage of darkness."

Cheyney's calm voice came over the intercom. "Six minutes out."

As Vic unbuckled and moved into kneeling position, he could hear the pilot briefing her crew who were already on their feet, watching the windows, looking out for RPG launches.

Far below Vic could see the pale glimmer of the snowy slopes of the whaleback western ridge of the Shah-i-Kot Valley.

Cheyney finished, "Anybody have any questions? No? Let's rock and roll."

Eleven years ago, 1515, Village Motel, Annapolis, Maryland

"Let's lock and load, baby," Sean said, squirting a shiny glob of lube on his hands. He rubbed his fingers together, warming the gel.

Vic shifted, trying to get comfortable — like that was even a possibility.

Sean ran his hand lightly over Vic's ass, stroking him, and then he parted his buttock cheeks, tracing a light finger down his crack — not quite teasing, but not invasive either. Delicately he touched the tight — and clenching tighter — entrance to Vic's anus.

Vic sucked in a breath. Fists punching sharp indentations in the slick, flowered bedspread and mattress beneath, he looked uneasily over his shoulder. "I don't know about this."

Sean's finger stopped that little stroking motion that was sending butterflies swarming into Vic's hot, tight belly. "Are you welching on your bet?"

Was he?

Vic stared at Sean's hard face. Sean would be pissed... but, yeah, he'd let Vic back out of it.

"Fuck no. I just... you do know what you're doing, right?"

"A damn sight more than you knew when you shoved that canon up my ass the first time."

Vic blushed. He'd heard loudly and at length how he needed to work on his technique that first time. Well, practice made perfect, and he didn't get any more complaints about his performance these days. Far from it. Nothing Sean liked better than taking Vic's dick up his skinny ass.

So why he'd had to suddenly make this into a big deal, turn everything around, insist on that goddamned bet on the Army-Navy Game — and why Vic had had to *lose* the bet.

"A deal's a deal," he said gruffly.

He faced forward again, uncomfortable at the way Sean's face colored up and his eyes shone more brightly in the subdued hotel lighting.

"You'll like it, Stoney," Sean whispered and Vic shivered as Sean's lips pressed briefly, like warm velvet, to his spine. "You'll see."

Cocky sonofabitch. No way was Vic going to like this, although he had to admit to a little curiosity given the way Sean carried on when Vic was fucking him. Racked and helpless — like it was just the best thing in the world to have Vic's dick shoving in and out of him. He'd even cried a little the first time — and not because Vic had hurt him. They'd both pretended not to notice.

Sean started fingering him again in that embarrassingly intimate, *knowing* way. Vic jumped.

"Jesus, would you try to relax?"

"I *am* relaxed!"

Sean laughed, and Vic reluctantly laughed too, although he was a little angry at being forced into this.

Okay, in fairness he wasn't being forced. Sean would accept it if he said he'd changed his mind. He wouldn't be happy but he'd take it. And he'd still let Vic have him. But... Vic couldn't do that to him because clearly this meant something to Sean. Proved something. God knew what.

He could feel Sean's dick, rigid as a snub-nosed lance brushing against his buttocks. His own dick was soft as a limp noodle. In fact if his genitals retreated any further from this assault he'd turn into a girl.

... that felt kind of good, the way Sean's finger was touching him there, stroking so lightly. The tip of his finger was slippery with oil and it pushed gently into Vic and then pulled out; he was getting a sort of rhythm going and Vic made himself relax into it. His sphincter muscle automatically gripped Sean's finger — biology kicking in — but the friction wasn't so bad. Wasn't bad at all if he was honest.

Yeah, that was nice...

And Sean was patient. And careful. He pushed his finger in deeply and continued stroking until Vic was relaxed enough to permit another finger to slip inside — definitely a weird feeling, but after the initial uncertainty of whether his body would permit this transgression... it sort of felt good. Sean was touching him expertly as though feeling for something...

Vic gasped as a jolt of pure pleasure lit up inside him. All hands on deck. Sean nipped his shoulder, and oddly that felt good too.

"Do that again," Vic ordered, unevenly.

Sean did it again and Vic gulped. Sean took the opportunity to slide another finger inside Vic's body.

He was sort of getting used to it now, and he liked the way Sean's fingers were twisting and stroking inside his body — weird though it was. He'd always liked Sean's hands.

Sean pulled his fingers out. The bedsprings squeaked beneath as he moved into position, and Vic felt the alien brush of latex as the blunt head of Sean's dick pushed at the door of his body.

The condom changed everything, made him self-conscious, made him remember what they were doing, what they were risking. He tensed, but Sean was soothing him with whispers and a caressing hand on his cock. Vic forced himself to relax, he wanted to get this over with now. Sean pushed in.

It hurt. Bright pain flashed behind Vic's eyes and he briefly considered murdering Sean for raping him, but even as the red tide of fury rose, the pain was easing and a strange quivering awareness replaced it. Not exactly pleasure but... well, not like anything he'd ever felt before.

"Sorry, sorry. It'll get better, you'll see," Sean was whispering, and his hands petted and fondled until Vic's dick was hard again, and he was relaxed.

The fullness, the sense of being overwhelmed by another body, was disconcerting, but even that wasn't... bad exactly. Just strange.

Sean moved, sliding in a little further, then pulling out. He cautiously rocked against Vic and Vic cautiously pushed back against him. Sean's thrusts grew stronger, and Vic shoved back harder, and now they had the rhythm of it, the push-pull, the rise and fall.

There was a temptation to wrestle for control, but he could feel Sean's urgency, his need, and after all, this was about giving Sean what he wanted, so Vic let go and just went with it, let Sean drive it, letting it build speed like a steam engine picking up until it was rocketing along on its own momentum and he couldn't have stopped it if he'd wanted to.

Strangely, he didn't want to.

Sean's cock thrust in and out, faster and harder, and then he changed the angle and Vic felt something like a fireball of intense, fierce physical delight roll up his spine and burst in the back of his skull. At the same time orgasm rushed up through him and he came in hard spurts of milky white.

Sean was still humping against him, making small, desperate sounds, and Vic, still telling himself he just wanted this over and forgotten, rolled his hips and tried twisting back. Sean arched, slamming in and out until he suddenly shouted and Vic could feel that pulse of liquid heat — contained — but there nonetheless.

They collapsed together, a sweating tangle of arms and legs, gasping for breath. Vic felt a crazy sort of triumph that he had managed this, managed to give Sean what he wanted. After he'd caught his breath, he rolled over, groggy with release and weariness, reaching for Sean, pulling him close. Sean crawled clumsily into his arms, burying his head in the curve of Vic's shoulder and neck.

He was murmuring something hot and emotional into Vic's skin, the meaning half-blurred by the thundering pulse in Vic's ears.

"What did you say?" Vic asked uneasily.

But Sean shook his head, denying the words.

Present day, 0220, Somewhere in the Aram Mountain Range, Kunar Province, Afghanistan

The chopper set down in a sparkling powder of fresh snow. Vic was the first one down the ramp and out into the thin, cold air, M4 held at ready. His team followed on his heels.

The silence in the makeshift LZ was almost eerie. Moonlight spotlighted snowy pine trees and surrounding rocky crags. Nothing moved.

"Where the hell is he?" O'Riley asked at last.

Vic shook his head, eyes raking the barren plateau for any sign of life. "Let's fan out. Have a look for him. He's supposed to be on his way."

They spread out, moving quickly across the mountain top. Not so much as a ground squirrel stirred.

Vic jogged to the edge of the clearing, looking down the mountain side. He could see the nubby carpet of pine trees and conifers. Not a glimmer of light from anywhere but the moon overhead.

"Where are you?" he asked softly.

The wind made a ghostly sigh through the funnel of rocks.

Out of the corner of his eye, Vic saw the flash of white light. A blast rent the night. Vic turned as a giant, invisible hand seemed to gouge into the earth in front of the nose of the chopper, sending snow and rocks flying his way. He hit the ground as shrapnel slammed into the side of the chopper and pinged against the rotary blades.

Mortar fire.

He looked for his guys and saw them flattened behind cover. Matturo yelled across the clearing, "Two o'clock. The bastards are firing mortars from over that ridge."

The ridge was on the other side of a gorge separating this mountain from the next.

One of the chopper's door gunners returned fire with his M60 machine gun, though it was doubtful he had a viable target.

Vic considered the ridge as another flash indicated a second mortar was being lobbed their way. Light, probably hand-held mortar, and far enough away to make that strike near the nose of the chopper more a matter of luck than strategy — which wouldn't help Vic's team if that luck held and they ended up stranded on this mountaintop — surrounded by al Qaeda. He remembered Marsden's words about not wanting another Roberts' Ridge. Marsden was going to piss himself when he got word of this. Although anyone could have predicted what would happen putting a chopper down in the middle of these mountains.

Not like there was any choice about it. From the moment Vic had heard Sean Kennedy was the fox in the snare, he'd been determined to go.

The second mortar hit beneath the mountain top. Snow and rocks and shrapnel flew into the night and then rained down while Vic, Matturo, and Riley hunkered under what cover they could find.

Matturo was swearing a blue stream when he popped his head up again. "If this frogman doesn't show up, how long are we planning on hanging around here?"

"Working on it." No small arms fire. So far, so good. The dividing gorge between this mountain top and the ridge where the insurgents were holed up would slow al Qaeda down only briefly. And these mountains were filled with bad guys to whom the sound of those mortars and machine gun fire would be reveille.

"Looks like they were waiting for us," O'Riley shouted.

Vic shouted back, "If they were waiting for us this place would be swarming with al Qaeda."

"Well, it won't be long now."

That was sure as shit true.

Another mortar exploded in the mountain below them. Vic could feel the mountain shake as the round thudded into its face.

"Any sign of our boy?" O'Riley called again from his position behind a scraggy evergreen that looked like Charlie Brown's Christmas tree. "I got nothing. Any sign of him?"

Vic looked across to Matturo. Matturo shook his head.

"Let's give him a little while," Vic said. "Maybe traffic was heavy on the 101."

O'Riley guffawed.

Every fifteen seconds another mortar round hit the hillside, usually beneath the crest but occasionally striking the cliffside above. Given the randomness of the impacts, Vic suspected the mortar team lacked a forward observer. What they did seem to have was an endless supply of ammo and boundless enthusiasm for their mission.

If Sean was trying to get up this mountain, the mortar fire would be one hell of a disincentive. And if he wasn't trying to get up this mountain ...

In the lull between rounds, Vic jumped up and zigzagged back to the Chinook, boots pounding gravel. Taking shelter on the other side of the ramp, he yelled into the chopper, "Somebody get on the radio and contact base. See if one of the CIA's drones can give us Kennedy's coordinates."

In the distance he could hear the mortar firing. The longest minutes of his life ticked by while he waited for an answer.

When it came, it was not good.

"They're not picking anything up."

Sean. Don't do this to me.

"He's not moving or they can't find him?"

Another eternity while he waited.

"They can't find him."

Okay. That could mean a couple of things. If one word defined the SEALs it was silence. And the fact that Sean had gone silent could mean the drone wasn't positioned where it needed to be or there was a problem with it or with the live feed. It could mean Sean was lying low somewhere where the surveillance drones couldn't see him.

It could mean he had been captured.

Or killed.

But Vic wasn't going to accept that until he had proof. He turned to jog back to the clearing but the pilot, Cheyney, appeared at the top of the open ramp. She called after him, "Captain Black! We can't hang around here any longer."

Vic threw back, "We're not leaving without Kennedy, so simmer down."

"I'll simmer *you* down, Stoney," Cheyney snapped. "Any minute one of these ragheads is going to show up with an RPG and punch a hole in my bird. We're taking off."

Vic thought fast.

"Fair enough. Leave me here. I'll meet you at the bottom of the mountain."

She made a sound that in another woman might have been considered a squeak. "*Leave* you here? Are you out of your goddamned mind? This mountainside is going to be crawling with hostiles within the hour."

"Someone needs to wait here for Kennedy."

"Look, Stoney, I don't like it either, but — "

"If he's here, I'll find him."

"*Stoney.* What are you — you know as well as I do that he's — that there's a good chance he's been captured or killed. The live feed isn't picking up any activity."

"No way."

"*No way?* What do you mean, *no way?* Stoney, no way can I leave you here. I've got my orders too, you know? And even if I didn't — "

He couldn't hear this. He liked her. They'd had some good times together, but… no. He said, "Katie, give me three hours. I'll head for the valley below. It's a natural landing zone. You can pick me up there at… 0500."

"That's getting way too close to sunrise."

"We'll still have a little margin."

She was shaking her head.

"Listen, if Kennedy's still alive we can't fly out of here and leave him on this rock with hundreds of insurgents closing in on him."

"And what if he's not still alive? Stoney — Vic — no one is writing off Kennedy. But there are other ways to handle this."

"If al Qaeda finds him before we do, they'll execute him. You know that."

"I know that. I also know …" Her voice trailed. "You're out of your goddamned mind."

"Three hours. That's all I'm asking."

"It's not that simple. We've got another storm front moving in fast. Snow is on the way. We're losing our window."

"Then you better not be late."

She was motionless for a long moment, a dark shadow against the blinking lights and movement within the chopper.

"I must be out of my mind. How the hell am I supposed to explain — ?"

But she was talking to herself.

Eleven years ago, 1345, Bancroft Hall, U.S. Naval Academy, Annapolis, Maryland

"So when were you going to tell me?"

The one look at Sean's face he'd risked had hurt too much, so Vic was staring out the window of their dorm in Bancroft Hall, staring over the summer-green tops of trees. It made it worse because Sean was trying so hard not to show anything — after all those times Vic had warned him his face gave too much away. "I'm telling you now."

"Now." Sean's voice was flat. "Okay. You're telling me now. We're … how many weeks from graduation? And you tell me *now* you're thinking about the Rangers?"

"If I can get in."

Sean jumped up from the bed and began to circle the room. "You're going to cross commission to the fucking *army*? Your family's been navy since your great-great-great crawled out of the ooze. And you're suddenly talking about becoming an Army Ranger? You did notice we're in fucking Annapolis, right?"

Vic turned then. "What do you *want* from me?"

Sean gaped at him. "What do I want? Well, Black, I guess I wanted what we've been talking about for three years. You and me in the marines together — "

"You jackass," Vic yelled. He got his voice under control with an effort. "And how did you think that was going to work, Kennedy? It's not even like we were going to be in the same unit. What the hell were you thinking? We were going to go steady? We were going get married?"

"What the hell was *I* thinking?"

"We're career military. We can't just… we're not the kind of guys who …"

"Come out?"

Vic stopped cold. After a silence that seemed as deep and raw as the Mariana Trench, he said carefully, "Are you out of your fucking mind?"

Sean just stared back at him with those clear, light eyes.

Vic said — making it just as plain and to the point as he could — "Maybe it's different for you. You got in here on an appointment and there's only your aunt to think about. My grandfather was an admiral in the Second World War. My dad — my whole family — is expecting me to live up to — " The look on Sean's face stopped him. Vic said roughly, "I don't mean that, Sean."

Sean was smiling now, and that fierce white curve of his mouth was far worse than the hurt that had twisted his face a moment before. "Why not? It's the truth. It's what you think. I'm glad you said it. It makes it — "

Vic grabbed his shoulders, pressing his mouth to Sean's stopping him from saying it. He didn't want to hurt Sean. That was the last thing he'd ever want. He'd have given his soul to take it all back, to erase the last half hour, to change the future. But regardless of what he said or didn't say, this was the way it had to be. There wasn't any other way for them. He'd always known it, and he'd told himself that Sean did too. That despite what Sean said, what they'd *both* said, Sean knew the truth as well as Vic did. But maybe Vic had been seeing what he wanted to see because Sean … had always had that stubborn, irrational streak of idealism. Or stupidity.

Sean tore free and got on the other side of the room. He was shaking — and so, Vic was surprised to note, was he.

"Listen," Vic said, keeping his voice low. "This isn't anything to do with how I-I feel — "

Sean yanked off the class ring he wore. Vic's ring, , because they had secretly exchanged their class rings as Second Class Midshipmen. He hurled it with vicious accuracy at Vic. The heavy ring hit Vic squarely on the bridge of his nose and bounced away.

Present day, 0240, Somewhere in the Aram Mountain Range, Kunar Province, Afghanistan

Vic was already a hundred meters down the steep, rocky slope when he saw the Chinook wheeling away like a great black bird. It silhouetted briefly against the enormous red moon and then was gone.

The mortar crew continued to take petulant shots at it until it had vanished, the sound echoing off the stone walls, and then rolling away into a silence as absolute as the grave.

Vic reached for a handhold and something skittered away from his hand.

Cautiously, and very quietly, half-walking, half-sliding he got down the steep hillside until he reached a trail of sorts. He kept his eyes peeled because Sean Kennedy was somewhere on this mountain and Vic was going to find him if it was the last thing he did.

Sean was smart and savvy and stubborn. No one knew better than Vic how stubborn Sean Kennedy was — if eleven years of radio silence were anything to go by. Sean wouldn't give up. He'd keep fighting to get to the LZ.

If he was able.

And so Vic continued down a ledge that would have given a mountain goat pause for thought.

There was a clack of stone on stone, the sound echoing like a gunshot in the stillness of the night. Vic froze. The sound came from about twenty meters in front of him. Someone scrabbling up the cliffside. He reached for his combat knife. If this was a fight, it needed to be a quiet one or he was liable to have all of al Qaeda down on him. And if it wasn't a fight… his heart thudded hard in a hopeful mixture of adrenaline and anticipation.

Silent and deadly, he sprinted forward, and as he watched, two dirt grimed hands — one wrapped in a blood-stained handkerchief — groped blindly along the edge of the cliff.

Vic was ready, ready for the worst and hoping for the best as the man hauled himself, panting, over the lip of the trail and dragged himself to his feet, swaying as he tried not to put weight on his right foot. Vic saw the sweat-dark hair, the stained headband, and the gaunt, bearded face.

"Sean," he said in a voice that sounded nothing like his own.

Sean Kennedy's head snapped up and he nearly stepped backward off the mountainside. Vic lunged for him, caught his arm and towed him forward. For an instant they were in each other's arms, clutching tight, and then they were apart, standing on what felt like the edge of the world, teetering, off-balance physically and emotionally.

"*Stoney?*" Sean said at last. "Is that you?"

"Yeah." Vic was grinning like a fool. "Yeah, it's me."

"Jee-zus. It *is* you." Sean closed his eyes for a moment. He opened them and peered owlishly into Vic's face. "*You're* the cavalry?"

"You were expecting the navy?"

"Ha." Unexpectedly, Sean's legs gave and he half-sat, half fell onto the ribbon of goat track, head dropping back with exhaustion.

Vic knelt beside him. "How bad are you hurt?" He patted Sean down — any excuse to touch him, if he was honest. To reassure himself that it really was Sean, that he really was alive. All the times he'd dreamed of this moment — none of the dreams had come anywhere near this terrifying reality.

Sean's shoulders had broadened and his body was the hard body of a man. Beneath Vic's searching hands — and the battered body armor — Sean was all bone and muscle. His face was much older ... a thousand years older, and something inside Vic grieved for that. The last time he'd seen Sean he'd been a lanky kid with hair the color of autumn and eyes younger than spring.

Eyes still shut, wincing beneath Vic's exploration, Sean said, "It's all relative. Was that my taxi I saw flying away a little while ago?"

"Just taking her for a spin around the block."

"I hope it's a short block."

Vic found where a bullet had grazed Sean's shoulder, a crease along his upper arm, another nick along his side where he'd been hit beneath the edge of his vest. An assortment of cuts and scrapes and bruises. Nothing vital had been hit and the blood was drying, crusting. It was as though al Qaeda had been chipping bits and pieces out of him for days. "Christ, how many times have you been shot?"

Sean opened his eyes, frowning into Vic's face as though he was having trouble focusing. "How far are we from the top?"

"About two hundred meters. But we're headed down."

"I don't think we want to head down. I've got Taliban fighters on my tail." He sounded remarkably calm about it.

Vic let go of him abruptly, pulled his binoculars from around his neck and threw himself down at the edge of the mountain, scanning the dark slopes below.

Nothing moved.

Not a flicker of motion.

"Are you sure?" he threw softly over his shoulder. Not that it was a mistake Sean was liable to make.

Sean said nothing.

"Sean?"

When he still didn't answer, Vic glanced around and saw that he was sleeping. He turned the binoculars back on the mountainside beneath them.

Nothing.

But that didn't mean they weren't out there.

He crawled back to Sean, hesitating for an instant at the sight of that strained and weary face in repose. He rested his hand on Sean's shoulder and instantly caught the gleam of Sean's eyes.

"We got to move."

Sean said, "I thought I dreamed you up."

"You dream about me a lot?"

Sean's laugh was stifled but it was his old laugh, and Vic's heart seemed to swell.

"Not anymore. I got bigger boogeymen to worry about than you these days."

Yeah, wasn't that the truth. Vic took the slam absently, already recalculating. "Can you walk?"

"I got myself this far didn't I?" And Sean began to gather himself, pushing upright, though accepting Vic's help to stand.

"What's the matter with your leg?"

"Sprained my ankle like the goddamned heroine in a monster movie."

It was just getting better by the moment.

"Well, we can't go up. I don't think anyone knows I'm on the mountain, but they're going to be wondering what that chopper was doing here. We can't risk landing topside again, but Grizzly 01 is going to meet us in the valley at oh five hundred."

Sean pulled away slightly to examine Vic's face. "You've got a chopper going to touch down in the valley?"

"Yeah."

"You're not kidding?"

"You know me better than that."

Sean was shaking his head in disbelief. "What time is it?"

"We've got two and a half hours to get down there."

"Too bad you couldn't have come up with this plan *before* I climbed up here."

"Sorry. Your line was busy."

"Is this pilot in love with you or something?"

"Isn't everybody?" Vic wrapped an arm around Sean's waist. "Put your arm over my shoulders. Can you make it like this?"

"I can try." Sean added grimly, "But if I can't I don't want you wasting time up here with a chopper crew waiting in that valley for you."

They moved slowly down the trail, Sean half hopping, trying not to lean too heavily on Vic.

"I think our best bet is the north face," Vic said. "It'll be a tougher climb but whoever is tracking you won't be looking for you over there."

"They won't be looking for me coming back down at all."

"We'll have to double back around to the LZ, and we'll lose some time there ...
." Vic was still calculating odds. "How much ammo do you have left?"

"Maybe 50 rounds."

SEALs typically carried 4000 rounds. Vic nodded, accepting this, not commenting on the battle that Sean had waged to get this far. "If we're lucky we'll lift out without a firefight."

They traveled along the narrow trail, having to stop at one point to go single file down a ledge that was like a knife edge. It would have been tricky in the daylight. It was harrowing in the dark. Vic kept one hand clutched on Sean's arm terrified that Sean would slip or misstep. Having finally found him again, no way was he losing him.

They finally made it across the ridge and Sean slid down. "I've got to rest."

Blood loss, shock, exhaustion. Yeah, he'd earned a rest. Unfortunately, they didn't have that kind of time.

"Take five," Vic said, although it was going to have to be more like take three. He squatted as Sean slid down the frosty rock face and leaned back. A couple of snow flakes drifted down.

Fuck.

Vic stretched his arm out. "Here, let's conserve body heat."

Sean gave a laugh that was mostly a snort, but he leaned into Vic. Vic folded his arms tight around him. He had always dreamed of this meeting as a new beginning. It was feeling more and more like an ending.

"I lost my entire team," Sean said suddenly, the words vibrating against Vic's chest.

Vic nodded, not trusting himself to words.

"We had a direct action. Take out Akhtar Shah Omar. Limited time on target."

Not recon then. Assassination. He'd wondered if it was something more like that. He thought of the boy he'd known at Annapolis. His eyes prickled. And how insane was that when he wasn't exactly teaching Sunday School himself. And anyone who knew him would be laughing their asses off. So much for the Stone Man.

There was a long pause and he wondered if Sean had fallen asleep again; he was breathing long, steady breaths — and then Vic realized that he was struggling with emotion.

"What happened?" he whispered against Sean's cold ear. Tempting to kiss him, but ... no. No. He'd lost that right a long time ago.

"We got walked on."

Walked on. Compromised on a mission. He let his ears brush the chilled shell of Sean's ear. "It happens."

Sean said muffledly, "It does. And we all knew what we needed to do. But ... it was this little girl. This little goatherd girl. And I couldn't do it, Vic."

"Couldn't do what?"

Sean looked up, his eyes looked wide and so clear they looked almost silver in the paling light. "It was my call and I said we had to let her go."

Vic said calmly, "Hey, what was the option there? You've got to follow the Rules of Engagement. She wasn't Taliban. She wasn't al Qaeda."

"No, she was fucking Heidi. And I let her go and she ran straight to the mujahadeen militia." He turned away and wiped at his eyes with his forearm. "And my men ended up dead."

For a few seconds Vic couldn't say anything. Finally, he said unemotionally, "Sometimes they're on our side. How'd you end up with the Taliban chasing you?"

"We had to fall back once the mujahadeen showed up. Basic move and shoot maneuver. Pitched battles aren't our thing."

No. SEALs were not main force units. SEALs worked best as shock troops. Stun the target with maximum violence, accomplish the most destruction with minimal effort, and then fade away in the confusion.

"We were okay, but naturally it made a little noise. The Taliban noticed and decided to join the party. We lost Bobby right away. Voss was our communications guy. He got hit trying to radio for help. They shot him a couple of times, but he stayed on the high ground trying to make comms. Salvio and I went to drag him back and Salvio got hit in the head. He died in my arms."

"Close your eyes and sleep for a couple minutes."

"No time."

But when Vic tugged him back, Sean leaned into him and closed his eyes. His breath was warm against Vic's throat, his hair brushed softly against Vic's chin.

Vic let him sleep ten minutes. About seven minutes longer than he should have but he justified it as a power nap.

Far down the mountainside he could see stealthy movement, hear the faintest scrape of boots on rock. Every sound carried in this cold, crisp mountain air. Taliban soldiers were slowly navigating their way up the uneven slope. They were being surprisingly cautious. Sean must have made quite an impact on them.

He had a way of doing that.

Vic said against Sean's ear, "Rise and shine."

Sean's eyes opened instantly. He nodded.

The next two hours were a test of endurance. Somehow they made it across the scraggy face of the cliff, literally crawling at points, and then climbed with excruciating difficulty down a series of boulders. Vic knew he was going to have nightmares about that climb for weeks to come.

Assuming he still had weeks to come and they didn't end up in pieces on the mountain in the next half hour or so.

By the time they shinnied down the final boulder, they were both shaking and soaked in sweat. Sean was needing more and more help although he never asked for it once.

Reaching the bottom, they dropped on their bellies and tried to recover their breath.

"Did you ever get married?" Sean asked suddenly, softly.

"No. You?"

Sean snorted.

"I mean … did you find someone … ?" *Who appreciated you, who treated you like you should have been treated, who had the brains to recognize what you were worth?*

"Oh, sure. I found a lot of people."

Neither spoke for a time.

Sean's voice was abrupt. "I heard you did."

"Did what?"

"Got married." He sounded just faintly impatient.

"No. Where'd you hear that?"

"Specs Davis. I ran into him a couple of years back. He said you were engaged."

"No." Stoney pointed to the tiny scar between his eyebrows. "As you can see, I'm still wearing your ring."

Sean stared at him and then laughed.

Vic laughed too, threw him a look beneath his brows. "It took two stitches."

Bullets raked along the flat-topped stone and they rolled apart. Sean dropped over the side and Vic followed, hearing the crash of him landing in bushes. He pulled his M4 spraying the hillside behind them, hearing screams of pain. He turned and followed Sean whom he could hear scrabbling down another staircase of stone.

The next few seconds were chaos. Vic kept moving and shooting — all the while aware of Sean less than a yard ahead. Bullets whined overhead. All at once the enemy was everywhere and the graying night was lit by muzzle flash and mini flares.

"Down," Sean yelled and Vic hit the frozen ground.

He heard the whisper of a suppressed shot and knew Sean was using his MK23.

He crawled into the brush. They both opened fire, ducking down as the Taliban opened fire again with machine guns. They shot, reloaded while the bullets buzzed and whizzed around them, hitting the rocks and ricocheting with lethal force.

"We've got to move," Vic yelled.

He felt rather than heard Sean's assent.

They took turns firing and covering each other's retreat the rest of the way down the slope in a run, crawl, walk maneuver.

They were never going to make it.

Vic felt a brief and furious grief that they were not going to have that second chance after all. Maybe he didn't deserve it, but Sean sure as hell did. He determined to take as many of these murdering bastards with them as he could.

But as they reached the ledge they heard the pound of chopper blades and looked upward to see the Chinook rocking into position above them. Time flies when you're having fun — and Cheyney was not a girl who liked to be kept waiting. The door slid open and O'Riley was throwing down a line while Matturo and one of the door gunners laid a steady covering fire.

Sean was turning to cover him and Vic shoved him toward the line. "Climb." He turned his M4 on the hillside.

Sean dragged himself up the line with what seemed to be agonizing slowness while the mountain fighters continued to fire between Vic's bursts of fire — and the protective fire of the chopper gunners.

When Sean had neared the top, O'Riley and Matturo leaned out and hauled him into the chopper.

Vic ran for the line, climbing hand over hand. The chopper was already rising and swinging him away over the mountainside. He continued to climb as from behind the ridge the mortars were launched again. Vic hauled himself onto the cold metal flooring of the chopper and gasped.

O'Riley and Matturo were beside Sean working fast to stem what looked like a gushing artery from his thigh.

Seeing that fountain of blood Vic felt the strength go out of him. He dropped down beside Sean whose face was blanched of color in the yellow dawn, his breathing rapid and shallow.

"How bad?"

"Bad enough," Matturo said. The tourniquet he was trying to fashion was already soaked with scarlet.

Sean's eyes opened. They looked black. He tried to smile.

"Don't you *dare* fucking die on me, Sean."

Sean asked faintly, "How come you came back for me, Stoney?"

Vic had to work to get the words out. "I was always coming back for you."

Present day, 1750, The Craig Joint Theater Hospital at Bagram Airfield, Afghanistan

"He's asking for you," the weary-faced surgeon said. "Five minutes. Don't tire him."

Vic rose. "Is he — " He abruptly ran out of air, but the surgeon followed him easily enough — it was a question he was familiar with by now.

"He's still critical but… that's one tough sailor. We're transporting him to Germany tonight."

Vic stepped into the trauma bay. There were four beds and a hell of a lot of state of the art equipment, and then he spotted Sean. He lay in a bed that looked like a miniature space pod and he was hooked up to a confusing web of monitors, an IV and oxygen. He looked very brown against the bleached sheets.

Vic leaned over the railing. He said softly, "Hey."

Sean's lashes flicked and rose. His pupils were huge with whatever drugs they were pumping into him. "Hey ..."

"You okay?" Vic asked anxiously.

Sean's face twisted a little and he bit his lip. "Please don't ... make me laugh."

"I just mean ..."

"Yeah." Sean's eyes closed again, his colorless mouth formed the word. "Stoney ..."

"I'm right here," Vic said, leaning still closer. He was aware of the medical personnel but only as so much equipment — stuff useful for keeping Sean alive.

"Thanks." It was so soft he barely heard it. "For coming back. I mean ... you know."

"I should have come back a long time ago." Vic said with sudden fierceness. "I was too big a coward. Not — not the way you think. I got over worrying about all that bullshit a long time ago."

Sean's face was so still. Was he even listening? It didn't matter. Vic had been waiting a long time to say it.

"I was ashamed, Sean. I let you down. I let us both down. I didn't think you'd ever forgive me, and I didn't have the guts to face you. You're such a tough sonofabitch."

Sean's face tightened in pain. "I forgave you a long time ago, you jackass." His eyes opened, starred with emotion. "I love you."

"I love you too," Vic said steadily and he didn't give a damn who else heard it so long as Sean believed it.

Sean gave a ghost of his old laugh. "And it only took you twelve years to figure it out?"

"I never said I was fast. Just faithful."

"Mmm." Sean was tiring, but he whispered, "You planning to do anything about it?"

"You know it," Vic said. He slipped his class ring off and gently slid it on the ring finger of Sean's lax left hand. "The very next time we meet."

HEART TROUBLE

I discovered the rough draft of the story that is now "Heart Trouble" while digging through boxes of old files. It was scribbled down on notebook paper, which is how I used to write everything. There were a lot of arrows and insertions and scratch-outs, but the basic story was complete and, I thought, rather sweet. What was interesting to me about this 20+ year old effort was that so many of the themes and motifs I still write about are delineated here. I'm not sure if that's a good sign or a bad sign.

"So what seems to be the trouble, Ford?"

The emergency room doctor took a second quick look at the chart to make sure he hadn't just called me by my last name. He didn't look a lot older than me, light eyes, a smooth sweep of blond hair, tall and broad shouldered. Not handsome. At least, not in a TV Doc kind of way.

Which was really the last thing I needed, being already at a considerable disadvantage. I was sitting on an examining table in E2 which was decorated by colorful posters of all the things that could — and probably eventually would — go wrong with you. My T-shirt was off and my skin prickled with goose bumps. The harsh light in emergency rooms is not flattering.

"I'm uh… afraid I'm having a heart attack."

"Okay. Well, your blood pressure was a little high when you came in. We'll try it again in a minute. Meantime…" He whipped his stethoscope around his neck and moved in closer. "Can you describe your symptoms?"

"My chest hurts. I'm having trouble getting my breath. My left arm keeps going numb…"

He placed the cap of the stethoscope over my heart and listened. "Are you having trouble getting your breath now?"

"Not now. No. Earlier. It comes and goes."

He smelled clean. Soap, unobtrusive aftershave, and antiseptic. His breath was cool and zingy with mouthwash. He had a tiny scar over the left side of his upper lip. You'd have to be close enough to kiss him to see it. I closed my eyes.

"Is your chest hurting now?"

I opened my eyes. "It feels tight." Tighter still with him leaning into me, so close we were exchanging breaths. What was his name? If he'd said, I'd missed it, and I couldn't read the plastic ID hanging from the ribbon around his neck. J-A-something. Jack? James? Jacques? Probably not Jacques.

"Pain?" His lashes flicked up and his serious gaze met mine. Serious and kind. Which was a relief because I felt like an idiot sitting there half-undressed with no visible signs of illness or injury while down the hall someone was yelling his head off.

"Not now."

"But earlier?"

I felt myself turning red. "Not pain. Not like that. Just pressure. Tightness."

He nodded thoughtfully. Take a deep breath."

I sucked in a deep breath.

"Exhale."

I exhaled.

"Again." He moved the stethoscope slowly over my chest, listening intently. His expression gave nothing away. He straightened, moved away, out of my line of vision. I jumped when he touched my back.

"Sorry. Are my hands cold?"

Cool. Not unpleasant. I shook my head.

"Inhale."

The same routine. Inhale. Exhale. Inhale. Exhale.

"That's good." He stepped around, put his hands on either side of my head and gazed into my eyes. His own were blue. Very blue. Maybe he wore colored contacts. I gazed uncomfortably back and I thought he made a smiling sound though his mouth didn't move. He kneaded his way down my throat and rested his hands on my shoulders for a moment, then stepped back and draped the stethoscope around his neck once more.

"Well … your blood pressure is up and your heart rate is a little fast, but everything sounds normal. I think we'll run an EKG to be on the safe side."

I nodded humbly.

He smiled. He had a very nice smile. Patients probably felt better just seeing him smile. "Relax for a minute, Ford." Then he was gone, striding out of the room, white coat flapping. I heard him talking to someone in the hall.

Relax? Yeah, right.

A few minutes later I was taped up to an intimidating machine which measured out my heart beats in tidy, green blips. I watched the screen nervously. Were the blips big enough? Steady enough?

"What's that doctor's name?" I asked the technician.

She smothered a yawn. It was close to midnight now. I was tired too. Panic will only take you so far. "Who? Oh, you mean Dr. Hoyle?"

"My doctor." Well, not *my* doctor. Although ... I considered that and there were a couple of quick blips on the screen.

"Yeah, that's Dr. Hoyle." She didn't seem concerned by the double blip on the screen. She was checking her watch. A moment later she excused herself.

I was left alone with my unhappy thoughts. It was cold in the little room and it felt dehumanizing lying there all hooked up to machines. I could hear voices in the cubicle next door. I thought I could recognize Dr. Hoyle's voice. Same tone of voice, anyway. Calm, deep, slow. Reassuring.

He was probably about ten years older than me.

After a time the technician returned, took the EKG readings, untaped me, told me I could put my shirt back on.

I put my shirt on and waited.

More screams and yells from down the hall.

I could see my reflection in the glass front cabinets. I looked insubstantial, transparent, ghostly. They probably got a lot of that around here. I frowned at my defensive posture. Even as a ghost I looked like I needed a shave and a haircut. I picked at the rip in the knee of my Levis, unraveling the denim further.

Dr. Hoyle was reading my chart as he pushed open the door. "Everything looks normal, Ford."

"Great." I know I sounded uncertain.

He glanced up, caught my gaze and smiled. "You're twenty-three, Ford?"

"Yeah."

"Has anything like this happened before? Chest pains? Numbness in your left arm?"

"No."

"What did you have for dinner tonight?"

"Nothing. It's not indigestion."

His brows rose. They were darker than his hair, a lot darker when they formed that forbidding line. He inquired coolly, "Did I suggest this was indigestion?"

"No, but I know people can mistake heartburn for a heart attack."

"Yeah. Not usually the other way around. So you skipped dinner?"

I nodded. Offered, "I had a few cups of coffee."

"Is there any family history of heart trouble?"

That lever threw open the floodgates. "Yeah." I felt winded again just thinking about it. "My grandfather died when he was thirty-five. Suddenly. They thought it was his heart. My uncle died of a coronary when he was forty. My dad has a bad heart."

Dr. Hoyle frowned and made notations on my chart. "What do you do for a living, Ford?"

"I'm a writer."

"Yeah?" Was that a flash of genuine interest? "What do you write?"

"Oh, books. Novels." I hadn't got to the point where I could say it casually. I still only half-believed it myself.

"So you're published? Would I find your books in a bookstore?"

"Uh... maybe. It's just one book." A gay book. So it would have to be a gay bookstore. And he probably wasn't... No wedding ring, but he probably wasn't.

"What's your book about?"

"It's about a boy. About a boy's life. Kind of a coming of age thing." Coming of age and coming out.

Dr. Hoyle was flatteringly interested. He said he wished he could write. He said he loved to read but all he seemed to read these days were medical journals. He asked all the right questions, and I stopped worrying about whether I was giving the right answers. Or that I wasn't letting Dr. Hoyle get a word in edgewise. I told him all about the reviews and the worry of living up to those reviews and how the next book was going — or wasn't going — and the writer's block. No, capitalize it. Writer's Block. Last known address.

"So, safe to say," Dr. Hoyle managed to interrupt at last, "You're under a fair amount of pressure?"

"Yeah. I guess."

"Are you sleeping okay? Eating okay?"

I shrugged.

"Getting any exercise?"

"Some."

"Like?"

"I swim. Nearly every morning."

"Swimming's good. How do you feel after you swim?"

"Good," I said.

"Dizzy at all? Weak? Any chest pain?"

"No. I feel good after I swim."

Dr. Hoyle made another note. "How's your health in general? When was the last time you had a complete physical?"

"It's been a couple of years."

"Any other stress in your life? Get along with your family okay?"

"Sure."

"How are things going financially?"

I wondered if he was worried I couldn't pay my emergency room bill, but then I understood where he was going with this line of questioning, and all *that* worry came pouring out too. I told him about the advance I'd spent, and the rent that had just doubled, and the buying groceries on credit cards which had turned out to be just as bad an idea as everybody always said. It was a relief to get it off my chest, to info dump it all on this attractive, attentive stranger with the kind eyes.

Dr. Hoyle let me run until I was all out of words, and then he said, "I don't think there's anything wrong with your heart, Ford. But because there's a family history of coronary disease I'm going to order some tests. Just to put both our minds at rest."

"Okay." No way. Not without health insurance. He was trying to be helpful, but what I didn't need were more bills to worry about. Even I knew that.

"Do you have a regular family doctor?"

"Yeah. Up north."

I'd wondered what the full impact of his smile would be like. It took him from attractive to downright handsome in nothing flat. It also shaved about ten years off him.

"I'll tell you what I think. In my expert opinion, you've experienced a text book case of an anxiety attack."

I felt my mouth drop open.

"You're under a lot of stress," he explained, as if I didn't know. "I think this is just your body's way of reminding you to slow down and take some deep breaths."

The relief was incredible. Like Christmas morning and the governor granting your reprieve all at the same time. I hadn't realized exactly how terrified I was until the danger was past.

"Then I'm okay? There's nothing to worry about?"

"I think you're *fine*." Was it my imagination or was there a special emphasis in the way Dr. Hoyle said "fine". "I'm going to prescribe something so you can get some rest. Who brought you in?"

"I drove myself."

"You thought you were having a heart attack and you drove yourself?"

"I ... uh ... it was late. I didn't want to bother anybody."

He let out a disbelieving exhalation. Not exactly a gasp. More like sucking in air to deliver his thoughts and opinions, but he restrained himself.

"I live alone," I defended. What I was really thinking about was that health insurance I didn't have — and the price of an ambulance ride.

"Well, Dr. Hoyle said, "is there someone we can call to come and get you now? A girlfriend?"

"I don't have a girlfriend."

"A boyfriend?" He was smiling, teasing me. It was West Hollywood, after all. But was there another question there? His eyes didn't waver. Was he asking me for a reason? Or was I projecting?

"I don't have a boyfriend," I was startled to hear myself blurt, "I haven't really come out."

Dr. Hoyle didn't bat an eyelash. "That's another source of stress, isn't it?"

"Yes. Yes, it is." God. It was such a relief to finally *say* it.

There was a funny pause while I absorbed what I had just done.

"I'll tell you what," Dr. Hoyle said with brisk kindness, "I don't want you driving just now. Not after all this. How about if I drop you off? I'm off duty — " he checked his wristwatch, "officially — as of three minutes ago."

I didn't know what to say, what to make of this. This couldn't be standard procedure, but Dr. Hoyle (what the hell was his first name?) seemed too professional to be coming on to a patient. Too straight, for that matter.

"You don't have to," I said awkwardly. "I could… call a taxi." And pay for it with what? I'd be paying for this emergency room visit for the next few months.

"I want to." He seemed perfectly serious.

"Are you sure?"

He assented.

"Well… okay. Thank you."

When he met me in the waiting room a few minutes later he had changed into a leather jacket and chinos. He looked mature and successful and I re-revised my estimate of his age again. Definitely older. One of the big kids.

A little intimidated I accompanied him out to the parking garage. He kept up a relaxed line of talk as though this were all routine. Maybe it was for him.

"How long have you been in L.A.?"

I replied, "About eighteen months."

"How do you like it?"

"I like it a lot. Are you a native?"

"Oh, yeah. I grew up here. I went to Hollywood High. UCLA."

"I almost went to UCLA."

"Why didn't you?"

"I ended up getting a scholarship to Berkeley." That had been a big factor, but the other factor had been how far away UCLA seemed from home and everybody I knew and loved.

Our cars turned out to be the only two left on the upper parking level. His was a battered, green Volvo. A few empty spaces down my Nissan Skyline GT-R gleamed dully in the fluorescent lights. A symbol of the money I hadn't invested wisely.

"I think we better drive yours," Hoyle said, "seeing that she's screaming *take me* to the pylons."

I laughed nervously. Tried to find my keys. "But then how — "

"I can call someone to pick me up and bring me back to my car."

"This seems like a lot of trouble…" Still searching my pockets. There weren't that many of them.

"It's no trouble." He watched my increasingly feverish hunt and suggested in that same kind voice he'd used back when I was his patient, "Do you think you left them inside?"

We went back inside and Hoyle directed the search for my keys which were finally located in the men's washroom. He took charge of me and my keys and we headed back out to the parking structure.

By now the drama of the night was catching up with me and I was feeling shaky and weird with reaction. Despite the fact that it was a spring night and not really all that cold, my teeth were starting to chatter and I couldn't stop yawning. I was simply grateful when, outside, Hoyle slipped his jacket off and put it around my shoulders. It felt heavy and smelled of leather and that astringent aftershave I was beginning to associate with him.

This time we didn't talk on the elevator ride to the top level. Hoyle unlocked the passenger side and waited, till I was inside and adjusting the seat, to shut the door and cross round to the driver's side.

He slid inside and started the Nissan's sometimes finicky engine with no trouble, shifted smoothly, backed up in a clean, precise arc, his well-cared for hands familiar and almost caressing the wheel. "Nice," he murmured.

I thought of his hands on me, impersonal in the emergency room — no, not impersonal. There had been kindness and caring there, but a distance that had not existed when he laid his jacket over my shoulders.

I shivered.

"Still cold?" He reached down, found the heater, flipped it on. "We'll get this prescription filled first and then I'll run you home."

Fine. I didn't have energy to protest if he'd suggested disco dancing for eight hours and then abandoning me on the streets and stealing my car.

"Okay?"

I nodded. Realized he wasn't looking at me. Cleared my throat. "Yeah. Sorry about this."

"Hey, just relax," he said easily. "It's all part of the service. I'm Jacob, by the way."

Jacob. It suited him. Low-key and grave and steady.

We stopped at an all-night pharmacy. "I can get this done faster," Jacob said and was out of the car and disappearing inside the building while I was still trying to decide if that was a good idea.

I fell asleep waiting, and resumed consciousness to find a strange man sliding in beside me. I started upright.

"It's just me," Jacob reassured, and there was something about his tone of voice and the words he used. It was like we'd known each other for years. Like we'd been crawling inside tight, dark places together for a lifetime.

"Jacob," I acknowledged huskily. His name felt odd coming off my tongue for the first time.

I saw the gleam of his teeth and eyes in the gloom as he smiled.

"So you want to tell me how to get to Larrabee Street?"

"Right. Yeah. It's Larrabee and Palm." I gave him directions.

As we drove through the dark, mostly quiet streets, I started to get anxious. What was supposed to happen now? Was he just giving me a lift home or was there more to this? What did he want from me? What did I want from him? Did I have to invite him up? Did he expect me to? Did I want to?

I didn't know him at all.

For all I knew he could be an ax murderer. Half the killers on those true crime shows were doctors.

My chest got tight again, my palms grew wet and clammy. My heart started jumping so hard I was surprised the seatbelt strap didn't move. "You can park anywhere along here," I told Jacob breathlessly as the complex came into view.

"You don't have parking?"

"Well, yeah… yeah. The parking is… "

He'd already figured it out.

He parked neatly in the packed garage. I felt myself going hot and cold with panic. Almost two in the morning. What next? What did he want?

"Is it okay if I use your phone?" Jacob asked.

Of course. The old can-I-use-your-phone routine.

Who was he? Jacob Hoyle. What was a name? I didn't know him. He hadn't said to anyone at the hospital he was driving me home. No one knew he was here. He could do anything to me and no one would ever know. Fantasies of rape and murder flickered through my foggy brain.

I stammered, "I … uh … I …"

There was a moment of silence. Jacob handed over the little white bag with my prescription — which I belatedly remembered he had paid for.

"I'll call from the Mobile station around the block. Can I see your window from the street? I want to make sure you get inside."

Numbly I pointed toward the courtyard. Like that would tell him anything.

"Okay."

Jacob got out of the car, locked the door and came around to where I was stiffly unfolding from my seat. He held the door for me, locked it, handed me my keys. I handed him his jacket. He draped it over his arm.

I dropped the bag with my prescription. He bent to pick it up. Our fingers brushed as we exchanged the bag once more.

"What do I owe you?"

"Nothing. When you get inside, turn the light on," Jacob instructed. "And I'll know you're in safe."

Safe. What a wonderful word. A word from childhood really because once you left home nothing was safe ever again. Everything was up to you, everything was on you, and you either made it or you didn't. But safe was a word like *home* and it conjured images of warmth, comfort, someone who cared ... .

"You can't see it from the street. My apartment faces the pool and the courtyard."

"Then I'll wait and you can wave from your balcony."

"Thank you, Jacob." I felt like an idiot. What the hell was I doing? I was being a jerk and this guy — this attractive, nice, caring guy was about to walk out of my life forever.

He acknowledged curtly. "When you get in, make yourself a hot drink. Something without caffeine. Take one of those tablets and go straight to bed." He smiled, though it was brief. "Doctor's orders."

I nodded. We walked out of the parking structure. I glanced sideways at him. He glanced sideways at me. His hair looked silver in the grainy light, his eyes black. He patted his pockets, handed over a card.

"If you want to talk sometime, give me a call."

"Talk?"

"I've been out a long time, but I remember how it feels."

I took the card and dropped my keys.

Jacob gave a muffled laugh and retrieved them. He handed them to me. "With anyone else, I'd think you were trying to say something," he teased.

A light went on in the abandoned warehouse of my brain.

Good thing I didn't write mysteries because we had walked out of the hospital together, his fingerprints were all over my car, he'd picked up and paid for my prescription, and now he was patiently standing in the lamplight for anyone to see. He couldn't be plotting anything too sinister.

I said nervously, "Jacob, why don't you call from my apartment?"

"Are you sure?"

I nodded. Embarrassingly, my teeth started to chatter.

"You really do need to get inside." He draped his jacket around my shoulders once more. It was like having his arm around me as we walked through the main entrance. We stopped at the security intercom, the gate opened, and then we were inside the grounds with fountains splashing to the right and the scent of jasmine and citrus mingling with smog. The palm trees and tall lamp posts threw bars of shadow across the stone walkways and dark windows.

"There's a koi pond in the back," I said.

"That's nice," Jacob said.

We went upstairs and I fumbled tiredly with my keys until I finally managed to get the door open. Jacob followed me in.

"Sorry it's such a mess," I said, finding the light switch.

Jacob shut the door and looked around himself. I imagined his place was probably as spic and span as an operating room. I pictured something modern and utilitarian. Steel frames and glass tops.

My living space, on the other hand, was a clutter of books, clothes, papers. The computer sat on the dining room table, screensaver rolling an endless view of outer space. The stereo was on but silent. Trash bins overflowed, the sink was full of dishes, there were books everywhere. The dining room walls were paneled in bookshelves — which was ultimately going to cost me my deposit, but so be it. There were books stacked on the floors, the counters, the tabletops, every conceivable flat surface including the top of the fridge.

Jacob's brows rose. All he said was, "I like it. Early Dewey Decimal, isn't it?"

"I'm a little obsessive," I admitted.

"Do tell." He grinned at me.

It was hard to believe he was standing there. Not that I hadn't had friends over, but not a friend like this. Not a friend who was maybe going to be more than a friend.

But was that the case? The minute the thought took form, I shied away from it. Too soon. Too soon to get my hopes up. Especially when I didn't know what my hopes were.

I walked into the kitchen alcove, still wearing Jacob's jacket and opened the empty cupboards. Shut them. Opened the fridge.

"Would you like a drink?"

"Sure." He was examining the prints on the living room wall. Vintage watercolors of the French countryside I'd bought as an exchange student. "These are nice."

"What did you want?" I asked doubtfully, still studying the empty shelves of the fridge. A couple of beers and a small, forgotten carton of fried rice. Not much else. "There's a bottle of chardonnay. I think it's pretty good. Or would you like an MGD?"

"I'll have a hot drink with you."

That was a nice way of reminding me not to mix booze and tranquilizers. "I don't know if I have anything without caffeine. I thought caffeine was one of the nine essential amino acids?"

"Do you have any milk?" Jacob joined me in the kitchen which seemed too confined to accommodate all that confidence and vitality.

"A little." I sniffed doubtfully at the blue and orange carton. Checked the label. "I guess this is still good."

Jacob took it from me, checked it. "This will do. Do you have any cocoa?"

"Ovaltine?"

"Ovaltine's fine." He was smiling. Laughing at me? It put me on defense, made me self-conscious. Maybe if we were meeting on an equal footing, but I'd been at a disadvantage from the start. It's hard to be charming when you think you're dying.

"The phone's over there." I nodded to the wall. I knelt to open the cupboard and started searching for a saucepan.

I felt his silence as well as heard it. Out of the corner of my eye, I watched him set down the milk carton on the counter and go to the phone. I heard him punching buttons.

Then, "Rob? It's me."

Rob. Well of course there would be a Rob. Nobody like Jacob was available. Not for long. Not in this city.

My throat tightened up. My eyes blurred. The bridge of my nose prickled. I stayed crouched down, hidden by the counter and sink. What the *hell* was the matter with me? I'd only just met him.

Stomach in knots, I listened to him arrange for Rob to come and pick him up.

Jacob hung up and I wiped my nose hastily and started rummaging in the cupboard again.

"It'll take him about thirty minutes. Is that going to work?" Jacob walked back into the kitchen.

Halfway inside the cupboard, I nodded, banged my head — hard — and withdrew, blinking away tears.

"Sure," I choked out. I made to wipe my face on my sleeve, realized I was still draped in Jacob's jacket and, to my horror, started to cry for real.

It was silent, mostly, but it's not like you can hide that. Not from someone standing two feet away.

"What's the matter?" Jacob knelt beside me. "Ford?"

"Nothing. I hit my head." My throat ached with the effort of restraining sobs — God help me, they tore out anyway.

What the hell was the matter with me?

"Jesus, how hard did you hit it?" He turned me towards him, tilted my head up, examining me. His hands were cool, gentle. Through the mist of tears I could see him frowning.

I gulped out, "I just don't feel so great."

"I know you don't." He did the completely unexpected then and folded me into his arms. Just a hug. Just… strong arms and a warm body. Comfort. Friendship. Just not being alone for a few minutes. In that instant it meant as much as someone throwing me a life preserver.

I cried into Jacob's shoulder, which was conveniently broad and built to withstand flood rains. Poor Jacob. No good deed goes unpunished. But he bore up pretty well, patting my back and every so often making a sound that fell somewhere between encouraging and shushing.

Eventually I managed to get myself back under control. Not so under control that I pulled away from him. Or loosened my own grip. "I'm really sorry," I managed. My eyes felt swollen. My face felt hot and sticky. No one looks good when they cry — and I hadn't been at my best before I broke down.

"Everything's going to be okay," Jacob reassured.

His jacket slipped off my shoulders. "This floor is none too clean," I warned him.

"Don't worry about it."

I gave myself a second and then confessed, "I don't know what's wrong with me."

"I do."

"I'm not like this. I swear to God this is *not* me."

I could hear the smile in his voice as he asked, "No? What are you usually like?" This time I didn't mind the smile.

I sat back. "Normal."

We were still close enough that I felt his laugh. "You seem nice and normal to me."

"Obviously you see a lot of nuts in your line of work."

"I do. I can spot them a mile off. Here's the deal," he said seriously. "You're probably batting about 378 on the Holmes and Rahe Stress Scale. You've got a lot of stuff going on right now. A lot of stuff you're working through. But you'll get through it. You just have to remember to take care of yourself."

I nodded. Pushed up to standing position. I think Jacob may have even helped. By then I didn't care. I couldn't remember ever being this tired and wrung out before. I was going to take his word for it that this was temporary and I wasn't having a breakdown. Just like I'd taken his word that I wasn't having a heart attack.

"Why don't we do this," Jacob suggested. "Why don't you get into bed and I'll fix the Ovaltine. I'm going to call Rob and tell him to hold off. I can sleep on your sofa. I don't want to leave you alone tonight."

I wasn't so sure about the sofa. I was sure I didn't want to be alone. "Yeah, sure. There are extra blankets in the hall closet." I gestured vaguely.

"Okay. I've got this." He fished the saucepan out of the sink of dirty dishes and turned on the faucet.

It was hard to think of anything he wouldn't be able to handle. I stumbled tiredly to my room, threw the clean laundry off the bed onto the floor, pulled my clothes off and added them to the pile. I dragged back the comforter and crawled between the sheets.

I moaned in relief. But a few seconds later I was wide awake and listening uneasily to Jacob rattling around in my kitchen. Shouldn't I offer to help? Shouldn't I make some effort ... ?

Jacob tapped on the half open door. "Can I come in?"

I sat up. "Yeah! Of course."

He navigated around the books and clothes, handed me the Ovaltine and offered a pill on the palm of his hand.

I tossed the pill back, swallowed some Ovaltine.

Jacob sat on the foot of my bed watching me. It felt natural. He didn't seem like a stranger anymore.

"I don't think I even thanked you for everything you did tonight."

"Part of it was my job. Part of it, I wanted to," Jacob said.

"Is Rob your boyfriend?"

"Rob's my brother."

The weight that lifted off my chest made me think I might make it to thirty after all.

"That's the first time I've seen you smile," Jacob observed.

"You're not seeing me at my best. I even have a sense of humor most of the time."

He was smiling. "Good."

I finished the Ovaltine, handed him the empty cup. We smiled at each other again.

"I work a lot of hellish hours," Jacob said. "It can be hard on a relationship."

"I work a lot of hellish hours too."

"I'm not a big party guy."

I pointed at myself. "Introverted writer. Not a big party guy either."

Jacob looked down at the empty mug. He said carefully, "You're going to be down for the count in about two minutes. Would you — did you want me to hang around till you wake up or should I just let myself out in the morning?"

He looked up. I reached out and took his hand. He squeezed my hand back.

I said, "I want you to stay."

CHAPTER TWO

MONTPELIER — Police Chief Ervil Collier is asking the public for help locating a Bear Lake Valley police officer who went missing earlier this week.

Lt. Glen Harlow, of Bear Lake, was last seen between 4 p.m. and 5 p.m. Sunday when he left Pocatello Airport for his shift. Harlow, who has been with the Montpelier Police Department for more than 10 years, never showed up for work and has not been heard from since.

Police Chief Collier said the department has been working since Monday morning to determine whether Harlow left the area voluntarily.

Harlow is described as Caucasian, 6 feet 1 inches tall, with slender build. He has brown hair and light blue or gray eyes. Police have not ruled out foul play.

"Anything is possible. We don't know," Collier said. "Officers have been kidnapped before or taken against their will. We're just trying to figure out exactly what happened."

Montpelier Crime Victim Advocate Marilyn Bennett said Harlow, who oversees day-to-day operations and personnel, is a conscientious, responsible officer, and his unexpected departure is "not typical."

"For something of this nature to happen obviously has us concerned, and his family is very concerned," Bennett said.

There is no indication that struggles at home, frustration or danger from his work as an officer, or threats contributed to Harlow's disappearance.

Harlow is a healthy, fit person who often enjoyed camping and fishing in his spare time, Bennett said.

The Montpelier Police Department is leading the investigation, with assistance from Bear Lake Valley Sheriff's Department. MPD will request assistance from State Police if Harlow is not located within 48 hours.

Collier stated that at this point, police don't have any leads. Harlow was last seen wearing light jeans, a dark blue hoodie, and Nike basketball shoes. He was driving a silver 2007 Nissan XTerra SUV.

"I'm asking Glen, if he's out there, to call us and let us know what's going on," Collier said. "I'm asking the public, if they've seen Glen, if they think they've seen Glen, to give us a call." Anyone with information can call Montpelier police at 208-847-4000.

The Montpelier Police Department is currently under scrutiny as the District Attorney office investigates charges of improper use of force within the department. Police brutality concerns led to the dismissal of two investigations led by one officer, who the Idaho State Lodge of the Fraternal Order of Police identified as Detective Lon Previn.

Collier said Harlow is not connected to the investigation into those two cases.

Glen Harlow had walked out of the Pocatello airport, climbed into his SUV, and vanished off the face of the earth. The last person to see him had been an airport security guard who had waved to him in passing.

Nash's request to officially assist in the investigation was refused. A missing cop, especially one who might be voluntarily AWOL, was not an FBI matter; nor was the MPD asking for Bureau assistance. So Nash took his unused annual leave and returned to Bear Lake Valley.

By then, it was thirty-six hours into Glen's disappearance. If Glen had not purposely disappeared, the window was closing on the chances of a safe recovery. If Glen *had* purposely disappeared, the window was closing. The suicide rate for police officers was almost double that of the general population. Officers were two to three times more likely to take their own life than die at the hands of a criminal. And most of the time, friends and family never even saw it coming.

Nash didn't want to let that thought form a picture in his mind, the picture of Glen sitting in his car out in the middle of nowhere with half his head blown away. But he'd examined a lot of crime scene photos through the years and it was too easy to imagine every awful detail.

"Glen was — is — a quiet guy," Chief Collier told Nash. "He could be moody. Off hours, he pretty much kept to himself."

"What kind of things was he moody about?"

They were in Collier's small and cluttered office in Montpelier. In 1896 Butch Cassidy's Wild Bunch had tried to rob the local bank, and it didn't look like Collier's bulletin board had been updated since. The chief took a mouthful of coffee and set his mug down with care. "I don't know. Like I said, he kept to himself. Mind if I ask your interest in this case, Agent West? You're a little out of your jurisdiction."

Are you out? Nash had asked, and Glen had grimaced and said, It's not that cut and dried. I'm not in the closet, exactly, but there isn't anyone to be out for either. You understand?

Yeah, Nash had understood. That's how it was for a lot of gay law enforcement in small towns and rural areas. No point making an issue of your sexuality if there wasn't any opportunity for sex, anyway.

It wasn't Nash's place to out Glen to his boss, not when Glen might still be coming home, not unless there was no other choice. Nash said, "I liked Glen. We hit it off. I feel sort of responsible, seeing that he disappeared after dropping me off at the airport."

"Yep, you're practically the last person to see Glen." Collier's dark, knowing gaze studied Nash.

Nash smiled. "You don't mind an extra pair of eyes, do you? I'm trained, willing, and available."

"It's your vacation," Collier said. He stroked his white mustache meditatively. "But you'd better damn well believe we're going to make sure you really got on that plane Sunday night."

Nash nodded, conceding the point. "I wouldn't think much of MPD if you didn't."

■ ■ ■ ■ ■

Montpelier was an okay little town. In fact, technically it was a city, but its population was in decline, according to the last census. Not what you'd call *cosmopolitan*. The surrounding community consisted of farms and wildlife refuge, the population was ninety seven percent white, and the median income was about thirty thousand. There were lots of parks and a few good restaurants and some really spectacular scenery.

It was a peaceful place, mostly. But then investigation always began with the victim.

On the surface, Glen Harlow's life was an open book. Or, an open webpage. In this case, the official website for the Montpelier Police Department. Nash had read the basics in his hotel room that first night after going out to dinner with the entire Montpelier police force.

Lieutenant Glen Harlow — Office 2B2: has lived in Bear Lake County for most of his life. He is a graduate of Bear Lake High School. Officer Harlow started his career in Law Enforcement when he attended the Idaho State University law enforcement program. He graduated from the program in May of 2001. He was hired in June of 2001 by Custer County Sheriff's Office located in central Idaho, where he worked as a dispatcher and jailer. Officer Harlow was hired by Montpelier Police Department in August of 2002 as a patrol officer. Since then he has attended several trainings; including detective & new criminal investigator course, the sergeants academy, incident command, and breath alcohol testing specialist course. Officer Harlow is happy to be working for the Montpelier Police Department and is looking forward to serving the citizens of Montpelier for many years to come. Harlow was appointed Interim Chief of the Montpelier Police Department from 6/16/2011 - 8/28/2011

Nash had liked Glen at first sight. Liked his looks — he was a very nice looking guy — and liked his style. Glen had an easy, quiet competency that appealed to Nash, who was a low key sort of guy himself. Glen asked smart questions during the training and made a couple of useful observations. He wasn't just opening his mouth to hear himself talk, unlike Officer Walker.

But it wasn't until dinner with the rest of the team that night, that Nash had realized Glen was gay. He wasn't a believer in gaydar, but he couldn't deny how accurate that unspoken awareness between gay men could be. It had to be more than eye contact or brushing fingers when passing the salt shaker. Whatever it was, it was pretty damn accurate. He'd known before they ever got to the apple pie and coffee that Glen was gay, and Glen was interested.

Unfortunately, everyone was interested — though not in the same thing — that first evening. The novelty of having a G-man in town had kept the entire police force at the dinner table till closing time.

"Goodnight," Nash had said wryly, shaking hands with Glen on the sidewalk outside the restaurant.

Glen's smile in the moonlight had been as rueful as Nash's was wry. "Night." Then, clearly on impulse, he'd asked, "Can I buy you breakfast tomorrow?"

Nash had smiled broadly. "Sure. What time do we have to be at the office?"

"Eight."

"Pick me up at seven."

That's how it had started. And before they were through their eggs and bacon the next morning, Nash had known he and Glen would be sleeping together that night.

Not that they had slept much.

But how well could you know someone after only a week? If a career in law enforcement had taught Nash anything, it was that no one ever really knew anyone else. Humans were the most unpredictable animals on the planet.

And the most dangerous.

CHAPTER THREE

"Everyone liked Glen," Marilyn Bennett said. The Montpelier Crime Victim Advocate was about sixty, plump and grandmotherly, iron gray hair piled in an elaborate bun, and inclined to be tearful on the topic of Glen.

Nash smiled sympathetically. "That's gotta be unique in the history of law enforcement."

"Well, you know." Marilyn dabbed her nose with a tissue. "I don't mean criminal offenders. But even then Glen had — has — a reputation for being tough but fair. Not like — " She stopped herself.

"Not like Officer Previn?"

She said stiffly, "Lon is a good man and a good officer."

"What happened between Previn and Glen? Glen is Previn's supervisor, right?"

"Nothing happened!" Her eyes were wide behind the square-framed glasses. "What on earth do you mean?"

"Previn's under investigation. There must have been some discussion between Glen and an officer under his command."

"Well, yes, but ... it was really up to Chief Collier to pursue the matter. And anyway, the State Police are handling the investigation now."

Ah ha! as the TV sleuths would say. Not a motive, but certainly grounds for conflict and tension between two coworkers. The kind of situation that could get very messy, very fast. No one knew that better than Nash. This was an angle that would bear further inspection.

So Nash let that line of questioning go, and said, "Glen was Acting Police Chief for two months in 2011. Why was that? What happened?"

"Police Chief Talbot died suddenly and Glen was appointed by the city council to act in his place till a new chief could be hired."

"Didn't Glen want the job?"

Her gaze fell. "Yes, I believe he did."

"But?"

Marilyn absently straightened the cut glass heart figurine on her desk. "*But* the city council felt he was too young for the position. I think he'd just turned thirty at the time."

Glen had been thirty-two. Young, but not too young. Maybe there had been other reasons the city council had passed him over. Nash could think of one.

"How did Glen take being passed over for promotion?"

"Oh, it wasn't like *that*."

Yes. It was exactly like that. But Nash said easily, "No, of course not. But I guess he must have had some feeling on the situation?"

"He never discussed it."

"How did he get along with Chief Collier?"

"Fine. I think Glen liked Chief Collier. And Chief Collier thought the world of Glen."

Maybe yes. Maybe no. Glen was a gay man working as a law enforcement officer in a rural area. Safe to say, he was adept at concealing his feelings.

Once again, Nash changed direction. "I know Glen is unmarried. Anyone special in his life?"

Marilyn stared at him for a moment. She shook her head.

"No? No one?"

She said, a little stiffly, "No one that I know of."

Interesting. Not because she didn't know anything, but because she apparently did.

MPD and the Bear Lake Sheriff's Department had taken all the prompt and proper steps in tracking Glen's last known whereabouts. Security camera footage from the airport verified that it was indeed Glen climbing into his vehicle and driving away.

Over and over, Nash watched the grainy, black and white image of Glen raising his hand in casual farewell to the security guard. There was no particular sign of tension or stress in the tall figure striding across Nash's monitor screen. Zero indication that Glen had been under any kind of duress.

It didn't reassure Nash. With each passing hour his sense of desperation mounted. He was too experienced not to know how this scenario was likely to play out.

It was not going to end well.

And it mattered to him. It really mattered. He tried to preserve his objectivity, look at it like Glen was just another case — yes, a case that hit home because they had known each other, were good... acquaintances — but who was he kidding? It was eating him up inside. The not knowing, the fear... he'd never been on this side of a missing person investigation before, and it was hell. Sheer hell.

There had to be more he could do.

But what?

MPD had checked his home and garage, and there was no sign Glen had returned after dropping Nash off at the airport.

Both MPD and the Sheriff Department had made the trek from Pocatello to Montpelier several times, and there was no sign any accident had occurred during the ninety minute drive. Glen was not in any hospital or jail or morgue. His parents had not heard from him. His brother in Montana had not heard from him.

Nash did the drive himself the first day he arrived, cruising at a crawl, scanning the mountain road for skidmarks, oil stains, grease spots, broken railings, any indication of accident.

Glen had been driving his own vehicle, so there was no GPS tracking device on it. His cell phone was now going straight to message, indicating the battery had died.

"What about Search and Rescue?" Nash asked Collier, his second day in Idaho. By then Glen had been missing for over 48 hours. "What about getting a chopper with infrared out here?"

"Getting it out *where?*" Collier asked with some exasperation. He looked as weary as Nash felt. "Have you taken a look around you, Agent West? We're surrounded by mountains and forest. We can't just send a chopper out into the wild blue yonder and say *start looking!* You know we have to be able to pinpoint some kind of search radius. "

"We're running out of options."

"Glen would be the first person to say we have to use our resources wisely."

Would he? Nash knew so little about Glen. But yes, Glen had not seemed like a man to lose his head in an emergency. Nash wasn't a man to lose his head either, but then he had never been in this position before. It seemed a lifetime since he had said goodbye to Glen, held him briefly for that one last time.

I should have held onto him.

Crazy thought. But if he had held Glen for even a few seconds more ... because that's how fast things changed. Second to second could mean the difference between life and death. A deer in the road, a driver passing on the wrong side, the flash of sunlight in your eyes.

And worse things.

Evil things.

Nash got control of his voice and asked, "What about the warrant for his bank records? Do you have that yet?"

"We'll have it by noon. We found a sympathetic judge. Same thing with his cell phone records." Collier's dark eyes studied Nash. "The fire department has joined the search."

Nash nodded.

"We'll find him," Collier said staunchly.

Neither of them bothered to say "alive" anymore.

∎ ∎ ∎ ∎ ∎

"He was a good guy," Officer Kent Dann told Nash over coffee at Edna's Café. Dann was the newest member of the MPD, with less than a year on the job. His collar was too big for him and he still had a smattering of acne on his forehead. "A little lonely, I guess."

"What makes you say that?"

Dann shrugged. "No wife, no kids, no girlfriend. He kind of kept to himself."

Unexpectedly, Nash's throat closed up and he had to force the words out. "Maybe he liked it that way."

Dann glanced automatically to the shiny gold band on his left hand. "Everybody wants the same things, right? A home. Family?"

"Someone to share the highpoints and the lowlifes?"

"Sure." Dann didn't hear the sarcasm. Maybe because Nash's heart wasn't in it.

No, everyone didn't want the same things — Nash had never wanted those things. Or, rather, he had always believed there was plenty of time for them. Later. His priority had always been his work, his job, his career. He had a beautiful house in Virginia he rarely spent time in. He had friends, all of them work colleagues. He had family he saw for the holidays, which was plenty for all concerned. Occasionally he had lovers, but no one he had ever wanted to settle down with.

You ever think of relocating? he'd asked Glen, Saturday morning. God. Was it only Saturday morning? It felt like a lifetime ago. They had been lying in Glen's bed, and Glen had been staring somberly at the ceiling, but his gray eyes — the same shade as the rain pecking against the windows — had slanted to meet Nash's. "It wouldn't be easy starting over. Not with all these hiring freezes."

True. Very true.

"How old are you?"

Glen's thin mouth had turned down at the corner, an expression Nash already recognized for amusement. He resisted the desire to reach out and trace the crease in Glen's unshaven cheek. "Thirty-four. Too old for the FBI."

Yeah, pretty much. Not technically, but yeah. He was unlikely to be hired over equally qualified and younger candidates. The fact he had even asked the question frightened Nash.

The fact that he persisted, frightened him more.

"What if a position, a good position in LE were to open up for you across country?"

Glen's brows drew together. "How good? What kind of position?"

Nash had shrugged. He was dangerously close to making promises he couldn't be sure of keeping. "I've got a lot of contacts."

"Yeah?"

Nash gave into temptation and traced his fingertips along the uncompromising line of Glen's jaw. That was one determined chin. "Yeah."

Glen said at last, slowly, carefully, "Collier is supposed to retire in two years. I'm next in line for Police Chief."

"That might not happen, though."

"True." Glen's mouth had twisted and he'd gone back to staring at the ceiling.

Now Nash understood that hint of bitterness.

Saturday night, over homecooked dinner — and a damn good dinner at that — Glen had said, "There's an FBI satellite office in Pocatello."

"I know. The Division Office is located in Salt Lake City."

Glen had smiled, his eyes lighting. "You looked it up."

"I did, yeah. But... from a career perspective, it's pretty much the equivilent of Siberia." The light had gone out of Glen's eyes, which Nash had hated to see. He'd tried to ease past the moment, "The scenery is nicer in Idaho."

"Yeah. We do have nice scenery." Glen was still smiling, but the smile just wasn't the same. Nash wished he'd never brought the subject up, never raised anybody's hopes, including his own.

The sex that night had been great. Every bit as energetic and passionate as before, every bit as satisfying. But Nash had felt something strangely close to disquiet. He was not an introspective man, but he was aware of feeling something uncomfortably close to longing. This was all they were going to have, and it wasn't enough.

But what was the alternative?

No, once he was back home, or better yet, back on the road, this would all be placed in perspective. A wonderful interlude. A welcome break from real life, but *not* real life.

They watched the gloomy-faced moon drift across the panes of glass in the bedroom window, and Glen had asked, "You ever get out this way other than the road shows?"

Nash had shaken his head regretfully. "No."

They had left it there.

Now Nash asked Dann, "What about this investigation into Officer Previn's conduct?"

"What about it?" Dann was instantly on defense.

"That must have caused some tension."

"Lt. Harlow would have backed Previn. He always backed up his officers."

"Is Previn often overzealous in the performance of his duties?"

Dann's face went red. "We're not G-men," he said shortly. "Sometimes we have to get our hands dirty."

"Ouch." Nash grinned.

After a moment or two, the tightness left Dann's face. "Okay. Sorry. Policing a rural community isn't like the kind of thing you're used to, Agent West. You're from a different world."

Nash let that go. "So Previn and Harlow got on well?"

"Sure."

"Did anyone ever threaten Lt. Harlow? Did he have any run-ins with anyone that you know of?"

"No. Most of the time Glen was in the office. A lot of what he did was management, administrative work." Dann started to add something, but stopped.

"What?" Nash pressed.

Dann lifted his shoulder. "I don't know. Maybe he missed being in the field. I think he was kind of bored. I don't think he was happy."

■ ■ ■ ■ ■

Working in law enforcement, you came to believe in the randomness of life. You couldn't help it. Bad things happened to good people. Good things happened to bad people. The sky fell on whoever happened to be standing there. Nash didn't believe — hadn't believed for many years — that there was a plan or a purpose or even a point.

It would have been nice to be able to tell himself some comfortable lie. That he had met Glen, cared for Glen, because he was going to be the one to find justice for Glen. But if the world really worked like that, then why wouldn't the purpose have been simpler, benign? That he was going to find Glen.

No. You couldn't let yourself start thinking that way. Next thing, you'd be getting mad at God. You'd be *believing* in God.

Things happened without rhyme or reason. Sometimes they happened to people you cared about. There wasn't any moral to the story. Maybe it wasn't even a story. Maybe it was just a sequence of unrelated events.

There were no photos on Glen's desk. A clean, white coffee mug read MY SON CAN ARREST YOUR HONOR STUDENT. Today's newspaper had featured an interview with Glen's parents. Nice people. Good people. They were unswerving in their belief that Glen was alive. That he had no enemies. And, contrariwise, that he would never walk away from his responsibilities, the people who loved him, the people who counted on him. Nash wished he had the guts to talk to them, but that would have been for his own sake, not theirs. What could he tell them that they didn't already know? That their son had been a fine man? A man worth loving? They already knew that.

There was a short stack of unopened mail and a couple of reports in Glen's inbox. A large, opal geode served as a paperweight.

The desk was organized, files neat, but not obsessively so. The drawers smelled faintly of Old Spice. The ghostly scent made Nash's chest ache.

It looked like Glen was caught up on his work — barring what had landed in his inbox over the last couple of days. The light was blinking on his phone. No one had thought to pick up the messages yet.

On the wall behind Glen's desk hung a number of framed certificates and awards. All that training and preparing for a job that the fucking city council probably wouldn't have given him anyway. And not because he was too young.

The small office was mostly dominated by a large, framed print photograph of a turquoise lake surrounded by blue mountains and pine trees.

"Where was that taken?" Nash asked Marilyn when she brought him coffee.

"That's Bear Lake. Pretty, isn't it? It's limestone that gives the water that color." Her expression was regretful. "Glen used to go fishing down there."

Three days and Glen was already past tense.

"Did Glen take the photo?"

"Oh no!" Marilyn chuckled at the idea. "Glen wasn't artistic. Glen was just a normal guy."

CHAPTER FOUR

Officer Lon Previn was a big man — and it was all muscle. Except for the mustache, which was formidable enough to have muscles of its own. A muscle mustache.

"Let's get something straight," Previn told Nash when he came in from patrol. "The only reason I'm talking to you now, is Collier told me to humor you. I have no idea where Harlow is. I never laid a hand on him."

"I gotta say, you sound pretty damned defensive," Nash observed.

"Maybe it's because you're going around hinting to everyone that I killed Harlow to keep him from ratting me out to the D.A."

"Uh, no. I can guarantee you I never phrased it that way," Nash said. "But since we're on the subject, did you?"

"No. I sure as hell did not." Previn scowled from beneath his black, curling eyebrows. "But for the record, Harlow was no angel. I could tell you a few stories."

"Go ahead. I'm all ears."

Previn opened his mouth, then closed it. "Yeah, right."

Nash spread his hands. "If you've got something, let's have it. Maybe it'll shed some light on what happened to Lt. Harlow."

"I've got news for you, FBI. Everybody here knows what happened to Harlow. They just don't want to say it out loud."

Nash kept his voice even. "What happened to him?"

"He drove out somewhere and ate his pistol."

"I see. And what's you theory on that? Why, in your opinion, would Lt. Harlow commit suicide?"

"Because he was a homo. Everybody here knows it." Previn's lip curled. "*You* sure as hell know it."

Nash's gaze drilled into the other man. "And that's an issue for you?"

"Don't try to turn this back on me. You asked, I'm telling you. I think Harlow capped himself. And I don't blame him."

Nash was a seasoned, maybe even hardened, agent of the law. It took a lot to get under his skin. Even so, it had been a long time since he'd confronted this kind of naked prejudice. Not because it didn't exist in his world, but because Nash was very good at passing for straight. He wasn't in the closet, it wasn't that; a neutral personality was the protective camouflage all good field agents instinctively donned, right along with the shades and suits. Keeping his private life private was the first line of defense against the ruthless, crazy, and sometimes terrifyingly intelligent perpetrators of the crimes he investigated.

But Glen? Glen would have had to put up with these attitudes and comments every single day.

Nash said, "Did we just walk into a 1950's flick? I didn't realize being gay was still considered grounds for suicide."

Of course that wasn't true at all. He'd never seen any suicide statistics on gay officers, but he'd have been willing to bet they were higher than the average — and the average was alarming enough: 91 percent of suicides were by males and, 63 percent of the victims were single.

"Maybe not where you come from," Previn said. "But Harlow grew up around here."

"Where men are men, and sheep are nervous?"

"Keep laughing. You wouldn't last a year out here."

"I might surprise you."

"You haven't so far."

"So that's your theory? Lt. Harlow drove off and shot himself because he was gay? If that's the case, how come he didn't leave a note? And why choose that moment?"

Previn gave him a long, contemptuous look before turning away. He said over his shoulder, "I guess you could answer that better than anyone."

Glen's bank records yielded nothing. There was no activity on his debit or credit cards, no checks had been cashed. He had a healthy balance in both his checking and savings, so it was unlikely money troubles were a factor in his disappearance.

"Did anyone check Bear Lake?" Nash asked Ryan Walker when he returned from dinner that evening.

"I drove out there myself Monday morning," Walker said. "But there's no way Glen would have driven that far out of his way."

"Why? He had a couple of hours before he was supposed to be on duty."

"You're not a fisherman, are you?"

"No."

"Just… take it from me. There wasn't time before Glen's shift to go fishing."

Nash never "just took it" from anyone. He gazed at Walker with dissatisfaction. What was he missing here? Walker was getting at something, but what?

Walker's eyes were hollow and red-rimmed, his face sallow. He looked exhausted. He looked like the image Nash had seen staring hopelessly back from the mirror in the washroom a few minutes ago. In fact, he and Walker were similar physical types. Tall, athletic build, clean-shaven, blond, blue eyes.

Nash said slowly, "How is it that you answered the phone at Glen's house Sunday night?"

A tinge of color crept into Walker's face. "I drove over there when he didn't show up for his shift." He added defensively, "It wasn't like him. I thought maybe he'd been taken ill."

There must have been a short in the wiring because it had certainly taken a while for the lightbulb to go on. "Why you?" Nash persisted.

"Why not me?" Walker's face was flushed now, his blue eyes bright with an emotion that looked a lot like defiance. He seemed to wage an inner battle before blurting out, "I had a key."

"You..."

The words were fairly innocuous. Maybe Walker meant only that he was the one who watered Glen's houseplants when he went camping. But even if the words could have been interpreted a number of ways, Walker's expression meant one thing and one thing only.

It rocked Nash. He hadn't seen it coming. There had been nothing in the week he'd spent with Glen to indicate there was another man in Glen's life.

"That's right," Walker was saying with quiet, fierce satisfaction. "I had a key."

He had been wrong. He had been wrong from the start, wrong about every single thing. There was nothing special or unique in what had happened between Glen and him. What had happened between Glen and him was the usual thing that happened when two single, horny guys were attracted to each other. Sex. That's all it was. All it ever was going to be.

But then Nash thought of Glen's face at the airport. Thought of Glen's hand gripping his that final time. "Did Glen know you still had a key?"

Walker's eyes widened. The defiance drained from his face. "No," he admitted.

"Nice."

"Whatever you're thinking, you're wrong. Glen wouldn't have cared. We still saw each other some nights."

Nash had to wrestle down that surge of unproductive and pointless jealousy. "What happened between you?"

"Glen decided — "

"No. The day Glen disappeared," Nash interrupted.

"Nothing. I never saw him." Walker said roughly, "I was on duty all afternoon, ask anybody. Chief Collier called me and told me Glen had never shown up. That's when I went over to his place. There's no way I'd have ever hurt Glen."

"Too bad we can't ask him," Nash said.

∎ ∎ ∎ ∎ ∎

First thing Thursday morning the phone company was able to narrow the radius of Glen's cell phone to a tower in northeastern Utah. By lunchtime Glen's vehicle had been located in the parking lot of the Greyhound bus station in Tremonton. State

Troopers found Glen's cell phone beneath the passenger seat. Glen's keys were in the ignition. There was no sign of Glen.

A crime scene team was going over the vehicle, inch by inch, but on initial examination it looked clean. No signs of violence, anyway. They had found trace amounts of marajuna.

No one at the bus station remembered seeing the XTerra arrive or knew how long it had been sitting in the parking lot. The security camera showed nothing, indicating the footage of the XTerra's arrival had already been recorded over — meaning the vehicle had been sitting in the lot for over 56 hours.

On Thursday evening, Chief Collier summoned Nash to his office. "We appreciate all your help, Agent West, but I don't think there's much more you can do here."

"I don't believe Glen just climbed on a Greyhound bus and rode off into the sunset."

"It's pretty hard to believe," agreed Collier. "But then again, stranger things have happened. We both know people do sometimes choose to disappear."

"He wasn't the type."

"I've known Glen a lot longer than you, Agent Nash, and I can't rule out the possibility that Glen walked away of his own volition."

You knew him longer, but I knew him better. That's Nash wanted to say, but he wasn't sure it was true. One thing he did know for sure, no one ever really knew anybody. Not entirely.

That wasn't to say you couldn't know the important things about them. He believed he knew the important things about Glen. "I suppose your theory is he hopped that bus after smoking a joint?"

"I don't know about the pot. I agree that doesn't sound anything like Glen. But Forensics hasn't found any sign of foul play. The keys are there, his cell phone is there —"

"So that's it? You're just going to *give up*?" Nash could feel a vein throbbing in his forehead. He was probably going to blow a blood vessel from the strain of controlling his fear and anger for days on end.

"Hell no, we're not giving up," Collier snapped, his own nerves frayed. "But clearly this case isn't going to come to a quick resolution, and I don't think you hanging around here harassing my officers is going to be helpful."

"*Harassing* them?" Heat prickled beneath Nash's collar. "Is that what they say I'm doing?"

Collier caught back whatever he started to say, and flattened his hands on the desktop. He said almost kindly, "Look, Nash, I know this case is personal. I know you've done your best to help, maybe you even *have* helped. But the fact is, we're not any closer to finding Glen than we were Sunday night. So unless you're planning to move to Bear Lake and take up searching fulltime… I think you need to start making plans to head home."

Nash was so tired he couldn't think straight. When was the last time he'd really slept? Back before he'd met Glen. Another lifetime ago.

He stared at Collier. He could see a mix of sympathy and uncomfortable awareness in Collier's dark gaze.

There was so much Nash wanted to say to him, to explain, to persuade, to convince him that they had to keep looking, couldn't give up... It was almost funny. How many times had he sat right where Collier was now? How many times had he confronted some desperate, grieving, terrified loved one who wasn't ready to face what everyone else already knew?

He didn't need to say a word to Collier, because Collier already knew everything he wanted to say.

Nash nodded.

CHAPTER FIVE

There was an old movie Nash liked. It was about a detective who, through the course of his investigation, fell in love with a murder victim. The movie was called *Laura*. Of course, being Hollywood, it all turned out to be a case of mistaken identity and the detetective got to live happily ever after with Laura.

Laura had lived in one of those swanky, sophisticated Hollywood sets. Glen lived in a redwood and stone house on Valley View Drive. Four bedrooms and three baths seemed a lot of house for a guy living on his own.

"He got a great deal on it," Officer Walker said, unlocking the door and letting Nash inside.

It was a nice enough house. Wood floors and skylights. Granite countertops, a wood-burning stove, all the mod cons. There was a great view of the mountains from the bedroom balcony.

Nash and Glen's rinsed breakfast dishes were still sitting in the sink. Nash's toothbrush was lying on the glass shelf in the master bath. He stared at it for a long time; he couldn't ever remember leaving his toothbrush anywhere. It was the first thing anybody packed, right?

"We shouldn't be here," Walker said from behind him.

"It's not a crime scene," Nash replied, as though he didn't know perfectly well why they should not be there.

Why *were* they there? Nash wasn't really sure. Taking a final goodbye? Probably not, since he had every intention of flying to Salt Lake City and driving out to Tremonton to follow up on the investigation of Glen's abandoned vehicle.

He could hear Walker opening and closing closet doors in the bedroom. Nash stared at his face in the mirror. He looked like hell. He looked like he felt. He looked like everybody looked in his situation.

I'm going to find — and kill — whoever hurt you.

He grinned ferociously at his reflection.

Scary.

"We should probably get rid of these." Officer Walker had appeared behind him again. He was holding a stack of *OUT* magazines.

"Leave them."

"Think of his mom."

If Nash started laughing, he would never stop. He clipped out, "Officer Walker, you know better. Do not disturb anything."

"Are you leaving your toothbrush?" Walker shot back.

Nash stared at his his toothbrush. Innocuous green stripes on white. His DNA splattered all over every bristle. "You're damn right I'm leaving my toothbrush."

"You're an idiot," Walker remarked, before vanishing back into the bedroom.

He was probably right.

Nash returned to the bedroom. A painting of Bear Lake hung above the neatly made bed — he had helped Glen make the bed — and he didn't have to close his eyes to see himself and Glen lying there, smiling at each other. He could still feel Glen's touch, still hear his voice, still remember the taste of his mouth, the scent of his hair.

Part of what had always touched him about *Laura* was how vulnerable the dead were once they could no longer protect their secrets. That was the truth. There were no secrets in a murder investigation. Which Glen would have understood. But what did Glen have to feel embarrassed about? He was gay. He was lonely. He had dry skin. That was about the extent of it. Okay, a taste for vinegar and salt potato chips, a fortune in fishing lures, an unnatural love for Linda Ronstadt.

Nash didn't know anything about Glen. Didn't know his favorite food, his favorite song, his favorite movie, his favorite color ... . Was he Democrat or Republican? Did he believe in God? Did he want kids one day? Did he prefer the left or right side of the bed? Did he shave before or after showering? In the end, weren't they all about equally important? If you wanted it to work, needed it to work, couldn't you make it work?

He kept coming back to this. In the end, hadn't he known everything that mattered? Hadn't he known enough?

That was the painful part. That too late he recognized that Glen had been the guy for him. He had learned nothing this week he hadn't already known about Glen. Glen was a decent, intelligent, hard-working guy. Every day he got up and did his very best to make the world a better place.

What the hell more could you ask of someone?

Okay, in fairness, unlike the detective in *Laura*, Nash had spent enough time with Glen to know he had felt more relaxed and at peace in Glen's company than he could remember feeling with another guy ... maybe ever. Glen had made him laugh. Glen had made his heart ache. Glen had cooked the best scrambled eggs this side of the Rockies.

"We should go," Walker called from the front room.

The wall in the hallway was lined with framed photos. A bridal couple from the Sixties, a couple of skinny tow-headed kids in cowboy hats and sheriff badges, a photo of Glen in police uniform looking young and solemn —

"We gotta go, Agent West," Walker insisted from down the hall. "Maybe you don't care about your job, but I sure as hell do."

He stared when Nash joined him. "So is that it? Now what? What will you do now?"

"Is there anything left to do?"

"No."

"Then I guess I've got a plane to catch."

Walker looked relieved.

On the way out, Nash paused before yet another photo of aqua marine water and pine trees. "This is Bear Lake?"

"That's right."

"Where?"

"On the lake."

"I can see that. Where on the lake?"

"Nowhere in particular."

"What are you talking about?" Nash asked impatiently. "It's a place. It's got a specific longitude and latitude. How could it not be somewhere in particular?"

Walker's face reddened. "It could be anywhere, that's all I mean." Meeting Nash's disbelieving gaze, he repeated, "It could be anywhere. That lake has an area over one hundred square miles. It all looks the same."

Nash nodded. Maybe it did all look the same to Walker. But three framed photos of the same exact composition of trees, mountain, and lake? You didn't have to be Ansel Adams to recognize a theme when you saw it.

Walker asked reluctantly, "You need a lift to Pocatello?"

"I've got my rental car. I'll turn it in at the airport."

"Great. 'Cause no offense, but it seems like leaving you at the airport is not a healthy thing to do."

"Yeah, no offense taken."

As an afterthought, Walker offered his hand. And as an afterthought, Nash shook it.

■　■　■　■　■

He found the site late that afternoon.

Nash had deduced, it turned out correctly, that several professional prints of a particular spot on the shore of Bear Lake meant the place was photographed a lot and was therefore reasonably accessible. The coffee shop attached to his hotel had a selection of pretty postcards, and sure enough, he found the exact arrangement of trees, mountains, and lake. The area was called Shoshone Point.

Why Shoshone Point should be important to Glen, he had no idea. Maybe the fishing was great there. Maybe Glen liked the view. The significance of the site was one more mystery, but Nash had no doubt Shoshone Point had been one of Glen's favorite places.

He figured it this way: after he and Glen said goodbye at the airport, Glen had felt pretty much like Nash had — like he had just made a huge mistake — so Glen, with a few hours before work, had headed out to the lake, to a place that obviously meant a lot to him. Not to go fishing, not to kill himself, just to clear his head before he had to be on duty. Because that's how Glen thought, that was the way his brain worked.

And there on the shores of Bear Lake, there at Shoshone Point, something bad, very bad, had happened to Glen.

Whatever that bad thing was, it had resulted in Glen's SUV being found in Tremonton, Utah. Tremonton just happened to be the closest bus station to Bear Lake, a mere two hours away. No way was that a coincidence.

Nash parked his rental car on the sandy shore and got out. The air was nippy and smelled of pine trees and wet grass and fish.

The water really was aqua in color, the lake living up to its name of Caribbean of the Rockies. In the summer, the lake was a popular tourist spot, but this was April and the wind-scoured shore looked cold and barren despite the tropical-colored water. The distant lodges and cabins appeared deserted. No lights shone in windows, no smoke drifted from chimneys. There were no boats on the lake, nobody fishing from the shore, no cars parked anywhere.

No sign of life as far as Nash could see.

He shaded his eyes, staring up at the watery sun, searching for any ominous circling of birds. But the cobalt sky was empty of anything but ragged, rolling, dark-rimmed clouds. He shivered. The wind off the water had a bite to it. Only a couple of weeks ago there had still been snow on the ground.

He began to walk slowly over the uneven ground, scanning the wet earth for tire tracks.

Near a small cairn of rocks, he found bleached and scattered bones. His heart stopped, but the bones were old and too small to be human. Still, it was a grim reminder that this area was home to everything from elk and mule deer to wolves and grizzlies.

"Glen?" called Nash. His voice sounded tentative, doubtful, and in a hard to explain way, that made him angry. He called again, with more force, *"Glen?"*

The word seemed to bounce off the surrounding mountains and fall flat on the grassy shore.

Nash moved on down the beach, still scrutinizing the clumps of grass and sedge for tracks.

According to local legend, there was supposed to be a creature living beneath those turquoise waters, the Bear Lake Monster. Maybe Glen had run into the monster. It made as much sense as anything.

That was a mistake, though. Looking for things to make sense. Finding a pattern wasn't the same as finding meaning, any more than an explanation supplied reason.

"Glen?" shouted Nash. The silence of pines and mountains seemed to swallow the word whole. He called again, loudly, stubbornly, "Glen?"

A few yards down he found the impression of a sports utilitiy vehicle's tires in the dried mud near a fallen tree. Nash knelt, tracing the tiny dashes and arrows of hardened soil, like a blind man reading braille. *Journey's end.* That's what these tracks spelled out. He could make out where the vehicle had parked, and where it had reversed in a wide and crooked arc, crossing its earlier tracks as it headed out across the hilly terrain.

Avoiding the main road.

Nash's heart thumped hard with excitement and dread.

He rose and continued down the shore in a slow lope, scanning the waterline and the uneven swells of grassy hill and rock.

He came upon a firepit, a ring of blackened rocks around the remains of charred driftwood. Empty beer cans littered the ground, and there were multiple, mostly obliterated footprints.

"Glen?"

He heard a faint cry, and turned, eyes searching the empty landscape. Nothing moved. Nash listened tensely, afraid he had mistaken a bird or an echo for an answer.

He tried to call out again, but his voice was so choked, the word was as much sob as syllable. Even so, he nearly missed the answering shout.

He stumbled up the bank, up the grassy hillside until he found himself looking down into a shallow ravine.

A man lay unmoving on the green slope. He wore blue jeans and a blue hoodie. His dark hair was soaked with blood and he held a pistol. His bearded face was tilted up as though he was watching the clouds tumbling overhead, but his eyes were shut.

Nash half ran, half slid down the slope, landing next to the supine figure.

His voice shook. "Glen?"

Glen's eyes, bloodshot and red-rimmed, opened. He stared blankly and something in his hollow gaze flickered into life. His cracked and peeling lips moved. "Nash?"

"It's me, Glen."

"This is ... a ... pleasant ... surprise," Glen got out slowly, painfully.

"Where are you hurt?" Nash's hands were trembling as he felt Glen over, careful to avoid an obviously dislocated shoulder, broken arm, the cracked —

"*Ribs!*" Glen sucked in an agonized breath.

"Sorry. Sorry it took so long. Sorry. How bad is it?" A stupid question. Nash was close to babbling.

Glen gulped out, "Can't be ... too bad. Be ... dead ... by now."

Nash shrugged out of his jacket and carefully laid it over Glen, sliding the pistol out of his unresisting grasp. He dug his cell phone out. No signal. Nash swore with quiet and restrained fury. "Be right back. Don't go anywhere."

Glen's eyes were closed. His colorless mouth twitched.

Nash bounded up the rocky slope. He kept walking until he saw the signal bars and called emergency services detailing the bad news: ribs, shoulder, arm, head injury, shock, exposure, dehydration ... None of which could outweigh the good news.

Glen Harlow was alive.

"They're coming. Help is coming. Hang on. Half an hour. Tops." Nash flung himself back down beside Glen and Glen's lashes stirred, though he didn't open his eyes.

He mumbled, "I hope ... you're real ..." The rest of it trailed away.

"I'm real. I'm not going anywhere."

Glen's mouth tightened.

"Don't go to sleep," Nash said urgently. "Glen, stay awake. You've got a head injury."

Glen started to laugh and then cried out. "*Fuck.*"

Nash was laughing too, unsteadily. "I thought you were dead."

Glen's head moved a fraction in negative.

Nash didn't know what to do, so he leaned over him, trying to cradle him, warm him, without moving him. Glen smelled like blood and sweat and, very faintly, Old Spice. His cheekbones were sharp, his skin gray, his hair matted.

"Glen," Nash whispered. Not the start of a conversation, just ... *Glen.* The miracle of Glen. Still here. Still alive. Still Glen.

Glen's colorless mouth curved. He said gently, almost inaudibly, "Nash, you're ... raining."

Nash hastily wiped his face on his own shoulder. "Yeah. Why the pistol?"

Glen's face twisted. "Trying ... to get ... rangers' ... attention."

"What the hell happened? We all thought — " No. Maybe he'd wait to share all that until Glen was stronger.

Glen's eyes opened. He frowned. He said more strongly, "Parked by the lake. Bunch of ... jackass kids were fooling around. Thought I better ... break the party up." He squinted as though trying to see past Nash's shoulder. "It's kind of ... fuzzy. One of the little shits must've hit me with a rock. Something."

"Thank God for that."

Glen's eyes widened. He said faintly, "Yeah. My lucky ... day."

Nash started to laugh. "I mean thank God it wasn't worse." That it had not been what he and everyone else had believed. The randomness of life had struck again. There had been no dark intent on Glen's part, no plot against him, no plan to harm him. No rhyme. No reason.

Yet... here they were, against the odds, together. And maybe Nash was getting soft in his old age – probably — but he couldn't help feeling that the very fact that they *were* here together, against the odds, meant something. That maybe this was the way it was supposed to work. That maybe the universe was trying to tell him something, and that the message lay in the very randomness of life.

He rested his face against Glen's cold one, very gently kissing Glen's eyelids, nose, corner of his mouth.

"Nice..." Glen breathed. "Thought you'd left, Nash."

"I came back."

Glen nodded a fraction. He was breathing in shallow, careful breaths. "Why?"

That was a great question, wasn't it? Nash cared enough for Glen to drop everything, even risk his precious, all-important job to race across the country when he'd thought Glen might be dead. And yet, the idea of doing the same thing when Glen was alive and well and could reciprocate had seemed impossible then, even crazy. Crazy to try to find a way to make it work with the man he loved?

The only crazy thing was that it had taken him so long to see the truth.

"You know why," Nash said softly.

In the shadow made by the cradle of his arms, he saw moisture glinting under Glen's lashes. "Yeah," Glen whispered. "I know."

THE PETIT MORTS

*In July of 2009, Jordan Castillo Price proposed an idea for
a shared world series. The Petit Morts would be themed
novelettes, ten to twelve thousand words in length, each story
a standalone and complete in itself. The framing element
would be "a Tim Burton-esque chocolate shop" originally
named Bittersweet (later Sweets to the Sweet) which would
appear in various cities, even various times, and act as a
catalyst for the unfolding and often strange romances. The
mysterious store owner, a character straight from mythology
but playing a different role from his usual one, would be
known to readers as Chance. His true identity would not be
revealed until the final story.*

*The concept was all Jordan's, and it fell to Jordan to write
Chance's overarching tale — including his own mysterious
"love" story. My five were written to be read within or without
context, and now that the Petit Mort series has concluded,
I've decided to share them in this collection. You don't need to
read the entire the Petit Mort series to enjoy the stories, but
the series is wonderful and, if you haven't read all seventeen
installments, I urge you to do so!*

SLINGS AND ARROWS

My college years are way behind me now, but they remain some of my best — and worst — memories. The weird thing about college is you're trying to make long-ranging decisions that will affect the rest of your life — before you're really experienced enough to know what you'll ultimately need or want. I wanted to capture that sense of an insular but temporary world, and how it feels when you begin to make choices that separate you from your friends.

No surprise that who we end up falling in love with often changes the dynamics of our entire social circle — even the course of our lives. That's the case here with Carey Gardner who finds himself falling for Walter Sterne, a man that most of the other students neither like nor understand.

It was a cold winter's night in Hartsburg.

A moon as dry and white as cork shone over the shadowed hills and dales of the Napa Valley, shone like a distorted clock face in the wine dark water of the Napa River. In the small town, shops were closing — window displays of red and pink hearts, overweight cupids — winking out. Down wide and shady streets, curtains and blinds were drawn across remodeled Victorian windows to keep out the chill rustling in the eucalyptus trees.

Over at the college, students walked in pairs or singly across the well-lit campus. The blazing buildings in Dorm Row pulsed with a variety of musical beats: The Flaming Lips vying with Lady Gaga for air space.

Carey Gardner, twenty-three, blond, cute, and brighter than he looked, pushed open the door to his dorm room on the third floor in Pio Pico House to find it, as usual, crowded with his roommate Sty's buddies watching TV.

"Yo, Bones!" Sty waved a beer in greeting.

"Yo," Carey responded, swallowing his irritation. The "Bones" joke was getting old. It was all getting old. For some reason Sty had taken Carey's change of major to anthropology personally. Sty was still clinging to his major in management and entrepreneurship, which, granted, was better than the physical education major of a lot of the other guys on the swim team.

"Where've you been?"

"Library."

"Dude."

There was pity in Sty's voice. Whatever. They'd started out friends — technically they were still friends — and they were rooming together by choice. Or maybe it was more habit. Either way, Carey was not being held prisoner in Suite E (commonly known as Cell Block 8).

The problem was, Sty was the same easygoing, fun-loving goofball he'd been as a freshman. And Carey... was not.

In order to graduate on time, Carey had to make up a couple of classes he'd blown off the first time around. His course load was heavy and his sense of humor was not what it had once been.

"Make way for Dr. Leakey," Sty ordered, and the interchangeable frat boy sprawling on Carey's bed, shifted to the foot of it and gave Carey a glinting look from beneath his shaggy bangs.

Yeah. Like that was going to happen. Like Carey was going to lie down, sheep to the slaughter, in the midst of these assholes.

"You're blocking the TV, dude," someone else said irritably.

Carey dropped his backpack under his desk, well out of the way of temptation — although it was unlikely any of Sty's pals would be tempted by anthropology books. Or any books that didn't have plenty of pictures of naked girls.

"Have a beer." Sty used the remote to turn down the sound on the TV to the vocal disappointment of an audience that didn't want to miss one single second of Olympic ski jumping.

"Thanks, but I'm — " Carey hooked a thumb over his shoulder to indicate he was on his way out again — although it was nine-thirty now and he had to get up for swim practice at five. They both did.

"Wait, wait." Sty bothered to push upright. "Something came for you." He jumped up and grabbed a large flat box wrapped in distinctive red paper with a black ribbon.

"What is it?"

"It's from that shop in the town square."

"What shop?" Carey asked slowly.

Sty lifted the box and checked the gold label beneath. "Sweets to the Sweet."

"Candy? I didn't order that."

Five pairs of gleaming eyes zeroed on Carey. In fact, he thought he saw a pair of yellow eyes shining beneath the bed. The promise of free chocolate was not to be taken lightly in this jungle.

"Well, if you didn't order it, maybe it's a gift. Maybe your parents sent it."

"Or your girlfriend," another of the jerk-offs put in.

Carey ignored him. He reached for the box; Sty handed it over reluctantly.

"You're not going to eat that whole thing yourself?" he protested, as Carey turned to the doorway. "You're in training."

"So are you, dude. I'm saving you from yourself."

"He's headed for Little Castro," someone cooed as Carey closed the door behind him.

On the other side of the sound barrier Carey took a couple of steadying breaths. *Not worth it.*

He knocked on the door to the left.

"Venido adentro!" The voice behind the door was muffled.

Carey opened the door to Heath and Ben's room.

Heath Rydell was lying on his bed in paisley boxer shorts reading the CliffsNotes to *The Mill on the Floss.* He was a tall, languid-looking young man with red hair and wide brown eyes. Ben Scully sat at his desk jotting down notes from a book titled *501 Spanish Verbs.*

"Hola." He was smiling. Ben was blond, broad-shouldered and blunt-featured. He wore jeans and a Hartsburg College tee shirt.

"Don't those douchebags ever shut up?" Heath inquired. It was a rhetorical question.

Carey held up the wrapped box. "I come bearing gifts."

At the promise of food, Heath, who looked like a consumptive and ate like a horse, sat up. "What is it?"

"Candy, I think."

"Where did it come from?" Ben asked, setting aside his book.

"I don't know." Carey flopped comfortably down on the foot of Ben's bed and slid the black ribbon off the box. "I guess someone sent it."

He ripped open the blood red paper and his eyebrows shot up. He lifted out the heart-shaped box. "Candy for sure."

"Wow," said Heath, scrambling over to the foot of his own bed. "Look at that thing."

"That thing" was an old-fashioned confection of red velvet, pink silk roses, and a black satin ribbon.

"That must be two or three pounds of chocolate," Ben said, impressed.

"There's a card." Heath got up and knelt beside the bed at Carey's feet, reaching beneath the blue comforter. "It fell when you lifted the box out." He handed the small white envelope to Carey.

Carey slid his thumb under the flap, slid the card out. He read aloud, "From your secret admirer."

Heath chortled as Ben inquired, "Who's your secret admirer?"

Carey shook his head.

The three of them considered the bizarre notion of Carey having a secret admirer.

"No offense, darling, but you're not the type."

Ben shot Heath an impatient look.

"It's true," Heath insisted. "Look at him."

They both studied Carey, who stared uneasily back at them.

"If he was any more vanilla he'd come in a bottle."

"Thanks!"

The other two snickered.

At last Heath said, "Are you going to open that or just fondle the ribbon all night?"

Carey snapped out of his preoccupation and slid the ornamental lid carefully off the heart-shaped box. The smell of chocolate — good chocolate — wafted through the over-warm room. He closed his eyes and inhaled. It was unreal, that scent. Like pheromones or something. Weight was not a problem for him, but he was in training, and this was ... *Jesus, that smelled good ...*

He resisted the temptation to bury his face in the box and graze; instead he bravely settled for a single dark chocolate and almond cluster, handing the rest of the candy around.

"Whoever he is, he has good taste," Ben said, his mouth full of marzipan.

"He? It's probably a chick," Heath objected. "You know who it is? It's probably that Nona chick from your anthropology class. She's got the hots for you, dude."

Carey shook his head. A three-pound box of fine chocolates — and these were very fine indeed — probably cost as much as a ten meal card at the cafeteria. Nona was always broke.

"Or what's her name. Pronzini."

"Kayla?" Carey said. "No way. She hates me."

"That's what you *think*. I think she's one of those chicks who acts out her attraction in misdirected aggression."

"One semester of psychology and he thinks he's an expert." Ben reached for the box of chocolates again. "By the way, Skeletor was looking for you earlier."

Carey nearly choked on his chocolate. "Walt was here? In this suite? What did he want?"

"Walt!" hooted Heath. "I want to see you call Walter Sterne *Walt* to his face."

Carey and Ben both ignored that, Ben answering, "He didn't say."

"Did he leave a number?"

"No."

"He didn't say I should call him at Professor Bing's office or anything?"

"No. Nothing. He was on his way out when I arrived," Ben explained patiently. "I happened to catch him on the stairs. He said he was looking for you but you weren't in. That was it. That was our entire conversation."

"What time was this?"

Ben looked at Heath. Heath considered while he munched. "Eight? Eight-thirty?"

Carey scowled thoughtfully.

"Are you in trouble or something?"

"Me? No. I ..."

"Hey." Heath sat bolt upright. "Maybe Skeletor left the chocolates for you!"

"Don't call him that," Carey said, pained.

"Why not. That's who he looks like. That's who he acts like." Heath quoted in a nasal Skeletor-like voice, "*I must possess all, or I possess nothing!*"

"He's been totally cool with me," Carey said. "I never would've gotten into Advanced Ethnographic Field Methods if he hadn't talked to Professor Bing for me."

"Gee, that would have ruined your life."

"It would have kept me from graduating. It's not offered next semester and it's a required class."

"He likes *you*," Ben said with feeling.

"Everyone likes Carey." There was a tinge of acid in Heath's tone.

"Holy crap." Ben stopped, staring down at the box of chocolates as though he'd tasted arsenic.

"What?" Carey asked uneasily.

Ben's bright blue eyes met his. "Nothing. I mean ... I was thinking ..."

"No wonder he scared himself," Heath put in, predictably.

"You were thinking ... ?"

"About the Valentine's Day Killer."

In the sudden silence he could hear the muffled sounds of TV and voices from the room next door.

"Huh?" Carey said at last.

"You've heard that story. Everyone has." Heath sounded bored, but his gaze was riveted to Ben's.

"Not me."

"It's an urban legend."

"What's the story?"

Heath was looking pointedly at Ben.

"This is way back in the seventies," Ben reluctantly took over. "It was like over a period of five years or something, right?"

Heath nodded.

"Every year, right before Valentine's Day, a girl on campus would get a big fancy box of chocolates from a secret admirer."

He stopped.

Carey prodded, "And?"

"The girl would be found stabbed to death on Valentine's Day."

"What?" Carey burst out laughing.

"Hand to God, dude."

"Sure it is." He waited for Heath or Ben to break the straight faces. Both continued to look solemn. "That is such total bullshit. You totally made that up."

"Swear to God, dude." Heath put his hand over his heart. "Swear. To. God."

"No. Fuck. Ing. Way."

Heath spread his hands and looked at Ben for confirmation.

"It's true," Ben said. Unlike Heath, Ben knew enough not to milk a joke to the last laugh, but he still wasn't smiling.

"Let me guess the rest. He was an escaped maniac from the local mental institution — and he had a hook for hand."

Ben and Heath spluttered into guffaws.

"No. Seriously," Ben protested. "They never caught the guy."

"Or gal," Heath interjected.

"What, he just stopped?"

Ben said seriously, "He probably graduated."

"To what? Mass murder?"

They all snickered uneasily.

Another blast of laughter and voices from next door filled the suddenly awkward pause.

"So… you two sent this box of candy, right?"

"You've got to be kidding," Heath said, and Ben looked blank and uncomfortable. "That's too pricey a joke for my budget. Although these are probably the best chocolates I've ever had." Heath considered the tray of nuts, creams, and caramels before him and reached for another.

They chomped in silence. From the other side of the suite they could hear music, the thudding of a bass. Sometimes Carey thought that was the toughest part of dorm life. The lack of silence. Although the silence in this room was plenty loud.

He said abruptly, "Right. Whatever. I think I'll go the library."

Heath said, "Weren't you just *at* the library?"

At the same time Ben said, "*Now*? It's ten o'clock." He was frowning, looking worried.

"The library stays open till three."

"Yeah, but you're the guy who can't stay awake past eleven."

"So I'll sleep in the library. I'm sure as hell not going to be able to sleep with those loudmouths in my room."

"Throw 'em out," Heath advised nonchalantly.

"Like that's going to happen."

"Tell Sty — "

"Look, I'll leave the chocolates with you."

"Oh." Heath subsided, shoving a pecan cluster in his mouth and reaching for *The Mill on the Floss* CliffsNotes once more. He said thickly, "In that case — "

CHAPTER TWO

The buildings and trees cast geometric shadows across the brick drive. The tall overhead lights threw down triangles of yellow illumination. Carey's footsteps echoed as he walked. There were not a lot of people hiking back and forth from the main campus to the dorms at this time of night.

He was not the nervous type. He was not even particularly imaginative. But you didn't have to be nervous or imaginative to notice what a long, deserted walk fifteen minutes could be at this hour. Especially after receiving an expensive gift from a possible stalker.

Lights shone brightly in dorm windows as he strode along. The occasional sonant floated through the night air. Now and then a pair of slow-moving headlights swept along the road above him, picking out trees and the cars parked along Orchard Drive.

He passed the outlying science buildings and the theater, went down the two short flights of stairs to the main quad.

Water from the fountain in the center shot up white and sparkling like liquid starlight in the night. A couple of shadowy figures sat on the cement bench that formed the basin of the fountain. They watched Carey walk past without speaking.

"Hey," he said.

"Hey," one of the figures muttered back.

Carey walked on. He felt more at ease now that he was in the center of campus. Not that he had been spooked before, really, but he wished Heath and Ben had kept their mouths shut. No way, not for one minute, did he believe that story about a Valentine's Day Killer. But he wasn't crazy about the idea of a secret admirer either, and it turned out that was for real.

The glass doors slid open before him. The library was brightly, almost garishly lit, after the weird shadows and artificial light of the night

Carey prowled the aisles and corners. With no finals pending, the library was relatively quiet. A weary-looking librarian filed oversized books. A few students studied or whispered at tables. A blue chair concealed behind a potted silk fern was occupied by a bearded kid in a green hoodie and sandals. He was snoring softly, his bag of illicit Cheetos spilling onto the carpet.

Carey went upstairs to where the study rooms were — mostly deserted at this time of night. He glanced in the small oblong windows of each closed door. Only one room was lit.

Walter Sterne sat reading at the long table. Most of the time the rooms were reserved by groups, but Walter was on his own, surrounded by a forbidding stack of books.

For an instant Carey studied him, wondering if he should interrupt, if he was about to make a total fool of himself.

Probably. But when had that ever stopped him?

Walter was Dr. Bing's teaching assistant. A grad student with a brilliant future, according to everything Carey had heard. Okay, not *everything* Carey had heard, because most of what Carey had heard was not so flattering. For all his brilliance, Walter didn't have a lot of friends or admirers. He was withdrawn and a little arrogant — and he looked it: tall and thin with a bleak, aquiline profile. He had black hair and he wore gold-rimmed spectacles that made him look older than he was. He was about twenty-six.

Carey tapped on the door, peering through the window.

Walter turned to the door. He did not smile. He rarely smiled. After a moment he nodded curtly, and Carey opened the door.

"Hey."

"Hi."

"I heard you were looking for me earlier."

Walter's expression didn't change, but his pale, bony face reddened. It seemed like he wasn't going to answer, but then he said, "It wasn't... no. It doesn't matter."

"Oh. Okay."

But Carey couldn't quite let it go. After all, it wasn't like Pio Pico house was on Walter's *way*. Walter lived in town. He had zero reason to be visiting the undergrad dorms, let alone Carey's suite unless...

Heart beating as fast as it did in those final seconds of waiting for the crack of the starter pistol, he said, "You must have had a reason."

To his amazement, Walter seemed to go a shade or two darker still. Carey stared into Walter's eyes, which were a very light brown and unexpectedly long-lashed. Walter stared back.

"It was merely an impulse," Walter said reluctantly.

Carey knew Walter well enough to know he didn't act on impulse very often. Unlike Carey.

"What was?"

"I..." Walter seemed to struggle internally, "thought you might want to go to dinner." Despite the accompanying shrug, Walter sounded formal. Most guys would have said *thought you might want to grab something to eat*. Walter probably wanted to sound casual, but... he didn't. He never did. Now he eyed Carey with a mixture of irritation and embarrassment.

Carey beamed at him. "I'd like to go to dinner, yeah. I didn't have time earlier."

"You mean *now*?" Walter sounded startled.

Carey's turn to flush, but he barreled on. He'd been waiting and hoping for this opportunity for a while. "Didn't you mean this evening?"

Walter considered. "I did. Yes."

"Well? Did you already eat?" He doubted it. From what he'd observed, Walter was one of those brainiacs who often forgot to eat because they were too busy working out the solution to world hunger.

"Er... no."

"Good. I'm starving."

It seemed to take Walter a few seconds to translate. Then, unhurriedly, he began gathering his books and books. "There won't be anything open on campus."

"I don't care if you don't."

"I don't care." Walter sounded terse. Carey was unsure if that was because Walter really didn't care or because he was so pissed off at having been roped into taking Carey to dinner that the added annoyance of off-campus barely registered.

Having unexpectedly gotten his way, Carey found himself unable to think of anything to say as they made their way downstairs and started out through the library doors. He was trying to remember if he'd ever had to coerce someone into taking him out before. He didn't think so, and he wasn't entirely comfortable with it.

Not given to chitchat, Walter made no effort to dispel the silence between them. Maybe he didn't even notice it. He seemed — when Carey risked a quick glance — preoccupied.

"Sterne!"

They turned as Kayla Pronzini hurried out the sliding doors after them. Kayla was short and stocky. She wore her glossy brown hair very short and favored knitted sweaters with cuddly animal motifs.

"I *did* turn in my paper on Evans-Pritchard, so I don't know what you're talking about." Her voice echoed loudly in the cement walkway.

Walter answered as calmly as if they'd previously been discussing this. "I didn't receive it. Professor Bing says he has no record of it."

"Professor Bing is wrong. His office was closed, and I shoved it under the door."

"Maybe you didn't shove it far enough." Walter sounded polite, but indifferent.

"I shoved it all the way under. There's no way it blew out again or anyone pulled it out."

The overhead lights turned the lenses of Walter's spectacles opaque. He said in that same even, automatic voice, "I suggest you print another copy and resubmit."

"And have it marked late?"

Walter shrugged. "That's up to Professor Bing."

"It *wasn't* late."

"You'll have to talk to Professor Bing."

"If you tell Professor Bing — "

"You have to take this up with Professor Bing."

"This is bullshit!" Kayla's angry tones bounced off the cement overhang. Her gaze fell on Carey and twisted with open dislike. "Is that so? Because you don't have any trouble interceding on behalf of your friends."

Carey opened his mouth, but Walter said calmly, coldly, "Good night, Pronzini." He turned and continued unhurriedly toward the quad.

"Asshole," Kayla said clearly.

Carey ignored her, following Walter's unhurried, loose-jointed stride down the stairs to the quad, past the fountain. He was thinking of Heath and Ben joking about the possibility of Kayla having sent those chocolates. No way was Kayla's antagonism for him a mask for deeper feeling. She couldn't stand him — and the feeling was pretty mutual. She was abrasive and confrontational, and frequently made dismissive comments about jocks. No, Kayla wasn't his secret admirer.

So who was? He studied Walter's uncompromising profile. As much as he'd like to think Walter was maybe as interested in him as he was in Walter, he couldn't see Walter shelling out a big wad of cash on a romantic gesture. He could always *ask*, of course, but if by chance Walter *had* left the chocolates, that might put him on defense. Carey didn't want him on defense.

"Is this liable to be a problem?"

"What?"

"You and me. Going to dinner."

Walter said crisply, "Not for me. I don't determine grades. Professor Bing does. So if that's what you're hoping for — "

It took Carey a second or two to process this. His heart seemed to slip in his chest as he realized what Walter was saying. He said at last, "That's not what I'm hoping for."

Walter's thin mouth curved in a derisive smile.

Carey gazed at him with disbelief, but Walter didn't say anything else, didn't look his way as they went up the steps to the faculty parking lot.

"I'm parked on Orchard Drive," Walter informed him.

"Okay."

As they made their way across the mostly empty lot, Walter continued silent and lost in thought. He could have been on his own for the attention he paid Carey, and Carey's former pleasure and excitement drained away.

By the time they reached the long flight of steps to Orchard Drive it had occurred to him that he had probably made a mistake in pushing Walter into taking him out.

He halted at the foot of the stairs. "Look…"

Walter, two steps up, stopped. Waited.

Carey said with difficulty, "I totally browbeat you into this. Anyway, it's late and I've got swim practice first thing tomorrow. Why don't we do it another time?"

It was too dark to read Walter's expression, but the outline of his body remained straight and stiff.

"Of course." He didn't sound surprised. He didn't sound let down. He didn't sound anything at all.

"Okay." Clearly he'd made the right call or Walter would say something now. Say that it wasn't late, that he hadn't been forced to ask Carey, that he wanted to have dinner with him, get to know him better.

He waited.

Walter said nothing.

Carey squared up to the disappointment. "Thanks anyway," he said lightly and turned away.

"Good night," Walter replied in that cool, colorless voice.

He could hear the quick light scrape of Walter's feet fading on the stairway behind him as he walked back across the deserted parking lot.

Disappointment gave way to irritation and embarrassment. Jesus. It's not like he had to beg people to go out with him. Plenty of people would be more than happy to go out with him if he wanted that. And the fact that he didn't want that, that he wanted someone who so obviously didn't want *him* said a lot more about Carey than it did Walter. By now Walter probably totally regretted the impulse that had made him seek Carey out in the first place.

And it was worse because Carey had probably put Walter in a weird position. As Professor Bing's GTA, Walter had to keep a certain distance from the students he worked with. He'd already done Carey a big favor by getting him into Ethnographic Field Methods when the class was badly overcrowded.

His face heated as he considered facing Walter in class tomorrow. Walter was going to think Carey was a total headcase dragging him out of his study room — basically forcing him to ask Carey out — only to have Carey ditch him in the parking lot.

Shit. But maybe Walter would take it as a kind of weird compliment. It's not like the idea had come to Carey out of nowhere. He'd picked up the invitation that Walter had already...

Withdrawn.

Yeah.

Okay, so now Walter probably did think Carey was flaky. Still. Not like Carey had asked him to dinner on Valentine's Day or done something dramatic like anonymously send a giant box of chocolates.

It really *wasn't* a big deal. Except he'd probably blown it. And he liked Walter.

A lot.

He started down the steps to the main campus. There was a footfall behind him. He glanced over his shoulder and to his shock there was someone right behind him — he hadn't noticed anyone at all. He had a fleeting impression of a tall figure at the top of the stairs. His foot skidded on a rock or an acorn. Carey was already startled and off balance, and turning his foot was all it took. He pitched forward.

With astonishment, he felt himself falling. The cement was shining in the moonlight as he crashed down the accordion of steps. Instinctively, he put a hand out to protect himself. Everything went black.

CHAPTER THREE

"Carey? *Carey?*"

The frantic voice at last got through. Carey opened his eyes.

He was on the ground. The very cold, very hard ground. Someone had laid their jacket over him. Bits of gravel were biting into his cheek. His head throbbed and he knew from the nauseating, twisting pressure radiating up and down his forearm that he'd broken his left arm. Either his wrist or his arm... but something was definitely broken.

"Can you hear me? Are you okay?"

The voice was familiar. Even so, it took him a few more seconds to place it. Ben. Ben sounding scared out of his wits.

"I'm okay," he gasped, and made the effort to sit up.

It didn't go so well.

"Did I throw up on you?" he asked a short while later.

Ben didn't hear, busy on his cell phone summoning help from the sound of things.

He disconnected and crawled next to Carey again. "How did you fall?"

Was that what had happened? He'd fallen? It was sort of fuzzy. He remembered... saying goodnight to Walter... *oh.*

Really not a good evening

"I don't know," he got out. "Slipped, I guess."

"Man, you're lucky you didn't break your neck." Ben sat down beside him and put a cautious arm around his shoulders. Carey leaned against him gratefully. The combination of pounding head and pounding arm was making him tired and sick.

"What are you doing here?" it finally occurred to him to ask.

"I left something in my car. I'm parked on Orchard Drive, so I was going to cut through the faculty lot. I'm glad I did."

"Me too."

"Relax," Ben said, sounding surprisingly authoritative. "Help is on the way."

○ ○ ○ ○ ○

"What's the last thing you remember?" Heath asked.

"Walking across the parking lot."

It was the morning after Carey's spill down the parking lot stairs. He was in the dining hall having breakfast with Heath and Ben. Mostly he was watching Ben and Heath eat. His stomach was still rocky.

Late night visits to emergency rooms are never a whole lot of fun. Last night's had been no different. The intern on duty — who looked about his own age — had pronounced mild concussion and a fractured scaphoid, which turned out to be a tiny bone in his wrist. The good news was fractures of the scaphoid near the thumb supposedly healed in a matter of weeks. The bad news was, Carey wouldn't be swimming until the bone healed. The worst news was, he needed a cast.

The cast stretched from right below his thumb to right below the elbow. It seemed like a lot of cast for such a little bone. He had a sling to take the weight off. It was mostly annoying at this point, although flashes of pain seared through the nerves and muscles of his arm.

Coach Ash had had a few things to say about swimmers who managed to injure themselves when they were supposed to be under curfew.

If Carey was honest, the last thing he could recall for sure was walking away from Walter. He wasn't about to bring that up. The memory of the way he'd had to maneuver Walter into asking him to dinner — and the alacrity with which Walter had gotten himself off the hook — was more painful than his wrist.

"I told you he was an aquatic animal," Heath told Ben. "I think he tripped over his webbed toes."

"So funny I forgot to laugh," Carey said.

He could feel the curious gaze of his friends. It was Ben who broached the obvious. "Yeah, but what were you doing all the way over in the parking lot? I thought you went to the library."

"I did. I was ..." He glanced at his wristwatch. "Hey, we're going to be late for class."

"*You?* Shit." Heath scooped up his books. "I'm across campus at the art building." He departed, a long-legged vision in purple jeans and tie-dye shirt.

"You ought to be in bed," Ben said, as Carey pushed to his feet.

"How hard is it to sit there and listen for an hour?"

"To Professor Bing? Very." Ben was grinning. "Want me to carry your books?"

"People will talk."

"Fuck 'em."

Carey laughed, but he carried his own books.

Truth be told, he didn't feel too hot. He would've liked nothing better than to spend a day or two licking his wounds, but he couldn't afford to fall behind again. He listened absently to Ben as they walked across the quad.

Ben was still talking as they reached the social science building. Carey couldn't have repeated a word he said. He was braced for seeing Walter, but when they entered the room, Walter was busy talking to Professor Bing, not looking for Carey at all.

Carey relaxed. Knowing Walter, he probably didn't even realize last night had been a big deal for Carey. Knowing Walter, he probably didn't even *remember* last night.

"What happened to you?" Nona asked. She was a tall and frail-looking girl with sad dark eyes and long, long hair. Gold heart-shaped barrettes held the front of her hair back from her pale face. Carey remembered Heath suggesting Nona was his secret admirer. Nona *was* attracted to him; he could tell. She was a quiet, intense sort of person — and sending anonymous chocolates did seem like the kind of thing that a girl would do. But... Nona?

"He fell up the down staircase," Ben joked.

Nona looked bewildered. She was Iranian, and her grasp of English hit an occasional pothole. Not that some of Ben's jokes didn't need translating even for native speakers.

Carey glanced down to where Professor Bing and Walter still stood conversing in front of the chalkboards. Walter casually glanced up to where Carey was standing. Their eyes locked. Walter looked away, then looked back, plainly startled at the sight of the cast. His mouth opened. Closed.

Carey turned back to Nona. "It's fine. A tiny fracture."

"Better get our seats," Ben said, and Carey nodded and preceded him up the wooden tiers to the row of seats in the back of the lecture room.

Maybe it was his aching wrist, or lack of sleep, but Carey found it hard to concentrate that morning. It wasn't only him. Ben was shifting in his seat and fiddling with his pen.

"For example, our own Valentine's Day," Professor Bing said, and there were a few snickers through the rows of seats.

Whatever the joke was, Carey had missed it. He glanced at Ben, who was frowning as he took notes, so maybe this was important after all.

"Our best guess is that the modern rituals of this day date to the ancient Christian and Roman traditions, with antecedents stretching all the way back to the fertility festival of Lupercalia, also known as Lupercalis. The rise of Christianity was responsible for a number of pagan holidays being renamed for and dedicated to the early Christian martyrs. In 496 AD, Pope Gelasius turned Lupercalia into a Christian feast day to honor Saint Valentine, a third century Roman martyr."

Carey risked a look at Walter. He had felt Walter's gaze throughout the lecture. The few times he let himself look, Walter was jotting down notes, his expression grave and absorbed. It was no different this time, and he suppressed a sigh. Nona, on his other side, smiled at him.

At the end of the lecture, Carey closed his notebook and slowly pushed his things in his backpack. "I've got it," he assured Ben who was standing by to lend a hand.

"Sure?"

"Yeah." He spared another look and saw Walter standing and talking to Professor Bing.

Ben was saying patiently, "Dude, you're going to take another header down these stairs if you don't — "

"Got it," Carey repeated with a quick smile — and one eye on Walter who was taking the tall stack of papers Bing was handing over.

Ben fo llowed Carey's glance. He mimicked softly, "Now I, Skeletor, am master of the universe ..."

Carey shot him an irritable look, shrugging his backpack over his good shoulder.

Ben gave him a lopsided grin. "Later."

"Later," Carey made his way without haste down the wooden tiers. The cast made him feel ungainly and off balance, and falling in a heap at Walter's feet would not do much for his image.

As he reached the bottom he found Walter had been watching his descent. "What happened to you?" he asked quietly, seeming to tear his gaze from the cast with an effort.

"I fell walking back to my dorm last night."

"*Fell?*" Walter sounded about as astonished as Carey had ever heard. "Fell how?"

"The usual way. Head over heels." If things had gone differently the evening before he might have teased Walter a little. He liked flirting with Walter, even if Walter's response veered between bemused and dismissing. But things hadn't gone differently. In fact, they had — and were — going nowhere at all, and teasing Walter was likely just another bad idea.

"You broke your arm?" In a minute Walter was going to say *That does not compute!* like the robot in *Lost in Space.*

"My wrist. The doctor thought I probably put my hand out to soften my landing."

"You don't remember?"

"I hit my head."

Walter scowled. "Other than the wrist, are you all right?"

"Other than the wrist, great," Carey responded tersely.

Walter was still scowling, black brows knitted as he mulled over whatever deep thoughts he was thinking, and Carey lost all patience — with himself first and foremost.

"I've got to go. I've got class."

Walter appeared to struggle over what he wished to say. Usually Carey found Walter's utterances worth the wait. Today, he didn't have the strength.

"See you around."

If Walter had an answer, he missed it.

○ ○ ○ ○ ○

By noon he was thinking he should have taken the doctor's advice and allowed himself a day to rest and recuperate. He felt like crap. His head was pounding, his arm was aching, and he felt weirdly, unreasonably depressed.

The worst thing was to give in to feeling like that. What he should do was get his ass in gear and go to the swim meet to cheer his teammates on, but even as he was thinking this he was walking back to the dorms — and realizing what a very long walk it was.

When he finally made it home, he climbed the stairs, and let himself into his room — Sty-free for once, as Sty would be on the bus headed for the meet — and stretched out on the bed. He had a class in applied anthropology that evening, and he needed sleep or he'd be useless.

Carey closed his eyes.

When he opened them again the room was in blue winter shadow. A bird was hopping along the windowsill. Its cheep-cheep was surprisingly loud, but that wasn't what had woken him. There was a small creaking sound. He glanced across at the door.

The doorknob was turning back and forth.

Sty had forgotten his keys again.

In that relaxed post-dream state, still mildly opiated, Carey watched calmly as the knob grated left. Then right.

He sat up. Called groggily, "Coming."

The handle stilled. Sty didn't reply. Carey stared at the door, an uneasy feeling prickling down his spine.

Sty would thump on the door or get the RA to come and unlock it. He wouldn't swivel the knob in that furtive way.

Besides, Sty was at a swim meet on the other side of the Napa Valley.

Carey rolled off the bed, crossed to the door in a couple of steps and yanked it open.

The hallway and suite living room were empty.

The door to Heath and Ben's room stood open, but there was no one inside. His candy box was sitting on the top of their mini fridge. Across the hall, he could hear the shower running in the suite bathroom.

He poked his head in the steamy bathroom. Heath was singing "Love Game" loudly and off-key.

"Got my ass squeeeeezed by seh-*eh*-exy Cuuuupid..."

There was no one else in the bathroom.

Carey ducked back out again.

Jerome, who lived in the room across from his own, appeared, bundled for the cold and carrying a load of books.

Carey said, "Did you see — ?"

"Did I see?"

"Was anyone on the stairs?"

Jerome looked at him like he was nuts. Maybe he was. "Sure. Lots of people."

Okay, so he never pretended to be Sherlock Holmes. Or even Watson. And, really, what was the big deal because someone had turned his door handle? It could have been the student maintenance service.

Except, in that case, where was the student or his maintenance equipment?

Carey's cell phone was ringing. He went back in his room, hunted around for it. Finding it, he flipped it open. He didn't recognize the number on the screen.

"Gardner."

"Hi. It's Walter."

He managed not to drop the phone. "Hi."

Walter had never asked for his phone number, but he probably had access to Professor Bing's records.

"I wanted to ask whether you had plans for tomorrow night," Walter inquired in that formal way, "and if not, would you like to have dinner?"

"Tomorrow night?" Carey asked, astonished and pleased.

"Yes."

"It's Valentine's Day."

"You have plans, naturally. I realized that you probably would — "

"No," Carey interrupted. "I don't. And I'd like to have dinner."

The pause sounded nonplussed. Walter said, "Good. I'll pick you up at seven."

Pick him up? As in come to Pio Pico house?

That could be tricky. Carey said awkwardly, "You don't have to do that. I can just meet you — "

The silence on the other end of the line shut him up.

Walter asked politely, "Where would you like to meet?"

Carey wasn't particularly insightful about other people's feelings, but he remembered Walter's skeptical smile at the idea Carey was with him for anything but ulterior motives. Maybe Walter was more insecure than he appeared. Maybe he thought Carey didn't want to be seen with him, whereas the truth was Carey had enough problems with the assholes he shared living space with without giving them this kind of ammunition.

But if it was a matter of his feelings or Walter's?

"Here is fine."

Another of those hesitations that felt like waiting for Walter to decipher critical code. Walter said, "I'll see you then."

After dinner, Carey and Ben parted from Heath and went to the library to study as they did most evenings.

"Remind me why we thought anthropology would be a good major?" Ben inquired when they stopped for a brief coffee break several hours later.

"I figured it would be drier than coaching swimming."

Ben's smile faded. He nodded at Carey's cast. "Are you really disappointed about missing so much of the season?"

Carey shrugged. "I guess I should be grateful I didn't break my neck."

"Yeah." Ben tossed his paper cup in the trash, and they went back inside.

"Are you about ready to head back?"

Carey lifted his head out of Mycenae's dusty history and stared at Ben. Over Ben's shoulder he spotted Walter on his way toward the stairs to the second floor study rooms.

Five seconds earlier he'd been barely able to keep his eyes open, feeling every ache and pain of his tumble down the stairs the night before. Now he felt newly energized.

"You go ahead," he told Ben. "I just got my second wind."

"You're kidding."

Carey shook his head.

Ben glanced around instinctively and spotted Walter climbing the staircase. "*Skeletor*?" he said in disbelief.

Carey snapped, "Oh, shove it."

Ben couldn't have looked more surprised if one of the framed paintings of the previous college presidents had snarled at him.

"Chill out, amigo. I didn't know, okay? I didn't realize you two had a thing going on. I thought you were being nice to the guy."

"We don't have *a thing*."

At least… well, they were going to dinner, so they had some kind of thing going on. Carey had no clear idea what. He wasn't sure Walter did.

"Right." Ben was shoving papers in folders, stacking books. "I hope you know what you're doing." His face was tight with anger and hurt feelings. Whether he was pissed because he thought Carey was lying to him or because he thought Carey was lying to himself, was unclear.

As he shrugged into his jacket, his gaze rested on Carey. "You don't look too hot. If you were smart you'd come back to the dorm with me rather than walking back on your own."

Carey remembered the disquieting loneliness of his walk the night before — not to mention his tumble down the stairs. Ben was probably right, but he said, "I'm going to give it another hour. I've got that human sexuality exam on Thursday."

"I don't think you'll have problems with that one." Ben sounded dry.

"I want to make sure I'm ready."

Unimpressed, Ben zipped his jacket. "Night."

"Night."

He waited till Ben disappeared through the automatic doors. He shoved his books in his backpack, pushed back his chair, and headed upstairs to the study room.

Walter was not in the study rooms — all of which were currently in use. He sat at a table facing the picture windows that looked out onto the wind-tossed night and appeared deeply engrossed in *Cultural Anthropology: A Global Perspective.*

Carey sat down across from him. Walter looked up, briefly, unencouragingly. His expression changed. It was more like micro expression than an actual altering of facial appearance, but his eyes warmed and his mouth softened.

Or maybe that's what Carey wanted to see.

"Hi."

"Hi." It was fine for a start. After that Carey was abruptly out of words. It was weird. He was not normally shy or backward, was not typically lacking in confidence, but something about Walter...

And it had been like this from the first time he laid eyes on him two years ago when he'd first flunked out of Professor Bing's Ethnographic Field Methods. When he got around Walter, Carey seemed to fluctuate between vampy and tongue-tied. It was a wonder Walter hadn't written him off as bipolar a long time ago.

As the pause began to strain, Walter said matter-of-factly, "Given your injuries, I thought you'd be making an early night of it."

"I planned on it."

"Cramming?"

"No. I saw you come up here."

Now Walter too was out of words. He licked his lips, an unexpectedly nervous mannerism that seemed endearing to Carey.

"What did you — ?"

At the same instant Carey said, "Could we — ?"

They both stopped. Carey laughed nervously. Walter looked self-conscious.

Carey readied himself for another plunge into frigid waters and said with calm desperation, "Could we go somewhere and maybe get a cup of coffee?"

Walter nodded. He looked down and started gathering his books and papers. There was nothing to read from his expression, and Carey's heart sank. He hoped to hell this wasn't going to be a repeat of the night before. Was he pushing too hard again? Probably. But he was so sure — or he had been —

Walter glanced up. "You look white," he observed with utterly unexpected gentleness.

The gentleness seemed to suck the air right out of Carey's lungs.

"Walt, am I... totally making a fool out of myself?"

Walter shook his head.

"Because when I'm *not* with you, I feel sure it's not just me. But when I *am* with you — and it should be the opposite, right? Like maybe I have stalker tendencies?"

Walter laughed. It was the first time Carey had ever seen him laugh — genuinely laugh — and he was afraid his astonishment showed. Walter's teeth were very white and very straight even if his laugh had a squished, flattened sound — like he was used to smothering it.

Walter said, "No. Not at all. Let's go somewhere we can talk."

○ ○ ○ ○ ○

They had coffee at a café in Hartsburg. It was the kind of place couples went for first-date dessert and cappuccinos. Cute and non-threatening. Ruffled gingham curtains and tablecloths, wooden toys on shelves, old-fashioned advertisements in frames on the walls.

They talked over cheesecake and coffee — primarily about anthropology — and then Walter asked abruptly, "Why did you change your mind last night?"

"I didn't think you really wanted to go to dinner."

Walter appeared to think this over. "I went to your dorm to ask you," he pointed out eventually.

"You did say it was an impulse."

"True." Further consideration. "I didn't regret it. I was glad you hunted me down."

"That's what it felt like," Carey admitted. "Like I hunted you down and tried to force you to take me out."

Walter shook his head. "No. It wasn't like that."

"Then I wish I'd shut up and gone with you. I wouldn't have broken my arm." It was a hassle being one-handed; he'd ended up having Walter cut his cheesecake into bite-sized bits.

Walter's expression grew serious. "How did that happen exactly? You were vague earlier."

"That's because I can't really remember. I remember walking away from you and crossing the faculty parking lot. I guess I slipped and fell down the stairs."

"Were you feeling dizzy, perhaps?"

Carey shook his head. "No. Nothing like that."

"But you're not sure?"

"I'm pretty sure of that," Carey said slowly. "I have this weird impression… like someone came up behind me."

"You mean you think someone pushed you?"

"No. I'm sure I'd remember that."

"Not necessarily. Not with concussion. Even with a mild concussion you might forget."

"I don't think so." Carey squinted, trying to remember. "I have this mental image of someone behind me, but if someone had been there, they would've called for help or stayed with me."

"Maybe."

Walter looked so bleak, Carey felt uneasy. Clearly Walter did not have his own faith in his fellow man. "There was probably no one there. The truth is I've been kind of jumpy lately."

Walter said, "Trouble with your classes?"

Carey smiled faintly. "Not this year. No, I don't know what it is exactly."

He did know, but he didn't want to bring it up. He had the uneasy feeling that if he seemed like too much trouble, Walter would back away, decide it wasn't worth it. Whatever *it* was liable to turn out to be.

"Did you want more coffee or cheesecake?" Walter asked courteously.

As much as Carey wanted to prolong the evening, he had eaten all he could manage. "I'm ready to explode now."

Walter smiled faintly.

The seconds passed and he didn't say anything. Carey bit his lip nervously. What the hell went on behind that mask of Walter's? When they were talking about class work or anthropology or politics, they had plenty to discuss — it was both stimulating and relaxing — but these abrupt, full stops were freaking Carey out. He was not usually insecure; he didn't like the feeling. At all. He stared out the window with its painted pink curlicues and red hearts.

Walter said slowly and carefully, "Would you like to come back to my place?"

Carey turned to him. "Yes."

Walter's eyes looked dark and unsure behind the specs.

"Yes," Carey repeated firmly.

Outside on the sidewalk a breeze was kicking a tin can along the sidewalk like a ghost child. You could almost hear the silent laughter.

Walter said, "It's going to be a full moon tomorrow night."

Carey, occupied in clumsily draping his varsity jacket over his shoulders, looked up. The moon did appear enormous over the roof and treetops. It turned the shingles and leaves to silver and shadow. Across the square the shops were all closed but one. The sign in the window caught Carey's eye.

"Look."

Walter obediently followed the direction of Carey's gaze.

Carey said, "They're still open."

"Did you want candy now?" Walter sounded puzzled, but patient.

"What kind of candy shop stays open 'til almost midnight?"

"I don't know."

A twenty-four-hour candy store? For all your junk food emergencies? That was weird, wasn't it?

"Can we check it out?"

"If you want to." Walter sounded reluctant. Did he think Carey was liable to change his mind about going home with him?

Carey smiled at him and Walter smiled doubtfully back.

They crossed the green, pushed tentatively on the door. The heady scent of chocolate wafted into the crisp night air. A little bell rang with silvery cheer, and the young man behind the counter looked up.

Whatever Carey had been expecting — plump middle-aged ladies in hairnets or bored teenagers — it was a far cry from this sleek, slim man with long black hair and harlequin eyes.

For an instant, as those wicked eyes met his, Carey felt disquieted.

"Are you still open?" Carey asked.

It was a silly question. Although there were no other customers, the shop was still lit, the door was still unlocked.

The man's mouth quirked. He said gravely, "What do you need?"

Not ... what do you want? What do you *need*? It seemed like a small but crucial difference. Deliberate. Portentous. (Assuming that word met what Carey thought it did.) Nothing about this young man seemed careless or haphazard, which was ironic because the name embroidered on his black chef's coat was "Chance." But from the cuff of Chance's herringbone pants to the red bandanna knotted around his throat, he seemed ...

Carey glanced at Walter, but Walter had moved away and was studying a display of red and lemon yellow Valentine's Day candy boxes with the same dispassionate interest he'd view artifacts from an ancient civilization.

"I received a box of chocolates yesterday and I was wondering whether you could tell me who sent them?"

The slanted brows arched. "Was something wrong with the chocolates?"

"No. The chocolates were great." For all that the clerk kept a straight face, Carey was certain he was laughing at him. "It's ... the card said it was from a secret admirer, and I ..."

"Don't like secrets?"

Carey thought it over. "No." He didn't.

Chance said softly, "Perhaps you shouldn't keep them."

"W-what?"

"We all have secrets." Chance smiled as Walter rejoined them. "Try this." He offered a small red paper cup with a piece of candy.

"Thank you, but I don't care for candy," Walter said.

Chance's arched eyebrows rose still higher. "You see?" he said to Carey.

"Not really."

"Secrets are the foundation of human interaction."

Walter made a sound. Not exactly a laugh, but he sounded amused. "You're talking to the wrong people. We're anthropologists."

This was getting weirder by the minute. The light gleaming off the polished red and black squares of the floor, the alchemy of fragrance — almost orgasmic in its intense complexity: vanilla and cocoa and... coffee and aged tobacco and wood-chips and cinnamon...

For an instant Carey felt dizzy, as though he'd peered into the future. He blinked at Chance who seemed inexplicably taller and darker. "Can you tell me who sent the candy?"

"I'm afraid that's confidential."

Carey had been prepared to hear that Chance had no memory of this customer, but how could the sale of a box of chocolates be confidential? "It's chocolate not... not confession."

"Sometimes it's the same thing."

Yes, this guy was definitely putting them on.

"Three *pounds* of chocolate."

"Someone must admire you very much."

Carey looked helplessly from Walt to Chance.

"Let's go," said Walter.

"Don't forget your chocolate." Walter opened his mouth and Chance nodded at Carey. "No, but *he* does."

CHAPTER FIVE

Walter lived in a block of 1950s apartments near the old railroad station. From the outside, the building did not look like much. But when Walter closed the apartment door and switched on the light, Carey was surprised to see that the open-plan rooms were done in airy, retro décor: Armstrong floors, chrome and Formica tables, straightline, square chairs and sofas upholstered in primary colors. There was a Swedish fireplace in one corner and an entire wall was given over to a series of metal and wood compartmentalized shelving.

"Wow. *Back to the Future.*" It was nice. Much nicer than he'd expected. What had he expected? Not the work of an interior designer, anyway.

"Are you cold? Would you like a fire?"

Carey glanced back. "Whatever you like." Walter handed him the small paper cup of candy and went over to adjust the thermostat. Carey set the paper cup down on a kidney shaped table. The idea of candy made him feel slightly queasy.

"What was that all about?" Walter asked. "At the candy store."

Carey had sort of hoped Walter wouldn't ask. He was afraid it made him sound like the kind of guy who attracted nuts — or was maybe a nut himself. "Someone sent me a box of chocolates yesterday."

"I gathered. And?" Walter's voice and face were neutral. He looked back at Carey and the lenses of his glasses formed two blank squares in the lamplight.

"I wondered who it was," Carey said lamely.

"A secret admirer."

"I guess so." Carey had been unsure whether Walter was listening to that conversation or not. He still wasn't clear, really. Maybe Walter was guessing. Maybe Walter...

No.

No. That would be too freaky. Carey didn't want his secret admirer to be Walter.

All the same he tried to remember if anything in the way Chance had looked at Walter had indicated prior acquaintance. Maybe that was why Chance had been so mysterious. His customer was standing four feet away.

He walked over to Walter's bookshelves and studied the rows of titles. In addition to the books there were a number of artifacts: a whale bone, obsidian arrow points, a carved wooden funerary boat.

He nodded at a small stone bust. "Polynesian, right? Is it real?"

Walter threw the bust a dismissing look. "Yes."

"Sweet. How much *does* the GTA gig pay?"

Carey wasn't seriously asking, but Walter was silent. Clearly Carey had once more wandered right past the No Trespassing sign. It was... startling. Walter — or someone close to Walter — had a lot of disposable income.

"Sorry. I only meant — "

Walter said flatly, "My father is very wealthy. He gives me lots of things to make up for the fact that he has no feelings for me."

Carey had no idea what to say to that. "Sorry, Walt," was the best he could manage.

"It doesn't matter."

Carey was the youngest of a big, loving family. Pennies had counted in the Gardner clan, but love and loyalty had never been in short supply. He said, "It must."

Walter stared at him and the harsh planes of his face softened for an instant. "I suppose what I mean is, I'm used to it. I've adjusted. My father and I have learned to make the best of the situation. He gives me lots of things I don't need and I accept them because it makes him feel better."

"Why — ?" It occurred to Carey that might not be a tactful question.

Walter said, "My parents are beautiful people. Were. My mother is dead now. They were both beautiful, charming, and successful. And they had me for a son. You can't really blame them."

"What are you *talking* about?"

Walter smiled. It wasn't the engaging smile Carey had seen a couple of times that evening.

Carey said, "I don't know what you mean, Walt. You're brilliant. I mean, it's common knowledge."

Walter laughed — and he sounded genuinely amused. "You're very sweet. Do you know that?"

"No," Carey said, uncomfortable at such an idea.

"They — my parents — wanted... different things for me. They wanted a different son. Someone like them. What they got was someone who just wanted to read books and go dig up old bones in foreign places."

"But — " Carey had no idea what to say to this. This was pain way beyond his scope of experience. Clearly Walter carried invisible scars, scars that must cut deep.

"I wish I hadn't told you that," Walter said abruptly. He took his glasses off, folded them up and set them on a copy of *Consuming Grief: Compassionate Cannibalism in an Amazonian Society*. "Now you're sorry for me. I don't want you to be sorry for me." He took Carey into his arms and kissed him with an easy cool expertise that left Carey breathless and shaken.

Carey had been assuming he would be the expert in this, that he'd have to take the lead. That appeared to be a gross miscalculation on his part.

He studied Walter's face, memorizing every feature — how long his eyelashes were, how unusual that shade of brown eyes. His nose was really sort of elegant. Walter bent his head and kissed Carey again, kissed him with such shattering and tender thoroughness that Carey couldn't remember what to do — except hang on and kiss back. Walter's tongue slipped inside his mouth, sweeter than any chocolate. He could feel Walter's hands on his shoulders, and the slick heat of his tongue probing gently. At the end of that kiss, Carey was surprised he even remembered his own name.

Walter whispered, "I don't know why you're here, but I'm glad."

"Me too."

"Want to go to bed?"

Go to bed. Carey smiled inwardly, nodded.

They went into the bedroom. It was probably as nice as the other rooms, but Carey was no longer paying attention to furnishings. He had a general impression of restful comfort.

The sheets were blue and gray plaid flannel, soft on their skin. There was a leather-padded headboard. He wondered if Walter was into kinky. Carey was pretty much every bit as vanilla as Heath had joked.

He watched Walter undress with swift efficiency. He did not seem self-conscious — merely businesslike — before he turned his attention to helping Carey. Here he was painstakingly careful; Carey was the one in a rush. At last he sprawled, naked and relaxed, on the brushed flannel, silently admiring Walter's strong, rangy frame. Maybe Walter was not his parents' idea of masculine beauty, but Carey liked what he saw: wide shoulders, narrow hips, long legs. Walter's skin was white and smooth — barring the blackness of his five o'clock shadow and the dark silk of his body hair. His nipples were rose brown and his cock, already stiff and erect, was heavy and flushed. A man's cock — nothing boyish or unsure there.

Walter knelt beside Carey on the bed. "What would be easier for you?" His hand ran lightly over Carey's collarbones. Carey shivered as a bolt of arousal shot through him. He stretched lazily, enjoying the brush of Walter's fingers on his sensitized skin.

What would have been easiest was if they didn't discuss it and just let it happen, but Walter was too meticulous, it seemed. That was okay. First times were always awkward.

He reached out and returned the caress, stroking hot, smooth skin and Walter gave a twitch, like a nervous horse. Carey whispered, "I think you're beautiful, Walt."

Walter gazed down at him with dark, unfathomable eyes. He said, "No one has ever called me Walt. I've never had a nickname before."

"Do you mind?"

"I don't think I mind anything you do."

Carey smiled, reached up to pull him down.

That was probably his last moment of control although things grew vague, Carey's wits scattered beneath Walter's sensual onslaught. He moaned his pleasure as Walter's hands caressed with greedy, worshipful thoroughness, his mouth kissing and licking and nibbling every inch of Carey. It seemed to Carey, slightly dazed beneath this ravishment, that there wasn't any part of his body that hadn't received due attention from Walter.

They moved against each other, tentatively, and then faster, feverishly, trying to get closer still, rubbing ... grinding ...

Carey would have been willing to take it as far as Walter liked; he'd never felt anything like this. His lungs labored for air beneath those breath-robbing kisses, his heart hammering away as though he were swimming too far beneath the surface to make it back in time, drowning in Walter's arms as Walter pressed him into the mattress, but in fact, this alone was enough. He could hear his own incoherent voice asking Walter for more — and Walter thrusting harder against him.

In all too short a time Carey arched and cried out, clenching his eyes tight as warm seed pulsed and shot in shockwave after shockwave of astonished delight.

Lost in the intensity of that release he was only vaguely aware when Walter tensed and gasped, his own tight control releasing blood hot and wet. He pulled Carey to him and hugged him so tightly, Carey gasped.

Instantly the steel-like bands eased. "Did I hurt your arm?"

Carey shook his head. "It's okay." He hugged Walter back as best he could, one-handed, and kissed him beneath his jaw.

It felt a long time later when Carey said, "That was ... I've never come like that. Never. I thought I'd detonate."

Walter snorted, amused. His face looked softer in the muted lamplight. He lifted a bare shoulder. "It's merely another form of athletics."

He wasn't being unkind, merely matter-of-fact, but Carey had to work to absorb the notion that what had been a mind-altering experience for him was how it always was for Walter. At last he became aware that Walter watching him.

Their eyes met. Walter looked serious, almost concerned. "I don't mean that it wasn't significant."

"No? What do you mean?" Carey propped his head on his good hand.

"That good sex is an acquired skill like any other. I know how to give you intense pleasure."

No doubt about it. Carey had been sobbing by the end, begging Walter — literally racked with something closer to religious rapture than sexual gratification. He said unemotionally, "You do, yeah. The clinical approach is sorta chilling, though."

Walter's brows drew together. "I don't mean…"

"It's kind of hard to know what you do mean, Walt."

Walter's lips parted. Without the glasses he looked younger, uncharacteristically defenseless. "I want to give you pleasure. I want sex with me to be so pleasurable you won't want anyone else."

"You do." Carey smiled crookedly. "I don't want anyone else."

"You don't even know me."

"You don't know me either."

A peculiar smile touched Walter's thin mouth. "I've been reading your essays and papers and tests all semester long. I know more about you than you know about me."

Carey smiled again. He was wondering if that was flattering or creepy? He was interested in Walter so it felt flattering, but it was a fine line, wasn't it?

"Guys like me don't end up with guys like you."

Startled, Carey studied his face. Walter appeared serious.

"Why not?"

Walter smiled faintly, brushed his knuckles against Carey's cheek. "It doesn't happen."

o o o o o

Carey's stomach was growling when he woke up. He was starving. His arm ached from his fingers to his elbow, and he remembered he didn't have swim practice because he'd broken it. And his belly and groin were flaky with the sugar glaze of semen. Memory came flooding back and he opened his eyes.

Walter was awake and smiling at him from the opposite pillow. He was wearing his glasses, so he'd been out of bed at some point.

"Hi." Carey was self-consciously aware that he needed to pee and brush his teeth — and probably not in that order.

"Hello." Walter leaned over and covered Carey's mouth with his own. "I don't know if I have anything to feed you."

"You'll do for starters," Carey said when he could breathe again.

Walter was still smiling. "Do you dream you're swimming?"

"Sometimes. Why?"

"I thought you might." Walter managed to suppress his smile, but it confused Carey. Nobody feels more defenseless than when they're sleeping, and he didn't like the idea he was being laughed at — even affectionately. He threw back the bedclothes.

Walter asked, "When's your first class?"

"What's today?"

"Wednesday."

"Ten."

"We should get moving."

Carey nodded. "I need a shower. Do you have a trash bag or something I can wrap my arm in?"

"I'll find something."

Walter left the bed and vanished into the next room. When they both returned to the bedroom, Walter had a white trash bag and twine. He sat next to Carey on the bed, carefully and methodically waterproofing his cast.

Carey scrutinized his downbent face. What long eyelashes Walter had. The glasses successfully masked the eggshell delicacy of his eyelids and the nearsighted softness of his eyes.

Walter's eyelashes flicked up. He asked, "Do you need help in the shower?"

Carey smiled, shook his head. He needed a little distance. He liked Walter a lot. Maybe too much because Walter remained an enigma. He clearly had a few hang ups — well, who didn't? — and he didn't seem to think this relationship was going anywhere.

Guys like me don't end up with guys like you.

Which — okay — Carey wasn't naïve enough to think sex equaled love, but he'd like to think that they could at least keep an open mind about it. Given how much he did like Walter — even if Walter was laughing at him while he was sleeping, and even if Walter considered sex nothing more than exercise, and getting Carey to want him a kind of challenge. Not that he thought Walter was manipulating him or anything, and after all, Carey had gone hunting Walter…

When he was done in the shower, Walter took his turn. Carey drank the orange juice and ate the toasted English muffin that Walter had left for him on the turquoise Melmac Mallo Ware.

○ ○ ○ ○ ○

On the drive back to the campus Carey asked, "Did you ever hear a story about someone murdering girls on campus?"

"On this campus?" Walter glanced at him.

Carey nodded.

"No."

"Someone was telling me about this Valentine's Day Killer. Every year he would send a box of chocolates to a girl and then she would be murdered on Valentine's Day."

Walter's expression was disbelieving — and disgusted. "That's ridiculous."

"I don't know. It's supposed to be true."

"According to whom?"

Good point.

Walter said, "You believe that whoever sent you the candy is stalking you? Planning to harm you?"

It sounded ridiculous when put like that.

"Er, no."

"It's probably someone who doesn't know how to approach you."

"Yes." Carey wished he'd never brought it up. Walter looked withdrawn again. Hopefully it was because he didn't like the idea of other people sending Carey valentines.

When they got to the college, there was the awkwardness of not knowing how to say goodbye. Carey knew it was for him to take the initiative on this kind of thing, but it wasn't easy. Walter had his forcefield up again, and somehow even picturing him naked and transfixed by orgasm didn't give Carey the confidence to broach that barrier. Whether intended or not, Walter could be intimidating as hell — and Carey wasn't confident Walter didn't want it that way. Maybe he preferred to keep a distance on campus. That made sense, but they hadn't discussed it, so how much of a distance would he want? Carey didn't want to make a move and get smacked down — and he was only too aware that Walter wouldn't hesitate if Carey crossed whatever the invisible line was.

He wavered, undecided, and Walter looked away from him and stared out the windshield.

That seemed clear enough. It wouldn't be so irritating if he felt he knew Walter as well as Walter seemed to think — based on a few essays and test scores — he knew Carey, or if Carey could convince himself that Walter was feeling anything remotely as emotionally vulnerable as he was.

He climbed out of the car and said lamely, "Bye. Thanks for breakfast and everything."

"I'll see you this evening."

Walter sounded cool and businesslike. They could have been planning a study group meeting. Carey nodded and shut the car door.

○ ○ ○ ○ ○

Sty was in their room, sorting dirty laundry to take home for the weekend, when Carey got back to Pio Pico House. Carey shoveled Sty's dirty socks off his bed and asked, "How'd the meet go?"

"Swept all sixteen events, Bones. One eighty to one oh eight. I guess somehow we're going to survive without you."

"No, no. Don't bother cheering me up."

Sty laughed. "You're out for the rest of the season?"

Carey nodded. He was trying not to think about it too much.

"Bummer. Did you eat all that chocolate?"

"I left the box next door." He eyed Sty speculatively. "Hey, did you ever hear this urban legend about Valentine's Day murders here on campus?"

Sty brightened up. "Ooh, yeah. Everybody's heard that story."

"I never heard it."

Sty shrugged.

"So what's the story?"

"This was like back in the Stone Age, dude. Every year the prettiest cave girl would get a big box of chocolates from an anonymous friend and on VD Day she'd be found *slaughtered*."

It just seemed so… unlikely. "And they never caught the guy?"

"Nope."

"You're shitting me."

Sty was scooping up all the piles of his clothes and shoving them in a big duffle bag, so God only knew what the sorting had been about. He glanced up.

"True story, dude. It's on the Internet." He tossed the duffle bag by the door and turned on his CD player. Led Zeppelin blasted out.

CHAPTER SIX

Carey hooked up with Heath for lunch in the dining hall. They found an empty table on the raised section. Heath carefully lowered his tray with its mountain of precariously balanced plates and food.

"So Ben says you were out with Skeletor last night."

"Don't call him that." Carey awkwardly carved off a slab of vegetarian lasagna.

"Carey, the guy is a fer-reak. What are you doing with him?"

"I like him."

Heath jeered, "You *like* him? What, are you in high school?"

"I'm going out with him," Carey said. "I'm dating him."

"You're nuts." Heath was no longer smiling. "If I were you, I'd talk to Ben. He doesn't want to say anything to you because he thinks you have a thing for Skeletor, but Ben has information you need."

"I'm not talking to Ben about Walter."

Heath glared at him. He said quietly but distinctly over the surrounding clatter of voices and plates and flatware, "Wake up, Gardner. The dude is a stalker."

"Bullshit." But Carey's heart was thumping with a mixture of dread and premonition.

Heath sat back in his chair. "Hey, fine. Suit yourself, Marine Boy. But don't say nobody warned you."

Carey nodded curtly and changed the subject. Unfortunately it wasn't so easy to squash the doubts Heath had raised. Walter *was* a little odd. So what? The most interesting people often were, right?

But so were the most dangerous people.

Even if Walter had sent those chocolates, it didn't mean he was dangerous. He sure as hell couldn't be the Valentine's Day Killer. He'd have to be in his fifties. Just because he — someone — sent chocolates signed "your secret admirer" didn't mean he was copycatting that old story. He hadn't even heard of the Valentine's Day Killer.

Unless he was lying.

Carey glanced at Heath and Heath was studying him with an unsettling sympathy in his eyes.

On the way out of the dining hall, he elbowed Carey. "Hey."

Carey looked at him.

"Just… you, me, Ben. We've been the three amigos, right? Friends since we were sophomores. Don't let this thing with Ske — Sterne ruin it for us."

Carey cleared his throat. "We're cool."

Heath nodded, and sprinted off on those long legs. Carey went to the library and signed onto the computers.

It took him no time at all to find what he was looking for. There was more than enough information on Hartsburg's legendary Valentine's Day Killer. In fact, looking at all these pages made Carey wonder how he'd never heard anything about it before.

He scanned photos and interviews with witnesses and police reports, and before long, he found the page that explained that the whole thing was a hoax.

In fact, the perpetrators of the hoax — former Hartsburg alumni — were so proud of their work they openly took credit for it these days. There they were, now bearded and respectable professors, grinning sheepishly over their gruesome urban legend and explaining how they'd come up with their more twisted ideas.

Carey read with a sense of relief — and embarrassment. As preposterous as the story of the Valentine's Day Killer had seemed, maybe he *had* been buying into it, and after his fall he had been a little spooked. Now he felt like a fool.

A relieved fool.

Carey grimaced, signing off the computer. Did Heath and Ben know the truth? Had they too fallen for the urban legend or had they been deliberately yanking his chain?

He was lost in his thoughts as he walked back to dorm row. A florist's van was parked outside Pio Pico House. Carey passed it and went inside the building that always seemed quiet, almost deserted this time of day.

In his room, he turned on music — Coldplay — and flung himself down on his bed, staring moodily at the ceiling.

Nobody said it was easy ...

Someone tapped on his door.

Carey sat up. "Come in."

Ben opened the door. He held up Carey's box of chocolates. "You better take these before Heath eats them all."

"Thanks."

Ben nodded. "Everything okay?"

"Why wouldn't it be?"

Ben shook his head. He said tentatively, "Do you have plans for tonight?"

"Yeah."

Ben didn't say anything. Carey said shortly, "Yes. Dinner with Walter."

Ben's eyes widened — maybe at Carey's tone. "Hey, it's not my business."

"No, it's not."

Ben put his hands up in a "chill, dude" gesture and went out.

Carey rubbed his forehead. He really didn't function well without his full eight hours, but even lack of sleep didn't explain his nervous restlessness. If he could talk to Walter instead of hearing everyone else's theories —

He rolled off the bed, went to his desk and punched the numbers he'd memorized into his cell phone.

He was prepared for the call to go to message, but Walter answered.

"Sterne."

"Hi. It's me. Carey."

"Hi." Walter sounded ... careful.

"I just ..." He just *what?* Walter had not said Carey could call him. Walter had not indicated any desire to chat. Walter had not shown any interest in hearing from Carey before their date that evening. His voice faded.

Nothing from the other side. As usual Walter was giving him nothing. Into the silence that had already stretched too far, Walter said politely, calmly, "It's all right if you changed your mind about tonight. I have a lot to do."

"Oh." Did that mean what it sounded like? That Walter wanted off the hook? Numbly, Carey said, "That works out then."

"Yes."

Carey was afraid Walter must have heard the sound of his swallow. All at once he was sick of it. Sick of feeling insecure and off-balance all the time. He didn't need this. He didn't have to beg someone to take him out. He said shortly, "Okay. Great. Thanks again for last night."

Walter sounded like a polite robot. "It was my pleasure."

Carey clicked off before Walter could.

For a few seconds he stood there feeling hollow. It was over, then? Before it had really even started? Maybe that was for the best. Anything you had to work this hard at couldn't be right.

Right?

He went next door. Ben had the music on unusually loud. Carey rapped on the door and after long seconds, Ben opened it. He looked like he'd been crying.

"What's wrong?" Carey demanded, shocked.

Ben shook his head.

"Did something happen?"

Ben shook his head again.

"Can I come in?"

Ben moved aside, wiping his eyes. He sat down at his desk and stared at Carey. "What did you want?"

"If you want to talk about it — "

"I don't."

What was it about Valentine's Day? It seemed like they were all on edge today.

"Heath said I should ask you about Walter."

Ben wiped his eyes again, impatiently. "You don't want to know."

"No, I don't. But maybe I should."

Ben stared at him. It made Carey uncomfortable.

"Walter left the candy for you," Ben said abruptly.

"How do you know?"

"I saw him. He asked me not to say anything. It was supposed to be a surprise."

"Walter?" It didn't seem like a Walter thing. Not the leaving candy — the asking someone to not tell. He couldn't imagine Walter confiding in anyone that much.

Ben nodded. "I didn't think anything of it at the time, but there's something not right with him, Carey. It's like he's obsessed with you. I mean, a few hours later he came back to see if you wanted to go to dinner."

"I don't think there's anything that weird about asking me to dinner."

Ben persisted, "I've heard stories about him, though. Like he's done this before."

"Done what? Asked people to dinner? Given them candy?" Carey was getting irritated. Why the hell had he asked if he didn't want to know?

Ben was also getting irritated. He seemed to struggle inwardly, before saying, "There's more."

"Well, what the fuck is it?" Carey asked angrily. "Stop hinting around and say it."

"I think Walter pushed you down the stairs the other night."

"*What?*"

"I saw him in the parking lot."

"I saw him go up the stairs."

"He must have come back down. I saw him."

"You're lying."

Ben shook his head.

"Yes you are." Carey stood up. "I saw his face in class the next day. There's no way he pushed me. There's no way he'd hurt me. He didn't have any idea — "

He stopped, considering Ben's face, that mix of mortification and bitterness. "You're lying," he repeated, realizing it was the absolute truth. Not mistaken, not misreading the evidence. *Lying.* "And if you're lying about that …"

Ben said nothing, just sat there watching him, looking dull and stricken.

"Why?" Carey asked.

Still nothing from Ben.

"You're lying about the candy. And that whole story about the Valentine's Day Killer is a hoax. Did you know about that? Were you deliberately trying to spook me?"

Ben started to speak, then seemed to catch himself.

"Why were *you* in the parking lot that night?" Carey asked. At the time Ben had said he'd left something in his car, but he'd never said what, and Carey had been wondering about that, off and on, though it hadn't seemed important until now.

"Heath thought he left his notes in his car."

Carey shook his head. "Is Heath going to confirm that? I don't believe you."

Ben began to cry. "I love you. I would do anything for you, and you don't even *see* me."

Carey opened his mouth, but he didn't know what to say.

Ben's wet eyes seemed to blaze with anger. "And then suddenly, out of the blue, it's Walter Sterne. That fucking *freak*. What's the matter with you?"

"Did you push me down the stairs?" Carey asked. The whole conversation felt unreal.

"*No.*" Ben jumped up too. "How can you think that? You fell. I never touched you. Maybe you heard me coming up behind you. I only wanted to talk to you."

"Why didn't you tell me?"

Ben gazed at him, mouth working. Carey sort of understood the feeling.

○ ○ ○ ○ ○

When Carey left Ben's room, he went back to his own, locked the door, and sat on the edge of his bed. He rested his forehead against his good hand.

After a time he became aware someone was tapping quietly on his door.

He jumped to his feet, went to the door, braced for the next lunacy, and yanked it open.

Walter stood there, hand raised. He lowered it, looking self-conscious.

Carey's angry confusion drained away. Hope flared.

"I — " Walter cleared his throat. "Earlier this afternoon. Did you really call to cancel?"

"No." Honesty compelled Carey to amend, "I don't know. I sort of... needed to talk to you."

"I was afraid you were calling to cancel."

Carey shook his head. "I thought you wanted me to cancel. It sort of sounded that way."

"No. Of course not. I — " Walter stopped himself.

Carey tried to read his expression, but it was going to take a long time before he was adept at reading Walter. The good news was, it looked like he was going to have a chance to work on it. He drew a breath. "I'm really not insecure. Probably the opposite. Maybe that's why I act like such a dumbass around you. I'm not used to not knowing where I stand."

"You come before anyone and everyone."

The stark simplicity of that left Carey wordless.

Walter's smile was painful to see. "I'm not usually like this, either. It's simply that I... feel so much for you. I know it probably seems strange to you, but even two years ago when I used to read your papers — before you flunked out of Dr. Bing's class — I thought you were... special. That we would get along."

He looked hopeful and miserable at the same time. "When you seemed to feel the same thing... it felt too good to be true. I don't know how to be with someone like you. I never have. So I keep doing these stupid things."

"What a pair," Carey said, but he was smiling.

Walter's smile grew hopeful — and then confident as Carey hooked his good arm around his neck and pulled him close.

○ ○ ○ ○ ○

The full moon shone down on the small town of Hartsburg. A *snow moon* the long ago Indians called it, though it rarely snowed here.

Beneath tidy roofs sated lovers slept sweetly in each other's arms.

The tree-lined square was dark now. The tall old-fashioned street lamps were haloed in fuzzy radiance, like candles lighting the empty streets and frosted lawns. A band of light showed beneath the blinds of Sweets to the Sweet like the gleam of eyes beneath heavy lids. Behind the closed blinds, Chance studied the symmetrical patterns made by the frost crystals on the black glass. Delicate feathers, frozen flowers, even crooked hearts among the snowflakes ... Condensation on energy-deficient windows or augurs of things to come? He tilted his head, considered ... a slow smile touched his mouth.

OTHER PEOPLE'S WEDDINGS

What I wanted to do was tell the story of a man whose day job was helping other people achieve their romantic fantasies — while his own hopes and dreams went without nurturing. At the same time I wanted Griffin Skerry to be a positive, optimistic person. Someone who had made the best out of the hand he was dealt. Technically he's lived all his life in a tiny town in North Dakota, but he's created a world for himself that mirrors in many ways the life he would have chosen if he'd left for New York and a career in fashion as originally planned.

"I'd rather be dead than wear this!"

Griff dropped the latest issue of Elegant Bride as Madeline Dalrymple burst from the dressing room cubicle, shot across the showroom floor, and slammed out the front glass door of Venetian Bridal Gowns. Her exit bore an unfortunate resemblance to a big purple balloon flying wild after being jabbed by a pin.

Mallory, Madeline's sister, appeared at the mouth of the hall to the dressing rooms, looking exasperated.

Sometimes Griff suspected that brides deliberately picked the worst possible dresses for their bridesmaids and maids of honor. Or maybe it wasn't deliberate. Maybe it was subconscious, a paying back of old scores, a testing of true devotion. The Watters & Watters strapless sheath of lilac layered over hot pink chiffon would have flattered Mallory's tall, slim, brunette beauty, but it made short, plump Madeline look like a Purple People-Eater after a good meal.

"Well?" Mallory said to Griff.

"Well?" Griff returned blankly, with an uneasy look at Sasha, co-owner of Venetian Bridal Gowns. Sasha raised her shoulders infinitesimally. After twenty years of dealing with brides and bridesmaids, she didn't bother trying to understand, she rode the whirlwind the best she could — and cashed in at the end of the ride.

"Go after her," Mallory ordered. "Are you my wedding planner or not?"

Mallory's idea of Griff's job description was a cross between a personal assistant and confidante. By the second week of accepting the job of coordinating Mallory and Joe Palmer's nuptials, Griff knew he'd made a deal with the devil. Possibly literally. But the Dalrymples were Binbell's wealthiest family, and the Dalrymple-Palmer wedding was going to be the social event of the season — plus he needed the money. In these days of economic hardship prospective brides might not be willing to cut costs on dresses or cakes or hair stylists, but hapless wedding planners all too often fell under the heading Optional.

This, however, was different. Griff was experienced enough to know Lord help the mister who comes between a bride and her sister. "I don't think it's my place — "

"Of course it's your place," Mallory snapped. "Whose place would it be? You need to get her in line before she wrecks my wedding."

"She's still wearing her three hundred and forty-five dollar bridesmaid dress," Sasha pointed out mildly.

Now and again co-ownership seemed like more trouble than it was worth. Griff choked back words he would regret once he started juggling utility bills on the space next door, and pushed out through the glass door. The jaunty notes of the Wedding March followed before the door closed and cut them off.

The L-shaped strip mall, locally known as Wedding Aisle, consisted of Venetian Bridal Gowns, Skerry Weddings, and Guy's Tuxedos. On the hook of the "L" was Betty Ann's Crafts and Supplies. It was, as they said, a match made in heaven.

Maddy's blue Sebring convertible was still parked between Griff's classic red VW Beetle and Mallory's BMW Z4, but there was no sign of the runaway brides-maid. He ducked his head inside Skerry Weddings, but Mallory was not hiding out there. He walked around the buildings to the end of the strip mall.

Maddy was walking up and down the asphalt drive behind Guy's, smoking a cigarette. She looked up with raccoon eyes at Griff's approach and snorted. She had stopped crying, which was a huge relief.

"Fuck, Skerry. Don't you have any pride?"

"Look," Griff spoke awkwardly. "Mallory's sorry if she didn't seem sympa-thetic, but it's too late to change the dresses. This is the final fitting."

"She's not sorry," Maddy spat out. "She wants me to look like a fucking circus freak. She deliberately picked the dress that would make me look worst. You were there. You saw. She could have picked the dress I liked, but oh no! It had to be some-thing only her and her anorexic friends could wear."

Griff managed not to sigh. It had seemed that way to him too, but experience had taught him the sister dynamic was a weird one. A decade of organizing other people's weddings had made him very glad he'd been born an only child.

He said patiently, "Mallory's wedding is the most important day of a woman's life, so naturally she wants everything to be perfect. The way she always imagined it. You'll see when your turn comes."

Maddy's tear streaked face screwed into an expression of disgust. "First bullet point: I am never getting married. And if I did get married, it wouldn't be in one of these big fat geek weddings. Second bullet point: her wedding day is not the most important day of a woman's life. Do you honestly believe that shit?"

Er... no. Not really. Not exactly. He believed in marriage, obviously. Believed in commitment. A wedding was an important symbol of commitment, a significant milestone, but the single most important one? No. How could it be when most women married men, and most men *didn't* consider their wedding the most important day of their lives?

Then again, he arranged weddings for a living so...

He was still trying to think of a compromise answer when Maddy said scornfully, "Don't you find it ironic that all these people who despised you and made fun of you in high school hire you to do their weddings?"

Griff flushed. He said defensively, "High school was... a long time ago. Everybody does things they regret."

"They don't regret anything they did," Maddy retorted. "They thought you were a joke then and they think you're a joke now. The gay wedding planner. They're laughing at you."

This attack caught him off balance — not least because he and Maddy were not close. There had been three years between them in school, and whether Maddy believed it or not, her family and her money ensured she had never truly been the social outcast she imagined. For a moment he was right back there. Right back in Mrs. Dodge's tenth grade biology class, struggling not to cry because no one wanted him for a lab partner. No, because Hammer Sorensen had humiliated him once again with a cruel but accurate imitation of Griff's light voice and slightly affected speaking manner. The horror of breaking down in front of the goggling, giggling class. Like falling in the snow in front of a pack of wolves.

He could practically smell the formaldehyde. Hear the whispers... But he wasn't fifteen years old anymore, and he hadn't cried since that day. Griff said shortly, "I don't think anyone would trust a day as important or an event as expensive as a wedding to someone they considered a joke. Are you coming back inside?"

Maddy raised her brows as though this sudden display of spine was unexpected. She flicked her cigarette to the asphalt and crushed it beneath her kitten heel. "I don't have a choice. Mommy Dearest will disinherit me again if I spoil Mal's big day."

True. Dilys Dalrymple's tight clutch on the Dalrymple purse strings was the ace up Griff's sleeve. He was leery of playing it, though, not least because it would require him having to deal with Dilys. She was more alarming than both of her daughters put together.

As she walked past him Maddy said, "You're good at what you do, Skerry. That's true. But my sister can afford the best in the entire country. Maybe you should ask yourself why she wanted you?"

○ ○ ○ ○ ○

Griff had given quite a lot of thought to that particular question. Especially because Joe had made it very clear he did not want Griff to take the job. Sometimes

Griff wondered if Mallory knew about him and Joe. But he was pretty sure if that was the case, Mallory and Joe would not be getting married.

He was still thinking about it as he pulled up in front of Sweets to the Sweet to see about the new wedding favors. Naturally good old Jordan almond flower favors had never been an option. Mallory had requested chocolate favors and then promptly shot down personalized chocolate bars, personalized chocolate wedding coins, heart-shaped dress and tux cookies, chocolate shell and starfish with personalized tags, wedding chocolate puzzle boxes, and dark chocolate flowers in lavender and pink foil. She had finally settled on handcrafted ivory calla lily favor boxes with four squares of Belgian chocolate. At $4.30 a pop times four hundred guests...

But one week ago, Mallory had abruptly changed her mind about the favor boxes. No explanation. Not even the threat of having to pay a sizable restocking fee had swayed her. She said only that she'd decided she wanted to "patronize local artisans," and had ordered Griff to work with the owner of Sweets to the Sweet.

Chance always made Griff uneasy. It wasn't anything he said or did, exactly. In fact, Chance was always, unexpectedly, nice to him. Unexpectedly, because the first day he'd walked into Sweets to the Sweet, Griff had heard Chance offering his frank and unvarnished opinion of Horace Plaice — to Horace's face. Not that Horace wasn't every bit as detestable as Chance observed, but he was also rich and influential — and one reason he was as grotesque as he was, was his passionate love of fine chocolate. But apparently Chance wasn't worried about pissing off potential clientele. It must be a lovely feeling.

Griff parked out front of the shop wedged discreetly between Nina's Café and Buckner's Books.

He went inside, the bell on the door ringing cheerfully. The scent of chocolate, rich, complex and seductive, greeted him. Chance looked up and smiled.

"Hello, Griffin."

"Hi, Chance." Griff was, uncomfortably conscious of that flutter of awareness in his chest — that tingle in his groin. What the hell was the matter with him? Even if Chance did happen to be gay, he wouldn't be interested in someone like Griff. He'd want someone like himself. Not that Griff could think of anyone like Chance. Not in Nowhere North Dakota, population nine thousand seventy-three.

Awkwardly, he said, "I only dropped by to check we're on schedule with the Dalrymple-Palmer wedding favors."

"You didn't have to come yourself." Chance's voice was velvety smooth as buttercream. That voice made the most prosaic of comments sound... beguiling.

"I — " Griff broke off as the silvery bell behind him chimed again. He glanced around and froze.

Hammer Sorensen stepped inside the shop. Big, blond, buff Hamar. The bane of Griff's school days. Yeah, Hamar — Hammer as he'd preferred to be called once they reached high school — had certainly had it all. The cool chicks, the cool car. You really had to give him credit: honor roll, varsity sports — and yet somehow he'd still found time to harass a nobody loser like Griffin and make his life a living hell.

It had been how long? Years since Griffin had last seen him at anything but a distance. Hammer was older, heavier now — but still handsome, still fit. No sign of the leg injury that had put an end to his career in professional football before it had ever really begun.

Griff faced front again. The muscles in the back of his neck clenched so tight he was afraid his head was going to start shaking like one of those bobble-headed dogs.

"Howdy, Sheriff," Chance drawled with a hint of mockery. "Come to verify the chocolate percentage in my bon-bons?"

Hammer chuckled. The hair rose on the back of Griff's neck. He remembered that easy laugh. Such an attractive laugh for such a mean bastard.

Hammer's deep voice said, "We're celebrating my grandmother's ninetieth birthday tonight. I thought I'd get her a box of your finest."

He was now standing next to Griff. Griff could smell his aftershave and the mix of cold air and leather jacket. He continued to stare straight ahead at Chance who had propped one elbow on the case and was smiling lazily at his second customer.

"My finest what? Creams? Nuts? Truffles? Divinity? Fudge ..."

"No hurry. I'll wait my turn," Hammer said. Griff felt his glance, felt Hammer looking his way with that light, curious gaze. He ignored him, continuing to gaze forward. As his gaze slowly focused on Chance once more, he recognized the wicked amusement in Chance's eyes.

Of course there was no way Chance could know the history between himself and the now-Sheriff Sorensen — Sweets to the Sweet was new. Or at least ... Griff couldn't exactly remember when the shop had opened for business. Anyway, for an instant he had the notion that Chance was at least aware of and entertained by the undercurrents.

Undercurrent. Singular. Because any current was all on Griff's side. Hammer was unlikely to recognize him after all this time. Griff was no longer the gawky, acne-scarred adolescent he'd once been. The braces were gone and laser surgery had taken care of the glasses.

"Hold that thought." Chance was smiling as though he had indeed read Griff's mind. He ducked into the back room.

Griff could still feel Hammer looking at him — the prolonged look that people gave you when they wanted to initiate conversation. He didn't recall Hammer ever being the chatty type. Maybe the bastard was up for reelection. He turned his back and strolled over to the glass case as though inspecting the trays of dark and milk chocolate. He continued to feel the weight of that gaze between his shoulder blades. Why didn't fucking Hammer turn his X-ray vision on the display before him and figure out what he was going to buy Mormor Sorensen for her birthday?

Chance returned with a tiny white box on a pink plate. Griff moved to the counter to examine it, temporarily forgetting Hammer's presence.

"It's perfect," he breathed. The two-inch white boxes were to be filled with dark chocolate hearts then wrapped in lavender or silver ribbon garnished with tiny sprays of autumn berries. "I've never seen anything so lovely."

"So long as you're happy."

"Truly happy." He heard the echo of his own voice and remembered Hammer's cruelly accurate mimicry. He cold-shouldered the recollection. "And they'll be ready — ?"

"Tomorrow afternoon. You can pick them up after the wedding rehearsal."

"Wonderful." Griff meant it. The wedding favors had been the latest in a long series of crises. He would be abjectly grateful when the Dalrymple-Palmers were safely wed and buried. "And the Jordan almond white Rachetti branches for the Stewart-Simpsons?"

"You can pick those up at the same time."

"Thank you so much."

Chance bestowed one of those dazzling smiles. "You're welcome, Griffin."

Griff turned to leave. His eyes met Hammer Sorenson's bright blue ones. Hammer appeared to be studying him intently. Griff gave him a direct, cold look and walked out of the shop.

CHAPTER TWO

Joe Palmer was medium height, slim, dark and handsome as a courtier in a Renaissance painting. He looked exceptionally good in the black Jean Yves Mirage tuxedo. The satin mandarin collar and single-breasted perfectly suited his rather sensitive and romantic looks.

He and Griff had been lovers, off and on, ever since Joe returned from Walden University. Not openly, of course. Joe was still in the closet. His parents were staunch Republicans and social conservatives — so was Joe. He just happened to like guys. As he had often reminded Griff, that didn't automatically make him a bleeding heart liberal.

Joe turned to the left, looking over his shoulder at the bank of mirrors and his elegant reflection. He turned to the right.

"What do you think?" he asked Griff.

"I think you're making a mistake." Griff hadn't meant to say it aloud, as much as he believed the truth of his words. He knew Joe didn't want to hear it. Knew, whatever happened on Saturday, it was over between them. Joe had made that clear.

Joe expelled an irritable breath and ignored him, still examining his reflection.

Griff said wearily, "I think you look great."

Joe grinned at Griff in the mirror. "Not too shabby, eh?"

Griff smiled politely. He could see his reflection behind Joe's. He too was dark, though taller and lankier than Joe. He was not naturally graceful like Joe, but he'd learned the value of good posture. He knew how to sit and stand. He watched himself critically in the mirror background while Joe posed and preened like a peacock. The unpleasant conversation with Madeline Dalrymple, followed by running into Hammer Sorensen, had stirred up a lot of unhappy memories. Griff was relieved to see there was no visible sign of the ugly, awkward boy he had been in the young man sitting still and straight in the fake-leather club chair.

"Mallory called to tell me Maddy had another meltdown," Joe said.

Griff shrugged noncommittally.

"She's going to ruin our wedding if she can."

"I think it's nerves. The dress is really ugly on her."

"Hey, that's her fault. She was supposed to lose weight before the wedding. She had six months."

Six months. Right. Griff had six months warning too. Six months ago Joe had come over for dinner and told him he was engaged to Mallory Dalrymple. Griff hadn't even known Joe was dating Mallory. In fact — as embarrassing as it was to admit now — he had thought things were going really well between himself and Joe. So well that he'd even imagined the day was coming when Joe might feel brave enough to come out of the closet.

"Want to grab a beer?" Joe asked as they left After Eight Formalwear — no good old Guy's Tuxedos for Joe. Griff looked at him in surprise. Joe smiled his get-away-with-murder smile. "What?" He shrugged. "Last splash, bro."

"I can't," Griff said. He was surprised at how calmly the words came out. He was surprised they came out at all.

Joe's eyes narrowed. "You're not still holding a grudge over the bachelor's party thing, are you? I told you, I had nothing to do with that. If Rick had realized we were friends, he would've invited you."

"No. I'm not holding a grudge. I have another wedding rehearsal to get to tonight. In fact..." He checked his wristwatch. "I'm late now."

"Well, maybe later?"

Griff stared at Joe. Joe stared calmly back.

"I don't think so," Griff said.

Joe's face hardened. "Your loss."

○ ○ ○ ○ ○

Jennie Stewart and Bryan Simpson were being married at the Little Brown Chapel on Big Bear Highway. The church was small and quaint and cute. A Valentine's and wedding card sort of church. They did a lively business in baptisms and weddings and funerals.

Griff hadn't known either Jennie or Bryan in school; they were quite a bit younger than him.

Before Mallory and Joe's wedding, Griff had considered weddings like the Stewart-Simpson upscale affairs. But nineteen hundred plus dollars on chocolates had clarified that point. Still, despite Jen and Bryan's relatively restricted budget, it was going to be a lovely, lovely wedding — and he was earning a lovely fee to match.

It was the kind of wedding he was proud of helping to put together. Jennie and Bryan were crazy about each other, and their happiness showed. They were pleasant to work with even when Griff had to talk Jennie out of her plan to release hundreds of butterflies outside the church. Butterflies in November in North Dakota? No way.

"They won't fly in temperatures less than seventy-two degrees," he'd explained.

"Can't we warm them up somehow?"

Visions of microwaved butterflies danced before Griff's eyes. He shook his head. "No."

"Well, what can we release?"

Mallory was having doves released outside the church by special handlers. Griffin forbore to mention this. He was supposed to guard the details of the Dalrymple-Palmer wedding with his life. He considered Jennie's question — and her parent's budget, which they had already exceeded. "Bubbles are fun. We can get little cake design bottles and everyone can blow bubbles outside the church. It's very pretty."

Jennie looked unconvinced.

"Bubbles are fun," Bryan had echoed with a hopeful eye on Jennie's face. It was refreshing to see how much Bryan adored Jennie, how much it mattered to him that her day be perfect.

"Paula and Chris did bubbles." Jennie was trying to be brave, but clearly she was suffering.

"Or balloons," Griff suggested. Yes, Jennie and Bryan were over budget, but Jennie was an only child and the Stewarts had already assured him they wanted their little girl to be happy on her day. "Balloons in the colors of your wedding palette. After you leave the church everyone releases a balloon into the sky. It's very dramatic. Makes for wonderful photos."

Jennie brightened immediately.

Well, sure. Wedding photographs were a vital part of any successful wedding. The photographs provided a visual history, which was useful since few people ever seemed to remember the details of their wedding days. Personally, Griff thought too many weddings suffered for the demands of self-important photographers. But… there was no arguing with it. He usually recommended Bob Tyrone, one of his oldest friends and a real professional, but Bryan's brother was a freelance photographer and he and Jennie had roped him into doing their wedding portraits. And, of course, Mallory had chosen her own hotshot photographer without any advice from Griff. Larry Lee was "documenting" every event leading up to the wedding, from Mallory's wedding shower to the reception.

The Stewart-Simpson photographer was present at the rehearsal, but that was because he was a member of the wedding party. He snapped a few photos, then he put his camera away and the rehearsal went off without a hitch.

Jennie and Bryan invited Griff to the rehearsal dinner, which was sweet, but not necessary. He was attending Joe and Mallory's dinner, too, but that invite had been in the nature of a royal summons. In fact, Mallory's insistence that Griff — like her personal photographer — attend every single event leading up to the wedding was driving him crazy. She acted like a ring of saboteurs were waiting for a chance to blow up her wedding — and that it was Griff's duty to prevent them. He'd blown off her three wedding showers, but there was no way of getting out of the rehearsal dinner.

Generally when Griff was invited to these things, he merely put in a quick appearance, but it had been a stressful day. Maddy's lashing out at him had sliced deeper than he wanted to admit, and the weird coincidence of seeing Hamar again had underscored his dissatisfaction. No, it was worse than dissatisfaction. It was loneliness, and it was more about Joe than anyone or anything else. Needing to postpone his eventual return to an empty, silent house, Griff had a couple of beers and stayed longer at the dinner than he ordinarily would. In fact, he had an unexpectedly good time, and was feeling pleasantly relaxed until he reached home and found Joe waiting for him in his living room.

Joe was stretched out on the couch, shoes off, watching TV. When Griff stopped in the doorway, he snapped off the remote and sat up smiling.

"What are you doing here?" Griff was uncomfortably aware that his heart was thumping in a mixture that was too many parts excitement to parts indignant.

Joe was smiling his naughty little boy smile. The smile that never failed to get under Griff's guard. "I still have my key."

"Joe." He stopped. This was so much harder than it should be. But he'd loved Joe for a long time. He couldn't just turn that off, couldn't just flip a switch. No one could. Still, this was wrong. Wrong on every level. "You should go." He firmed his voice. "And you should leave the key."

Joe rose. He stood there gazing at Griff, giving him plenty of time to change his mind. Griff hung onto his resolution as best he could. Joe's eyes were dark and mournful as they met his own.

"I know you still love me, Griff," Joe said simply. "I love you too. So all you're doing is hurting us both by denying us one last night."

Griff turned away but when Joe took two steps and put his arms around him, turning him, Griff didn't fight. Joe leaned his face against Griff's, and Griff could smell the mingled scent of breath mints and bourbon as Joe murmured, "Come on, Griff, we deserve a chance to say goodbye the right way."

It was strange and bittersweet to make love knowing it was for the last time. Joe was the most passionate he'd been since the very beginning, kissing Griff all over with his hot, hungry mouth while whispering his unique mix of crudities and compliments. Griff closed his eyes against the sting and kissed Joe back.

Afterwards, Joe rose and pulled on his clothes, not looking at Griff. He tucked his shirt in, zipped his trousers, buckled his belt. Still unspeaking he sat on the edge of the mattress and pulled on his socks, rose and stepped into his shoes.

He walked to the door and paused. Without looking around, he said, "I know you don't understand, Griff, but I can't be like you. I care about what people think about me."

"I care what people think."

Joe shook his head. "No you don't. Not really. You never have. Oh, you want them to hire you. You want them to think you do a good job planning their damned weddings. But you don't care if they like you or if they're laughing behind your back. You know who you are, and I guess you're happy with that."

Griff opened his mouth. He shut it again. If Joe really believed that — well, maybe it was better if Joe did believe that. If they all believed that.

CHAPTER THREE

Friday was frantically busy. Griff was on the go from the instant he rolled out of bed, checking the weekend weather report while he drank his coffee and ate his pre-packaged cheese blintzes.

Temperatures... sunny, dry, and cold. Highs of 40F and lows of 17F. Normal for November, in other words.

He showered, shaved, dressed in Lucky Brand straight-legged jeans and a Thomas Dean woven sports shirt in a gray print. Clothes were important to Griff. Having fallen squarely in the geek category growing up, it was a matter of pride to him that he was always perfectly groomed and in style — Updated Traditional, to be exact. It was funny that Joe, who knew him probably better than anyone, honestly thought he didn't care what people thought of him. Oh, he knew folks in Binbell didn't understand him, and never would, but he wanted them to see that he was successful and he wanted always to appear... sophisticated and elegant.

Well, as sophisticated and elegant as a boy who'd never made it out of North Dakota could be. Griff always tried to live as he imagined he would have if his dreams had come true, if he'd won that scholarship to the Fashion Institute of Technology and moved to New York City as he'd planned growing up.

He was on his cell phone before he left the house. The Dalrymple-Palmer dove handlers had concerns about the possibility of high winds, and the florist for the Stewart-Simpsons reported an emergency shortage of the orange Star 2000 roses that formed the focal point of the bride and maid of honor bouquets. Griff talked the birders down and suggested Desert Spice roses as a substitute.

"Or what about those 'Oranges and Lemons'?"

"We'll do our best. Sometimes I miss the old days and plain white roses and ivy. Oh, speaking of which," Shireen of Aristo's Flowers said, "your idea for dried leaves in Mallory Palmer's bouquet was inspired. They're gorgeous."

Nice to know someone noticed. Maybe Griff wasn't smiling when he arrived at Skerry Weddings, but he was feeling much more cheerful than when he'd opened his eyes that morning to see the indentation of Joe's head in the pillow next to his.

Maybe Joe had been right. Maybe they had both needed the opportunity to say goodbye one last time, knowing that it really was goodbye. Sort of like a funeral. Rituals served a purpose. Funerals and weddings and birthdays and lots of other milestone events. So maybe he had needed that goodbye fuck. If so, why did he feel so… empty this morning?

Probably low caffeine levels. And no time to top up before his eleven o'clock meeting with prospective clients at his office. He opened the blinds, turned on the music — Pachelbel's Canon — and squirted lavender mint air freshener around the office. He was turning on his computer when the clients arrived.

He'd been recommended to Dani Mulder and her mother by Mallory. Dani was budgeting for a 30K wedding, which was good news considering the fact that the average price of weddings was down about six thousand dollars. However, he didn't get a good vibe from Dani — she was asking for a lot of discounts and bargains while at the same time dropping brand names as though Crate&Barrel was going out of business. She made it clear she was going to consult other planners before she decided on anything, but Griff's percentage would be a smidge over three thousand, so it was worth smiling pleasantly while Dani continued to rattle on about artisan cakes and engraved wedding invitations.

Dani's mom, Lesli, watched him all the time with her pale green eyes. Something about her narrow stare reminded Griff of Maddy's scathing comments the day before. It had been a long time since he'd fretted over what people might think about him — a long time since there had been anyone in his life besides Joe whose opinion really mattered to him. He disliked this feeling of being on defense.

He was glad when the meeting was over and Dani and her mom sauntered off in their mother-daughter Rock and Republic skinny jeans. Griff jotted a question mark beside Dani's name in his day planner, jumped back into his VW and proceeded to Marguerite's Bakery, which was handling both of his wedding cakes.

Mercifully, at Marguerite's, everything was running smoothly on schedule. The Stewart-Simpsons were serving an assortment of mini wedding cakes, which made for lovely, cost-saving table décor as well as delicious desserts in a variety of flavors. The individually iced and decorated cakes were pricey, but since the Stewart-Simpson reception had a relatively contained guest list, it worked with their budget.

The Dalrymple-Palmers were naturally going in a completely different direction. The four layer white cake was frosted in Wedgwood blue fondant and dusted with tiny white gum paste flowers and pearls.

"It works out to about nine-fifty a slice," Marguerite remarked as they studied the masterpiece.

"Money is no object."

"Must be nice." They exchanged smiles. Marguerite had been happily married for twenty-nine years.

After verifying that the wedding cakes were on track for delivery, Griff jumped back in the car to see how the reception venues were coming along.

The Stewart-Simpson wedding was being held at eleven in the morning with reception immediately following at Binbell's largest hotel. The Dalrymple-Palmers were saying their vows at five-thirty in the afternoon with a formal reception following two hours later at the country club in the neighboring town. It was going to be an incredibly challenging — and stressful — day for Griff trying to stage manage two large weddings. He'd done it once before, but both weddings had been relatively small events.

Still, he felt calm, even confident. This was what he did and he was good at it. And the busier he was, the less time he had to think about the fact that Joe was marrying Mallory. For better or for worse.

At the Binbell Majestic the banquet room was still in use for a business seminar. The event staff was in a holding pattern, waiting for the signal to move.

"The client is supplying special pale yellow tablecloths," Griff reminded Krysta, the Majestic's special event coordinator. "So don't use the ivory ones, and definitely not the white."

"Check."

"The florist will make the drop at eleven — right after they finish at the church."

"Check."

"But the main centerpiece for each table will be the mini wedding cakes."

Krysta made a note on her clipboard. "Got it."

"Those will be delivered between ten and eleven."

"Check."

Griff had been working with Krysta for five years now. The Majestic was a very popular choice for wedding receptions. He suddenly wondered what she thought of him. She was always friendly and professional, but maybe she thought he was a pain in the ass. Maybe she groaned every time he called. Maybe she thought he was a joke too.

He realized that she was waiting for him. "I guess that's it," he said.

Krysta smiled. "It's going to be a beautiful reception. All your weddings are lovely, Griff."

After finishing at the Majestic, Griff grabbed lunch while he looked over his day planner and checked his messages. There were three calls from Mallory. He listened to them while he ate his gyro and stared out the window of Santa Lucia's at the wind-scoured dun hills.

It really was a very long way from New York.

He felt almost light-headed when he remembered the things he and Joe had done the night before. Absurdly, it had been the best it had ever been, maybe because they both accepted it was goodbye. And Joe had, for once, been affectionate. Even loving. After he'd left, after the sound of his car driving away had faded into silence, Griff had lain there dry-eyed and still. It had hurt too much to cry. At that instant he had realized that he was never going to have what most people had. He was never going to marry. No wedding for him. And all those silly, secret fantasies of what he'd like someday...

No one to come home to, no one to share the good times and the bad, no one to care for him in sickness and in health, no one to love, cherish, honor, no one to worship with his body...

Better to accept it right now.

He'd felt quite calm when he finally drifted to sleep. Stoic. He felt less stoic listening to Mallory's raspy voice on his voicemail saying, "Griff, can you please double — no, triple check that all the guys pick their tuxedos up tonight?"

He sighed. He'd have done that without being asked. He knew firsthand Joe's pals weren't the most reliable guys on the planet.

Next message. "Griff, I'm starting to have serious doubts about the crabmeat stuffed prawns. I really think we should have gone with the filet of salmon."

"You gotta be kidding me," he muttered, checking the next message.

"Griff, you have to get Maddy under control. She is going to ruin our wedding!"

Our wedding. Right. And how the hell was he supposed to control Maddy if her nearest and dearest couldn't?

Appetite gone, he finished his lunch, got back in his car and started the long drive to the next town and the Indian Hills Country Club.

The folks at Indian Hills had everything under control. The banquet room was already set up with pristine linens, shining flatware, and gleaming china. Hurricane lanterns of various sizes were positioned on the tables. All that was missing was the garden of flowers that were due to be delivered tomorrow afternoon.

Griff signed off on the arrangements and reaffirmed the final details for the open bar, the butler service hors d'oeuvres during the cocktail hour, the red and white wine for the tables, the champagne for the toast, the valet parking — and taxi service for those too drunk to drive home.

○ ○ ○ ○ ○

"Now the minister is very insistent that we always..."

Griff nodded politely to Mrs. Culpepper, the church's own wedding planner. She was a plump, middle-aged woman who smiled too much and clearly felt hiring an outsider was a slur on her abilities. She made her wishes known in the form of the-minister-always-insists.

When he'd let Mrs. Culpepper set him straight on the way it was all done back in the day, he excused himself and went outside to see if any of the wedding party had arrived yet. A tall lean man with weary, weathered good looks was fiddling with a camera. Griff guessed that this was the big city photographer, Larry Lee.

"We haven't met. I'm Griffin Skerry. The wedding planner."

"Larry Lee. I'm the photographer." They shook hands.

"We haven't worked together before. Are you based locally?"

Larry smiled at the idea. "No." He added, "I'm an old friend of the family."

Griff was curious as to what Larry Lee was charging his old friends, but he couldn't think of how to ask.

"Do you do a lot of weddings?"

Larry Lee shrugged. "A few. Not my favorite thing. It's a lot of work for the money. Especially nowadays."

"Love in the time of recession."

Larry Lee laughed. "That's about the size of it. I mostly do landscapes and freelance work. Calendars, greeting cards, that kind of thing. I've made a name for myself, but it's not a big name."

"I guess it's like any art. You do it mostly for the love of it."

Larry Lee smiled, but whatever reply he might have made was lost to Griff because Joe and Mallory pulled into the parking lot in Mallory's BMW Z4.

Griff put on his game face and went to meet them — narrowly avoiding being run over by Madeline, who screeched into the lot, stereo blasting.

Madeline parked next to Mallory's car and the two sisters got out and promptly began a low-voiced argument. It was cut short by the arrival, one car after another, of the rest of the wedding party. Mallory smiled graciously for the procession of cars. Madeline lit a cigarette and stalked into the church.

○ ○ ○ ○ ○

The rehearsal went smoothly enough — documented by Larry Lee's high-powered 35mm Nikon. It was not the light-hearted event the rehearsal for the Stewart-Simpsons had been, but there were no problems. Griff anticipated that the wedding would run as smoothly as a military operation, but that was as much due to Dilys's field marshal skills as his own abilities.

When the rehearsal was over, they all headed over to the Majestic for dinner. Joe's parents were paying for the meal, and Joe had handled the arrangement without consulting Griff. That had been during the phase when he had been adamantly against Griff taking the job of wedding planner. Griff hadn't been over the moon about it either, but as he'd tried to explain, what possible reason could he give for refusing? Besides, a wedding like this was a professional coup. And last, but hardly least, he needed the money.

The meal was traditional fare — steak and potatoes — uninspired but sure to please the majority of guests. Griff found himself seated with a couple of ushers, college friends of Joe's, who ignored him after the first few polite comments. That was fine by Griff, he planned on getting away as soon as possible. The last thing he needed was to sit there watching from across the room while Joe fawned over Mallory, smiling and nuzzling the back of her neck.

He ordered a cosmopolitan, to the barely concealed amusement of his table companions, and tuned out the discussions of football and hunting deer and swans. His gaze wandered with his attention. He could see Larry Lee and Dilys, Mallory's mother, in deep conversation. Dilys had that ferocious smile that always reminded Griff of a friendly mink; he didn't envy Joe having Dilys Dalrymple as a mother-in-law. , he didn't envy Joe anything.

He thought again about Joe's comment that he didn't care what people thought. Joe meant it as a criticism, but wasn't it the opposite? Wasn't it a sign of maturity to stop caring so much about what other people thought? Not that Griff didn't care about his professional reputation, but he counted a victory that he'd stopped letting the opinions of people he despised influence his choices and actions.

He thought of Hammer Sorensen again — and a nearly forgotten memory returned to him. It was years past now. He'd pulled open the glass door to the bank for a guy on crutches, and the guy had looked up — and it was Hammer Sorensen. Hammer's bright blue eyes in a face that looked older and lined with pain. It was after he'd broken his leg in college — putting an end to his dreams of a career in professional football.

How strange that Griff had all but forgotten that. He remembered the shock of that moment, and he remembered the chaotic mix of his own emotions: pity but also a bitter satisfaction that Hamar's arrogance and ambition had come to nothing — and sickness with himself that he should be glad of such a thing.

He had been unable to find words, staring as he held the door.

And Hammer had stared back with those hard blue eyes and nodded curtly as he hobbled past.

"You're being summoned," the guy on his left said, snapping Griff out of his disturbing reflections.

Griff looked up and Mallory was now sitting next to her mother in the chair Larry Lee had vacated. She was beckoning impatiently to Griff. He rose and went to join them.

Dilys said quite coolly, as though she was simply making conversation, "I'm having serious doubts as to whether you are entitled to your entire fee, Mr. Skerry. Or any fee at all, frankly."

"I'm sorry?" She didn't appear to be kidding. He looked bewilderedly at Mallory.

"Do you know what she did?" Mallory demanded in answer to that look.

"Who?" He looked back at Dilys. She had resumed eating her shrimp cocktail, still eying him with that unwavering dark stare. Her neat white teeth sank into the plump gray flesh of the prawn and tore it in half. She looked like something from the X-Files. , she looked a lot like Mallory.

He swallowed down rising nausea.

"My pathological lunatic sister," Mallory said impatiently. "Do you know what she's done now?"

Griff shook his head. He scanned the tables and spotted Maddy, already well on her way to being shit-faced. It seemed pretty much business as usual.

"She got a tattoo," Mallory informed him. "Right here." She gestured to the top of her own slender shoulder. "A butterfly. A big, fat blue and yellow butterfly."

"Oh."

Dilys swallowed a lump of shellfish and said, "Not easy to disguise."

"No." He was already mentally reviewing the options: body makeup, some kind of stole or mini shawl... lace wouldn't work with the dress but some kind of chiffon... not too sheer...

"I told you she was going to pull something like this. I told you you'd need to deal with her."

Griff stared at Mallory in disbelief. He heard himself say the words he had sworn he would never say to any client no matter how challenging. "That's not my job. Controlling your sister is not my job."

"Your job was whatever I needed done, and I needed you to keep Maddy in line. I warned you how many times — "

She broke off as her mother suddenly rose.

"Excuse..." Dilys turned away — lurched away, really. Griff wondered how much she'd had to drink. He and Maddy watched her fumbling her way through the closely positioned tables as she made her way toward the restrooms.

Frowning, Mallory pushed her chair from the table and rose. "Don't bother showing up tomorrow," she told Griff. "We'll take it from here."

"You'll take it from — " He knew his jaw was hanging open; he couldn't help it. He'd met a few prize-winning clients in his time, but the Dalrymples deserved their own special award. "I've literally put in four times the man hours on this wedding that I normally do. I damn well plan on getting paid for it."

"Prepare to be disappointed."

"Prepare to have your ass sued."

Mallory smiled, unimpressed. "I'm not Joe. Don't fuck with me, Griffin. You'll never know what hit you."

CHAPTER FOUR

"Everything is ready to go," Chance said. "Are you sure you have room in that little car of yours?"

"Sure." Griff absently sized up the stack of cardboard boxes. "I've done this a million times."

Would he still be doing it once Mallory and Dilys Dalrymple finished bad-mouthing him to all their ritzy friends? Griff knew only too well how this kind of thing worked. The truth was pretty much irrelevant once the gossip mill built up steam and the blacklisting began. He remembered very clearly how it had worked in high school.

And what had been the deal with Dilys? If she was sick, sure as hell they were going to claim food poisoning, and even though Griff had absolutely nothing to do with the rehearsal dinner, somehow the rumor would be that he had organized the entire thing. In fact, he'd be lucky if in the final version of the story he wasn't cooking the meal.

"Something wrong?" Chance asked.

Griff realized he'd been standing there staring at the boxes.

"No," he said. Chance smiled. Was he really that bad a liar? "Client trouble."

Chance raised his expressive eyebrows. Something about that sparkling, knowledgeable gaze led Griff to say, "The Dalrymples aren't happy with me." He heard it with disbelief. He had very strong feelings about criticizing clients with other vendors.

"Do you think they're ever happy with anything?"

Griff considered this. "I don't know." He wondered how the hell Joe would survive with those piranhas. But Joe had climbed into the fish tank voluntarily. He had to remember that.

"I doubt it," Chance replied. "Anyway, I wouldn't worry about it."

Easy for Chance to say. No one would dare criticize him or his wonderful chocolates.

His wonderful chocolates. An idea occurred to Griff. A possible bargaining chip. He picked up the tower of boxes. "You're probably right. Good night."

"Good night."

○ ○ ○ ○ ○

When Griffin pulled up in front of his house the porch light was shining in welcome, and there was a police car parked out front, blue and red lights flashing in the crisp, cold night.

As he parked in the driveway, the cops — two uniformed sheriff deputies — got out of their SUV and walked across to meet him, boots crunching on the dead leaves.

"Griffin Skerry?"

Griffin froze. "Yes?"

"Please come with us."

"Why?" His heart pounded in alarm. Cops waiting on your doorstep. Never a good thing.

"Sheriff Sorensen wants to speak to you."

"About what?"

"Sheriff will explain."

Griff stared at their wooden expressions. To his immense relief, they did not put him in handcuffs, but his legs were shaking as he followed them to the police car, climbed in the back. At least he did not appear to be under arrest, and that was one for the plus column. He sat stricken and wordless as the car cruised along the silent streets, the streetlamps throwing crossbars across the road, the chatter on the police radio filling the silence.

His heart was racing like a locomotive. What could this be about? It had to be bad, very bad, for the sheriff's department to roust him out of bed — well, he should have been in bed — this time of night. He remembered the terrible night, not long after he'd graduated from high school, when the then-Sheriff had come to inform him his mother had died in a car crash. He was almost relieved he had no one to lose now.

"Is it something to do with the shop?" he asked the back of their heads. A break-in? A fire? Vandalism? But surely they would tell him if that was the case?

Neither man looked around. "Sheriff will explain," one of them said.

The Sheriff. That meant Hammer Sorensen. Griff's heart thumped harder in alarm. Hamar. His oldest enemy. His oldest friend, for that matter. Former friend. This was bound to be a horrendous meeting. What had Mallory done? Accused him of something? Like what? He couldn't think of anything that would warrant calling out the sheriffs. What if Dilys had been suffering from food poisoning? What if they were blaming him? It was crazy, but something was certainly going on. But Joe would speak up in that case. No way would Joe let Griff be arrested for ... well, whatever this was.

Had they figured out what he planned to do with the wedding favors?

Round and round Griff's thoughts chased. Then they were at the sheriff station and Griff was being escorted through the harshly lit hall and bustling main office to a smaller office with glass walls, the blinds closed tight. Hammer Sorenson was sitting behind a desk. He was on the phone when Griff was escorted into his office. He nodded at the deputy, nodded for Griff to take a chair, and listened to whoever was on the other end of the phone.

Griffin looked at Hammer and looked away. Somehow looking at Hammer hurt his eyes. It was like staring into the sun. Uneasily, he glanced about the office. It looked like pretty much any office. Bookshelves, filing cabinets, bulletin board full of information that would only make sense to the owner of the bulletin board. On the wall were a couple of framed photographs of running football players — Hammer during his brief college career, Griff guessed. Maybe that dream hadn't panned out, but Hammer was still doing well for himself. He was the youngest Sheriff the town had ever had, and he seemed fairly popular in what was an unpopular job.

"Call me when you know for sure." Hammer put the phone down and gazed across at Griff. He was not smiling, but that was no surprise.

"Hello, Griffin. It's been a while."

"Why am I here?" Griffin burst out.

"I want to ask you a few questions."

"About what?"

Hammer said calmly, "This is the way it works. I ask questions and you answer them. And when I'm finished, if you have questions, maybe I'll answer them in return. Get it?"

"Got it."

"Good. I understand you had a run-in with Mallory Dalrymple this evening."

Griff drew a sharp breath. It was exactly as he'd guessed. Mallory was making good on her threat by means of a preemptive strike against him.

"It wasn't much of a run-in. She's threatening not to pay my fee for planning her wedding."

"And that upset you, I guess?"

"Of course it upset me. It's my livelihood!"

"Lower your voice."

Hammer didn't say it in a threatening way, but Griff could imagine how quickly that even tone could turn harsh, berating. He folded his arms. It seemed cold in the office, but maybe that was his incipient nervous collapse.

"So you were angry with Mallory. And you decided to get back at her."

Oh God. It was the wedding favors. They were accusing him of theft. In fact, nineteen hundred dollars was probably grand theft or something with serious jail time attached.

"It wasn't like that," he pleaded. "I was only taking out some insurance. They were trying to stiff me. My fee is worth a lot more than nineteen hundred dollars."

Hammer's eyes flickered with somber emotion. Disappointment? Disillusion? He asked flatly, "What insurance?"

"The wedding favors." Didn't he know? He had to know. "I do have them. They were in my car."

In the pause that followed his words he could hear the hum of voices in the main office. It seemed very late for a small town sheriff department to be so busy, but it was Friday night. Perhaps there were a lot of drunk driving arrests.

Hammer said finally, politely, "I'm sorry?"

"I was going to hold them until Dilys forked over what she owes me — my contracted fee. I'm within my rights. I have a contract. I was going to call Dilys in the morning and tell her that I needed my check in order to deliver the favors to Indian Hills. If it wasn't for the fact that the Dalrymples are the richest people in town, you wouldn't be hassling me about this. You'd be going after them."

Well, maybe not. Hammer was looking at him like he thought Griff was out of his mind. At last he asked with what sounded like unwilling curiosity, "Why were they threatening not to pay your fee?"

"They blame me because Maddy went out and got a tattoo."

"Maddy..."

"On her shoulder. I didn't see it. I just heard about it, but it will show. The bodice of the dress comes to here." Griff drew a line across his chest.

Hammer covered his mouth with his hand. His blond eyebrows rose politely.

"I would've found a way to conceal it, but they fired me this evening, so it's their problem now. I only want to be paid for all the work I did."

Hammer nodded thoughtfully. He removed his hand from his mouth. "Tell me about the dinner tonight."

"It's exactly what I told you." An unpleasant inkling popped into Griffin's mind. "I didn't have anything to do with the dinner. That was outside the scope of my responsibilities. The groom's family ho — "

"That's not what I asked."

It was food poisoning. Why else would he keep hammering on the dinner? Griff swallowed hard. He said, hoping his voice sounded steadier than it felt, "Has something happened?"

"Like what?"

"Like did someone get… food poisoning?"

Hammer's face hardened into forbidding lines. "Why do you ask?" Now Griff knew not to trust the evenness of his tone. Hammer was angry.

"Because when I was sitting talking to Mallory and Dilys, Dilys had to excuse herself from the table. I thought maybe she was ill."

Instead of picking up from there, Hammer asked bluntly, "What's your relationship to Joe Palmer?"

Heat rose slowly, remorselessly, through Griffin's body. He felt his face turning red hot, felt his body shaking with a mixture of humiliation and rage. It was Mrs. Dodge's biology class all over again.

He ground out, "Why?"

"Are you having a sexual relationship with Joe Palmer?"

"How would that be any of your business?"

"Are you?"

He said with a defiance he didn't feel, "You'd have to ask Joe Palmer."

"Joe Palmer says you are. Or, rather, you were."

"Wh-wh-what?" stammered Griff. "Joe said that?"

"That's right. What do you say?"

"I don't know why he'd say that. Why won't you tell me what's going on? What's happened?"

"Dilys Dalrymple is dead."

"Dead?" He knew Hammer was watching him for his reaction, but he didn't have to fake the shock and horror. "From food poisoning?"

"We don't think it was food poisoning," Hammer said pleasantly. "We think it was good old-fashioned poison poisoning."

Distantly, Griff was aware that Hammer had set a cup of coffee in front of him. He did not remember Hammer leaving his desk, but he must have because he was sitting down in the big chair again, the leather creaking beneath his lean weight. He picked up his own cup of coffee and sipped noisily.

"You want to rethink your statement?" he inquired.

Griff shook his head. He reached for his coffee, grateful for the warmth of the liquid. It wasn't a caramel macchiato, but it wasn't instant either. "I told you the truth. I told you everything. Are you sure Dilys didn't die of food poisoning? People do die of it sometimes."

"They usually don't instantly die of it."

"Oh." Probably not.

With a sort of harassed impatience, Hammer said, "We think the poison was introduced via her shrimp cocktail. But that's a guess at this stage. It's what she was eating when she was stricken."

"But why would everyone think I had anything to do with it?" Griff was both angry and indignant.

"Well, let's see," Hammer said with irony. "You were arguing with the victim a few minutes prior to her collapse, and you're the only person in the room who didn't eat his shrimp cocktail."

"I'm allergic to shellfish."

"Since when?"

Their gazes tangled and tore away. "I don't know," Griff said. "Since high school, I guess."

"Either way, you're everyone's favorite suspect."

"Me?" Griff repeated slowly. He remembered Hammer saying Joe had admitted he and Griff were lovers. Joe had accused him of murder. He couldn't seem to think beyond it. When he thought he had his face under control, he looked at Hammer again.

Hammer was sipping his coffee and staring out the window at the starry night. He looked calm and thoughtful.

Griff cleared his throat. "I guess I better call a lawyer?"

"Why's that?"

"If I'm under arrest for murder — "

"Have I arrested you?"

"Well …"

Hammer sighed. "Unless you've changed a lot over the years, I don't think you murdered anyone."

"I have changed a lot."

"Haven't we all. But I don't think you've changed that much."

"Then why am I here?"

"Because three people have accused you of murder — and I find that very interesting."

"Who?"

"Mallory Dalrymple, Madeline Dalrymple, and Joe Palmer."

Griff's hand was shaking. He put his coffee cup down. "Joe accused me of murder?"

Hammer nodded. He glanced at Griff and looked out the window again, for which Griff was grateful.

He heard himself ask, "How was Mormor Sorenson's birthday party?"

Hammer's gaze returned to his, softened. "It was great. You should have stopped by. She would have loved to see you. They ask about you now and then, momma and Mormor, when they start reminiscing about the old days."

"What do you tell them?"

"That you hold a grudge."

Griff snapped to attention, spilling his coffee. "How fucking dare you." His voice wavered and broke.

Hammer's blue eyes met his. "Come on, Griffin. I recognized you yesterday, and I know you recognized me. Is there some reason we can't act like grownups? High school was a long time ago."

Griff stood up. "If I'm not under arrest and you don't suspect me of murder, can I go?"

Hammer said wearily, "Yeah, you can go. I'll drive you. I have to get back to the crime scene. You still living in the old neighborhood?"

The last thing Griff wanted was to get into a car with Hammer and spend the next eleven minutes trying to make conversation — or worse, avoid making conversation — but what choice did he have?

"Yes."

He waited in silence as Hammer rose, shrugged on his jacket, and led the way out of the office. Griff paid no attention to the officers Hammer spoke to or the instructions he gave. He felt numb. Detached.

At last Hammer nodded to him and they went out the brightly lit entrance into the cold November night.

CHAPTER FIVE

"I don't see why anyone would kill Dilys." Griff finally, broke the silence. What did it mean when murder was the most neutral subject you could find to talk about?

"Loved by everyone, was she?"

"No, but the idea of killing her is … crazy."

"So who in that bunch is crazy?"

Griffin was shaking his head.

"Okay, tell me about Palmer."

"Joe?" he asked warily, "Why?"

"How long has Mallory known about you and Joe?"

"I didn't think she did know. I'm sure Joe didn't think she knew. But before I left the Majestic, Mallory said something to make me think — " Griff swallowed hard, "that she did."

"When was the last time you and Joe were together?"

Griff's voice was almost inaudible. "Last night."

Hammer said nothing — had no right to say or think anything — but Griffin sensed disapproval. Or maybe he was projecting. He wasn't proud of what he'd done with Joe. He'd told himself he needed the closure, but he wasn't happy about sleeping with Joe on the eve of his wedding. It had provided closure in an unforeseen way — he had lost all respect for Joe as well as himself. It had been the end.

"According to Mallory, she's suspected for some time that you were trying to seduce Joe."

Griffin couldn't help it. He started to laugh. He knew it was the reaction of overstrained nerves, and that he sounded like he was losing it, but he couldn't help it.

"All right, all right," Hammer said gruffly. "I know. Pull yourself together."

Griff stared at his profile. "You know? You don't know. You probably think the same thing. That it's possible to turn someone gay by association or by harassing them long enough."

"Don't be an ass," Hammer muttered.

"What does Joe say?"

"Palmer says you've been seeing each other off and on — mostly off — for the past five years. He said he experienced confusion over his sexual identity in college, and that's why he allowed the friendship with you to progress even though he knew you took it too seriously."

"That's bullshit. I tried to break it off with him a couple of times and he always ..." His voice shook. He stopped. Tried again with a pretense at calm, "Joe is a coward. He's always been a coward. He's afraid Mallory will dump him now. Or maybe he's afraid he'll come under suspicion." He added bitterly, "And what the hell does any of this have to do with Dilys's death?"

"Nothing." Hammer looked briefly from the road to meet Griff's eyes. "I thought you ought to know. I guess you already do."

Astonished, Griff held his silence. He was surprised to find his face warm, his pulse tingling.

"Maybe the poison wasn't intended for Dilys," he said at random. "Did you ever think of that?"

"Well, if it had been Mallory who died, you would have been the number one suspect."

Griff shook his head. "No. Mallory dying wouldn't have changed anything. Not now."

Neither of them spoke again as the SUV turned down quiet streets and sleeping neighborhoods until they reached Griff's block. Hammer parked in the driveway behind Griff's VW.

"Is that where the hostage chocolate is?"

Griff nodded.

Hammer made a sound that might have been a laugh — or a snort. He turned off the car engine, staring out the windshield.

"Hasn't changed a bit, has it?" He was looking at the house next door to Griff's. The house where he had lived growing up. The Sorensens had moved about the time Griff and Hamar started high school.

Griff lifted a shoulder. "Thanks for the ride."

"Can I come in?"

"What? Why?" Griff's heart, which had been feeling lifeless as lead as he contemplated the full extent of Joe's betrayal, jumped into action. Fight or flight response.

"I'd like to ... talk to you. Off the record."

"All right." Griff could hear the reluctance in his voice. Knew that Hammer could hear it too. But what did he expect?

He got out of the SUV, not waiting for Hammer, but knowing he was right behind him anyway. He unlocked his front door, stepped inside and turned on the lights.

Hammer stared around the living room. "Jesus. Well, this has sure changed."

The small living room with all its fussy details and moldings had been painted white — even the hardwood floor. Griff had tossed out the old furniture he'd grown up with and replaced it, carefully chosen piece by piece, with wonderful objects: austere wrought iron lamps, fat comfortable chairs the color of sunshine, a gilt wheat-sheaf coffee table.

He felt a flicker of pride as he saw the room through Hammer's eyes. Yes, this had changed. Over the years he had renovated and redecorated every room in this house and it looked — even though he was biased — every bit as lovely as anything in *Elegant Homes* or *Better Homes and Gardens*. In the summer he planned to start redesigning the garden.

This old house was more than his home, it was his haven. He rarely got a chance to show it off. And no one was in better position to appreciate how much he'd achieved than Hamar.

"Did you want coffee or something?" He watched Hammer still gazing about himself.

Hammer's eyes refocused on him. "No, thanks. I want to talk to you."

"More questions?"

Hammer shook his head. All at once he looked grim.

"About what?"

"About... us. About how we used to be friends and then we weren't."

Griff folded his arms defensively across his chest. "What is it you think you could tell me that I don't know?"

"Why I was such a shit when we had been best friends for so long."

"I know why."

Knowing didn't change anything. Didn't change the facts, didn't change the hurt. He and Hamar had lived next door to each other from the time they were small kids. Hamar was part of his earliest memories. Their mothers were best friends and shared their first and only pregnancies. Their offspring had shared playpens and sandboxes. They had slept next to each other in kindergarten and shared lunchboxes in elementary school. In junior high, which had been hard on geeky little Griffin Skerry, Hamar had been his self-appointed protector. And in high school Hamar had become "Hammer" — and Griffin's worst nightmare.

"It wasn't all the things you must have thought."

"You mean like I was a nerd and you were a jock?"

"I mean, because you told me that summer you were gay."

The laughter died out of Griff. "I know. I know it didn't have anything to do with *me* being gay. I finally figured it out a few years later, but if you think I'm going to sit here patiently while you come out to me, sorry. Save it for someone who gives a damn."

Hammer stared for what seemed like a long time. He shrugged. "Okay. I thought I owed you that."

Now that was funny. Griffin spluttered a tired laugh and led the way to the front door.

CHAPTER SIX

The phone startled Griff out of a confused dream in which Joe and Hammer were arguing about where the water feature in Griff's backyard should go.

He sat up, took the princess phone off its hook and croaked, "Hello?"

Hammer Sorensen said, "The poison used to kill Dilys Dalrymple was cadmium."

"The color?" He thought in alarm of the bright cadmium yellow walls of this very bedroom. Surely Hammer wasn't going to try and make some weird connection

—

"The chemical compound. It's very toxic. It can be ingested or inhaled. It's not water soluble, but it does dissolve in acid foods such as fruit juice and vinegar — or tomato juice."

"So it was the shrimp cocktail?"

"Yep. The shrimp cocktail was loaded with it. More than an ounce was dumped into Dilys's goblet. And she was a very slender woman and a heavy smoker, which aggravates the effects of the poison."

"It's not anything that could fall in her goblet accidentally?"

"No way. However it was introduced, it wasn't by mistake."

Griffin cast his mind back to the yesterday evening. To the seating arrangements at the dinner. Maddy had been sitting next to her mother, but had changed her seat almost immediately. Anyway, Maddy might have issues, but she wasn't psychotic. Besides, she'd surely have a better opportunity than a crowded dinner. Ditto for Mallory. She'd been sitting next to Dilys when Griff had sat down to speak to them, but she was merely lighting as she made her rounds of the room and the tables. Her own seat had been next to Joe and her maid of honor.

Hammer had told him he was off the hook, but had he now changed his mind? Griff asked worriedly, "How fast does this poison work?"

"If ingested? Very fast. It causes almost immediate nausea among other things. It's hard to kill someone through ingestion because the victim's body rejects it so fast, but like I said, it was a massive dose and her smoking complicated things."

"What is cadmium? Where does it come from?"

"It's a chemical compound used in dental cement, glazes, paints, insecticides, and photography."

"Photography."

"You got it."

The memory snapped into Griff's brain. Larry Lee sitting next to Dilys while they spoke quietly, intensely — all but oblivious of those around them. "Oh, my God," he gulped. "It's Larry Lee. The photographer. It has to be."

Oh thank God, thank God the Dalrymples had hired their own photographer.

Hammer replied cheerfully, "Yep. It sure is."

"He confessed?" Maybe it was as easy as TV. It all certainly felt as unreal as TV.

Hammer chuckled. "No. No, we've got a ways to go to prove our case, but we've got our man. And we think we've got our motive."

Griff peered at the brass alarm clock on his night table. Four-thirty in the morning. Hammer and his small town police force must have worked all night.

"But why? Why would he do such a thing?"

"Turns out when Dilys Dalrymple was Madeline's age, she ran off to Mexico and got married to one Lawrence Lee. And she never got divorced. Or changed her original will."

"Yes, but…"

"Yeah. But all criminals are not geniuses. In our conversations with Larry Lee last night he asked a bunch of questions about probate and codicils. He figured he was being pretty slick talking to a bunch of hick cops, but those questions started me thinking. It didn't take much digging to find what I was looking for."

"Wait a minute. He killed Dilys to inherit the money she inherited from her second husband — before she got around to changing her will?"

"That's what I think happened."

"But if Dilys was still married when she married Hank Dalrymple, her marriage wasn't valid."

"Right." He could hear the amusement in Hammer's voice.

"So she probably didn't legally inherit. The money probably should have gone straight to her kids or something?"

"You got it." Hammer was openly laughing, a deep sound that sent a shiver down Griff's back. "That's why it's going to take a little work to corner him. He thinks he had a motive, even though we know he didn't."

Griff reclined back against the bank of pillows. He wondered why Hammer was calling him with this news. He said cautiously, "So it's over? I'm totally… off the hook?"

"You're off the hook."

He considered this quietly. "Thank you for telling me."

"Yeah. Well…"

That about summed it up. Griff waited to see if there was more. Did he want there to be more? It occurred to him that Joe would not be getting married in a few hours after all. Dilys's death was bound to mean a postponement. Maybe a long one. Maybe so long Joe and Mallory would never get married. Once that would have meant something to him.

"Griff?"

He made an inquiring sound.

"See you around," Hammer said finally.

After a beat, Griff said, "See you."

○ ○ ○ ○ ○

February was not a good month for weddings.

Flower prices were always at a premium and most brides were smart enough to know that if they arranged to have an anniversary in February they were bound to be stinted on Valentine's Day. But there was always at least one happy couple in Binbell who simply couldn't wait for spring. The Martinez-Robinsons were that year's couple, and Griff was checking up on the wedding reception favors.

The Martinez-Robinsons were opting for white chocolate lollipops tied with yellow silk ribbons. Connie's Confections was doing a nice job, but it wasn't anything like what Chance would have done at Sweets to the Sweet.

Griff could almost taste the cool satiny creaminess of Chance's white chocolate as he stood there gazing at the dark windows and the FOR RENT sign of the empty shop between Nina's Café and Buckner's Books.

"When did he close the place?" a familiar voice asked.

Griff turned and was surprised at the flash of pleasure he felt at the sight of Hammer Sorenson standing on the salt-crusted pavement behind him. The lights from the other shop windows turned the sidewalk amber, and Hammer's skin and hair gold.

Griff shook his head. "I don't know. Chance never mentioned he was closing. One day he was… gone. No one seems to know anything about it."

"That's too bad. That chocolate was addictive. And I don't even like chocolate."

"I do," Griff said wistfully. He glanced at Hammer again, racked his brain for a neutral topic of conversation. "I heard you finally arrested Larry Lee for Dilys Dalrymple's murder."

Hammer assented.

"That was good work."

"I think so." Hammer spoke with a hint of his old arrogance. He asked after a pause, "Did you ever get paid for the wedding?"

Griff shook his head. "No. Mallory felt that since she and Joe ended up getting married by a justice of the peace, she didn't owe me anything."

Hammer grunted. "What did you end up doing with all those wedding favors?"

"Ate them. Froze them. Gave them to people for Christmas."

Hammer laughed. Griff laughed too.

They both turned back to the empty rental space. Any second now Hammer was going to say goodnight and head back to his office — or home to dinner. Griff was unsettled to realize how much he didn't want that to happen. He tried to think of something to talk about.

Almost as though he read Griff's thoughts, Hammer said abruptly, "I know it's late for asking, but did you have plans for tonight?"

Griff stared, mildly affronted. "Do you know what today is?"

"Sure. Valentine's Day."

"What makes you think I don't have plans?"

Hammer's smile seemed askew. "I figured you probably did have plans, which is why I didn't ask sooner."

"Oh, I see. So if I hadn't happened to be standing here — "

"Well, now that's a funny thing," Hammer interrupted. "As it happens, I was looking for you. I have something of yours. I just had a feeling you'd be here."

"What do you have of mine?" If Griff had left something in the sheriff station, he hadn't missed it in all these months.

Hammer reached into his pocket and pulled out a small piece of paper. "Mormor was going through her things a few days ago and found this." He handed it to Griff. Griff stared down at the small faded heart-shaped paper. Glitter floated gently down. A little boy Viking was shyly proffering a heart with the words "Will You B Mine?"

He turned it over. A childish hand had scrawled XOXOXO Griffin.

"I looked but I didn't see an expiration date on this," Hammer said.

Griffin continued to stare down at the dog-eared paper. He felt his mouth tugging into a smile. You just didn't expect to see a Viking wearing that much glitter; probably all the other little Vikings gave him a hard time.

He looked up at Hammer — was surprised at how serious he looked as he waited for Griff's answer.

Casually, Griff said, "Let's talk about it over dinner."

SORT OF STRANGER THAN FICTION

We used to take a lot of long drives when I was a kid, and as we'd pass those little population-one-thousand towns off the freeway I used to wonder what it would be like growing up in a place like that. Even today some people spend their whole lives in the same place with a lot of the same people. I think there might some comfort to that — assuming you like those people.

Ethan has spent his entire life in Peabody, California, but until Michael Milner opens up a martial arts studio next door to Red Bird Books and Coffee it never occurred to him the greatest adventure might be in his own backyard.

His name was Michael.

Not Mike. Not Mikey. Certainly not Micky.

Michael.

Like the archangel.

Michael Milner of Milner's Martial Arts. Two doors down from Red Bird Books and Coffee in the self-consciously rustic Viento Square mini mall. He'd been in business six weeks, which was a long time given the economy — and a town the size of Peabody. That was two weeks longer than Paper Crane Stationery had lasted. He wasn't packing them in like the candy shop, but he seemed to be doing all right. He had students. Mostly skinny boys and girls needing to be kept busy during their summer vacation.

Michael looked like an archangel too. He was built like a runner or a knight of old. Tall, lean, wide shoulders and ropy muscles. His hair was nearly shoulder length — when he didn't have it tied back — and of the palest gold. Not that Ethan — who owned the book store half of Red Bird Books and Coffee and hoped to be a published author one day — would have normally used that kind of hyperbole to describe Michael, but *blond* just didn't seem to cover that particular shade which somehow brought to mind the gleaming tips of arrows or reverberating harp strings. Michael's eyes were blue, the blue of a cloudless sky or the color you believe water is when you're a little kid. His face was beautiful. Really beautiful. Elegant, almost exotic, bone structure — at least on the one side of his face.

The right half of his face had been destroyed at some point. Smashed and burned, it looked like, though Ethan was no expert — and he tried very hard not to stare. They — whoever *they* were — had tried to rebuild Michael and they'd saved his eye, but the skin looked like it had been stretched too tight over reconstructed bones. It had a stiff, shiny, inflexible quality. Since Michael was mostly expressionless, it wasn't as noticeable as it might have been if he'd been the smiley, chatty kind.

Ethan figured he'd had about thirty words out of Michael in the weeks since he'd opened the dojo. it was more like one word thirty times — *Thanks* when Ethan handed him his change.

It was Chance from next door's Sweets to the Sweet who had told Ethan that Michael had been Special Ops in Afghanistan.

"How'd you find that out?" Ethan asked through a mouthful of divinity fudge. Chance was generous with his samples. Maybe that was why Sweets to the Sweet had been a hit practically from the moment the doors opened.

Chance raised a negligent shoulder. He reminded Ethan of a cat. Sleek and graceful and inscrutable. Chance and his boutique chocolates seemed even more out of place in Peabody than Michael Milner's kajukenbo lessons.

"Do you know what happened to his … ?" Ethan put a hand to his own right cheekbone rather than complete the sentence. It was probably in bad taste to ask such a question but it wasn't possible to pretend he hadn't noticed. He found Michael fascinating. He wanted to know everything about him. He told himself it was his writer's imagination wanting fuel for the fire.

"Why don't you ask him?" Chance had returned too innocently.

Ethan had retreated instantly from the suggestion. Of course he would never ask — who the hell *would* ask that kind of question? Even if his previous attempts to be friendly to Michael hadn't fallen flat. Michael was unfailingly polite and unfailingly distant. On the rare occasion that he bothered to make eye contact with Ethan, he seemed to see something slightly off center that made him narrow his gaze.

Ethan swallowed the last heavenly bit of white fudge. How was it that everything in Sweets to the Sweet was *so* delicious? He half suspected Chance of adding addictive substances. It wouldn't surprise him. He made Ethan a little uncomfortable sometimes — like now when he was studying Ethan as though he could see right into the secret corners of his mind. The places Ethan himself was afraid to explore too closely.

"I should get back." Ethan rubbed his fingers, trying to remove the lingering sugary sweetness. He headed for the door.

"Ethan?"

Ethan glanced back.

Chance smiled that sly smile of his. "He's not married."

○ ○ ○ ○ ○

"What's the matter with you?" Erin asked when Ethan returned to the bookstore.

Ethan wiped his forehead. "Nothing."

"You look like you have sunstroke."

It was hot enough for sunstroke. Summers in Peabody were like vacationing in Hell. Minus the scenery.

"It's just ... hot."

"Understatement. Here try this." Erin leaned across the counter and handed over a tiny paper cup with chilled pale green liquid.

Ethan took an incautious sip. He was still badly shaken by the encounter with Chance. It wasn't that he was closeted exactly. Being the only gay man in Peabody — the only gay *person* as far as he could tell — his sexuality was as irrelevant as if he'd taken a vow of chastity. Erin, his twin sister, was straight and had pretty much the same problem. With a population of 339, there were not many unmarried eligible people of their age in the little desert town.

No, it wasn't that Chance had correctly identified him as gay. Heck, Ethan had originally wondered if Chance might be gay. It was that Chance had correctly identified Ethan's interest in Michael. Ethan himself had strenuously avoided recognizing his interest for what it was, but he could no longer avoid the truth. The fact was he ... well, he had a thing for Michael.

Had it bad. Bad enough that other people had noticed.

Had Michael noticed?

Ethan nearly choked as the mint green slime slid down his throat.

"What do you think?" Erin asked.

Frozen Nyquil? Chilled hemlock? One could never be sure with Erin. Ethan cleared his throat. "Uh ..." He took another sip to avoid having to answer. It seemed to be mostly ice, mint with perhaps a hint of coffee. Whatever it was, it wasn't very good. But then most of Erin's experiments weren't. She was a passionate and spectacularly ungifted barista. Luckily for everyone in Peabody — and the financial stability of Red Bird Books and Coffee — she stuck mostly to the premixed recipes.

"Hmm. I don't know."

"What do you think it needs?"

"Chocolate?"

Erin brightened, looking past Ethan. "Here comes Michael."

Ethan stiffened. A hasty glance over his shoulder offered a view of Michael pushing through the front door of Red Bird Books and Coffee. As usual, when he spotted Ethan, Michael's face grew more impassive than ever and he got that squint like Ethan was a foreign particle that had flown into his eye.

If Chance had so easily recognized Ethan's attraction to Michael, it was more than probable that so had Michael. No wonder he looked pained every time he spotted Ethan.

Ethan mumbled an inarticulate hello and retreated hastily for the back of the store and the comfort of the stock room.

Michael usually came in twice a day. In the morning he ordered a medium house blend. In the afternoon he ordered a fruit smoothie. Sometimes the mixed berry with acacia and sometimes the citrus cooler with passion fruit. Once a week, usually on Friday, he'd buy a book. Those brief Friday encounters had been the high point of Ethan's week for the last month and a half.

He lurked in the back for a few minutes waiting miserably for the coast to clear. He could hear Erin's cheerful voice and a lot less frequently, the dark, blurred tones of Michael, and then Erin called, "Ethan, what are you *doing* back there? You've got a customer."

Ethan groaned silently and walked out to the front.

"Were you working on your book?" Erin teased.

Ethan scowled at her. Erin found the idea that Ethan was seriously trying to write a book endlessly entertaining. She'd told everyone they knew that Ethan was working on A Novel. He could see their customers laboring over some polite question to ask — besides *how's it coming?* Except Michael. He had greeted the intelligence of Ethan's literary aspiration with raised eyebrows and a reminder of no strawberry in his mixed berry smoothie.

Now he stood at the book counter holding a copy of *History Man: The Life of R. G. Collingwood*. He looked up at Ethan's approach.

Usually Ethan couldn't shut up around Michael, chattering away about a lot of stuff Michael obviously didn't give a shit about. Today he took the hardcover Michael handed him, rang it up quickly.

"Twelve seventy-three." He stared determinedly down at the cover photograph of the English countryside.

Michael got out his wallet and selected the bills. A ten and three ones.

Ethan took the bills, made change, and handed the coins over, trying to avoid physical contact. He was horribly, painfully conscious of how transparent he'd been all these weeks. God. Like a teenager with a crush. No wonder Michael made a point of being as standoffish as possible.

Michael dropped the coins in the Jerry's Kids container on the desk next to the cash register.

Ethan realized he hadn't bagged the book. He grabbed a bag, shoved the book inside, and handed the bag to Michael, who took it unhurriedly.

"You didn't read this one?"

Ethan's head jerked up. He stared at Michael. He couldn't have been more startled if the bonsai tree on his counter had addressed him. As far as he could recall, it was the first time in six weeks Michael had initiated conversation between them.

"Who, me?" Ethan said brilliantly.

"You've always got something to say about the books. You didn't read this one?"

The books were all mostly used at Red Bird Books and Coffee. Ethan ordered a few paperback bestsellers, but he preferred the old books. According to Erin, the bookstore was just Ethan's excuse for buying and reading all the books he wanted. She wasn't far wrong.

"I read it. It's good." Ethan made an effort. "You'll enjoy it."

Michael nodded politely. He turned and left the store.

"Bye, Michael!" Erin called as the door swung shut behind him. She looked across the floor. "What's the matter with you?"

"Nothing."

"Did something happen?"

"No."

"You acted like you were mad at being disturbed. *Were* you working on your book?"

"No I didn't and no I wasn't."

"I thought you liked him?"

"I don't like him!"

"Come off it. If you were a puppy, you'd be on your back and wriggling every time he walks in here."

Ethan's temper, generally mild, shot up like the red strip of fake mercury in the giant thermometer outside the Bun Baby Restaurant. His voice rose with it. "*Like* him? I'm so sure!"

The door to the shop swung open. Ethan registered the chirping bird, saw out of the corner of his eye that the door was moving, but it was too late to stop the angry words already spilling out. "I think I can do better than the Phantom of the Dojo."

Erin's stricken expression told him what he needed to know. He turned to the front of the shop expecting to see Michael, and sure enough Michael stood in the doorway, frozen in place — just as the scarred half of his face was frozen.

Ethan swallowed. Even as he was trying to tell himself that Michael could only have heard half of that outburst and no way could connect it to himself — and that "Phantom of the Dojo" could mean anything, didn't have to be a reference to a scarred and tragic monster — he knew he was sunk. If Michael *hadn't* heard enough, Erin's patent horror filled in the necessary blanks.

The longest two seconds of Ethan's life dragged with agonizing slowness. Neither he, Erin, nor Michael moved. Neither he, Erin, nor Michael spoke. Ethan's fervent prayers for the earth to open up and swallow him went unanswered.

If he'd been the one to overhear that ugly comment, he'd have backed up, closed the door, and never returned to Red Bird Books and Coffee. Michael stepped inside, closing the door after him, and crossed to Erin's counter. The wooden floorboards squeaked ominously beneath his measured footsteps. Ethan's heart thudded heavily in time to the thump, creak.

"I'm working late tonight. I thought I'd get one of your sandwiches." Michael's voice was even, without any inflection at all.

It was the bravest thing Ethan had ever seen.

"Sure!" Erin said brightly. Too brightly. "What kind did you want? Tuna fish on whole wheat, chicken salad on sourdough..." She babbled out the options.

"Tuna on wheat."

Ethan couldn't stop staring at the uncompromising set of Michael's wide shoulders, the straight way he held himself. His throat felt too tight to speak, practically too tight to breathe. He'd have felt sick about anyone hearing him say something that stupid and cruel, but for Michael to have heard it...

Erin was still gabbling away as she got Michael's sandwich.

Shut up, Ethan willed her. *You're making it worse.* But silence would've probably been worse. It would have been a dead silence. Michael hadn't said a word since he'd requested his sandwich. The back of his neck was red. It probably matched Ethan's face, which felt hot enough to burst into flame. Now there was a solution to his problems. Spontaneous combustion.

As though feeling the weight of Ethan's gaze, Michael turned and gave him a long, direct look.

That look reduced Ethan to the size of something that could have taken refuge beneath the bonsai tree. After an excruciating moment, his gaze dropped to the counter. He scrutinized the schedule of California sales tax beneath the clear plastic desk blotter as though he was about to be tested on it.

When he looked up again, Michael had his wallet out.

Erin waved his money away. "Oh, no. On the house!"

Ethan could have put his head in his hands and howled. Why didn't she just sign a confession in blood? Couldn't she see that undid all Michael's efforts to put things back on a normal track?

Her eyes guiltily met his own across the floor. Had she been a mime making sad eyes and upside-down smiles she couldn't have more clearly conveyed distress.

"Thanks," Michael said. "But no thanks." He handed her a bill and Erin, her face now the shade of her hair, quickly made change.

Michael unhurriedly took his change and his sandwich. He nodded to Erin.

The bird-bell cheeped cheerfully as the door swung shut behind him.

CHAPTER TWO

"Oh my God, I think he heard you," Erin gasped as soon as the door was safely closed.

"Ya think?" Ethan wavered, undecided, then darted out behind the counter and headed after Michael.

The dusty heat of the afternoon hit him like a thousand needles. His skin prickled. Sweat broke out over his body.

Michael was already at the dojo entrance, keys in hand. His profile, the good side of his face, was stern and beautiful.

"Michael?"

He turned at Ethan's call, but his expression didn't change. Ethan forced himself to continue down the wooden walkway, past Sweets to the Sweet. It was a bad idea to pursue this, of course, but not doing anything was equally bad — and gutless.

He stopped about a foot from Michael and said, "I want to apologize."

Michael shrugged. His eyes held Ethan's levelly. Ethan had never seen eyes so fiercely blue. "Why? It wasn't meant for me to hear."

It was a relief that he didn't pretend not to know what Ethan was talking about. Ethan was grateful for that courtesy — and mortified all over again. He got out, "It was a stupid thing to say."

Michael shrugged. "Yeah. Well, I know how I look, but I'm grateful to be alive. I'm not ashamed of my face."

Ethan said painfully, "I am, too. Grateful you're alive, I mean."

Michael made a sound somewhere between a laugh and a snort. Not unkindly but as though Ethan were a harmless kook. He nodded, the conversation clearly at an end, and went inside the dojo, closing the door after him.

Ethan walked slowly back to the Red Bird.

"What happened?" Erin demanded.

"Nothing. I apologized."

"Jeez. What did he say?"

"He said he knew how he looked but he was glad to be alive."

Erin winced. "He was in Afghanistan. Did you know that?"

Ethan nodded. "Chance told me. He said Michael was Special Ops."

"He was part of some hush-hush mission to stop the Taliban kidnapping the Pakistani ambassador. His team's truck hit an IED."

"Did he tell you that?"

"Eventually. In drips and drabs. He's not much of a talker." Erin made a face. "But I am."

The door opened and they both jumped as guiltily as if they'd been planning the overthrow of the town council. It was just Beth Miller and her three monsters. Ethan and Erin hurried to fill orders for comic books and fruit smoothies.

The remainder of the day passed without incident.

At five o'clock, Erin grabbed her Peanuts lunch box from the back room.

"Is your serial killer stopping by tonight?"

"Don't joke about that." Ethan glanced uneasily at the door. He didn't want to take a chance on being overheard again. Speculating aloud on this particular topic could put them out of business. If Peabody could be said to have a first family, it was the Hagars of Hagar's Truck and Tractor Equipment. Karl Hagar was the scion of the dynasty.

"I'm just saying what you think."

"I don't think Karl is a serial killer. I mean, yes, he is a little … weird."

"I'll say." Erin shivered. "I don't know how you can all stand to read those gory stories of his."

"You could say that about half the bestselling crime writers out there."

"Well, who knows what those people would do if they couldn't get it all out in their writing."

Ethan rolled his eyes. He did find Karl's writing disturbing — as did the other four members of the group — but there was no doubt Karl was very talented. Even gifted. He was probably the best writer in the group. Even better than Ethan, as much as Ethan hated to admit it.

"Well, but he does have that outlet," he pointed out.

"Maybe it's not enough."

"This is a creepy conversation," Ethan protested, laughingly.

"I haven't been able to get that story out of my head. The one about the young guy who poisons all the patients in the nursing home where he works."

That *had* been a disturbing story. Not least because it was so sympathetic to both the victims and the murderer.

Erin added, "You know, the Hagar ranch isn't far from where those men were found."

"Oh, come on. You can't go by that. If you want to get technical, their bodies were found closer to Lena's property."

Lena Montero was another member of Ethan's writing group. She was in her seventies now, but she lived way out in the boonies.

"You just don't want to consider the possibility because he's a Hagar."

"No shit. That's one household we don't want to go to war with. Anyway, Karl doesn't strike me as the serial killer type."

"How do you know? Serial killers look just like you and me."

"They have red hair?"

"Ha ha."

Ethan's hair wasn't red. It was brown with reddish highlights. Erin had the red hair. Red hair and green eyes. Ethan's eyes were hazel. He knew himself to be reasonably attractive, but Erin was beautiful. Everyone always said she should have been a model or an actress — usually after they'd sampled one of her original coffee drink recipes.

"Seriously," Erin said. "I was reading an article in *Reader's Digest* and most serial killers are not the dysfunctional weirdoes you see on TV. A lot of them can pass as perfectly normal."

"That leaves Karl out."

She laughed, and Ethan reflected that he probably shouldn't encourage her. She was liable to slip and say something in front of Karl.

"Anyway, be careful tonight and have fun!"

Erin went out into the sunny evening, and the door swung shut with a friendly chirp behind her.

Ethan got his copies of the group stories out and began to browse through them. This was always their quiet time of day. He and Erin took turns manning the shop for the three hours between five until closing. An occasional customer might wander in from the Interstate, but the good citizens of Peabody were generally having dinner and settling down to a night of reality TV.

He made a few notes on three of the stories, and then he started reading Karl's. It was the first chapter in a new novel, and, yes, it did seem to be about a serial killer. This time the serial killer was a sweet little boy with a twin sister.

The further Ethan read, the more unhappy he was. Not that he and Erin were ringers for the kids in Karl's book, but they were the only fraternal twins in Peabody and Karl's physical descriptions hit too close to home. Jeez, Erin had her faults, but she wasn't a sociopath, and far from exhibiting serial killer tendencies, Ethan got lightheaded at the sight of blood.

There was a great deal of blood in the first chapter of Karl's novel as little Iain Dearie dispatched the family cat and then went after the neighbor's baby. Happily the chapter ended with dear little Iain stuck in the shrubbery. Maybe he would stay there for the next seventy thousand words.

Ethan shuddered, drew a happy face on the first page, and went next door to visit with Chance.

He nearly bumped into Pete McCarty on his way out of the candy shop.

"Hi, Pete," he said tentatively.

Pete looked straight through him and walked away toward the parking lot.

Anna McCarty, Pete's wife, had stepped out onto the wooden walk behind him. She hesitated, then said uncomfortably, "Why hello, Ethan. How are you these days?"

"Hi, Anna. I'm good. How are you and..."

It was unexpectedly hard to finish it. He and Erin had grown up next door to the McCartys. Up until last year they had looked upon Pete and Ethel as an informal aunt and uncle, but now everything had changed.

Anna ignored his swallow. She said brightly, "How's Erin? Is she seeing anyone?"

Ethan shook his head.

"No? Well, you tell her I said hi."

Ethan nodded.

Anna hesitated for a fraction of second. "I'd better skedaddle. You know how Pete hates to be kept waiting."

Ethan nodded again.

Anna bit her lip. She patted his arm and hurried off, clutching her box of candy.

Ethan watched her go, watched her plump figure cross the parking lot, watched her climb into the SUV beside Pete. He appeared to give Anna a piece of his mind. And from the look of things Anna was returning it with interest. A few seconds later, the SUV roared past Ethan and out of the parking lot.

He gritted his teeth as the SUV disappeared down the road, and pushed through the door to Sweets to the Sweet.

The usual heady fragrance greeted him, a warm blend of cocoa, butter, and citrus. Somewhere Ethan had read that just the scent of chocolate acted as a male aphrodisiac and he could totally believe it when he walked into Sweets for the Sweet. It didn't hurt that Chance was the guy behind the counter.

"Just in time," Chance greeted him. "Try this."

Ethan came forward and took a tiny bite of a dark chocolate flower. He blinked at the unique flavor, the bite of spice and dark chocolate. "What is it?"

"Ginger, wasabi, and black sesame seeds."

"It's great. Unusual."

Chance smiled that enigmatic smile of his, and tucked back a silky strand of dark hair that had worked loose. "What happened between you and Michael?"

"Er, nothing," Ethan said guiltily. "Why?"

Chance nodded at the glass window. "I saw you tearing after him when he left your shop. I wondered what you'd said."

That was just ... uncanny. How could Chance have guessed that Ethan had said anything?

"I — "

"Did you decide to ask him about his scars after all?"

"Of course not!"

Chance studied him as though making his mind up whether that was true or not. He smiled lazily. "Just wondered. I could see Michael was upset."

"You ... could?" Ethan couldn't imagine how that would be. He found Michael as unreadable as the sandstone bluffs that overlooked the valley.

"I know Michael pretty well by now." Chance seemed to watch Ethan. What was he looking for? Signs that Ethan was jealous? He was, a little.

"Erin was teasing me and I said something stupid."

Chance's eyebrows angled up. "What did you say?"

"I … it doesn't matter."

"I didn't realize you had such a terrible temper." Ethan could hear the mockery in Chance's voice, but it was friendly mockery. At least, Ethan hoped it was. It was hard to tell with Chance.

"I don't. I just … I think it's the heat. I haven't been sleeping well."

Chance continued to regard him as though he could see right past that lame excuse, see right into the Ethan's heart. He murmured something that could have been commiseration or amusement. "Well, I wouldn't worry. It'll work itself out."

Would it?

It seemed unlikely.

To keep himself from saying anything else, Ethan popped the last bit of dark chocolate flower into his mouth. The spices stung his tongue, and then melted into sweetness.

○ ○ ○ ○ ○

"It's all these people who want something for nothing. Illegal aliens. They're the ones bringing the rest of us down."

They're not the only ones, Ethan thought.

John Dylan was fifty and heavy-set. He wore his dishwater blond hair pulled back in a ponytail. His day job was "postal delivery specialist," but he had dreams of being a paperback writer.

Then again, so did everyone else in the Coffee Clutch writing group.

"I don't like your racist remarks," Lena Montero said. She was small and brown and as tough as a rusty nail.

"I'm not a racist," Dylan said. "I'm just not broken up over some wetbacks dying in the desert when they shouldn't have been here to start with."

Uneasily recollecting Erin's theories on how the vagrants had died, Ethan looked sideways at Karl.

Karl's gaze slid to meet Ethan's. His mouth quirked into a faint smile.

Karl was two years younger than Ethan. He was blond and tanned and hand-some. He looked like a police cadet or the poster boy for Hitler Youth. In school, Karl had been a star athlete but a loner. Ethan had been aware of him, but had zero contact. Karl moved in a very different crowd from Ethan. He'd been surprised when Karl had shown up two months ago asking to join the Coffee Clutch.

Surprised, but pleased to gain another member. Especially one who could really write. Greater familiarity with Karl's work had spoiled some of the pleasure. It wasn't easy reading the violent and gruesome fantasies that poured out of Karl's brain.

Studying the stark perfection of Karl's face, Ethan couldn't help thinking that in a movie or a book Karl would always be cast as the cold-blooded killer. Real life generally wasn't so tidy.

The group ended. Everyone said goodnight. Ethan locked the rear door. He turned the OPEN sign to CLOSED, emptied the register, deposited the day's take in the floor safe in the back office, and dragged the trash bags to the front.

The trash dumpsters were at the far end of the parking lot.

As Ethan dragged the trash bags over to the dumpster, he noticed that Michael's pickup was still parked in front of the dojo. Another car was parked on the far side of Michael's truck. Was he giving someone a private lesson that evening?

Ethan raised the lid on the dumpster, swung the first trash bag, and tossed it over the rim. It landed with a dull thud.

He turned to grab the second bag and realized someone was standing behind him. Right behind him. Ethan hadn't heard footsteps, had no warning, but there he stood, fair hair gleaming in the silvery, summer moonlight.

CHAPTER THREE

"Jee-zus!" Ethan jumped back, knocking into the dumpster. The lid banged down. "What are you doing, Karl?"

Karl didn't say anything.

The hair stood up on the back of Ethan's neck.

"What do you want?"

By moonlight, Karl's expression was frightening. His eyes looked black.

There was nowhere for Ethan to run. He was already backed against the dumpster. *This can't be happening*, he thought, and just as the disbelieving words took shape in his mind, he spied movement behind Karl. A pale figure strode toward them through the darkness.

Ethan's heart leaped with relief even before Michael called crisply, "Is there a problem?"

Karl spun with a kind of wary precision.

"Everything okay, Ethan?" Michael asked, still in that hard voice. He sounded more than ready to deal with it, if everything wasn't okay.

"Everything's fine," Karl answered.

"Ethan?"

Ethan got out, "Yes. Everything's fine. I was just … ." He grabbed the remaining trash bag, heaved it into the dumpster, and turning back to Karl said with an effort at normality, "What did you need, Karl?"

Karl seemed to have forgotten about him. He was still staring at Michael. Ethan took advantage of that distraction to scoot past him, walking toward Michael. Michael, too, ignored him, staring at Karl. Did they know each other?

If so, neither was saying anything.

Karl said, "It'll keep," and for a second, Ethan couldn't even remember what the question had been.

Karl walked past Michael to his car. He didn't say goodnight, he didn't say anything at all. He went to his black TR7 sports car, and got in. The engine started, a hornet's buzz in the warm night.

"What was that about?" Michael asked. He was still watching Karl as he backed up the car, swung around, and sped out of the parking lot.

"I don't know," Ethan admitted. "He just freaked me out popping out of nowhere like that. But I probably freaked him out reacting like I thought he was a…"

Serial killer.

Damn Erin for planting that thought in his mind. He gave Michael a sheepish smile.

"He was waiting for you in his car. I noticed him when I was closing up the dojo. I wondered why he was just sitting there, and when you came outside, he got out of his car to follow you. I could see you weren't expecting him."

Ethan had jumped so high it was a miracle he hadn't knocked himself out on the moon. It would have been hard to miss that panicked reaction — even in the dark.

He firmly put aside the knowledge of what Michael must think of him — after the "Phantom of the Dojo" remark he probably couldn't get a lot lower in his estimation. "It was probably nothing, but thanks for coming out here."

That would have been kind and conscientious anytime, let alone after the afternoon they'd had.

Michael nodded curtly.

"I should probably take some kind of self-defense course."

Michael made a *yeah right* sound. "What you should do is take a minute or two to check your surroundings before you walk out here late at night. Erin too. You both usually close up after the rest of us have gone. We're not that far from the freeway."

Right, that never-ending conveyor belt of potential customers and crazies, also known as the Interstate. From where they stood they could see the constant moving flash of lights coming and going through the scrubby barrier trees.

"Chance is usually here," Ethan said.

Even now the windows of Sweets for the Sweet were cheerfully shining like a beacon in the night.

"Yeah, he is," Michael said thoughtfully. "But somehow I don't see Chance running to your rescue."

Ethan laughed. "Probably not." Chance would probably be too busy in his kitchen cooking up more amazing addictive confections to notice if all of Viento Square burned down around him.

Michael was turning away, crisis averted, conversation over.

Without giving himself time to think, Ethan blurted, "Michael, you want to go grab a drink somewhere?"

His face burned in anticipation of the imminent rejection. He meant it simply as a friendly gesture, but Michael would almost certainly misread it, and even if he didn't, he'd shown zero interest in forming any friendships. Or even acquaintanceships.

To Ethan's surprise, Michael hesitated. "Where?"

Good question. Ethan had thrown the offer out there; he hadn't expected to be taken up on it. Options in Peabody were limited, and he knew with certainty that Michael would not be up to driving any distance to one of the other little towns along the Interstate. Denny's served wine and beer, but it would be full of noisy — and nosey — high school kids at this time of night.

"The Drifters?"

"*The Drifters?*"

Michael's astonishment was understandable. The Drifters was a grubby hole-in-the-wall mostly patronized by Peabody's redneck career drinkers — and the occasional biker gang.

Ethan had been there twice in his entire life, and he had no particular desire to go back, but he thought Michael could tolerate the toxic testosterone levels.

"Sure. They've got a good selection of import beers."

"The Drifters it is." Michael turned away.

They were going to the Drifters. It took Ethan a second to register it. They were *going.* "Okay, I'll... see you over there." He was equal parts excited and alarmed as he jogged back to the store and finished closing up. Why on earth had Michael agreed? What the hell would they talk about? Could Michael possibly be — no. But at least it seemed unlikely he knew Ethan was attracted to him. That was a huge relief. It was like having his ego handed back to him on a platter.

By the time he got back outside, Michael's pickup was already waiting in the driveway, exhaust drifting in the summer night, and again Ethan felt a surge of gratitude that Michael hadn't just driven off. Not that there could be any real threat to him, but the bracket of shops that made up Viento Square was eerily empty at night, store windows lit like museum exhibits.

He followed Michael's red tail lights down the highway, turning left before the railroad crossing, and then down the narrow road that led to a small white building between the feed store and the Mobil station. A blue neon cocktail glass poured its winking green bubbles into the starry night.

Michael parked at the back of the lot. Ethan edged his prim Toyota in between a row of gleaming motorcycles knowing if he happened to scrape one he would die before the night was over.

By the time he'd finished parking, Michael was out of his truck and waiting for him at the door of the bar. He was dressed like Ethan, jeans and a T-shirt, but somehow he looked like he belonged at the Drifters — or at least like no one would challenge his right to be there.

The two previous times Ethan had been to the Drifters he'd been carded even though he'd been at school with George, the bartender, who knew full well Ethan was twenty-eight.

Michael didn't say anything as Ethan joined him. In fact, he seemed a little distant, but maybe that was Ethan projecting. He pushed open the door and the sound of country music flooded the night. Garth Brooks.

Inside the bar it was dark and smoky. The greatest source of light in the room was the jukebox. No one was smoking, so it was probably twenty years' worth of accumulated tar and nicotine haunting the structure. The bar was lined with men in cowboy hats and baseball caps hunched over bottles of beer. A few heads turned their way and then turned back. It wasn't exactly a warm welcome but no one hissed at them.

In the farthest and darkest corner of the room was a crowded table. Ethan had an impression of beards, shades, and a lot of leather.

"Grab a table, I'll get this round," Michael said. "What did you want?"

"Pauli Girl." Ethan didn't particularly care for beer, but his father had always drunk St. Pauli Girl, so when he did have beer, he always picked that.

Michael headed for the bar.

There were a number of small, empty tables. Ethan picked one well away from the biker corner. He sat down and folded his arms, trying to find some place to stare that wouldn't seem rude. He felt awkward and conspicuous. He reminded himself that this wasn't a date.

Michael came back with two bottles — no glasses, and Ethan made a mental note not to identify himself as a candy ass by asking for glasses when his turn came to get the next round.

Michael hooked a foot around the chair leg, dragged it out, sat down and placed the open bottles on the table.

"Thanks," Ethan said, reaching for his bottle and automatically wiping the mouth.

"Come here often, do you?" Michael inquired gravely, and as Ethan found the gleam of his eyes in the gloom, it occurred to him that Michael might have a sense of humor. That was dangerous. It not only made Michael more real, it made him a lot more appealing.

"Er, no."

Michael's teeth flashed in a white, very brief smile. He was sitting slightly angled toward Ethan so Ethan couldn't see the scarred half of his face. What would it be like to be that handsome, to have that power, and then lose it? Not naturally fade away with age, but have half your face torn off.

The jukebox started up again with the same Garth Brooks song that had been playing when they walked in. "Standing Outside the Fire."

Michael put the bottle to his mouth and drank. Ethan followed suit and stared at the large girly calendar on the wall behind Michael. What *was* the appeal of naked girls on tractors? It just looked… uncomfortable. He glanced at Michael again. Michael was staring into space.

There were a lot of things Ethan wanted to ask him, but he wasn't sure if they'd be viewed as intrusive or not. Michael seemed so private.

Ethan looked around the bar. He recognized a couple of faces. Dave Wilton fleetingly met Ethan's eyes, before turning away. Of course, Ethan had never had much in common with Dave, but it was easy these days to put that coolness down to Pete McCarty and the Starbucks thing.

Did Michael know about that? Ethan glanced back at Michael who was looking more tuned out and distant with each passing moment. If there was going to be any conversation, Ethan was going to have to initiate it.

"So," Ethan said, and Michael's eyes jerked his way. "What made you settle in Peabody? You're not from around here." No way could Ethan have missed Michael Milner while he was growing up.

"No." Michael set his bottle on the table.

Ethan waited. Michael said reluctantly, "After I got out of the service — the hospital — I was trying to figure out what to do with the rest of my life."

"Were you career military before … ?" Ethan stopped awkwardly, but Michael didn't seem offended.

"That wasn't the original plan, but I enjoyed the military." He lifted a shoulder. "I could have stayed in after I got this, but I felt like it was time to do something else."

Ethan nodded. There couldn't be that much of an age difference between them, but every time he was around Michael he became conscious of his lack of life experience. All Ethan had ever really wanted was to sell books at his mom and dad's store. That, or be a librarian, but Peabody didn't have a library of its own.

"Some friends of mine wanted me to go into their sailboat rental business. I was on my way up north to check it out when I got off the freeway to buy gas."

"And you decided to stay?"

"This place appealed to me. I liked that it was quiet and out in the middle of nowhere."

"It's a long way from the ocean, that's for sure."

"The boat business wasn't my idea. It was just … something to focus on when I needed it."

Ethan nodded. He could understand that only too well.

Michael said with sudden curiosity, "When I was looking at rental spaces for the dojo, the realtor was badmouthing you because you'd refused to be bought out by Starbucks."

Ethan's heart sank, though maybe it shouldn't have come as a surprise. "Mr. McCarty. He's still upset."

"Yeah, he did seem irate."

Ethan tried to smile. It wasn't exactly cheering to hear Pete went around bad-mouthing them to anyone who would listen — including people who might just be passing through town.

"Pete wanted us to let our lease expire so that Starbucks could buy out the Red Bird."

"Why would you?"

"A Starbucks would attract freeway business to Peabody."

The scarred half of Michael's mouth curled. "And it'd mean a big fat commission for Pete?"

"Yeah, but I guess you could argue — Pete did — that it would be good for everyone in Peabody. It would mean jobs."

"What about your job? And Erin's?"

Ethan nodded. It would have cost them their livelihood and perhaps eventually their home. But it just hadn't seemed to matter to Pete. Then Ethan had compounded that sin by getting 215 signatures on a petition to stop Starbucks from moving into Peabody at all. Ethan had taken the petition to the town council and the town council had agreed that Peabody was not large enough to support two coffee houses. Pete had been furious. He had still not forgiven Ethan and maybe never would.

"I liked that about you," Michael said, as though reading his mind. "It was one reason I settled on Viento Square."

Ethan hoped the poor lighting concealed his blush. Before he knew it, he was telling Michael all about how he and Erin had grown up thinking of the McCartys as extended family and how hard it had been since the falling out over Starbucks. That had been a real eye-opener. Ethan still couldn't get over the fact that Pete and his business cronies were honestly outraged that he had fought for his survival. The fact that Pete and the others had been outvoted and overruled didn't alter their resentment one iota.

"That's human nature." Michael took a pull of his beer.

"I guess." Ethan brooded for an instant. "It's when I realized what greed could do to people like Pete that I decided to write *Death in a Very Small Town*."

"Yeah, your sister mentioned you're writing a book. That title sounds familiar."

"*Death in a Small Town* has been used a few times. But not *Death in a Very Small Town*."

"Hm." Michael's gaze seemed to weigh him. "Are you sorry you fought McCarty on it?"

Ethan shook his head. "No. We couldn't give up the Red Bird. It's not just our livelihood, it's our ... inheritance." Then he had to explain about how his parents had been killed four years ago coming back from the first vacation they'd taken on their own in twenty-five years.

By the time he finished bringing Michael up to date on his entire history, it was last call. Embarrassingly, Ethan, who really wasn't much of a drinker, had forgotten all about getting the second round. Worse, he'd been so busy telling his life story, he'd barely let Michael get a word in edgewise. Not that Michael had tried to get a word in, but it would have been nice to throw the occasional question his way. If only in an effort not to look like a total egomaniac.

"I've got this. What did you want?" Ethan rose belatedly.

But Michael was rising too, shaking his head. "Thanks, but I've got an early start tomorrow. I need to get going."

Ethan looked at the Budweiser clock on the wall. He'd been talking for nearly three hours straight. No wonder Michael couldn't wait to escape.

"Oh my God," he said, and it was truly heartfelt. "Why didn't you tell me to shut up an hour ago?"

Michael had a nice laugh. It was the first time Ethan had heard it and he seemed to feel it in his solar plexus. "Nah. You were fine." But Michael didn't deny that Ethan was a blabbermouth and Ethan blushed again. The worst part was he'd spent three hours with Michael and basically didn't know anything more about him than he had that morning — and it was totally his own fault.

He followed Michael outside. The stars were brilliant in the black sky.

The bikers had vanished at some point during the evening and Ethan's Toyota sat by itself next to the chain link fence.

"Night," Ethan called as Michael walked back to his truck.

"Night, Ethan."

Just hearing Michael say his name made his heart skip. *Oh you have it bad*, Ethan told himself once he was in his car and buckling his seatbelt. *He probably thinks you're...* but there his imagination gave out. It was very hard to know what Michael thought about anything.

He watched Michael's pickup trundle slowly past his rear window, bump onto the paved highway and disappear into the night.

CHAPTER FOUR

"Listen to this." Erin read from the paper, "Kern County investigators are trying to determine the identity of a man whose body was found Thursday in the desert eight miles from the town of Peabody. The man was found just before 7 a.m. north of Highway 19, according to a release from the sheriff's department. Deputies at the scene were unable to determine the cause of death and requested homicide investigators. The identity of the deceased has not been confirmed and an investigation is ongoing. An autopsy will be conducted. This is the third body to be discovered in the vicinity of Peabody over the past six weeks. Anyone with information regarding the incident can contact Det. Ricardo Cabot or Sgt. Tony Guinn at 999-313-3859. Tips can also be left anonymously at 1-800-712-7123." She looked up from the paper. "That makes three. Three in six weeks. It says so right here."

Ethan, busy changing out the fragile vintage paperbacks in the swivel bookcase, replied, "That doesn't mean a serial killer is at large."

"What *does* it mean, then?"

"How should I know? It doesn't even say how he died. It could have been heat exposure. It's 114 out there right now."

"All *three* of them?"

"Where does it say that all three of them died from the same cause?"

"It doesn't have to. This is obviously more than a coincidence. You have to call the sheriff's department and tell them about Karl."

Ethan stood up. His sister was starting to make him nervous. "Tell them *what* about Karl?"

There was belated cheeped warning and the door swung open as Erin said in clear, carrying tones, "That he's a serial killer."

Ethan turned to face his doom, but it was only Chance.

"Who's a serial killer?" Chance inquired with great interest.

"No one," Ethan insisted. He glared at Erin. "*No one.*"

"Karl Hagar," Erin told Chance. "He writes all these creepy, gory stories about murdering people for Ethan's writing group."

"Murdering people for Ethan's writing group? Is that one of the requirements?"

Erin laughed. Ethan couldn't see the humor. "She doesn't know what she's talking about." To Erin, he said, "You're going to get us sued."

"By who?"

"By the Hagars, if they find out you're going around accusing Karl of being a serial killer."

"You should see the stuff he writes," Erin told Chance. "It's sick."

"Ethan?"

"*Karl.*" Erin was laughing again.

"It doesn't work like that," Ethan tried to explain. "That's just imagination. Writers ... they make stuff up."

Erin quoted wisely, "Write what you know."

"Yeah, but that's what I'm saying. It doesn't work like that. You don't have to be a detective to write mysteries, and you sure don't have to be a murderer. Most writers don't live what they write. Most writers are like ... me. They don't get out a lot. They make stuff up. It's all imagination and — and the creative process."

Erin seemed to have her heart set on Karl being a psycho. "He couldn't write like that if he didn't have firsthand experience."

"That's research. That's imagination. That's what being a writer is all about."

"When did these killings start?" Chance selected a variety of Pez candies. Why, when he surely had access to all the candy he could ever desire?

"Six weeks ago."

"*Ah.* So I could be the killer. Or maybe Michael. We've both only been here about six weeks."

"Michael is *not* a killer," Ethan said.

Hot embarrassment flooded him as both Erin and Chance laughed in response to his vehemence.

○ ○ ○ ○ ○

In the afternoon Michael came in for his usual fruit smoothie. Ethan had missed him earlier as Erin had run out of milk and he'd needed to make an emergency trip to pick up a couple of gallons to tide her over until the next delivery.

His stomach did its usual nervous belly flop at the sight of Michael. It was worse today because he was very conscious of what a lousy impression he must have made the night before. Thank God, it *hadn't* been a date. Michael would judge him less severely as a neighbor and potential friend. Hopefully Michael thought of him as a potential friend. It was hard to know since Ethan hadn't let him get more than a few words in all night.

"What do you think about Karl?" Erin asked, after Michael placed his order for a citrus cooler.

"What about Karl?" Michael shot Ethan a wary look as though he was unsure of what stories Ethan might be telling.

"Nothing about Karl," Ethan said. "Erin is convinced Karl is ..."

"A serial killer," Erin finished.

"You *can't* keep saying that," Ethan warned her. "We don't need any more enemies in this town."

"We don't have any enemies."

Michael, not easily detoured, asked, "Why do you think Karl is a serial killer?"

"You should see the stuff he writes for Ethan's group. It's sick."

Ethan was miserably aware he should never have let Erin look at Karl's stories. He'd gotten in the habit, when they were bored and the customers were few and far between, of reading stories from the group to her. She often had good insights. But her dislike of Karl's writing, and her suspicion of him personally, was beginning to be a liability.

Now she was describing the story about the nursing home poisoner to Michael. What Michael made of it was impossible to know. The scarred, frozen side of his face was turned Ethan's way.

Erin finished up with, "And *why* would he be waiting for Ethan in the parking lot after the Coffee Clutch group?"

At that, Michael's expression did change. He gave Ethan a funny look. Ethan didn't know what to make of it.

A few hours' distance had already given the bizarre encounter with Karl an unreal aura. Ethan said, "He could have been out there for a lot of reasons. Maybe he thought he forgot something inside the shop."

"Why didn't he come to the door, then?"

"He could have had some question he didn't want everyone to hear. He's very reticent in the group. He knows the rest of them don't like his stories."

"The rest of *them*? You hate his stories too."

"I know, but I can't say that. I'm the moderator."

"Chance thinks it's all a big joke," Erin complained. "What do you think, Michael?"

"I think Chance isn't in any position to point fingers."

Ethan said curiously, "He says you two know each other pretty well."

"Chance and me? No way. Not my type."

Not my type? It seemed a funny way of putting it. Of course, people used that phrase all the time and didn't mean it literally. Ethan really needed to stop trying to find signals where none existed.

"I think you should go to the police," Erin said.

"With *what*? The fact that he writes weird stories? The fact that he surprised me in the parking lot?" He realized he was looking at Michael, waiting for Michael to weigh in on this. Poor Michael. Why was any of this his problem?

Michael said, "What's your instinct tell you?"

Ethan frowned, consulting his inner oracle. "I don't know that I have instinct. I think civilization has bred it all out of me."

Michael made a sound that fell somewhere between amusement and impatience. "You were scared last night."

Funny that he didn't mind Michael knowing he had been scared. Not that Ethan could have hidden it. "Yeah, but I think that was mostly because Erin put the idea in my head. That and then reading the chapter of Karl's new novel."

"Chance said that we'd have all the same doubts whether Karl was a serial killer or not."

"If we're wrong and we accuse Karl of *anything*, the Hagars will ruin us. We couldn't survive a lawsuit."

Erin handed Michael his drink. Michael sipped from the straw with the good side of his mouth. Not looking at Ethan, he said, "If I were you, I'd just ask him what he wants."

○ ○ ○ ○ ○

It was Erin's night to stay late. Ethan left her with warnings to take the trash out while it was still daylight and to make sure no one was lurking in the parking lot.

"Don't worry. It's only men being killed," she told him cheerfully.

Ethan sighed and left her to it.

Michael's truck was already gone for the day. Ethan noted its absence with an internal sag of disappointment. Which made no sense at all. All day he'd been hoping for some sign that... well, what? He was impatient with himself for wishing whatever it was he wished: that last night would be a turning point in his relationship with Michael? It had been. But of course, he wanted more. He wanted Michael to feel the same way he did, and that was ridiculous.

There was no reason to think — hope —

Just because someone wasn't married didn't mean they were gay. Look at Erin. Beautiful, smart, fun, straight ... and not a single marital prospect on the horizon. For all Ethan knew, Michael could have been married. Maybe his wife had left him after his face was destroyed. He absently embroidered this sad scenario as he drove home. By the time Ethan reached the big old comfortable two-story house he'd grown up in, he'd saddled Michael with a faithless prom queen high school sweetheart and two point three children now being raised by their grandparents.

He made Fritos casserole for himself and Erin, put hers in the fridge, and ate his standing over the sink. He rinsed his plate. Taking out the pot of iced coffee they always kept chilling, he poured a glass and carried it out to the aboveground swimming pool in the backyard.

He plugged in the cord to the little plastic Chinese lanterns that hung in a large square around the yard. They glowed cheerfully as he skimmed the glassy water, removing the dead bees and moths. The black cloud-shaped shadows cast by the tall apple trees gradually dissolved into the deepening dusk.

For a time Ethan swam in the shady water. The evening was still very warm and the water pleasantly tepid. A bat twittered overhead.

He had stopped to drink his now-watery coffee when he spotted headlights moving slowly through the trees, coming up the road to the house.

His spirits soared even as he warned himself that this could be a belated UPS delivery or someone asking for directions. He climbed out of the pool and dried hastily, pulling on his jeans over his damp trunks. He finger-combed his hair out of his face as he walked down the gardenia-lined path along the side of the house.

He was rounding the corner when he spotted the car parked in the sandy circle in front of the lawn. A black TR7.

Ethan froze.

Karl.

He drew back and leaned against the side of the house, thinking rapidly. What on earth could Karl want? Why was he there?

If I were you, I'd just ask him what he wants.

No kidding. It was ridiculous to be skulking around like this just because Erin had a vivid imagination and Karl was maybe too effective a writer. But nothing Ethan could think of would entail Karl driving all the way out to Ethan's home.

Then again, the idea that Karl might intend him harm was preposterous.

For one thing, why pick Ethan? If, by some weird chance, Karl did have something to do with those transients dying in the desert, it still didn't make sense that he would suddenly focus his homicidal interest on Ethan.

Ethan was being a tool, and he knew it. In fact, if anyone was behaving suspiciously, it was Ethan. Karl had walked up to the porch and was politely ringing the doorbell. Ethan was the one skulking in the bushes and gawking.

There was no reason to react like this. None. Which didn't change the fact that he would've preferred not to be on his own for this meeting.

"Were you looking for me?" he asked, coming up behind the porch.

Karl jumped — much as Ethan had the night before — and turned as Ethan reached the steps. He looked yellow in the porch light.

"Ethan. Hi."

Was it Ethan's imagination, or did Karl sound strained?

"Hi." Ethan gestured vaguely. "I was swimming out back."

"You have a pool?"

"Yeah. It's just one of those aboveground deals," Ethan hurriedly qualified. Safe to say their venerable Doughboy was probably not Karl's idea of a real swimming pool given the in-ground pool on the Hagar property. "We've had it for years."

"I guess that's why you're tanned even though you're inside all day."

Ethan didn't really think of himself as tanned. He rarely got in the pool before five-thirty in the evening. It was an odd thing for Karl to comment on, wasn't it?

Neither of them spoke

"Would you like an iced coffee?" Ethan really couldn't think of anything else to say other than *what are you doing here?* and that felt too blunt.

"Coffee?" Karl's pale brows rose.

"Iced coffee."

"Sure."

Ethan led the way around the back — the front of the house was locked — and Karl followed him inside after briefly checking out the pool.

Karl prowled around the kitchen while Ethan got out a clean glass. The sound of crickets was loud through the open windows.

"When does your sister come home?"

Ethan glanced at the clock. "She has her scrapbooking class tonight. She'll be home around nine." Belatedly, he realized he should have said Erin was due home any minute. But that was only if he believed himself in danger, right? And he didn't. Karl was acting perfectly normal — within the parameters of the oddness of his visiting Ethan.

Karl said nothing.

Ethan opened the fridge and pulled out the jug of cold brewed coffee. "How's business?"

Karl began to give him a precise accounting of how business was. The Hagar controller probably couldn't have been more accurate as far as facts and figures. It was kind of surprising in someone who was as imaginative and descriptive as Karl, but people's contradictions were often the most interesting thing about them.

"That sounds interesting," Ethan said politely, when there was finally a pause. He handed a glass to Karl.

Karl took his iced coffee and sipped it. Ethan became conscious of the wet trunks beneath his jeans and how close and confined it felt in the shabby, over-warm kitchen. The smell of Fritos casserole was overpowered by Karl's aftershave.

"We can talk out back," he said.

Karl followed him outside. Through the distant trees Ethan could see the lights of the McCarty house. He wondered if the McCartys would help him if he came pounding on their door. Once he would have taken that for granted.

"It's quiet out here," Karl observed.

"Yeah." A mosquito buzzed past his ear and Ethan slapped at it.

Karl cleared his throat.

Ethan glanced his way. Karl stared straight ahead at the pool, which now looked black as an oil well.

"Was there something you wanted to ask me?"

"I…" Karl's voice gave out in a squawk that in other circumstances might have been funny. Whatever this was, it was obviously awkward.

Ethan waited nervously.

"I wanted to hire you," Karl said at last.

"*Hire* me?"

Karl nodded. "As a writing coach. I was hoping you'd work with me one on one."

This was so far removed from Ethan's uneasy, anxious speculations, it was almost surreal. "But I'm not a writing coach."

"You run the critique group. You sell books."

"But that's not like being a writing coach. Anyone in the group could give you as good, or better, feedback as me."

"I don't think so. I don't care what Lena Montero or any of the rest of them have to say. They don't know anything."

"Neither do I, really," honesty compelled Ethan to say.

"You know more than the rest of us. Anyway, I'd pay you."

Money always being an issue, Ethan asked, "How much were you thinking?"

"I don't know. What do you think is fair?"

"I have no idea." Ethan sipped his coffee to give himself time to think. "I guess I could look it up, but what you ought to do is see about enrolling in the junior college in Modesto. You could work with actual writing instructors."

Karl said decisively, "I don't want anything that formal. I don't have time to take a bunch of classes."

It wasn't that Ethan couldn't use the money, but the idea of tutoring Karl made him uncomfortable even without analyzing why. He was trying to formulate some diplomatic but convincing reason why he couldn't accept the job, when the glide of headlights through the trees down the lane caught his eye.

It was still too early for Erin, so who the heck was this?

His heart did another hopeful leap, like a goldfish in a too-small bowl. If nothing else, this interruption would give him a chance to postpone answering Karl.

"Hey, look, here's someone else." He rose, feeling like someone in an amateur theater production. God knows, he'd sat through enough performances of *Our Town* and *Oklahoma* in support of Erin.

Karl didn't move.

"I'll be right back," Ethan said as it became clear Karl wasn't going to budge.

Karl took a long swallow of his drink and didn't reply.

So … okay. Ethan left him and padded barefoot around the side of the house again. He stepped out of the trees as Michael's white pickup pulled neatly up beside Karl's TR7.

CHAPTER FIVE

Ethan's heart thumped. He couldn't think of a single reason Michael would come to see him other than Michael *wanted* to see him, and that was the best news he'd had all evening.

"Hi," he called as soon as Michael climbed out of his pickup.

Michael glanced around, spotted Ethan walking toward him. "Hi." He nodded at Karl's TR7. "I guess you've got company."

"Not exactly. Karl dropped by." Ethan wanted to make it very clear that he had not invited Karl.

"Ah." Well, it wasn't exactly *ah*. It was more or less a grunt, but the impression was the same.

Whatever it was, it didn't sound promising. Ethan said quickly, "You want to come around to the back?"

Michael hesitated. "Please?" Ethan added. "We're having iced coffee and talking."

"Iced coffee?" It was polite if doubtful.

"I could fix you something else." He wasn't exactly sure what. Crystal Light? Warm milk? The never-opened twenty-year-old cognac that had belonged to his father?

"I brought you Pauli Girl." Michael leaned back in the truck and lifted out a brown paper bag.

Ethan's spirits shot up still higher. Michael was definitely paying a social call. He hadn't blown it the night before. "Thanks!"

Somehow he was going to have to get rid of Karl without insulting him, because Ethan needed this time with Michael. He just … did.

He led the way to the back where Karl was still sipping his iced coffee. The little lanterns bobbed gently in the night breeze like colored moths. At the sight of Michael, Karl put his glass down and stood up.

"I don't know if you two have officially met." Ethan started off cheerfully enough, but even in the shadowy light he could see that Karl was not thrilled. "Karl, this is Michael Milner. He owns Milner's Martial Arts."

"I know who he is." Karl's voice was tight.

Ethan finished lamely, "And Karl is one of the Hagar boys. From, you know, Hagar's Truck and Tractor Equipment."

"Hi," Michael said.

"I need to get going." Karl was looking at Ethan as if Michael was invisible. "Thanks for the coffee."

"You're welcome." Something was obviously wrong. Ethan didn't really think Karl was disappointed he'd missed an opportunity to kill him, so what was his problem?

"I'll just — " He intended to walk Karl to his car, but Karl went striding off into the darkness, leaving him standing there.

"That was weird," Ethan said, turning to Michael.

"What was weird?" The scarred half of Michael's face looked mutable and unworldly in the uncertain light.

Ethan explained about Karl trying to hire him as a writing tutor, his gaze following the disappearing tail lights as the TR7 hurtled down the dusty road like a rocket.

"On the bright side, I don't think he's planning to kill me." He was kidding, of course.

"Do you really not see what's going on here?"

At the sharpness of Michael's tone, Ethan stared at him.

"No. What's going on?"

Michael expelled an impatient breath. "The guy is trying to ask you out."

"Ask *me* out?"

"You're not going to pretend you're in the closet?"

Ethan's mouth moved, but no sound came out. That was probably just as well since it wouldn't have been anything very intelligent. He was astonished on so many levels. Astonished that Michael *was* aware that he was gay. Astonished that Karl was apparently gay. Astonished that Michael must be gay too — mustn't he? — to have realized that Karl was interested in Ethan? And most of all astonished that he had missed all of that.

"You honestly didn't see it?" Michael asked while Ethan was still floundering.

Ethan shook his head. "Karl Hagar is *gay*? Somehow it was easier to imagine him as a serial killer. How do you know?"

"How do you *not* know?" Michael retorted.

"I guess I just never thought about it."

"Really?" The disbelief wasn't polite. "Because from the way you look at me, I'd say you've thought about it a lot."

Instantly Ethan felt as though he'd been dipped in boiling water. "Sorry," he mumbled.

After a second or two, Michael relented. "If it was a problem, I wouldn't be here."

"Oh. Right."

Well, that was the good news, wasn't it? Michael knew he was interested and here Michael was. All these highs and lows in the space of minutes; Ethan was beginning to feel like he was suffering from emotional whiplash. He looked at the paper bag Michael held, and said, "I've got a bottle opener inside."

"I've got a bottle opener."

Michael reached in his pocket, pulled out a Swiss army knife and sat down in the Adirondack chair vacated by Karl. He opened the sack, pulled out a bottle, opened it and handed it to Ethan.

"This is where you grew up?"

Ethan nodded. He sat down in the other chair and put the bottle to his lips. The beer was cold and fizzy. It tasted crisp and slightly hoppy. He thought he could get to like it.

"And you've lived all your life in Peabody." It wasn't a question so much as Michael arranging the facts in his mind, perhaps determining why Ethan was so blank on the finer points of romance.

Ethan made a face. "I know. Pathetic, right?"

"Not if you're happy here."

Ethan considered that as he drank his beer. He was not *un*happy, but he was lonely. Oh, he was friendly with a lot of people, but he wasn't really close to them. It had been the same in school. Erin was better at forming friendships. She belonged to a lot of clubs and social groups. She always had something going. Ethan didn't think she had time to be lonely. He hoped not, anyway.

He knew enough not to talk about loneliness to the guy he was hoping to spend the night with, and he made a determined effort to turn the conversation back to Michael.

"Where did you grow up?"

"La Crescenta. It's in L.A. County."

Ethan had never heard of it. It sounded ... affluent.

He dropped his empty to the grass and took the second beer Michael handed him. "Where'd you go to college?"

"UCLA. You?"

"Bakersfield Junior College. I always planned on going to a real university, but after Mom and Dad ..."

"Sure. You and Erin had to keep the Red Bird running." Michael had no doubt heard all he wanted on that subject.

"Yeah. Well, no. We could have sold out then, and I guess we would have gotten an okay price for it. Enough for each of us to go off and start someplace new. But we didn't want to. We grew up thinking this would all be ours one day."

Michael glanced around the large yard, the old house, and the open fields that stretched beyond.

"It probably doesn't look like much, but — "

"It looks like a home," Michael said. "It looks like a place where people have lived for a long time and been happy."

"That's exactly right." Ethan smiled, pleased that Michael recognized what had always seemed obvious to him. This was home and worth fighting for. He finished his beer and said tentatively, "Would you want to swim?"

Michael's eyes seemed to shine in the gloom. "Among other things."

Ethan laughed. It was probably a nervous-sounding laugh, but he was happy and excited. More happy and excited than he'd been in a long time. He pulled off his jeans and tossed them to the back of the lawn chair. He tried not to stare as Michael rose and stepped out of his Levis in three quick moves.

Even without staring he could see that Michael's body was silvered with scars. He was still beautiful though, and the fact that he seemed unselfconscious about the scars made him even more beautiful in Ethan's opinion.

Anyway, it wasn't Michael's scars he couldn't keep his eyes off. His gaze naturally gravitated to the neat bulge beneath Michael's white briefs. How big was Michael? There was one way to find out, of course.

Emboldened by curiosity or maybe more alcohol than he was used to, Ethan shucked his swim trunks and then levered himself up over the side of the pool. The water was cooler now — though not cold — and silky soft. The moon drifted across the black surface like a giant lily pad.

"Skinny dipping in the moonlight?" Michael sounded amused.

"Sounds like a song." Sounded like a dream come true, in fact. Ethan watched while trying to appear not to be looking as Michael peeled off his briefs and dropped them on top of Ethan's trunks before splashing down beside him in the water.

Broad shoulders, narrow hips, long legs ... and Michael had looked perfectly well-endowed in the glimpse Ethan'd had. Nothing missing or damaged structurally, thank God.

Michael struck off toward the opposite side of the pool in clean, long strokes. He surfaced, shook his wet hair back. "This is great."

He did a couple of brisk laps across the broad diameter of the pool while Ethan floated and simply enjoyed Michael's open pleasure. When Michael changed direction and swam toward him he felt a momentary unease. His memories of high school swim class weren't fond ones. He'd been in a class with Dave Wilton and Kurt Hagar,

Karl's older brother, and he'd always taken the brunt of the inevitable roughhousing. He didn't doubt he'd take the brunt in any wrestling match with Michael.

But when Michael's arms closed around him, it was playful and easy. He didn't drag Ethan beneath the water before he had time to catch his breath, he didn't accidentally-on-purpose bang his elbows or knees into any soft parts of Ethan's anatomy. He wasn't trying to overpower Ethan, and Ethan stopped wrestling and wrapped his arms around Michael's shoulders.

He could see the glimmer of Michael's smile as Michael hoisted him up, and he could feel the prod of Michael's erection against his thigh. It was kind of a turn-on to know Michael could feel him as well, although the thought was immediately followed by uncertainty over how he compared with other guys Michael had been with.

Michael fell back in the water, dragging Ethan with him. As they sank down, Michael's mouth closed on Ethan's. It was too fast and too wet and too bubbly to be romantic, exactly, but Ethan was vividly conscious of Michael's warmth and strength. The next moment they were laughing and splashing away from each other.

○ ○ ○ ○ ○

Though it was still in the high eighties, it felt cold by the time they climbed out of the pool. They toweled off and pulled on their jeans and shirts. They picked up the empty beer bottles and went inside. The house, by comparison, still felt warm and a little stuffy.

"When does your sister get home?" Michael asked as they went through the living room with its overstuffed plaid chairs and sofas, and pseudo Duncan Phyfe tables.

It seemed to be the question on everyone's mind. Ethan looked at the clock over the bookshelf. "We've got the house to ourselves for about an hour."

He led the way upstairs to his bedroom. Michael said nothing as he followed Ethan down the hall with its threadbare carpet and gallery of family photos.

Ethan felt for the light switch and the room was illuminated. It was almost disorienting, this sudden merging of his old dreams with his new. Until he saw the room through Michael's eyes, it hadn't occurred to Ethan that maybe it was time to start living in the present. Not that it was a child's room. Even when Ethan had been a little kid, he had not been particularly childish. The shelves were full of books. Travel posters and maps of places he had never been to — and probably never would now — adorned the walls.

His boyhood had been spent planning for a future and his adulthood had been spent in the trappings of his past. He had never really considered it before.

Michael moved slowly around the room lifting a model airplane, examining a map of the Sahara. Ethan sat down on the edge of the bed — it seemed newly, embarrassingly prominent as though positioned to be front and center stage — watching, waiting for the moment when Michael would finish exploring.

As though reading his thoughts, Michael came toward the bed. "So have you ever ... ?"

Ethan shook his head.

"*Never*?"

"There wasn't anyone around to practice with."

"But when you went to college?"

Ethan could feel his face getting red, but it was better if they just got this out of the way. "I didn't know how to ..." *Ask*. Nor did he know *who* to ask, as should have been obvious from his inability to read what was happening with Karl. "Sorry."

"Don't apologize."

Michael climbed onto the bed beside him and Ethan let himself fall back. It almost felt like he was moving in slow motion, he was so aware of every movement, every look between them.

Michael leaned over him, his hands slid beneath Ethan's T-shirt, raising it, and Ethan obediently raised his arms to let it be pulled off. He should probably be reciprocating, right? He reached up to slide the open shirt off Michael's broad shoulders. He liked the feel of Michael's skin, smooth and still cool beneath the warm cotton from their swim. Even the touch of Michael's scars was not displeasing to him, and he hoped he was communicating that as he gently traced the cobwebbed lines.

Michael's eyes lingered on the pulse beating at the base of Ethan's throat. He brushed it with his fingertips and smiled faintly.

"I feel like I'm dreaming. I didn't even think you liked me," Ethan admitted. As he said it, he realized it was a stupid comment. Maybe he had grown up in the boonies, but he wasn't so naïve that he didn't know you didn't have to like someone to have sex with them. Michael's options were as limited as his own — as were Karl's — so assuming that this was the start of anything, except maybe an occasional roll in the hay, was a good way to get his heart broken.

"You're not very good at reading people."

Was that true? Ethan wasn't sure. He'd always thought himself a reasonable judge of character. "Well, in fairness, you don't give a lot of clues."

Michael's mouth quirked, the scarred half, lopsided.

"*Do* you like me?" He couldn't help that asking probably made him sound insecure. He preferred knowing upfront.

"I like you." Michael's voice was low. "I liked you the first day I saw you. You were sitting on the floor surrounded by books, and you looked up when I opened the door and smiled right at me. It felt like you had been waiting for me, like you were welcoming me home."

Ethan sucked in a breath. Just *that* was so much more than he'd hoped for.

Michael added, "And I've got a perfectly good coffee maker at the dojo."

Ethan started to laugh. "Do you?"

Michael nodded, shrugging the rest of the way out of his shirt. He gathered Ethan into his arms. It was better than Ethan had imagined, and he had a vivid imagination. The startling, solid human reality of skin and hair and breath as they held each other, pressed closer was better. One of Ethan's flip flops fell to the floor, the other bent back and sprang free.

"Boing," gasped Ethan.

Michael laughed against his mouth. His weight pressed Ethan into the pillows, but it was reassuring, not threatening. Ethan could feel Michael's heart pounding — nearly as hard as his own. He lifted his head from the pillow, kissing Michael deeply, partly as a distraction from his own lack of technique, partly because he couldn't get enough of kissing Michael.

God. To finally kiss a man. To finally kiss *this* man.

Michael's mouth opened to his kiss, hot and wet, Ethan drank him in, submerging himself in the kiss as they had submerged in each other's arms in the night-cooled water of the pool. Michael's mouth was bigger than a woman's, a suggestion of bristle around the softness of his lips. He met Ethan's kiss with an openness, a hunger that seemed distinctly unfeminine — not that Ethan had a lot of experience kissing women either. He was surprised to hear Michael making little sounds again: not moaning, exactly, but a roughened breathing. He realized that he was the one making those excited sounds and promptly shut up.

Michael shifted sideways so that he wasn't crushing Ethan, his thigh no longer nudging aggressively into Ethan's crotch. Ethan wanted to touch him, but he felt uncertain as to what Michael would permit. Not that he seemed standoffish. His hand stroked Ethan's chest, his fingers trailing over Ethan's nipple. That wasn't something that had ever figured into Ethan's fantasies, but it felt nice. Startling, but nice. He copied the motion, pressing Michael's right nipple between his thumb and forefinger. Michael sucked in a breath.

It felt good to be able to deliver pleasure as well as receive, nice to control some of what was happening, because the jolts of sensation going through him every time Michael scratched his thumbnail against the sensitive tip of Ethan's nipple was cutting the current between his brain.

"Michael. God..."

Michael squeezed the little nub, and Ethan could feel it stiffen into a hard point. "You like that?" His breath was warm against Ethan's damp skin.

Ethan made an inarticulate response, feeling blindly for the back of Michael's neck, pulling his head down. He could feel Michael's smile against his chest and then Michael's tongue flicked out. Ethan gasped and arched up. That wet rasp of tongue on him ... it was like all his nerve endings were exposed.

When Michael's teeth closed on his nipple, raw sound tore out of Ethan's throat. It sounded like protest and Michael raised his head.

"No?"

"No. I mean, *yes. Please yes.*"

Michael's teeth clamped with peculiar delicacy on the tiny peak and he bit down. Ethan moaned and tried not to thrash as he wordlessly urged him on.

Thank God he didn't have to say it aloud. Michael seemed to translate his little gasps and moans with no trouble. He ground his teeth very gently on Ethan's nipple and then he transferred his attentions to Ethan's other nipple.

Ethan's fingers wound in the long hair at Michael's nape, soft as silk, still damp from their swim. He wasn't guiding Michael, he was hanging on for dear life beneath that intense pleasure.

Finally, Michael's mouth worked its way up to Ethan's again, and Ethan let his hand drop to absently massage his deliciously abused nipple, savoring the kiss.

"What would you like?" Michael asked. The warm words were murmured against his flushed skin. "Tell me."

Despite the cooling night air stirring the curtains, Ethan's skin felt hot, especially through his jeans where their lower bodies touched; the brush of Michael's hand through denim felt like a brand.

Michael lightly stroked his thigh, waiting perhaps for some signal — beyond the obvious signals Ethan's body was sending for him.

"Anything."

"*Anything?*" Michael repeated gently. "We can do better than that."

Ethan was willing, though "anything" sounded pretty good to him at the moment. His groin felt heavy and hot, his jeans increasingly restrictive. He could feel Michael was hard. No question there. Ethan slipped his hand between the join of their bodies to stroke the shape he could feel within the soft denim. Michael's eyelashes flickered, watching him. He made an encouraging sound as Ethan traced the length of his cock, trying once again to judge how big he was.

Michael's fingers worked the rivets of Ethan's Levi's. Ethan closed his eyes, focusing helplessly on the lovely moment when Michael opened his fly and slipped his hand inside. *Oh God. Yes.* That was what he'd wanted, needed, longed for — for what felt like his entire life. Instinctively Ethan pushed up into Michael's hand.

"Yes?" Michael murmured.

Ethan nodded. Talk about rhetorical questions. Michael sat up and divested himself of his own jeans in a couple of strong kicks. They landed beside the bed with the rest of their clothes as Ethan awkwardly followed suit — awkwardly because his cock was now so stiff it was presenting logistical problems.

He stared down and blinked. He'd never been this close to another man's erect penis in his life. Michael's cock slanted up from the soft dark tangle of pubic hair to brush the smooth, brown skin below his navel. It looked sleek, and hard, indefinably weapon-like — and about the size Ethan had guessed. Michael's balls were shadowed in the lamplight.

"Did you want to fuck me?" he asked. It took nerve because Michael's cock looked the size of a cruise missile. But Michael had been patient so far, putting a lot of effort into pleasuring Ethan. He'd like to do that for Michael. It couldn't be as impossible and painful as it looked or no one would do it.

"Would you like to fuck me?" Michael countered.

"Are you — ?" Ethan's voice cracked like the teenager he'd once been. "Seriously?"

"Yep." It was terse but Michael gave one of those brief, crooked curves of his mouth.

"How?" It came out baldly. He thought he'd die if Michael laughed, but Michael showed no sign that Ethan had said anything stupid.

"Do you have a condom?"

Ethan nodded, scrambling to the side of the bed and rifling through the odds and ends there. He pulled out a foil-wrapped packet and handed it to Michael.

Michael took it without expression. ", I've got one in my wallet. Why don't you find something we can use as lube?"

"Lotion? Suntan lotion?"

"Sometimes that stings. Do you have any cooking oil? Preferably not something currently being used for french fries."

Michael was teasing him, getting him past the embarrassed moment of realization that the condom was past its safe use date. Ethan nodded and headed downstairs, trying to tell himself it was no big deal. Michael already knew he wasn't getting any.

He went through the cupboards, found the olive oil, and started upstairs again. He glanced down at the green and gold label and had to bite back a laugh at the words *Extra Virgin.*

That about summed it up.

CHAPTER SIX

It was a relief when Ethan got back to the bedroom to find that Michael seemed content merely to kiss and caress. He didn't seem to be in a huge rush and that eased some of Ethan's performance anxieties. He could see why Michael was probably a good martial arts teacher.

After a time when Ethan was enjoying himself again, aroused and no longer self-conscious, Michael pulled a little away and said, "Do you still want to?"

Ethan nodded. He couldn't believe Michael was really going to let him do this, but Michael rolled onto his stomach, cradling his head on his arms. "Okay. Just be sure to use plenty of oil. Inside and out."

Inside and out. The thought of that seemed to stop Ethan's heart in his chest. He put the condom on. Once upon a time a long time ago he had practiced this very thing, and he still remembered how — although it was too painful to recall all that fruitless preparation. As he poured the oil into his palm, he could see that his hands weren't steady. He stroked the one firm, white globe of Michael's ass and left it glistening. There were scars on Michael's back, but his butt was as soft and innocent looking as a baby's.

"Nice. Go on," Michael encouraged.

Ethan leaned forward and very carefully parted Michael's buttocks with his free hand until he could see the rose brown entrance of his anus. He swallowed hard as Michael drew one knee up slightly, giving him better access. Ethan touched a tentative, slick finger to the clenched muscle. Michael's skin was warm, damp beneath the muscular curve of his ass, but dry between his cheeks. Ethan smoothed the oil over him, and then recalling Michael's instructions and his own youthful lurid reading, pressed a cautious fingertip inside.

He closed his eyes at the startling heat. He could feel Michael's sphincter muscle gripping on. He twisted his finger experimentally, and Michael made a sound.

"Am I hurting?"

He could see the beautiful half of Michael's face. Michael gave a small shake of his head. "No way. Feels good."

How could this part feel good? Ethan always thought it only felt good if you hit the prostate gland — which had to be here somewhere — but Michael was smiling and drawing his leg up higher, so Ethan must be doing something right.

"How many fingers ... ?"

"Hmm? Oh. One is fine. Even though it's been a while, I'm ..." Michael didn't finish the thought, but Ethan inferred that Michael's level of experience meant he didn't require the same preparation Ethan might.

The idea that one day Michael might be doing this to him sent a little shudder of delighted apprehension through Ethan.

Michael's breath caught. "That's nice."

Ethan touched the firm little lump again and Michael jerked and moaned. God, Michael's body was so hot and tight around his finger. Ethan was suddenly desperate to feel that grip on his cock, aching with need.

He drew his finger out, wiped it on the sheet and applied more oil to himself. Michael was panting softly, watching him out of one blue eye. He blinked.

"Listen," Michael said, and Ethan eyed him attentively. "We're okay here, but if you were to do this with someone else ... don't use olive oil. It breaks down latex."

"Oh." That put a little damper on Ethan's enthusiasm. He didn't want to think about doing this with anyone else. He didn't want to think about anything but this moment. And Michael didn't give him time to consider it, lifting up and repositioning so that Ethan could kneel between his legs. Ethan absently stroked his rubber-coated cock with one hand, hesitantly reaching out with the other to touch Michael's taut buttock.

"Is there anything in particular ... ?"

Michael gave a breathless laugh. "Take your time. You're a big boy."

He was?

Gratified, Ethan inched forward and began to guide himself into the narrow entrance of Michael's ass. It was tight, deliciously so, like nothing he'd ever felt. A couple of inches in, Michael grunted. Ethan felt the unmistakable feeling of muscle clenching around his cock. He stilled, waiting. Michael let out a breath and relaxed.

"We're good. It's just been a while. Go on."

Ethan shoved in farther. In fact, it would have been nearly impossible not to. His balls touched Michael's flesh, Michael's thighs pressed against his, Michael's smooth naked skin rested against his crotch. Ethan could feel the blood beating in his cock, feel each pulse.

He *had* to move. He was going to go crazy if he didn't.

Michael made it simple by pushing back against him and wriggling his hips. The grip of his body felt like a living glove around Ethan. Cautiously, Ethan pulled out and thrust in again, and the intensity of that set his nerves on fire. Little sparks skipped and danced from the top of his scalp to the tip of his cock.

He had to steady himself, hands on Michael's hips as he thrust into him. Michael pushed back and they were starting to find a rhythm to it, a sensual sawing, swaying into it, swinging back...

Vaguely he was aware of Michael, balancing on knees and one hand, reaching beneath himself to stroke his cock. That was probably something Ethan should be attending to, but it was hard to think past the incredible sensation of that tight, slick dragging caress. Sparks flared behind his eyes — and in his groin. God, it wasn't taking long at all.

He would've liked to kiss Michael again, liked to be held in his arms, but that wasn't possible in this position, and no other position would be possible because it was happening now. He wrapped his arms around Michael, holding him tight, wanting to feel his heart beating against Michael's own. He jerked his hips frantically, crying out against Michael's bare skin as he came.

○ ○ ○ ○ ○

Ethan opened his eyes. Moonlight illuminated the map of the Sahara, angled the planes of Michael's sleeping face.

A wave of happiness flooded him. For a few contented moments he simply enjoyed *being*. Michael's arm was looped casually about his waist, Michael's breath warm against his forehead. Ethan listened to the crickets chirping merrily, the night sounds, the feel of Michael's heart beating against his own.

They hadn't been dozing long. Ethan realized he hadn't heard Erin come home. He glanced at the clock beside the bed. She was nearly two hours late. Worry flickered into life. They made it a rule to let each other know if they were going to be late.

Ethan eased out from beneath Michael's arm and went downstairs to get a glass of water.

He was leaning against the sink, gazing out at the moon, when he heard Erin's car coming down the lane.

He emptied his glass and waited. In a little while he heard her key in the front door. When she walked into the kitchen her cheeks were flushed and her eyes shone brightly.

"Do you know what time it is? Where were you?"

He wasn't sure she even heard him because she said at the same time, "Is that Michael's truck out front?"

Ethan nodded.

"That's great!" She walked straight through to the living room, leaving Ethan no choice but to follow her.

"Why didn't you call?"

Erin blinked at this uncharacteristic heat. "You know it's my scrapbooking night."

"You're two hours late!"

"So? I went out for coffee afterwards." She was looking around the living room obviously expecting to see Michael, and clearly puzzled to find the lights turned down low.

"With who?"

Erin threw him a mildly exasperated look. "Tony Guinn."

"Isn't he married?"

"Divorced. Where's Michael?"

"Oh. Well…" Ethan rubbed the back of his neck. "I have to tell you something."

Erin's brows rose at his tone. "What?"

"I…"

"What?"

"It's about Michael."

"What about him?"

"It's just… we've never talked about this stuff."

"You and Michael? What stuff?"

"You and me. Well… about me and…"

"For God's sake, Ethan!"

Ethan drew in a long breath. "About me being gay."

Erin was staring at him as though she'd never seen him before. "Oh for — ! Is that supposed to be a news bulletin? What did you imagine I thought was going on with you?"

He relaxed. "I wasn't sure you knew. I mean, it's never really been an issue."

"Well, I should hope not. You're my brother. It was kind of hard to miss the fact you never went out with any of my friends no matter how much they hinted." Her face changed. "Wait a minute. You mean, it *is* an issue? You and Michael are … ?"

Ethan nodded. "At least I think so," he qualified quickly.

Erin's face broke into a huge smile. "Ethan, that's wonderful!"

"Shhh." He looked uneasily over his shoulder at the staircase.

"Is it a secret?"

"I don't know what it is yet. At least... I know what I *think* it is, but I don't want to scare him off."

"Aw." She squeezed his arm. "You won't scare him off. It's going to work out. I thought from the first there was something there. Chance knew it too."

"Chance?"

Erin nodded. "He's very observant." Her expression changed. "Erm, listen, Ethan. You're not going to like this, but I told Tony about Karl."

Tony Guinn had been Erin's boyfriend in high school. Ethan had never quite understood why they'd broken up, but Tony had gone on to marry Petra Walsh, who had been prom queen their senior year.

"*Why*? I told you not to spread that around."

"Because Tony's now a sergeant at the sheriff's department. If you'd been listening to me this morning you'd know that he's working the case of those men they found in the desert."

"Please tell me you didn't." Ethan closed his eyes. "Please tell me you did *not* do that."

"Ethan..."

Ethan opened his eyes and glared at her. "Did you tell Tony you thought Karl was a serial killer?"

Erin's chin rose. "I just told him that Karl might bear watching. That's all. I told him about Karl's stories — "

Ethan moaned and put his face in his hands.

" — and I told him that Karl cornered you in the parking lot last night."

Ethan dropped his hands. "He didn't. He was... what did he say?"

"Who?"

"Tony."

"He said it was interesting and he'd look into it."

Ethan moaned again.

Watching him, Erin said, "Well, Chance thought it was a good idea."

"Chance? How did Chance get involved in all this?"

Erin shrugged. "I don't know. He just... does."

"And Chance told you to go to the police?"

"Yes. Well, no. I happened to mention Tony, and Chance suggested that talking to someone informally about Karl might be the way to go. It made sense. Tony will be discreet. I told him you were afraid of Karl retaliating."

"Oh. My. God."

"What?"

Ethan shook his head. "I can't deal with this right now. I can't. I'll talk to you in the morning."

"Okay. Good night." Erin sounded maddeningly untroubled. In fact, there was a lilt of laughter in her voice as she called, "Sweet dreams."

○ ○ ○ ○ ○

A lonely tumbleweed bounced across the parking lot at Viento Square and rolled off into the desert as Ethan pulled in.

Michael had left him early that morning with a kiss but not offering plans of a future get together. He had not yet arrived at Viento Square, but Karl's TR7 was parked outside the bookstore.

Ethan winced, seeing it. He thought of Erin going to Tony Guinn with her suspicions. Well, he knew who was to blame for that.

The lights to Sweets for the Sweet were on, and though it was only seven in the morning, the sign in the window read OPEN.

Karl got out of the car as Ethan came down the wooden walkway. Karl looked as pale and sleepless as Ethan felt, although in Karl's case the cause was probably not nearly as pleasant.

A few feet from Ethan, Karl said brusquely, "I wanted to talk to you."

Ethan squared his shoulders. "Karl, I thought about it and I really don't believe I'm the right person to try and tutor you." He added honestly, "Whether it's instinct or what, you already know more about writing than I do."

Karl threw an uneasy look around the empty parking lot. "That isn't what I wanted to talk to you about. Can we go inside?"

"Okay." Ethan hesitated before unlocking the door and leading the way into Red Bird Books and Coffee. The smell of coffee beans and paperback books greeted them. "What's wrong?" He was very much afraid he already knew what was wrong. He wished he could spare both of them this.

"Nothing's wrong. I just wanted to … ." Karl's voice faded out. He swallowed, said, "I'm gay."

"Oh." Ethan knew Karl deserved more, but he also knew Karl was probably going to bitterly regret this revelation in a couple of minutes.

"And you're gay. I *know* you are."

"Yes." Ethan thought about Michael. He smiled. "True."

"And I thought maybe we could… I mean, it makes sense." Ethan opened his mouth but Karl rushed ahead, "We're the only two queers in five hundred miles."

"That's not a good enough reason for … whatever it is you're thinking. Besides, it's not true."

Karl's face seemed to flatten. "If you mean Milner, forget it."

"I just mean roughly ten percent of the population — "

Karl burst out, "I've heard all that bullshit about same-sex attraction in hetero-sexuals. The only thing that matters to us is where we live, and where we live we're the only two of our kind. We're the only two that matter."

That was a warped view on so many levels that Ethan hardly knew where to start. And what was the point of getting into a debate when the simple truth was even if he and Karl were the last two gays on the planet, he didn't like Karl enough to spend any more time with him than he had to?

He tried to say kindly, "Karl, thank you for trusting me enough to come out to me. I appreciate what you're saying, what you're offering, but that's not what I want."

"If you're thinking Milner, you're way off base. All he'll want is a quick fuck."

It hurt. How could it not since it was exactly what Ethan feared? But he knew firsthand where Karl's anger came from. He kept his tone steady. "What happens with me and Michael doesn't have anything to do with what happens between you and me. I see you as a friend."

"That's not how I see you."

"But wouldn't that be the place to start?"

"No."

"Well, I'm sorry, but — "

Karl turned on his heel and walked out without another word, slamming the door shut behind him and cutting off the bird chirp.

It felt like a very bad start to the day.

Michael's truck pulled into the lot half an hour later. He got out, walked toward the dojo. He was looking at the windows of Red Bird Books and Coffee. Catching sight of Ethan, he gave that broken grin. Ethan smiled in response and lifted his hand. Michael lifted his hand too.

Ethan's heart lightened once more. It didn't matter what Karl or anyone thought or didn't think. It was going to be okay. It was going to be terrific.

At ten Erin breezed in, humming a little tune. She went straight to her counter and began mixing her caffeinated potions.

"You're in a good mood," Ethan told her over the whir of the blender.

She grinned at him. "Then I guess it's catching."

He grinned back, nodding.

He was rearranging the vintage Harlequin Romances when she brought him a small paper cup. "I think I've got it now."

Ethan studied the pale green liquid doubtfully and tossed it back.

"What do you think?"

"What is that? Absinthe mocha?"

She giggled. "It's mint chip surprise."

"What's the surprise? Wormwood?"

"What do you think it needs?"

"Chocolate." He couldn't help adding tartly, " Maybe you should ask your pal Chance for more advice."

The door chirped and Michael walked in right on time for his morning medium house blend.

He looked straight at Ethan and nodded politely.

Remembering the "perfectly good coffee maker in the dojo," Ethan smiled widely back.

○ ○ ○ ○ ○

"Oh. My. God."

Ethan looked up from the crossword puzzle. "What?"

Erin raised her head. Although she was staring straight at him, she appeared to be seeing someone else.

"*What?*" Ethan asked again. He was on the verge of figuring out a nine-letter word for "love."

"The sheriffs made an arrest in the deaths of those men they found in the desert."

"They *were* murdered?"

Erin's gaze slid away from his. "Erm, not exactly."

"What exactly?"

"They've arrested Dave Wilton and his brother for toxic dumping."

"Do I want to know the rest of this?"

"No, seriously. They've been dumping waste from their disposal units in the desert and it sounds like it's poisoned the water hole near the Hagar property. The coroner thinks the three men who died might have drunk or bathed in the water."

"That's horrible."

She nodded, still reading and frowning.

"So Karl didn't have anything to do with it."

She continued to read. "Probably not."

"And you'll make sure you ex-boyfriend doesn't say a to Karl?"

"Yep."

"Erin."

She looked up. "Yes. I'll make sure." She looked down again, but she was smiling. "It'll give me a good reason to see him again."

Nine-letter word starting with an "A" ...

Erin gasped, once more breaking Ethan's concentration. "But he must have known all along!"

"Who?"

Erin's cheeks were pink. "If the coroner reached his findings yesterday, Tony must have known the whole time we were talking last night. He was just ... just ..."

"Wanting to have coffee with you." Ethan laughed at Erin's face. "Or maybe just trying to keep you from making it!"

CRITIC'S CHOICE

I have little patience with romances where the conflict is all based on some big misunderstanding or an artificial issue two intelligent people could resolve in about five minutes of honest dialog. My characters usually screw up big time and then the challenge is to see how they might realistically resolve those problems. I believe sincerely in the power of love — and that being able to forgive is one of the best gifts you can give yourself.

In "Critic's Choice," Cris still loves Rey, but he's been badly hurt and the idea of taking another chance on love is more frightening than having to watch an all-day Godzilla marathon.

What the hell had he been thinking?

The minute he saw Rey's car, Cris knew he'd made a mistake.

That 1964 fire-engine red Mustang convertible symbolized everything that had gone wrong between them six months ago. That was not the car of a guy who planned on settling down anytime soon. That was the car of a player. A player in every sense of the word.

Hey, nothing wrong with that. Unless you were trying to build some kind of relationship — life — with the player in question. In which case, if you had any brains at all, you'd pay attention to the signs, which happened to be about as obvious as bad news in a goat's entrails.

Well, it was too late now.

Cris slammed his own car door shut and walked briskly up the flagstone walk to the house. The landscaping consisted strictly of grass, dark green hedges, and tall Tuscan-style cypress trees. But there all resemblance to sunny Tuscany ended. There were no flowers, no fountains, no color or life at all. It reminded him a bit of Forest Lawn. The estate itself was nearly large enough for a cemetery. Twenty-nine acres set in the hills above Sunset Boulevard.

Cris spared a grim smile for the hunched stone gargoyle peering around the dormer window three stories above. From the outside at least, the house looked exactly as you'd expect Angelo Faust's home to look: creepy.

But creepy in a severe and stately way.

The wind, one of those legendary Santa Anas that periodically scoured the Southland in the late summer and early fall, whispered through the maze of hedges. Unease rippled down his spine. He hated the wind. Would always hate the wind.

The mansion entrance consisted of forbidding wrought iron scroll double doors. Cris touched the doorbell and jumped at the sepulchral moaning sounds that bounced off the portico. That got a quiet laugh out of him at both his own reaction and the sense of humor behind the trick doorbell. The Whiterock Estate would have been a huge hit with the neighborhood kids. If there had been any kids — or neighborhood — in walking distance.

The doors swung open soundlessly. A very tall, very bony man in black trousers and black turtleneck studied Cris for a few unimpressed seconds.

"Hi. I'm Crispin Colley. I have an ap — "

"Oh, yes." The tone was more like *Oh, no.* "Mr. Faust and the other *gentleman* are in the screaming room."

Was this human fossil Faust's PA? Butler? A misplaced zombie from one of Faust's later films?

"Screaming room?" Cris let the inflection that suggested *gentleman* was doubtful, pass.

The fossil raised a single disapproving eyebrow. "*Screening* room."

Cris had excellent hearing, sharpened through years of listening closely to fuzzy, terrible old movie soundtracks. He began to be amused.

"I didn't catch your name."

"I didn't throw it at you. I am Neat."

"I'm sure you are."

Neat didn't crack a smile. "This way, Mr. Colley."

Cris followed Neat down the vast center hall. Three tall archways adorned by carved woodwork and decorative moldings offered a glimpse of a grand staircase and two corridors leading east and west.

Baguès crystal chandelier, wrought iron wall sconces, a marble bust of Louis XIV, a large marble-topped table, silver candlesticks, cloisonné boxes, and marble benches ... it was nice to see that Faust had fared better financially than some of his contemporaries.

Neat, sounding like a bored tour guide, said, "To the west is Fhillips' Grand Ballroom, the Garden Retreat, Gentleman's Study and Salon d'Art. The east corridor leads to the Library, Drawing Room, Morning Room, Solarium and the Salon de Thé."

"Impressive."

"Possibly."

Cris bit back a smile, but his amusement faded as he realized he was going to have to face Rey in a minute or so. It was irritating to realize how nervous he was. He'd known when he accepted the offer from Dark Corner Studios that Rey was the other commentator on the voiceover of the legendary *The Alabaster Corpse*. The film's director, Paolo Luchino, was long since dead, so Rey would be offering his insights along with Faust, who had starred in the film. Cris wasn't sure why the studio thought they needed a third opinion, but he wasn't about to turn down the project. If it wasn't a problem for Rey, it sure as hell shouldn't be a problem for Cris.

"The theater is this way." Neat turned off another hallway, this one lined with framed posters of Faust's most famous releases, starting with 1956's *The Island of Night*.

There was no poster for *The Alabaster Corpse*, but then it wasn't one of Faust's major works. It was a cult favorite, having caught the critical attention of film historians and reviewers in recent years.

Cris knew all Faust's films. He'd seen them all many times growing up, and he'd watched them all again before he'd written *Man in the Shadows*, the one and only filmography of Faust's work. The filmography Faust had declined to authorize or even be interviewed for. In fact, given how steadfastly Faust had refused to contribute to the filmography, Cris had been more than a little surprised to be invited to take part in the project. Surprised but thrilled. Dark Corner was repackaging and releasing Faust's early films in a sumptuous five disc collection. The studio must have backed Rey's choice, which underscored just how much clout Rey had these days.

Rey, on the other hand, was an obvious choice for the project. The critics — with the exception of Cris — were hailing him as the new Wes Craven. There was even a rumor that Rey might be luring Faust back to the big screen.

Good for Rey, if it was true. Cris didn't grudge him his — well, maybe he did a little. Better not to go there.

Speaking of going places, they had reached their destination.

An open door led into a home theater papered in old-fashioned red and gold stripes and complete with slanted floor. Thirteen plush theater seats were arranged in a half moon. Crimson draperies hid the screen.

"Mr. Colic," Neat announced.

"Colley," Cris corrected automatically. Though he was looking straight at the elderly man who rose and came to greet him, his focus was on the room's other occupant.

Rey.

Cris's heart sped up just as though he'd received a bad shock, just as though he hadn't known the whole time that he was going to see Rey again. He was not looking at him, not even watching him out of the corner of his eye, really, and yet he was painfully conscious of Rey's motionless figure. Cris suspected that even if he closed his eyes and turned around three times he'd be able to pinpoint Rey's exact location in any room. *Reydar*.

He forced himself to concentrate on the man before him. There had been a time when the opportunity of meeting Angelo Faust would have wiped out all other considerations. That needed to be true again if he was going to get through this afternoon.

Even at seventy-something (assuming the age on his official bio was close to being correct) Faust was unnervingly handsome, almost angelically so. The surprise was that he was so much smaller than he looked on the screen. Of course, people did shrink with age, but Faust couldn't have been much over five eight even in his youth. He was about five six now. His hair was still — well, no, that was a wig, — was thick and black and curly as it had been in his youth. His eyes, those wonderful expressive light eyes, were still bright, still so blue they made you blink.

"So you're Crispin Colley." Faust didn't offer his hand or a smile. He scrutinized Cris with those amazing eyes, and his expression suggested skepticism.

"It's an honor, Mr. Faust," Cris said, and he meant it. To finally meet Faust... all his intentions of playing it cool, keeping a little professional distance, went flying right out the window. He offered his own hand. "I've been a fan since I was... gosh. Forever."

Oh God. He was *gushing*. But maybe it wasn't a bad thing because Faust unbent slightly and shook hands, albeit briefly.

"Christ, you're young."

He wasn't really. He was thirty-three, but thanks to genetics and a very fast metabolism Cris looked younger. Sometimes it was an asset. Sometimes it was a pain in the ass. Not as much of a PIA as it had been in his twenties.

He opened his mouth to make some disclaimer, but Faust waved it aside. "No, no. I merely expected... someone different."

Who? Cris managed not to ask the question. He probably didn't want to hear the answer.

Faust turned away. "I think you know Mr. Starr."

"Rey," Cris said automatically.

Not for the first time, Cris wondered what it was about Rey. He was good-looking, but not in a Hollywood way, not in a stop-you-in-your-tracks way. He was a little over medium height, square-shouldered and compact. His face was strong and sensual. His eyes were a very light hazel, his hair dark. His hair was longer, but other than that he looked disconcertingly unchanged. What had Cris hoped to see? Shadows and pallor? Some sign that Rey had suffered a little over their breakup? Suffered as Cris had?

"Cris." Rey was holding out his hand. It seemed a little formal, a little weird to be shaking hands with someone you'd once — but really he didn't want to start thinking like that. Did *not* want those images in his mind any more than he wanted to slo-mo through *Texas Chainsaw Massacre*.

Cris pressed his palm to Rey's, tightened his fingers. The mechanics of a handshake. The last time he'd touched Rey it was to take a swing at him. The swing had not connected. Rey had grabbed him and then let him go, and they had never spoken directly — let alone touched each other — again.

It was strange to hold hands, to feel that warm, strong grip, even for a few fleeting seconds. Strange, the memories that seemed to be waiting in the wings to rush the stage of this moment.

It was Cris who let go. Cris who stepped back.

"How do you like the setup?"

"What?" A second later it dawned on Cris what — duh — Rey meant. "Nice. Very nice. It will be great to see this on 35mm at last."

Rey turned to Angelo, though he was still addressing Cris too. "Okay, just to run over the basics. The plan is to record this as a feature-length, screen-specific commentary in one session this afternoon. The studio is hoping for an extempore but informative audio track. They've been slammed for the commentary on some of the other releases in the Tales from the Vault series, so they're hoping to recoup a little credibility here."

"Once again looking to me to bail them out," Faust said.

Rey didn't even blink. "Angelo, you're doing anecdotal stuff and reminiscences. Cris, you're doing the film background, significance to the genre, et cetera, and I'm talking about the film from a technical aspect. Is that pretty much what everyone expected?"

Cris nodded.

Angelo said, "No drinking games?"

Rey laughed. "Maybe later in the film."

Angelo winked at Cris. Cris smiled back with as much enthusiasm as he could muster. Everyone liked Rey. He was easy to get along with. Sincerely charming. He liked people and they liked him. The fact that he was a two-timing, cheating adulterer was beside the point. It really *was*, because other than the fact that Rey couldn't keep his pants zipped, he was a great guy — and a very good director. Including Crispin in this project had been typical of him. He liked to stay friends with his ex-lovers. Hell, when it was possible he liked to stay friends with people he'd fired from sets. He was a nice guy. A nice but tough guy. That was the word in Hollywood.

They weren't in Hollywood now, though.

"We have two options. We can watch the film first, make notes, and then record our commentary on the second viewing. Or we can just view it cold and say whatever pops into our heads."

"I haven't seen this film in over thirty years."

"It's a *great* film," Cris couldn't help saying, and that time Angelo beamed at him. Yes, it looked like the ice was breaking. Too late for Cris's book, but it would make for a better audio commentary.

"Personally, I think it'd be great to get your first reactions on seeing this film again after all that time." Rey turned to smile at Cris. "And knowing Cris, he's already viewed the film a couple of times and made his notes on it."

Given the fact that Rey was smiling, and that making digs wasn't his style, he probably didn't mean that in a derogatory way, but Cris was nettled all the same. It just underlined the difference in their styles. Cris liked to do his homework and Rey liked to wing it. Or, in other words, Cris was staid and uptight and boring and Rey was creative and innovative and exciting. No news there.

"If it'll float your boat," Angelo said breezily.

Cris recognized that too-grave expression on Rey's face and his own mouth twitched in an automatic, quickly repressed, grin.

"Anybody have any other questions?"

Cris shook his head.

"Then let the curtain rise."

They took their seats in the front row behind three mic stands. Rey sat down next to Cris and began to explain how to use the high-powered mics. Angelo sat on the other side of Rey.

It was too cozy with all of them lined up in the front row; Cris would have preferred they spread out a little, but it would have entailed repositioning the mics and in any case, would have surely looked ridiculous. Why *weren't* they doing this in an editing bay at the studio? Not that he seriously objected to getting to visit Angelo in his lair.

Angelo pressed a button on the remote control. The overhead lights dimmed.

He pointed the remote and the crimson velvet curtains slid slowly open to reveal a 130-inch screen.

Rey settled back and stretched his long legs out. His arm brushed Cris's on the rest. He asked quietly, "You have enough room?"

Cris moved his arm away. "Yep. I'm good."

Rey smiled at him.

Don't. Just don't. Cris smiled politely back and stared straight ahead.

Angelo pressed the remote again.

Anticipation of the movie relieved some of Cris's uncomfortable awareness of his proximity to Rey. Whether he liked it or not, it did feel very natural sitting here like this. They had watched a lot of films together.

Angelo pointed the remote again.

The screen before them stayed gray and blank.

Angelo swore and pointed the remote behind him at the light in the small projection room behind them.

Still nothing.

Rey began, "Is there something I can do?"

"No." Angelo hit intercom in the center console. "Neat!"

Silence.

"What the hell is he doing?"

A rhetorical question if there ever was one.

"Why don't I take a look?" Rey began. "I have a lot of experience with everything from projectors to — "

"No. No. Absolutely not." Angelo punched the intercom button again. "*Neat!*" With an exclamation of impatience, he rose and left the theater.

"Run, Neat," Rey murmured as Angelo disappeared down the hall.

Cris acknowledged with a little huff of amusement.

A couple seconds passed. It was so quiet he could hear Rey's wristwatch. How weird was it to sit here side by side alone in the dark? But to get up would be obvious. Cris forced himself to relax his limbs, to at least offer the illusion that he was at ease and perfectly comfortable — and wasn't jumping every time his arm brushed Rey's.

It wasn't easy.

And it didn't help that he was trying to present this picture of ease to the person who knew him better than anyone else in the world.

"How've you been?" Rey's voice sounded abrupt.

"Fine. You?"

Rey nodded. He turned his face and Cris caught the gleam of his eyes. "You look good." The glimmer of his smile was rueful, flattering. "You look great."

"Thanks." Grudgingly, Cris added, "Congratulations on the Saturn Award nomination."

"Thanks." Rey rubbed the edge of his thumb against the tip of his nose. One of his little mannerisms when he was bored or nervous.

He clearly wasn't nervous, so … good. Polite chitchat out of the way. Cris slid lower on his spine and stared up at the in-ceiling speaker system.

"I heard you're working on a book about Hammer Film Productions."

"Just Hammer Horror. The gothic films."

"You'll be going to England for research, I guess?"

Cris nodded.

"When? I'm going over in October for the British Horror Film Festival."

"I haven't decided." Cris continued to study the shadowy ceiling with its decorative moldings and seven mounted speakers.

Hopefully Rey would get the message. It probably wasn't very sophisticated of him, but Cris didn't want to be a good sport about their breakup. He appreciated being included in this project, but he didn't want to be friends with Rey. He didn't want to let bygones be bygones. Rey had broken his heart and maybe that was a cliché, but it still hurt like hell. He still wasn't over it. He was still angry — although that probably wasn't rational. Like being mad at a cat for chasing mice.

They could work together. Cris was a professional after all. A grownup. But they weren't going to be pals. He wasn't going to be another Teddy or Evan or Mark or Phil.

He couldn't handle it. He wasn't built that way.

The speakers suddenly crackled and ominous organ music poured from the sound system overhead. Both Cris and Rey jumped — and then laughed sheepishly.

A hooded figure flickered on the screen, time code numbers burned in at the bottom of each frame. The figure began pouring potions from jeweled flasks. The camera panned slowly to skulls littered on the floor of a tomb. The hooded figure hurried past and spared a kick for one of the skulls.

Cris had always loved that shot. It was so outrageous. Especially for 1963.

Rey reached the remote control as the credits flashed up. He pressed and the screen froze on the image of the hollow-eyed flying skull.

Angelo returned. He was a little out of breath but impressively spry for a man of his age. He took his seat. "What did I miss?"

"We're fine. We can re-sync the audio. I just want everyone to remember that the mics are hot. So if you don't want it potentially on the audio track, keep it to yourself."

"Got it," Cris said.

Angelo waved a lazy hand.

Rey pressed the remote. The credits began to roll, the jagged graphics looking like the black and white embodiment of a migraine.

CHAPTER TWO

"Hey, I'm Rey Starr and I direct horror films, some of which you may have seen or at least heard of. It's my great honor to introduce one of my all time favorite scary movies, *The Alabaster Corpse*. I'll be doing the audio commentary on this classic shocker, and I'll be joined by the film's star, Hollywood and horror legend Angelo Faust."

Rey paused. Angelo said nothing.

Rey continued, "This is a rare privilege. Angelo and I are sitting here with Crispin Colley, noted film historian and critic for *Phangloria* magazine. Cris is also the author of *Man in the Shadows*."

Rey nodded to Cris.

Cris leaned forward. "Nice to be here, Rey."

"Friends, Romans, Countrymen," announced Angelo. He giggled.

Cris threw a quick look at Rey.

Rey cleared his throat. "It's unusual to see the kind of prologue we're watching now in a horror movie — in any kind of movie of the period, . The director, Paolo Luchino, was trying to make sure the audience understood that we're watching a story about the decay of society rather than just a standard horror flick."

"*Si*," Angelo said, and rattled off a string of Italian.

Cris studied the tip of his Kenneth Cole boots, and tried not to laugh. Angelo was definitely a wild card. Watching the film first and roughing out a general script probably would work better, but Rey liked to fly by the seat of his pants. And he generally got good results, so ... .

"The film was made in 1963. It was based on a novel by James Gasper called *Death Merchant of Venice*, which came out in 1960. Although Gasper's novel was critically panned, it was a huge bestseller, and just watching these opening scenes, which follow the book closely, you can see how visual and dramatic a story it is."

"The film was shelved for two years," Angelo said. "I was very disappointed about that. It was supposed to be my big breakthrough. A lot of people in Hollywood saw it. Everyone had their own private projection rooms in their homes, and everyone kept saying it was going to be a smash hit, and the real beginning of my career, but the head of Europix didn't like the film, didn't understand it, and it was locked away.

"Finally, Carlo Grossi, the picture's producer, decided *fuck all that, fuck the American release.*"

Cris felt Rey's wince at the objectionable F-word, though he didn't attempt to curb Angelo's enthusiasm.

"The film opened in a little theater in London of all places, and got terrific reviews, became a tremendous success as a nihilistic classic. Then, of course, the American studio wanted their piece of the pie and the film was finally released over here. Two years late. I have to say American audiences never really did *get* it the way European audiences did. But the American filmgoer is generally simple-minded, don't you think?"

Rey said, "Er..."

Cris grinned inwardly. Poor Rey.

The plot of *The Alabaster Corpse* was pretty generic. The usual fiendish madman was busily preying upon lovely young girls in 1960s Venice. Dragging them off to his tomblike lair in the crypt of a monastery submerged beneath the canals — one of the best all time horror movie settings in Cris's opinion — the fiend murdered the damp and unlucky mini-skirted damsels, embalmed them, and finally posed them like classical statuary in the garden of his palazzo. Unfortunately for the cloaked fiend, he set his screwy sights on the tour guide fiancé of a nosy reporter — played by Angelo.

Cris tuned back in to hear Rey say, "Angelo, you were saying earlier you haven't seen this film in thirty-plus years?"

"That's right. Not since the director yelled *cut!* After filming was over, I came back to the States, back to Hollywood, and Jack Mart of Universal called me right away and asked me to do *Haunted Red Sea.*"

"*Red Haunted Sea,*" Cris murmured automatically. He didn't mean to correct Angelo — it was the last thing he intended — but he was obsessive about accuracy and it just... popped out.

There was a pause. Angelo said, "No, I don't think so."

Rey's knee bumped Cris's. Not that Cris was crazy enough to argue with Angelo, let alone on tape.

Angelo, sounding a little annoyed, continued, "Anyway, *that* became my big breakthrough. I made that picture with Anita Boyd. What a mouth on her! I forgot all about *The Alabaster Corpse*. I never liked to see my own work." He leaned over and said pointedly to Cris, "I never read my reviews."

"No, I don't read mine either."

"Make that three," Rey said.

They all laughed, though Cris's was a little strained. He'd met Rey when Rey had contacted him over his review of the remake of *The Mummy of Soho*. Rey had loved that review. Nearly as much as Cris had loved the movie.

"Cris, did you want to add s — "

But Angelo was now off and running on the beauties of Venice. "Have you been there? If you do ever go, my recommendation to you is you lose yourself in the city for a few hours. Wherever everyone else is headed, you go the opposite way. That's how you discover Venice. The real Venice. Not that gondola ride and glass-blowing crap. I don't think it can have changed that much."

Rey forged steadily on. "Now, in this shot we have — "

"Why don't we stop the movie here," Angelo interrupted.

"Uh…" Rey leaned forward and hit the record button. "Okay. What's up?"

The film continued to play on the screen in front of them.

"It's lunch time."

Cris nearly laughed at the expression on Rey's face. Priceless. For all Rey's fooling around when he was off the clock, when he was working, he was all business.

Rey checked his watch. "It's eleven."

"That's right." Angelo rose. "I'm an old man. I like my meals on time."

Rey looked at Cris with an expression that on anyone else would have to be described as "helpless."

Cris, still struggling to keep a straight face, shrugged and stood up.

○ ○ ○ ○ ○

They dined in the loggia off the main dining room. It featured high ceilings, tile floors, and an enormous arched leaded-glass window that looked over the mansion's windy south terrace. Cris could almost smell the creamy blossoms of the olive trees painted in the full-size wall mural of a sunny Tuscan garden.

Angelo sat at the head of the table, which was appointed with simple but elegant white linens and white china. Rey sat directly across from Cris, and each time Cris looked up, Rey's eyes met his. It made him uncomfortable, but it also set his blood pounding. He knew that look of Rey's.

"One thing the Italians do very well is lunch," Angelo said as Neat moved around the table, ladling creamy soup into each bowl. "In Venice they like a lot of fish and vegetables. Neat, let's have the Torrontes with our meal."

Neat muttered something that sounded uncomplimentary, and departed. He was back a short while later with a bottle of white wine and crusty, warm bread. The wine was crisp, the bread delicious dipped in olive oil.

Angelo directed his comments solely to Rey, though he kept all of their glasses topped up. Cris sipped his wine and kept his mouth shut. It seemed clear that Rey and Angelo knew each other pretty well.

The soup was really excellent. Cris spooned it slowly and watched the clouds scudding over the palm trees. The wind seemed to be picking up. No wonder he felt tense and off-kilter. He forced himself to concentrate on Rey and Angelo's talk of films and art. When had Rey met Angelo? It must have been fairly recently, but it was typical of Rey to win over even a difficult personality like Angelo.

The soup and bread was followed by chicken Florentine. In some peculiar way the chicken and spinach reminded Cris of the Florentine-style pizza he and Rey used to order in on summer evenings and eat while they watched movies on the land-scaped rooftop deck of Rey's house high atop the Hollywood Hills ridgeline. The movies were projected onto the house's exterior wall and the image quality had been pristine. Not that the viewing experience was what Cris missed most about those evenings. Nor the pizza. Nor the fabulous smog-enhanced sunsets.

Who had Rey invited over for pizza and movies last summer?

"I did read your book, you know," Angelo said suddenly.

Cris shook off his unproductive speculation to find both Angelo and Rey gazing at him. "Oh. Yes?"

Angelo topped off their wine glasses yet again. "It would have been a better book if I had cooperated."

"I know," Cris said regretfully.

"It wasn't bad, though." Angelo held his glass up as though judging the clarity of the deep red liquid. "I'm amazed you got that old buzzard Macy Carl to contribute. Although you shouldn't have believed half of what he told you."

"I tried to verify when and where possible." Cris was careful to keep his tone neutral. It *was* sort of aggravating, given how many times he'd tried to approach Angelo, but that was genius for you. You couldn't expect the Angelo Fausts of the world to operate on the same wavelength as everyone else.

"You even had *Vulcan's Shadow* listed in there. I didn't think anyone remembered that picture."

"Nothing escapes Cris's attention." Rey's hazel eyes met Cris's.

Was that supposed to be funny? Was Cris supposed to have reached the stage where he could chuckle over the memory of finding another guy's zebra print thong beneath the passenger seat of Rey's car? The car currently parked out front of this mansion?

"I've got a good memory too."

"Yes, you must." Angelo handed around a box of chocolates. The gold box label read *Sweets to the Sweet*.

Cris slipped the lid off. "Is this that new place on Wilshire?"

"I wouldn't know," Angelo made another of those airy gestures. "People send me things. Little presents. I'm not forgotten. Even now my fans remember me. Not that there are so many left. We're none of us getting any younger."

"This film collection will change that." Rey put a hand over his glass to prevent Angelo from refilling it yet again.

Cris selected a piece of chocolate and took a cautious bite. He closed his eyes in instant bliss. Real chocolate. The real thing. Cocoa, butter, sugar, cream ... and nuts. It was the kind of stuff he secretly loved. None of that trendy stuff everyone served now flavored with green tea and wasabi. These chocolates reminded him of his early childhood when everything had still been safe and happy. This was the real thing. Rich, sweet, peculiarly satisfying — especially with the merlot they were now drinking.

"What's your personal favorite of all your films?" Cris asked, emboldened by the wine and Angelo's relative approachability.

"*Haunted Red Sea*. What's your favorite of my films?"

But enough of me. What do you think of me? It was such a classic example, Cris's gaze automatically went to Rey. Rey's mouth pursed in that way he had when he was trying to keep a straight face.

"*Murder Tavern.*"

"One of my later efforts."

"I think my favorite's *Fatal Hour*. Frances Sullivan did a masterful job making that script human." Rey reached for a piece of chocolate.

Angelo's forehead wrinkled. "But that was a spoof."

Rey assented. "That's what was brilliant about it." He took a bite of chocolate. "Wow. What's in this stuff?"

He and Angelo bickered amiably for another minute or two and then Rey charmingly but firmly shepherded them back to the screening room. Angelo insisted on bringing the wine bottle and the box of chocolates, which he placed on the table near the bank of mics.

They were no sooner seated than he was on the intercom ordering Neat to bring more glasses.

Rey's expression was wry, but after all an element of spontaneity contributed to the success of some of the greatest commentaries out there. Who could forget Monty Python's *Soundtrack for the Lonely: A Soundtrack for People Watching at Home Alone.*

Cris had to admire the tact and patience with which Rey dealt with Angelo, but there was no question Rey was good at his job, and a lot of that job was about effectively dealing with people.

The film had continued to play while they were in at lunch. It had reached the climactic scene between the reporter played by Angelo and the cloaked fiend played by Gin Todesco.

Rey checked his notes. "Take it back to T.C. 012213."

Angelo was speaking into the intercom, requesting Neat.

Silence.

There was more punching of buttons, muttering, and then finally Angelo departed cursing quietly.

Rey picked up the chocolates and offered the box to Cris, who selected a truffle.

"Are you seeing anyone?"

Having his mouth full of chocolate gave Cris a few seconds to consider his reply. "Yeah."

Rey's eyes narrowed. "That didn't take long."

Cris stared at him in disbelief. A number of responses went through his brain. He kept his jaw clamped on them all.

Rey stretched out his legs, leaned back in the comfortably padded seat. "But then you always were all about the white picket fences."

"Fuck off." Cris said under his breath, aware that Angelo was going to walk through that door any minute. Rey seemed to have no such concern.

"Why? Have you changed your mind about what you want?"

"No. Have you?"

Rey had an odd expression. "You didn't stay around long enough to find out what I wanted."

"It felt more than long enough from where I stood."

Overhead, the organ blasted out its ominous intro. In front of them, the now familiar images flitted across the screen as the movie began to roll again. Cris stared stolidly at the screen as Angelo returned to the room.

He flung himself down into his chair. As an afterthought he reached for the remote and dimmed the room lights once more.

Rey pressed record. "Cris, I know this film is one of your favorites. Can you give us an idea of where it ranks with other classics of the period?"

Cris sat forward. "The sixties were a particularly rich period for horror movies. We start the decade with *Village of the Damned*, Mario Bava's *La Maschera del Demonio* and *Little Shop of Horrors* and end with *Night of the Living Dead* and *Rosemary's Baby*."

"*The Birds* in '63."

"*Mill of the Stone Women*."

Rey was laughing. "From the sublime to the ridiculous. I've never understood what you see in that flick."

"It's a great flick!" Cris was laughing too, his earlier anger forgotten as they gained the safety of common ground.

"You just dig the windmills."

"I do, yeah. The windmills are original, visually haunting. The whole film is atmospheric and stylish. The use of Technicolor is surprisingly effective. You don't expect it. Those eerie blues and fiery reds. Arrigo Equini's art direction and Pier Ludovico Pavoni's photography are nearly impressionistic. It's one reason why I regret Paolo Luchino opted for black and white in *The Alabaster Corpse*."

"You two used to live together, is that right?" Angelo interjected.

Cris snapped back to unpleasant reality. "Turn it off," he told Rey, and Rey jumped to hit the recorder.

When he was sure he was no longer being recorded Cris said, "We need to set some ground rules."

"What did I say?" Angelo seemed surprised.

Cris's attention was all on Rey. "I know you like that whole cinéma vérité approach but I'm not going to be part of some — "

"I know that."

"Our personal life — *my* personal life — is not up for home entertainment viewing."

"You don't have to say anything else." Rey said. "You already know this isn't scripted. Conversations... naturally evolve."

"I don't want any conversation evolving in this direction."

Rey's face tightened. "Okay. Relax. We've all got the message."

Angelo said huffily, "If I've overstepped — "

"You haven't," Rey said.

Cris refrained from comment. It wasn't Angelo's fault. It wasn't anyone's fault, really, but that didn't change the fact that no way was he discussing his personal life on this film's commentary track.

"I find it interesting." Angelo directed his comment to Cris. "In my day you couldn't be a known homosexual in Hollywood and still have a career. You're luckier than you know."

"Great. Let's go with that." Rey kept a wary eye on Cris. "I mean, of course, keeping it general and focused on Angelo. There's no secret that we're gay, right? Regardless of what happened between us, we're not in the closet."

Cris nodded. Both Rey and Angelo relaxed, which left him feeling unhappy and uncomfortable, as though he'd flipped out over nothing. Doubly embarrassing, because it probably looked like he wasn't over Rey if he couldn't casually laugh off the fact that they'd once lived together.

"So you're coming out officially?" Rey was talking to Angelo. "You're going on the record?"

Angelo snorted. "Is it supposed to be news? Does anyone give a damn what my sleeping arrangements are these days?"

Rey hit the record button again.

"Fuck off," Cris's recorded voice said quietly, fiercely.

Rey lunged for the recorder again. "What the hell?" He looked bewilderedly at the buttons. "I-I don't get it. I must have hit rewind when I thought I'd hit play. Or record when I thought I'd hit ..." he trailed off, still frowning at the buttons.

"How much did we lose?" Angelo asked.

"I'm not sure. I can't understand what happened."

"Take two." Angelo waved a vague hand. "Let's just go from here."

Rey looked at Cris. Cris shrugged. It was almost worth the wasted time to see Rey this flustered.

Rey let out an exasperated breath and carefully pressed record. "Let's talk about the homoerotic overtones in this film and a lot of your other films, Angelo. The friendship between your character, Dino Raniera, and the police inspector ..."

"Christian Tavella," supplied Cris.

Rey threw him a quick smile. "Right. Played by the talented Gabriel Caswell, who died so tragically young."

"He was a hop head," Angelo said casually.

Cris, who had reached for another piece of chocolate, choked, then coughed to try to cover.

Rey drove determinedly on. "The relationship between the cop and reporter is probably the most important in the film. I know the first time I watched it, I was struck by that friendship, which seems much more intrinsic to the plot then the relationship with the Bella Philbrook character."

"Don't you think we should rewind the film?" Angelo inquired. "That was a very good bit of acting you just missed commenting on."

Cris couldn't help laughing out loud at Rey's expression. Rey threw him a quick, uncertain look.

It was going to be a long afternoon.

CHAPTER THREE

The wind was still gusting in warm, tired sighs when Cris left the Whiterock mansion after eight o'clock that evening.

Against the odds, the film commentary had ended up going pretty well, but he still felt hungry, tired, headachy from too much wine, and a little depressed. Angelo had invited him to stay for a late supper, and if Rey had taken off, Cris would have grabbed that opportunity. But Rey had also been invited to supper and seemed inclined to accept, so instead Cris had said goodnight.

By the time he was walking down the flagstone steps to his car, he was sure he had made a mistake. When was he going to get this kind of opportunity to talk with Angelo Faust again? He was letting Rey scare him off — and it was especially foolish because Rey had been friendly, even deferent at times.

And yet ... he couldn't bring himself to turn around and go back inside.

Cris had nearly reached the bottom courtyard when he heard a whisper behind him. He glanced over his shoulder. There was nothing there. It was the wind making that unsettling sound, like a cloak dragging along the stones.

He felt a flicker of impatience with himself. He was not easily spooked. A lifetime of watching scary movies had pretty much hardened him to anything resembling *atmosphere*, but he was edgy tonight. Edgy for a lot of reasons. And letting it get to him.

As he continued down the stairs, he pulled his keys out, and tossed them from hand to hand as he crossed to his car.

The wind fluttered and scraped as though something invisible was scuttling behind him. Cris resisted the temptation to turn around and take another look. Funny how underused wind was as a device within the genre. Granted, he had particular reason to hate it, but the only movie he could think of off the top of his head was *The Red House* with Edgar G. Robinson and Judith Anderson. In that film, the wind made a creepy and effective ploy: the rising murmur of old ghosts crying for justice.

Well, there was *Horror in the Wind*, but that was entirely different. He smiled, remembering — until he reflected that the last time he'd watched that one had been with Rey.

He unlocked his car, got in, and sat there for a few seconds, feeling the gusts shake the vehicle. After a few seconds he recalled himself, and turned the key in the ignition. As he started down the drive, the headlights picked out the smooth indifferent face of the classical statuary behind the hedges. The blank, blind faces reminded him of the macabre garden in *The Alabaster Corpse*.

The road uncoiled in loose, black loops, snaking down through the arching tunnel of trees. It seemed a long way to the gate. Longer than it had seemed when he'd driven up that morning.

Cris's eyes were on the road, but his attention was back at the mansion, as he relived each frame of the afternoon in his memory. Mostly what he remembered was the painful delight of seeing Rey again after all this time. Maybe more painful than delightful, but ... there was no denying it had shaken him.

Well, he had loved Rey. Loved him so much it had frightened him sometimes. And no wonder given the way things had turned out.

His headlights died.

One moment the road was illuminated in the ghostly haze of his high beams, the next moment he was flying along in complete and utter darkness. The trees beside the road stood like darker shadows against the night.

Then, the car engine cut out.

The only sound was the tires gliding along the road and the wind.

"What the ... ?"

Cris checked the blacked-out dashboard, pumped the gas to no effect, and quickly steered to the side of the road. The car rolled to a silent stop.

The engine ticked, strangely loud in the windblown silence.

The battery usually gave some warning before it went. Cris knew this because he'd had plenty of experience. Which meant — shit! — the alternator. Much more expensive. Terminally expensive, in fact.

Cris tried the key again, knowing it was the wrong thing to do.

Nothing. Not a damn thing.

The dashboard remained dark and dead.

He got his cell phone out.

His initial relief that it still worked — and why wouldn't it? — faded at the sight of the single lonely little bar. No signal.

"Oh come *on*."

It wasn't freaking Black Hills Forest, even if it did look like it here in this Delphian tunnel of trees.

For another disbelieving couple of seconds Cris sat motionless.

Okay, well... he couldn't be that far from the front gates. The only problem was, it was about four miles to help if he figured in the walk back to Loma Vista Drive, then east on Doheny Road, then the march back to Sunset Blvd. The chances of anyone picking him up this time of night — anyone he'd be willing to climb into a car with — were growing slimmer by the minute.

No. Better to walk back to the house. It couldn't be much more than a mile away.

He climbed out of the car, ignoring the instant and instinctive unease at finding himself at the mercy of the elements.

One element. Wind.

The trees around him groaned as though they were being tugged by their roots. The leaves rustled noisily overhead, millions of whispering tongues. Cris closed his ears to them, locked the car, and started back toward the house.

Once he was outside the tunnel of trees, he tried his phone again.

Still nothing.

Ohhhkay. Maybe a little trope-ish, but people did break down on lonely, deserted roads and their cell phones failed to work. That was why movie tropes became... tropes. The recognizable reality within the fiction.

Cris started walking again, firmly ignoring how dark and isolated it was, considering all those colored, twinkling lights in the valley down below.

He walked with an uneasy eye on the creaking, swaying trees lining the road. He was slightly amused at his own reaction to the dark, but he'd never pretended to be the outdoors type. Not that you could really call a Beverly Hills estate, no matter how isolated, The Outdoors.

His heart jumped at the sight of distant lights shining through the trees. Then he realized he couldn't possibly be that close to the main house. Besides, the lights were too far to the north. It couldn't be the carriage house. Maybe a caretaker's cottage? Faust seemed like a guy who'd have a caretaker on the payroll.

Cris was distracted by the appearance of bright headlights coming swiftly down the road toward him. He heard the familiar growl of a sports car. Not any sports car. A vintage Mustang.

Rey.

He hadn't stayed for dinner after all. Cris moved to the middle of the road, waving as the headlights swept the road, spotlighting him.

The Mustang braked in slow swoops, swerving neatly to the shoulder and gliding to a stop.

The top was down. Rey rose from behind the windshield. "Hey. What happened?"

Cris approached from along the side of the road. "My car broke down." He hooked a thumb over his shoulder indicating where he'd left his vehicle. "Can you give me a lift down the hill?"

"Of course. Hop in."

Cris, came around, opened the Mustang door, and slid in.

Rey faced him. "You sure this isn't just a ploy to get me alone?"

"Very funny."

Rey's grin was white in the moonlight. "I can dream, can't I?"

Cris spluttered but refrained from comment. Too dangerous.

After a pause Rey said, "You're very hard on my ego, Cris."

"The fan club's plenty big enough without me."

Rey started to answer. Cris said, "Are we going to sit here trading witty dialog all night or can we get moving?"

In reply, Rey shifted the stick into drive. They bumped off the shoulder of the road and the Mustang molded itself to the road as they sped away.

"You left in a hurry this evening," Rey observed as they rounded the first bend.

"Places to go, things to do."

Rey decelerated into the next curve, accelerated out, headlights swinging across the black road. "So what's the matter with Chitty Chitty Bang Bang now?"

Cris acknowledged the crack with a reluctant quirk of his mouth. "Who knows? Maybe the alternator. Maybe a belt slipped. You're the mechanic of the family."

Cris heard the echo of *the family* and shut up.

"You should trade that heap in."

"Not all of us need something new and different every five minutes."

"Why do I get the feeling we're not talking about your car?"

Cris gazed out the side, watching the pale tree trunks flash by. He was reminded of Rey's white picket fences dig and annoyed with himself for that sour — and revealing — comment.

Not getting a response, Rey asked, "Who's this guy you're seeing now? Anybody I know?"

"No."

"How can you be sure? I know a lot of people."

Cris laughed. "No kidding. In every sense of the word."

"Ouch." Rey started to add something but stopped as Cris's car appeared in the Mustang's headlights a few yards down the hillside.

Rey tapped the brakes, slowing. "Do you want me to take a look at it?"

"No. If you can just drop me off somewhere on Sunset."

"I can do better than that — "

"I don't need you to do better than that. Just drop me off at the first pay phone."

"Why don't you just use your cell phone?"

"Oh my God. You know, I never even thought of that! Because I can't get a signal."

After a distinct pause, Rey said, "I don't ever remember you being such a surly bastard."

Cris made a face that Rey probably couldn't read in the dark.

They continued on down the hill, and Cris's misery escalated with each yard. Why *did* it have to be like this between them? Why couldn't Rey have been everything he'd seemed at the start?

More importantly, why couldn't Cris stop feeling this way? It was over. His mind was made up. Why did he still have to feel —

"Jesus fucking *Christ.*"

Cris wrenched his gaze forward in time to see one of the giant oaks by the side of the road come crashing down ahead of them. Leaves and dirt drifted in the wind, white on black, the image as stark as a film negative.

Rey hit the brakes, but it was too late. Cris felt the impact as one of the front tires hit something — a rock? A branch? — and exploded.

Belatedly, he remembered he hadn't put his seat belt on, realized that he was probably — ironically — going to die with Rey, and then the Mustang was careening across the narrow highway. Numbly, he watched a wall of tree trunks loom up on his right. He tried to brace for impact.

Rey twisted the wheel, hand slapping over hand, tires and brakes screeching. The Mustang spun out, made almost a full circle, and skated to a lurching stop.

Slowly, in shaking disbelief, Cris let go of the dashboard and sank back in the bucket seat. His blood beat a dizzy tempo in his temples, his heart hammered in his throat. All that adrenaline and no place to go. He felt almost sick in the wake of that violent surge.

He had been so sure. The wind ... the car out of control ... exactly like before ... like his mother ...

Rey was speaking to him, voice urgent. "Cris? Are you okay?"

Cris turned his head and stared at him.

"Are you okay?"

Cris nodded. He turned back to stare at the fallen tree. Leaves and twigs still floated lazily on the breeze.

Rey jumped out and walked to within a few feet of the tree. Cris shoved open his door and followed.

Side by side, they stared at the fallen giant, the huge snarled roots dropping great clods of earth. The fender of the Mustang just reached the leaves and outstretched twigs.

A few seconds earlier and they would've been under that monster. It seemed unreal, impossible that they weren't — nearly as unreal and impossible that the tree should have come down at all — yet here was the evidence a mere inches from their windshield.

"Talk about a freak accident," Rey said, his voice sounding bizarrely calm. "That oak must be a couple of hundred years old and it picked *now* to come down?"

"It's the wind. The fucking wind."

Rey reached out and gave his shoulders a quick, hard squeeze. Cris squeezed him back. Whatever was wrong between them, he was very glad Rey was okay.

That they were both okay.

Rey let him, go, pulled his cell out and was checking for signal — with predictable results.

"*Shit.*" His gaze was black in the glare of the Mustang's headlights. "I don't believe this. What now?"

Cris shook his head. "I guess we walk back to the house. I sure as hell don't feel like hiking down to Sunset Boulevard in this."

"No." Rey put his phone away, considered bleakly, and then went back to the Mustang. He retrieved his keys from the ignition. "So much for me coming to your rescue."

"It's the thought that counts."

Rey laughed.

They started up the winding road, the occasional pebble skittering from underfoot.

It was cold, but not unpleasantly so. The main nuisance was not being able to see more than a few feet ahead — and the wind, which made conversation difficult. Not that there was a lot to talk about.

Was there?

"Cris — " Rey began after what felt like half an hour or so.

"How long do you think we've been walking?" Cris asked at the same instant.

"Ten minutes?"

"It feels longer."

"You're out of shape."

That was probably true. Without Rey there to nag his ass he didn't swim or jog or play squash anymore. He still went for walks on the beach, that was about it. They were shorter walks these days.

He refused to let the memories hurt. "The thing is, right before I spotted your car, I saw lights through the trees. Now I don't see them anywhere."

"You mean over there?"

Cris's gaze followed the direction Rey was pointing and sure enough, there was the friendly winking glitter of light through moving leaves. He stopped walking.

That was weird. How had he missed those lights?

"Yeah. That's it."

"What do you think it is?"

"Guest house? Gamekeeper's cottage?"

Rey made a sound of disbelief. "Well, whoever it is, they seem to be home."

"Maybe their phone's working."

In accord they climbed the low bank and cut across the grass. Through this stretch the trees provided a natural windbreak, and it was quiet enough to hear themselves speak — assuming they had anything to say.

Once again Rey opened his mouth.

Once again, Cris interrupted, "You know, if this was a movie, we would've died in that accident and we wouldn't know it."

Rey switched whatever he had started to say. "Like *Carnival of Souls*." He sounded amused.

"Yeah."

"But it wasn't an accident. I stopped in time."

"We *think* you stopped in time. But in fact…"

Rey laughed. "If this was a movie, there would be someone waiting for us — moonlight gleaming on his knife blade — in that little clump of trees ahead."

Cris shuddered and laughed quickly. Rey gave him another of those casual sideways hugs — letting him go quickly this time, feeling Cris's instinctive resistance.

"How are the dreams?" he asked

"Under control."

Rey was the only other person in the world who knew about the dreams. The only person Cris had ever trusted enough to tell, to share that weakness. To hear him speak of them now seemed unsettling, almost a betrayal. But that was silly. Why would Rey instantly forget just because they weren't together?

"The wind doesn't bother you anymore?"

Cris said aloofly, "Sometimes."

His bad dreams had never been about vengeful ghosts or psychos with knives. Those things didn't frighten him. No, the dreams — nightmares — had been about loss and loneliness. Sad, ordinary, shabby little dreams. Dreams about waiting and waiting for someone who never came. Waiting on a night like this, a night when the wind howled like a hungry animal, and when the doorbell finally rang it was police officers. In his dreams he relived the death of his mother, relived waiting for his father to show up and save him from foster care, relived moving from family to family, afraid to let himself love.

Now Rey was part of the bad dreams.

But for all that had happened between them, he'd never tell Rey that. Never hurt him with that. Regardless of how it had all turned out, Cris couldn't forget how it had been for those months, how it had felt to belong to someone, to have someone of his own. That had been his own personal concept of heaven... waking up from the old bad dreams to find himself in Rey's strong arms, hearing Rey comfort him with the sweet, foolish things you could only say in the dead of night. It had meant everything knowing that at last there was finally someone to rely on, to trust.

Into the silence that had fallen between them, broken only by the thud of their feet on the grass, Rey began tentatively, "Cris..."

Cris shook his head. "Don't."

"Can't we at least be friends?"

He knew Rey well enough to know that it was meant sincerely, that there was no intent to hurt. So he checked the bitter words and said only, "No."

"You can't — it's not right — to cut me off without a word. To not let me at least explain — "

There was genuine pain in Rey's voice. Real and deep hurt. It was hard to hear. It undermined Cris's anger to know that Rey was suffering too. He preferred to think of Rey as hard and callous and unrepentant. But that was unrealistic. Just as unrealistic as Rey thinking a few sincere words of explanation could make it all better. For all that Rey was tough and savvy, there had always been that streak of naiveté. Maybe because Rey had grown up secure and loved; it was bound to make a difference. Rey truly believed that there was no problem so big or so complex that talking it all out couldn't set it right.

Cris knew better. There was no fixing some things. There was no fixing this. He said again, "No."

This time Rey didn't protest, didn't try to argue. He walked beside Cris without speaking, although Cris could feel all the unspoken arguments buzzing in Rey's silence.

It was probably due to his preoccupation that Rey stepped wrong and went sprawling. He landed face down, full-length on the grass. It was so astonishing, and he looked so uncharacteristically uncool, flailing as he went down, that Cris nearly laughed.

He caught it back in time, alarmed when it Rey didn't move for a couple of seconds.

"Rey? Are you okay?" He knelt.

"Shit," Rey muttered. He began to push up and then yelped.

"What's wrong?"

Rey sat up, shifted awkwardly, painfully onto his butt. He swore. "Talk about scenes from bad movies."

"What? What is it?" It was impossible to see in the darkness.

"I can't believe my goddamned luck. I think I sprained my ankle."

Cris drew back, resting on his heels. "You're kidding."

Rey shook his head. His big hands circled his ankle. What Cris could see of his downturned face was screwed up with pain.

He put his hand on Rey's shoulder, squeezing in comfort. "How bad? You want me to go ahead and bring help?" The lights of the caretaker's cottage, or whatever it was, weren't far now.

Rey rocked forward and back. He shook his head.

"You can't walk on a sprained ankle."

"It's not that bad. If you'll give me a hand I can make it as far as that house."

"Are you sure?"

Rey nodded, reaching out an arm. Cris put his shoulder under Rey's arm and helped him to his feet. Rey stood swaying, his arm hooked steadfastly over Cris's shoulders. Cris slipped his own arm around Rey's waist.

"I've finally got you where I want you," Rey got out from between clenched teeth. It was a line straight out of *The Alabaster Corpse*.

Cris made an amused sound, although he didn't find this particularly funny. "I think this is a mistake. You can't hop on one leg for a mile."

"Mile? It's only a few yards." Rey gave an experimental hop and Cris had no choice but to move with him.

It was distracting, no doubt about it, to have Rey plastered against him, shoulder to shoulder, flank to flank, hip to hip. Rey's muscular arm clutched Cris's shoulders. The light scent of his perspiration mingled with that of his aftershave. The aftershave was new. Something expensive and musky.

It troubled Cris, though he didn't know why.

"Is it pretty serious, you and this other guy?" Rey sounded breathless, probably from all the hopping.

"It could be."

Hobble. Hop. "You don't have any doubts?"

"About what?"

Hobble. Hop. "Ouch. About us?"

Cris stopped walking. "No. I don't have any doubts."

He tried to put a little distance between them — did they really have to be melded together to move forward? — but Rey clung like a limpet. "And yet you were sure we could stay together forever. Forsaking all others. That was the rule, as I recollect."

"You proved me wrong."

"Maybe *I* was wrong."

Cris shook his head. "No. You were right. For you. I still believe it's possible to be in a committed monogamous relationship. Straight guys do it all the time. I refuse to believe being gay means being sexually promiscuous."

"I never said that."

"Yeah, you did. You said monogamy was an unrealistic expectation for an adult, sexually active male."

The wind rifled through the treetops, throwing silver shadows over Rey's face. He bit his lip as though he was in pain.

"Why don't you wait here and let me get help? It's not that far to this cottage or whatever the hell it is."

"No." Rey's arm tightened. "This night is too fucking weird. We need to stick together."

Cris laughed. "What do you think could happen here in what's technically Angelo Faust's front yard?"

"It's just wrong," Rey said stubbornly. "Your car going dead. That tree coming down. Lights out here in the middle of nowhere. It's all wrong. At the least, you have to admit it's very weird."

"Maybe you should stop watching all those scary movies."

"Funny." Rey took another hobbling step. "Come on."

Cris shifted his arm to better support Rey's weight and they shuffled on.

As they drew closer Cris could make out the yellow light shining from behind diamond-paned windows. A gold and red sign hung above a rustic-looking door. *Sweets to the Sweet.*

"It's a shop," Cris said in disbelief, stopping short. "It's the candy store."

"It looks like they're open."

"But... how can there be a shop here?"

"We must have wandered off Angelo's property."

That wasn't possible. Cris opened his mouth to object, but Rey had let go of him and was hobbling to the front door.

Surely it would be closed. But even as Cris's thought took form, Rey was pulling the door open.

He held it for Cris.

Had he hit his head? Was he unconscious and dreaming? Because this was... nuts.

Hesitantly, Cris walked forward, stepped past Rey into the shop and registered the lush and complicated aura of chocolate. His eyes widened even before he saw the cases and shelves. That smell was more than fragrance, it was atmosphere, it was ambiance, it was... alive.

He stared at the glass cases, at the trays of gorgeous, handcrafted candies. He remembered that he hadn't had dinner and that he'd drunk more lunch than he'd eaten. Maybe that explained —

"Whoa." Rey's comment sounded heartfelt.

"What is this place?"

"Sweets to the Sweet." Rey was studying one of the black and gold boxes.

"But it's like something from … I don't know … Hansel and Gretel?"

Rey grinned. He called out, "Anyone here? Hello?"

"Don't say that!"

"What?"

"It's the equivalent of *Who's There?* and that's fatal."

Rey laughed. "Don't worry. I'll stay out of the basement."

"Shh. Wait." Cris's hand closed on Rey's arm. "I'm not kidding. There's something — "

The lights went out.

The last image Cris had was Rey frowning as he turned. Cris's breath caught raggedly.

He felt the breeze as the door behind them, still standing open to the night, suddenly flew forward and slammed shut with a force that shook the small building.

For a strange wracked instant, Cris wondered if he was going to suffer some kind of psychotic break, just completely short out in a surge of pure, unadulterated panic. He must have made some naked sound. Rey's arms locked around him, held him tight. His voice was warm and definite against Cris's ear.

"Don't. Don't, Cris. I won't let anything hurt you. I swear it."

It was like missing a step, only to have a hand reach out of the darkness and save you from a headfirst tumble. The solid relief of it was far greater than the shame of giving into animal fear. He hung on to Rey.

The door behind them swung open again and leaves swirled inside on a blast of wind.

"What *are* you doing?" inquired a light, male voice.

Vaguely, Cris was aware that Rey had stepped in front of him, partially blocking him from the newcomer.

The overhead light flashed on. A young man with long dark hair stood in the doorway, keys in hands. "You're going to have to find some other place for *that* sort of thing. We're closed. I was just locking up."

His voice was very pleasant, but the bright light reflecting off the windows and glass cases made it difficult to get a clear view of his face. Cris could see that he wore jeans and a leather jacket, that his hair was long and dark, but beyond that he had only an impression of shining eyes and a pale face.

"We didn't realize anyone was still here. Could we use your phone?" Rey asked. "Our car broke down."

That was certainly easier — and a lot more believable — than explaining what had happened.

The young man said, "Sorry. This windstorm must have knocked a couple of phone lines down. My phone's been out all evening. Can I drop you somewhere?"

"You can't get out through the gate," Cris told him. "One of the old oaks came down. It's blocking the road."

"I go out through the back."

Cris and Rey exchanged uncertain looks. "Could you drop us off at the main house?" Rey asked.

"Sure. Why not? My car's just around the back." He gestured for them to follow. They stepped outside, waiting while he turned out the lights once more and locked the front door. "My name's Chance, by the way."

"Rey," Rey said. "This is Cris."

"Hi, Rey. Hi, Cris." Chance gestured for them to follow. "This way."

"You're really out in the middle of nowhere," Cris commented as they rounded the small stone building and spotted Chance's black VW. "Do you get a lot of business?"

"I always get a lot of business." Chance opened the VW door. "Just squeeze in the back there, Cris. Rey, you can ride shotgun."

CHAPTER FOUR

"How's Angelo?" Chance inquired as the VW whipped through the obstacle course of trees and shrubs. "I need to pay him a visit, but things keep cropping up."

Cris's head grazed the ceiling of the car as they bounced over a rut. He unstuck his eyelashes, saw gleaming red eyes captured in the crazily sliding headlights, and squinched his own shut again. He was vaguely aware that he was clutching Rey's shoulder with his right hand, but he didn't care. He didn't even care when Rey gave his hand a reassuring pat.

"Is there a road through here?" Rey was asking doubtfully.

"Of course." Chance spun the steering wheel and they hurtled around a giant oak. "There's always a road. You just have to look for it. Oops. Sorry about that."

Cris fell against the side of the car interior, righted himself, and cautiously opened his eyes again. There was a scrap of paper attached to the visor over Chance's head. Despite the darkness of the car's interior, he thought he could almost make out the words.

Chance said, "If you limit your choices to only what seems possible or reasonable, you disconnect yourself from what you truly want, and all that is left is compromise."

"What?" asked Rey, tearing his gaze from the wall of trees rising before them.

"Cris was trying to read my quote of the day." Both Rey and Cris gasped as Chance's hand left the wheel so that he could point up at the paper pinned to his visor.

The VW bounced as it left the grass and hit the paved drive. Cris's head bonked the ceiling again. Rey threw him a quick look.

They sped on up the road unfurling like black smoke before them.

"Quite a storm," Rey said, seeming to feel some conversation was required.

"I've seen worse. How about you, Cris?"

"Yes."

"Here we go." Chance said cheerfully as the VW tore into the lower courtyard. He circled twice as though seeking the exact right parking place and jerked to a halt. "Safe and sound."

Rey got out of the car, and pulled the seat forward for Cris, who unfolded painfully. "Are you coming in?"

"Not tonight," Chance said. "But give Angelo my best."

Cris looked back over the slanted seat, but all he could see was Chance's Cheshire grin.

"Thanks for the ride." He could hardly believe they were standing there in one piece. His legs felt weak with the relief of being on solid ground once more.

"Not at all. Sweet dreams!"

The VW was in motion even before Cris pushed the door shut.

"And I thought the night was weird before," Rey said as the VW's buzz died away into the night. "If I didn't know better — "

"I'd say Angelo spiked our soup with hallucinogens."

Rey laughed. "Something like that."

"You're not limping," Cris observed as they headed for the stairs.

Rey misstepped. "Yeah. Well, my ankle's a lot better now. I must have just strained it."

Cris stopped walking. "Wait a minute."

Rey stopped too.

"Were you *faking*?"

"I ... yeah. I was."

Cris's jaw sagged. "Are you fucking *kidding* me?"

"Er ... no."

"*Rey.*"

"I know." Rey's face was apologetic. "Sorry."

"Sorry? That's so ... *so childish.*"

"It was. I know. Too many bad movies."

Cris scraped the windblown hair from his eyes. "Why? Why would you pretend to sprain your ankle? My God, it took us twice as long to walk up that hill."

Rey said shortly, "You know why."

"Oh come on."

Rey's face was set in stubborn lines. "I miss you. I miss you all the time. Is that so hard to believe?"

Cris missed Rey too, but he didn't want a part time lover. And he didn't want to be with someone he couldn't trust.

"It isn't hard to believe," he said quietly. "But it's beside the point."

Even in the moonlight he could see how that hit Rey, and he had to look away.

In silence they went up the flagstone steps and rang the doorbell. The ghostly moans echoed through the house.

No one came to the door.

"Do you think Angelo's in bed?"

Rey rang the bell again. "The entire staff can't be in bed. Besides, the lights are still on."

Cris winced at the macabre cries reverberating off the stones of the portico. At last, lights came on from old-fashioned sconces. The iron scrollwork doors opened.

Neat stood before them, weaving slightly. His hair stood up in tufts and he was wearing a dressing gown and slippers

As though on cue, one of the small decorative gargoyles slithered from the roof over the walkway, knocking its way down the tiles to fall in front of them with a dusty thud.

Neat peered nearsightedly down at the broken gargoyle and then looked at them.

"What are you doing back here?"

"Sorry to wake you. Our car broke down," Rey said.

Cris couldn't stop looking at the broken statuary. If that thing had landed on one of their heads, the unlucky guy would have been brained ...

"Why hello there!" Angelo appeared behind Neat. He was also in a dressing gown — embroidered black silk in his case — and leather slippers. "The party's not over after all!"

He sounded three sheets to the wind, in Cris's opinion. Not that there was anything wrong with that in the privacy of his own home, but he was a little startled when Angelo slung his arm around Neat's shoulders and smirked at them.

Rey launched into an explanation of their adventures, but Angelo waved this away, beckoning widely them to follow.

Rey looked at Cris. Cris shrugged.

They followed Neat and Angelo as they wove their way downstairs to a beautifully appointed wine cellar. A large wooden table sat in the middle of the room. On it were several open bottles of wine. The table was set for two with bread and cheese and olives and meat.

"We were just having a little snack," Angelo informed them. It came out more like *werejushhavinglilshnack.*

Neat eyed him, then wearily pointed to a sideboard. "Get yourself plates and glasses."

They moved to obey. Cris could see this whole scenario was tickling Rey's sense of humor. It *was* funny now that they were back to the relative safety of Angelo's house of horrors. He wouldn't have wanted to be on his own, though. Suddenly Cris remembered that terrifying moment in the candy store when reality had seemed to snap. Rey's arms had fastened around him and for an instant Rey had seemed to be the only thing tethering him to sanity.

He glanced at Rey and Rey, feeling his gaze, looked back and smiled. Warmth washed through Cris. Yeah, it was embarrassing to have come so noticeably unglued over a little windstorm, but it had meant a lot that Rey had been there for him — and that he didn't think any the worse of Cris for his meltdown.

He remembered too when the door had flown open and Rey had stepped in front of him. Rey hadn't known what was on the other side of that door — and he hadn't cared.

Cris carried his plate to the table and sat down. All at once he was starving.

In the end, the evening was one of the best that Cris could remember. Angelo reminisced and told a number of funny stories — especially funny given how much wine they were drinking — and boozily confided to Cris that he'd enjoyed his book and was sorry he hadn't cooperated. Even Neat, who turned out — among other things — to have been Angelo's private secretary for most of his career, had a number of dryly entertaining tales about their travels.

Every time Cris looked across the table, Rey seemed to be looking his way, smiling, sharing a private joke with him.

Finally Angelo invited them to spend the night and call for a tow truck in the morning when the phone lines were back up. Neat briefly disappeared and then returned to escort them to their rooms.

"No one can hear you scream," Neat informed Cris after Rey had closed the door of his room.

"What?" Cris stared.

Neat looked at him like he was losing it. "Your. Room. Is. In. This. Wing." He clearly enunciated each and every word.

"Oh."

Neat led him a short way down the hall and pushed open the door to a room furnished in dark wood and shades of blue and gray. "Good. Night," he said with that same exaggerated care.

"Deep screams," Cris bade him.

Neat smiled primly and closed the door.

Alone, Cris stood for a moment listening to the wind outside. He went to the window and looked down. Carefully placed spotlights illumined cypress trees and a

Grecian-styled swimming pool. He watched the silvery water ripple in the wind for a few moments, before turning away.

He turned out the light, undressed, and climbed into the large and surprisingly comfortable bed. The sheets smelled freshly laundered

Despite his fatigue, his brain kept turning over the events of the evening. He couldn't tune out the knowledge that Rey was just a couple of doors down the hall. It was hard to believe that Rey, who couldn't help jumping everything in pants and claimed he still had feelings for Cris, wouldn't make some move.

Cris considered this idea irritably and realized that at least part of his irritation was that Rey had given no indication that he had any such idea.

He remembered again that strange moment — was there a moment that hadn't been strange? — in the candy shop when Rey had instinctively moved to protect him.

Of course there hadn't been any danger, and Rey had probably realized that before Cris —

He stopped himself. Why was it so important to try and convince himself that the gesture had meant nothing? That Rey's feelings for him meant nothing? Rey had his faults, but he wasn't shallow and he wasn't cowardly.

Cris stared moodily up at the shadowy outline of the molding. He could feel a draft from the window across the room, the wind still whispering to him, telling him he would always be alone.

He closed his eyes. He didn't want to think about any of this, didn't want to start remembering. Where had he read that the nervous reflex of worrisome thoughts before sleep had been conditioned into man's Stone Age brain to keep him from falling too deeply and dangerously asleep?

That's all this was. His unconscious effort to keep a T. rex from having him for a midnight snack.

And yet here he was, once again remembering the night his mother died. He'd been nine. The woman from upstairs had been staying with him. Funny he couldn't recall her name, because she was the one who usually babysat for him when his mom worked late. His father had taken off when he was three. Cris had only the vaguest memories of him. He wasn't even sure whether they were true memories, or stuff he'd made up to comfort himself. It had been just him and his mom for as long as he could remember.

That night he had been waiting up to show her a clay dish he'd made at school. What had ever happened to that little dish? Lost in the aftermath, probably. He had waited and waited, but she never came. It was a cold, windy November night, and to the day he died, he would never forget the melancholy jangle of the chimes blowing on their little porch.

Finally the police had come and told them, Cris and the lady whose name he could never remember, that there had been an accident and his mother was dead.

That was all. Worse things happened to people. He had gone into foster care. It wasn't that bad. No one had hurt him. But no one had loved him. He had not come first for anyone. No one had fought to keep him when he was moved to other homes and other families. For a long time he had reassured himself that none of it mattered because his father would come for him. Once his father knew what had happened, he would come for him…

But his father had never come. He'd never heard from his father at all. Maybe his father had never known. Maybe he had known but hadn't cared. It was hard to say which scenario hurt more, but in the end it didn't matter. In the end it was all the same.

It had gotten a lot better once he was an adult and on his own. Being alone wasn't nearly as lonely as being with people who didn't love you. And for a time he had thought maybe he would find someone of his own to love, but somehow it just never quite worked out.

Until Rey.

And it turned out Rey couldn't be happy with just Cris.

But Rey did still care for him, was willing to step in front of a T. rex for him…

Cris jerked back to alertness. He realized he had been on the verge of falling asleep. He'd heard something. What? The draft from the window stirred the draperies, moved the door in its frame. He raised his head, listening.

Not the wind. Someone was tapping at his bedroom door. He threw back the covers and went to the door.

Rey stood in the hallway. He was still dressed. "Hey."

Cris, standing in his underwear, blinked at him. "Uh, hey."

"Can I come in?"

Well, this was certainly predictable. "Rey…"

"I didn't come here for sex."

"I should hope not. Sex is a death sentence in horror movies." The truly irrational thing was Cris felt a twinge of disappointment. About the sex, not the death sentence.

"You know, we're not in a horror movie."

"After the night we've had, I'm not so sure. Why *are* you here?"

Rey flicked him a funny, self-conscious look. "Because. Because you have trouble sleeping in strange beds, and because it's a windy night and you hate the wind."

True. All of it true. It touched him. It was probably meant to — he knew first-hand how very good at seduction Rey was — but… it was effective, nonetheless.

He said more sturdily than he felt, "Thanks. I'm okay though."

A glimmer of Rey's charming grin. "Okay, then you can protect me."

Cris rolled his eyes, started to shut the door, but Rey stepped forward, slipping his arms around him, halting Cris's automatic retreat.

It felt good to be in his arms again. Too good. Cris said dryly, "That's more like it."

Cris sighed again, but not as loudly as before.

"I've missed you."

You already said that. But Cris stopped himself. Why shouldn't Rey say it again? It was what Cris was thinking too.

Rey touched his hair lightly. It felt good. It felt familiar. "You can relax. I'm not going to do anything you don't want."

Cris grunted, but he was quietly processing. Rey had a partial erection that he was politely doing his best to avoid imposing on Cris's crotch, and he was confining his caresses to Cris's hair. That was certainly different.

After a couple of peaceful minutes, Rey's fingers stilled. He leaned over and kissed Cris's temple.

"Good night."

Cris said at last, "'night."

He could feel Rey's body relaxing, growing heavy against him. Lying here like this brought back a lot of memories, good memories of nights when they'd lain awake talking till dawn. The sex had been good too, the best, but it had been the companionship Cris longed for most.

For the first time he considered his own part in their breakup. Had he been too emotionally needy? He wasn't sure. Rey had never come right out and said it, but now Cris wondered. He'd recognized the depth of his feelings for Rey right away and he'd started pushing for commitment.

Maybe it was growing up in foster care. Maybe he *had* pushed too hard and too fast for security, stability.

That still didn't excuse what Rey had done. He could have just talked to Cris. Told him he was pushing too hard.

Right?

"Okay?" Rey sounded half-asleep.

Cris nodded. He blinked uncertainly into the darkness.

It appeared they *were* simply going to go to sleep.

CHAPTER FIVE

The room seemed gilded. Lovely, flickering autumn gold. It danced over the polished furniture and turned even the dust motes to something magical.

Sunrise. Ah, the traditional end of a horror film signifying the return to the natural order of things.

Cris smiled faintly. He turned his head. In sleep, Rey's face was relaxed and young as it never was when he was awake. His erection was prodding Cris's hip, but it didn't bother Cris. He'd had a night of surprisingly pleasurable dreams — most of them featuring Rey.

In fact, he gave a gentle push of his hips.

Rey's eyelashes flickered.

Cris gave him another nudge. His own body had been up and awake for some time. He leaned in, turned Rey's bristly cheek his way and kissed him deeply, thoroughly. Rey's arms came around his shoulders, his hands rubbing the muscles of Cris's back, kneading his spine as their tongues met. Cris murmured, surprised at the pleasure it gave to taste Rey again. He arched back into the willing and ready arms.

They kissed again, deeply, wetly. Cris's fingers twined in Rey's hair, Rey's hands brushed lightly down to cup Cris's buttocks and pull him closer.

Cris nodded encouragingly, just in case there was any doubt that he was fully vested in this. He liked the feel of Rey's smooth, flat chest against his own. Running his hands over Rey's muscled back, he slipped his tongue between warm parted lips.

Rey responded with tightened arms, his mouth working hungrily against Cris's.

Rey stroked one hand down Cris's flank, then slipped his hand between them, curving his palm around Cris's cock. Cris murmured huskily and pushed forward into the warm grip. "Yeah, I want it...that feels..."

His own hands grew more restless, more urgent. He found Rey and did his best to reciprocate. It was awkward with hands bumping against hands, and hard to concentrate when Rey was touching him just the way he liked, giving him just the right amount of pressure at just the right speed.

He thrust hard into the slick tunnel of hands Rey made for him. Beneath his own frantic, quick breaths he could hear Rey's choked moan, and he tightened his hold, trying to give at least a fraction of the pleasure he was getting. His hands pumped Rey's stiff cock faster, their voices blurring together.

And there it was. That hot, sweet release like no other, spurting between Rey's fingers, and Rey coming a few heartbeats after . . . .

○ ○ ○ ○ ○

Cris left the steamy bathroom. He picked his Levi's up, shook them briskly, and pulled them on. Finding his cell phone, he checked for the signal. Beauty.

He glanced over at Rey, still lying on his side, sheet modestly draped over his hip. Rey was frowning.

"The bathroom's all yours."

"Jesus. Can't you take a minute to . . . ."

Cris stopped. "To what?"

"To talk."

"About?"

Rey's frown deepened. "There isn't anyone else, is there?"

Cris stared at him.

"You wouldn't have made love — "

Cris's brows arched. "Made *love*?"

Rey stared.

"It was just sex. And I quote."

Rey whitened. "You don't mean that."

"Why wouldn't I mean it? That's your philosophy, isn't it?"

Rey sat up. "Why are you doing this?" The pain on his face was too real, too raw to ignore. It drained Cris's resolve.

He sat down on the edge of the bed. "I'm not... I'm trying to be a realist."

"I don't want you to be a realist. I want you to be you."

Cris laughed. "Great. Thanks." He shook his head — mostly at himself.

Rey covered his hand with his own. "What do you want?"

Cris felt the warm strength of the fingers laced with his own. He tried to imagine freeing himself, telling Rey that this morning had truly been the last time, that they would never hold each again, never kiss again. "I want the last six months never to have happened. I want the thing with Terry never to have happened."

"The thing with Terry meant nothing."

"It meant something to me."

"I know." Rey grimaced. "I screwed up. I can't turn back the clock, but I promise you I'll never screw up again. At least... I'll never screw up that way again. I may screw up other ways."

"Rey, you know me well enough to know I *can't* — "

"Listen to me. I want to be with you. I want that more than anything. Everything happened so fast between us we never really discussed our expectations until we were already moving in together. When I realized you believed that we'd be exclusive — "

Cris tried to free his hand. "What did you think moving in together meant?"

"I don't know. I just wanted to be with you all the time. I *should* have realized before, I know, but I wasn't thinking that far ahead. It wasn't even that I *wanted* to be with someone else. I wouldn't have moved in with you if that was the case. But knowing that I couldn't, that that part of my life was over... it's like deciding to give up smoking. All you do is think about cigarettes."

"Yeah, I get it. I got it six months ago. You weren't ready to give up that part of your life."

"But I was. That's the thing, Cris. I *was* ready. My head had to catch up with my heart, that's all."

"Which head was that? Because — "

"I'm serious."

Cris sighed. "Why didn't you tell me? Why didn't you talk to me? Why did you have to do that? And then let me find..." His voice gave out. Six months later it still hurt enough to knock the wind out of him.

"I don't know," Rey said. "It was stupid and gutless. I knew if I even suggested an open relationship, you'd be packing your bags."

Cris didn't deny it. "You still should have told me."

Rey's mouth twisted. "The truth? If I'd told you what I was feeling maybe you would've decided you had a right to screw around too. I couldn't take that."

Cris's laugh was short. "Well that's honest. Twisted. But honest." He didn't want to know the answer but he had to ask. "How many times was it? How many times did you cheat on me?"

Shamefaced, Rey said, "Just the once. I swear to God. I didn't go looking for it. Terry was coming on to me all the time."

"But you struggled madly? Yeah, I've seen that movie."

"Listen. Even if it doesn't change anything for you, let me say it. I owe you this much."

Cris pulled his hand free and that time Rey let him. "Interesting way of looking at it. You owe me the opportunity of forcing me to listen to you spill your guts so you can clear your conscience."

"That's not what I mean. It's not an excuse. It's an explanation. Terry was offering and I figured maybe I'd get it out of my system."

Cris nodded. "How'd that work out for you?"

"You know how it worked out. Terry decided we were starting an affair and before I could get rid of him, you found out about the afternoon at the beach house."

"That's the way I remember it too. Glad we cleared that up."

"I fucked up."

"Literally."

"But I've learned from that. I'm not saying it was a good thing, but maybe it was a necessary thing. It helped me understand that it's you I love and that what we had was real and it was meant to last."

"It didn't."

"It should have. It still could. I want you back, Cris. And I think, as angry and as hurt as you are, you still love me too."

The lie would have taken more energy than Cris possessed. He stared, silent, ahead.

Rey put his arm around Cris's shoulders. "You know what? You're telling me everything you're afraid of. What do you *want*?"

Cris was silent. Everything he was afraid of was the same thing. That Rey would fuck up again and break his heart. He wasn't sure he could survive being hurt that much twice. As for what he wanted? He wanted safety, security, commitment. And he wanted Rey. And he wasn't sure those things were mutually compatible. Rey without safety, security, commitment was a frightening proposition. But safety, security, and commitment without Rey would be like being buried alive. He might as well be one of the statues in *The Alabaster Corpse*.

"I love you," Rey said. "I'm not perfect, but I'll always be here for you."

Studying Rey's face, the sincerity there, Cris remembered his thoughts before sleep the night before. Remembered that Rey had braved monsters for him and held him safe against bad dreams. Rey loved him. No, he wasn't perfect, and perhaps they would hurt each other again, but he believed Rey when he said he would be there for him.

It was as much as anyone could hope for. Life was not a movie after all.

He took a deep breath. "I want ... us to try again."

Rey's arms locked around him. His kiss was sweet.

○ ○ ○ ○ ○

Angelo was at breakfast when they went downstairs to say goodbye. He was reading the paper and holding his coffee cup up to Neat to refill.

Both men stared as Cris and Rey walked in.

"The tow truck is on its way," Rey said. "We thought we'd — "

"What the hell?" Angelo stared and then turned to Neat. "I thought they left last night?"

Neat shrugged. He finished filling Angelo's coffee cup.

"Well," Angelo said. "Nice to see you again, of course. You said something about a tow truck?"

"The Auto Club is on the way. Cris's car broke down last night and my ..." Rey stopped. "I'll call you later," he finished.

"Of course. I'll look forward to it." Angelo waved them off vaguely.

"I'm telling you," Cris said as they headed for the vast center hall with its three tall archways, "this was the weirdest — "

"Tell me over breakfast," Rey said. "We've got plans to make." His gaze slid to meet Cris's. Cris smiled back, but his smile faded.

He stopped.

"What's wrong?" Rey asked, stopping too.

"Oh no."

"What? What is it?"

"You don't think this is one of those *it was all a dream* endings, do you?"

JUST DESSERTS

*This is another of my personal favorites, but I think Ridge makes
a lot of readers uncomfortable. Sometimes bad things happen to good people.
Sometimes bad things happen to bad people. Not everyone can make
lemonade out of the lemons life hands out. We all do the best we can
with the tools we've got.*

Murder had its drawbacks of course, but once the idea came to Ridge, it was hard to get out of his mind.

It began with the argument over the cable bill. Raleigh objected to paying for cable when he was never home to watch TV or use the Internet. It didn't seem to dawn on him that the only reason Ridge was stuck home watching TV and surfing the net was because Raleigh had been driving the car that plowed into the tractor and left Ridge in a goddamned wheelchair.

Ridge reminded Raleigh of that fact — in words of one syllable so Raleigh could understand — and Raleigh turned the usual shades of red, white, and blue and then agreed to pay Comcall their exorbitant rates before he stormed out, leaving Ridge to sit at the study window watching his cousin fling himself in his Mazda MX-5 and blast off down the cracked and weed-rutted drive.

There was sour satisfaction to be had in winning their latest skirmish, but some of Raleigh's barbs had hit home. They worked their way in deep.

You're not a prisoner. It's your choice to sit here all day. If I was the one that got crippled, I'd try to show some dignity.

Ridge's sense of injustice swelled and burst. As luck would have it, he was working on an In Sympathy design at the time. He stared down at the purple and blue line drawing of a Black Prince water lily, and the idea seemed to float into his mind.

The idea that… the world would be a much better place without Raleigh Baneberry.

The world, in general — and Ridge's world, in particular.

For long moments he sat there, his hands shaking with adrenaline and anger, and he realized with a flash of dazzling clarity that he was right. Not only right but reasonable. Plus, this was something still within his power to achieve. He could do it. He could get rid of Raleigh.

No. No euphemisms. He'd had enough of greeting card sentiments.

He could kill Raleigh.

He could murder Raleigh.

Ridge tested the words, tasted the concept on the palate of his conscience. He found it delicious. *Delicious* after the months of indignity and pain. Mental pain, of course. Oh, blah, blah, blah. But more to the point, physical pain. Physical pain like Raleigh could never imagine, let alone bear.

In fact, for a few pleasant seconds, Ridge toyed with the fantasy of not killing Raleigh at all, simply leaving him somehow helpless and tethered and in excruciating, agonizing pain from his waking moment to the first troubled dream of the unending night.

But no. Totally unrealistic. Besides, Ridge wanted his inheritance. The inheritance that was now Raleigh's because he had murdered Uncle Beau when he crippled Ridge. Or as good as. It was when Uncle Beau had received the terrible news that his two nephews had been in a possibly fatal car crash that he'd suffered a massive heart attack and died that very night. Died with his new will — which was, in fact, his old will — unsigned.

And though Raleigh knew the old man had fully intended to make Ridge his heir once more — and even old Mr. Maurice of Maurice, Maurice & Morris had tried to shame him into doing the right thing — Raleigh had clung tight and tenaciously to the letter of the law. Raleigh had prevailed.

And he was going to die for it.

But how?

How?

It had to be something that couldn't be tracked specifically back to Ridge.

Fortunately, all kinds of people would be happy to see Raleigh out of the way. Ridge had the best motive, no doubt, but he'd likely be dismissed as a serious suspect. He was a helpless cripple, after all, and he'd had three weeks to see how a man in a wheelchair was generally overlooked and dismissed.

Of course, his disability did limit his options. He couldn't drive, so he couldn't run Raleigh down in a hit-and-run accident. He couldn't walk, so he couldn't disguise himself as a burglar and overpower Raleigh.

Hadn't he once seen an episode of *Columbo* where a fragile invalid had pretended to mistake her victim for a prowler and shot him through the heart? That might work. The drafty halls and broken windows of Baneberry Castle would help sell that one.

Complicated, though. And messy.

No — shooting, stabbing, and blunt instruments were probably out. An accident would be best, but given Ridge's physical limitations, an accident might be hard to arrange.

Which left … ?

Ridge backed his chair from the desk and wheeled it over to the ceiling-high bookshelf. There it was. Eight shelves up. *Poisons: Their Properties, Chemical Identification, Symptoms, and Emergency Treatments.* He set the brake on his wheelchair, gripped the thick mahogany shelf with one hand, used the other to push himself up. He sucked in a sharp breath at the burning sensation of ground glass at the base of his spine. The pain radiated up through his back and down his legs. But he only needed to stand long enough to snatch the book from the shelf. Prize in hand, he lowered himself again to the padded seat.

He nearly shot out of his chair as the doorbell rang.

Unexpected as it was, the feeble tinkle sounded like the heavy chimes of Big Ben. *Boom. Boom. Boom.* The sound of the old-fashioned bell rang through the long and crooked halls, sprinted up the peeling staircases, and cannonballed out the cracked and broken windows.

The shock of it held Ridge immobile for a long moment.

They did not get visitors.

The last visitor who'd rung that bell had been the coroner.

They rarely got deliveries. Most days they didn't even get mail. Long ago, Ridge had set the local post office straight on the irresponsible filling of their mail slot with junk letters and catalogs for things no one in their right mind needed.

The doorbell chimed again.

Ridge wheeled vigorously across the room, down the hall to the door. The simplest things were a pain in the ass when you were in a wheelchair. You couldn't just yank open a door without banging it into the footrest of the chair. Whatever it was you were doing, you had to position the chair. You had to consider whether you needed to set the brake. You had to remember to keep your hands, arms, elbows and feet within the framework so you didn't pinch them between the chair and another object. When reaching or stretching or leaning, you had to consider whether you were in danger of overbalancing the chair. Or tipping yourself out of it. You had to consider whether you were rolling yourself into a position you wouldn't be able to roll out of. That was one of the big things to remember in Baneberry Castle.

So Ridge opened the door partway, using his free hand to back the chair while hanging onto the handle.

A young man in khakis, a navy polo, and tennis shoes stood on the doorstep squirting Binaca into his mouth. The peppermint scent drifted on the breeze. Ridge sneezed.

"Oh. Hi." The young man leaned over and offered a self-conscious smile through the door opening.

"Yes?" Ridge asked sharply. He had never been fond of the golly-gee school of charm.

On closer inspection, the young man wasn't quite as young as Ridge had thought. He was probably in his early thirties, no more than a couple of years younger than Ridge, though Ridge was looking a hell of a lot older these days. Chronic pain did that to you.

"I'm Tug Gilden." When Ridge frowned more deeply, Tug said uncertainly, "From our house therapy services?"

Ridge scowled. "*Whose* house?"

Tug seemed to think it was a trick question. He said cautiously, "Our house?"

"Who *are* you?"

"Tug Gilden." Tug smiled hopefully. He was very cute. Not tall but compact and well-made. Tanned, muscular arms, muscular thighs, untidy blond hair cut in crisp waves, wide eyes that matched that expensive shade of Ralph Lauren blue, a smattering of adorable freckles across a boyishly snub nose.

Ridge was pretty much thinking hate at first sight. "Are you insane or am I?" he asked coldly.

"Well... ." Tug seemed to give it his full consideration. He said slowly, "Neither, I guess."

How delightful. Huckleberry Hound had come to visit.

"Go away." Ridge slammed the door shut.

He gave the wheels a long, hard shove backward, which caused the front of the chair to fishtail to the right, spinning nearly around in a complete circle. The book fell off his lap. Ridge swore. He kept forgetting to use short strokes when reversing. It was a lot harder to propel a chair backwards because the chair's center of gravity was in front of the casters.

The doorbell chimed again. Tug's voice said distantly through the thick wood of the gothic design door, "I think we got off on the wrong foot, Mr. Baneberry."

The wrong foot? This idiot was a natural.

The desire to tell him so to his face got the better of Ridge. He shoved the right wheel, twirled left, and yanked for the door handle. The door opened and naturally banged into the chair, rolling Ridge back a few inches.

"God damn it to hell!"

Tug cautiously poked his head in. "Mr. Baneberry, your insurance is paying for this."

"If they're paying for *this*, I think I'll sue them!"

Tug craned his head around the edge of the door, spotted Ridge and chuckled. "This is like that who's-on-first thing, isn't it? Let me try this again. I'm from Our House Therapy Services. Your application for in-home physical therapy was finally approved by your cousin's insurance company. So here I am."

That was excellent news, of course, but somehow it didn't feel like excellent news. "When did this happen?"

Tug wrinkled his cute little nose. "Last week?"

"And you just show up here? Without a word of warning? You don't call and set up an appointment? You just show up here." He seemed to be on a loop. Ridge stopped talking.

"But I did call. I called and spoke to your cousin a couple of days ago. He set up this appointment."

Ridge opened his mouth. He could think of nothing to say. Well, not to Tugboat Danny anyway. He would have plenty to say to Raleigh when he finally stumbled home in his usual drunken stupor. "I'm sorry you've had a wasted trip," he managed. Once upon a time he'd been a polite, even occasionally charming person, and he still vaguely remembered how it was done.

Tug — and what kind of a name was Tug? — appeared unreasonably disappointed. "I'm sorry. Did I catch you in the middle of something?"

Ridge remembered what he'd been in the middle of when the doorbell rang. *Why no, I was just plotting to murder my only living relative.* He threw a quick look at the book now blocking his left wheel. "I ... er ... ."

Tug said quickly, persuasively, "You know, this first meeting is just fifteen or twenty minutes. Not long at all. We'll just introduce ourselves and talk about how you're feeling and then we'll set up your regular treatment schedule." As Tug spoke, he inched the door open a bit at a time so that by the time he finished he was all the way inside the house and smiling down at Ridge.

That was one of the things Ridge hated most. Having to look up at everyone. He was six feet tall when standing, but he couldn't stand for more than a few seconds nowadays. He frowned at Tug. Tug smiled confidently down at him, and Ridge noticed he had dimples.

Of course. Because Tug was designed for maximum annoyance.

Uneasily, suspecting that it might be no use, Ridge said, "I'm very busy. I'm working."

Tug noticed the book still lying on the floor. He stooped, picked it up, handed it to Ridge without seeming to glance at the title. "Well, then, we should get going," he said. "You do want to get better, right? Your doctor filled out that prescription, you filled out all that paperwork, and the insurance company finally shifted their lazy asses and put it through the system. We've lost enough time already."

That was all perfectly true. It was just that after the shock of Uncle Beau's death and three agonizing months in the hospital and three weeks of Raleigh being master of Baneberry Castle, Ridge had given up on ... pretty much everything. It was disconcerting to have the possibility of hope thrust back at him.

But Tug continued to smile down at him with all that bright and shining certainty, and Ridge felt a tug — ha! — of something he hadn't ever expected to feel again.

"Oh very well," he said ungraciously.

To which Tug replied, "Great. Why don't you show me to your bedroom?"

○ ○ ○ ○ ○

"This is some room!" Tug stared up at the marble gargoyles leering from the nine-foot-tall fireplace façade. His gaze traveled to the ceiling with its ornate carved moldings and medallion. His brows rose in wonder.

They were all "some rooms" at Baneberry Castle. The place had been designed in 1901 by the architect Bradford Lee Gilbert. Originally, nearly one thousand surrounding acres of meadow and forestland had guaranteed the Baneberrys their privacy, but by the 1940s most of the land was gone. Now only the moss-covered castle, ringed by a dense swath of tall, ancient trees and wild grass, remained. *Remains* was about right. *Ruins* might be closer to the facts.

Tug turned to observe Ridge lift himself from the wheelchair and take two shuffling steps to the bed. He didn't try to help, didn't say anything, just watched as Ridge eased himself onto the bed and pulled off his T-shirt.

Ridge got himself spread-eagled on the faded gold coverlet and waited. He was already regretting the impulse that had led him to agree to this examination. Maybe it was being in his bedroom — this bedroom — with another man, maybe it was the fact that the other man didn't look or sound like a doctor. But this felt too weird, too intimate. And Ridge felt too vulnerable.

"I've seen your charts and your X-rays. You should have more range of movement than this."

The bed dipped, box spring objecting, as Tug sat down on the edge of the mattress. He rested his hands on Ridge's scarred, tender back. Ridge tried not to jump, but it was startling to be touched with anything but clinical impersonality. Tug's touch was ... kind.

It made him angry. Angry to be grateful for kindness.

"I've got an advanced degree in physical therapy and I'm licensed by the state of Georgia to practice. I specialize in musculoskeletal injuries, in particular injuries to the spine." Tug was still talking, but all the time he talked he was gently, carefully stroking Ridge's back.

"How's that feel? Pain?"

"Course there's fucking pain."

"On a scale of one to ten?"

Ridge snarled, "Eleven."

"Well, that's not good," Tug said as patiently as if humoring a cranky little kid.

He continued to run his hands in smooth, rhythmic strokes from Ridge's lower back to his neck, where the pressure gentled as he circled around and returned to the base of Ridge's spine. "We got to do something about that."

Under Tug's ministrations, Ridge's knotted muscles relaxed, and some of his tension eased. This was supposedly an examination, but Ridge had had plenty of examinations, and none of them had been as pleasant as this.

"Would you like to ask me any questions?"

"Like what?" Ridge asked.

"Like how much experience do I have?"

"How much experience do you have?"

"About five years."

"Great."

Tug made a sound too quiet for a laugh but too loud for a smile. "Okay, well, why don't I just answer the questions you should be asking me? We're going to try some different things, massage and hydrotherapy and ultrasound, and if those don't work, we'll try other things. I'll give you some exercises to do on your own, and we're going to work together as well. Don't worry about the equipment because I'll bring most of that with me. You've got a swimming pool here, right?"

Ridge almost laughed at that. "Nobody has used that pool in years. It's a swamp."

"Yeah? Well, you're going to want to get the swamp cleaned up because you need to start swimming."

"Swimming!" Ridge tried to laugh. "I can't even walk."

"You don't need to walk to swim. Anyway, we're going to get you back on your feet."

"Are you saying I won't need a wheelchair anymore?" He wanted to scoff, but his voice came out thick and husky.

Tug stroked his back in that calming way. "I'm not going to bullshit you, Ridge. You're still going to need the chair, especially when you're tired or have to travel any distance. But we're going to get you a lot more mobility and a lot less pain."

Ridge considered this silently. He felt winded by hope. It was almost worse having something to look forward to.

"One thing we need to see about is getting you a walker. And better wheels. Although pushing that old clunker around is probably one reason you've got such nice upper body definition."

It was just an observation, not flirting, of course, but Ridge's face warmed. It was difficult to believe there was anything attractive about him now.

Tug was still chattering about different kinds of wheelchairs, like it wasn't a sensitive subject. Ridge said shortly, "There isn't money for a better chair. This is all we can afford."

"We'll see about that." Tug said with annoying assurance. "So you're probably wondering how often we'll need to meet and how long each session will last. Right?"

"Right," said Ridge, who was only thinking how nice it was to be pain free for even a couple of minutes. Tug's hands were not particularly large, but they were warm and strong and agile. Ridge couldn't help wondering what it would feel like to be touched by Tug in other ways.

Just academic curiosity, because, despite the fact that Tug gave off a subtly gay vibe, he didn't seem like the brightest bulb in the box, and that relentless cheerfulness was bound to drive someone to murder. Even if they weren't already at that point.

Ridge gave a smothered laugh.

"See, you're starting to feel better already," the clueless Tug said. "Just making the decision to take action makes you feel better, right?"

"You bet," Ridge replied.

CHAPTER TWO

The unrealistic sense of well-being stuck with Ridge all afternoon and even into the evening until Raleigh got home. Ridge brought up the swimming pool needing to be cleaned and repaired as soon as possible, and Raleigh, predictably, refused.

"Where do you think the money for that will come from? That pool is huge. It's as big as a small lake." Raleigh's eyes were bloodshot and he was not quite steady on his feet as he spoke to Ridge from down the length of the dining room table. They were not having dinner together. Raleigh had developed a habit of keeping some large piece of furniture between them whenever they spoke.

Maybe he subconsciously felt the threat from Ridge. Or maybe he was trying to block out the sight of Ridge sitting in a wheelchair.

"I don't care where the money comes from," Ridge retorted. "My physical therapist says I need the pool for my treatment."

Raleigh looked away from him. "That pool will have to be drained and cleaned. It probably needs a new pump. Who knows what all it needs? It's going to cost a fortune."

"I'm supposed to swim every day, if possible."

"Well, it *isn't* possible, Ridge. Can't this therapist take you to the YMCA or something? Isn't there a pool at the treatment center?"

"I'm not going back there! I just got *out* of the hospital. And I'm not going to the YMCA when we've got a perfectly good pool in our backyard."

"We *don't* have a perfectly good pool!"

"We will when you get it cleaned and repaired."

Raleigh's face twitched and worked. He rapidly blinked his red-rimmed eyes like he was trying not to cry. Some people, seeing his perennially pitiful state, might think he was eaten alive with guilt for killing his uncle and crippling his cousin, but no. Raleigh always felt sorry for himself when he drank too much. He always had.

He said in a low, unsteady voice, "You keep thinking there's all this money, Ridge. But there isn't. There wasn't much to start with, and that's nearly all gone. There was Uncle Beau's funeral — that wasn't cheap. There was — "

"Then maybe you shouldn't have bought yourself that brand new yellow bumblebee of a sports car."

"I had to have a car!"

"That's right," Ridge said. "Your car was totaled in the accident. Along with me."

Raleigh did the light show, paling and flushing and then purpling as his own temper kicked in. "I know you want me to feel guilty about the accident, but that won't put money in the bank."

"*Want* you to feel guilty?" Ridge gripped the arms of the wheelchair so hard the veins stood out in his hands and forearms — and probably his throat and face too. He was beside himself with rage. "You *are* guilty. Who the fuck else *is* guilty if not *you*?"

"I didn't make y'all get in that car. It was your choice to drive with me when I'd been drinking."

"I didn't know you'd been drinking!"

Raleigh screamed right back at him, "I'm *always* drinking!" Then, strangely, he was calm. He sounded quite reasonable as he said, "It doesn't matter whose fault it was, the truth is, there's no money. Whatever there was, is gone. Fact is, I'm thinking of selling the castle."

Ridge sat back so hard in the chair it rolled a few inches. "*Sell* Baneberry Castle?" He felt faint at the idea. "Sell the castle?"

Raleigh nodded defiantly. "It's the only thing that makes sense. There isn't any money to keep the place up. It's falling down around our ears. If I sell it, there'll be plenty of money." He added tentatively, "For you too, Ridge."

"I don't want money!"

"We have to have money. We can't survive without money."

Could you have a stroke at thirty-seven? Ridge thought maybe he was having one. The blood pounded so hard in his head he couldn't hear what Raleigh was saying, though he could see Raleigh's mouth was still moving.

If he'd had a weapon at hand, Ridge would have killed him then. But there was nothing lethal within grabbing distance, though he did throw the nearest bronze candlestick at his cousin's head.

Raleigh saw it coming and ducked in plenty of time. "You're crazy, Ridge. You're out of your mind. What did you think was going to happen? Look around you. The place is a fucking crypt."

"Then what was it all for?" Ridge cried. "You cheated me out of my inheritance — "

"It was mine as much as yours!"

"You know Uncle Beau was changing his will back."

"He *didn't* change it. He left the castle to me."

"You know there was a new will!"

"And there could have been a will after that. He was always changing it."

The most terrible thing of all was that Ridge was going to cry. He was fighting it for all he was worth, but the tidal wave of panic and fear and rage were too much for him. What the hell was going to happen to him? He was going to lose the only home he'd ever had and he was helpless. He was practically paralyzed in a fucking wheelchair. He didn't earn enough to cover anything. Especially now that he had all these goddamned special needs. He couldn't take care of himself. He was going to be out on the street living in a cardboard box.

"You don't have the right," he got out. He wiped his arm across his eyes and nose. "You have to… the will says you have to provide for me… like I'd a had to provide for you." Goodbye to dignity, goodbye to pride, goodbye to coherency. He could barely get the words out between desperate little-kid gulps for breath.

"I know that. I *will*." Raleigh's eyes were wet too. "There'll be money for you too, Ridge. Money for both of us. You could go to one of those places where they'd take care of you and you'd have all the swimming and treatments you need. We'd both have what we needed."

Raleigh's words slowly infiltrated Ridge's brain. Now it was Ridge's turn to be calm. Calm and cool. Ice cold, in fact. "A nursing home, you mean? A place for old people and sick people that smells like disinfectant and urine? Where I wouldn't have any privacy or control of my life?"

"*No.* Someplace nice! Someplace you could be happy!"

It was at that exact moment that Ridge determined to kill Raleigh for real.

He continued to sit there, staring at the baked beans on the chipped Wedgwood plate while Raleigh talked on and on. Ridge didn't answer Raleigh, didn't hear a word he said. Eventually Raleigh got bored flapping his jaw and walked out.

A short while later Ridge heard the Mazda rocket out of the front courtyard. The angry whine of the engine died away like a mosquito in the summer evening air leaving only the sound of crickets and the occasional ghostly creak.

"Coward." Ridge's voice sounded oddly loud in the empty house.

But that was typical Raleigh. Too gutless to face the consequences of his actions.

Or maybe he had a girlfriend, although that was hard to believe. Any girl stupid enough to want to be involved with Raleigh was surely already in jail or an institution.

Ridge leaned on his hip, extracting Tug's business card from the pocket of his jeans. He wheeled himself into the kitchen and dialed the phone.

He was expecting an answering machine, so Tug's friendly "Hello" nonplussed him for a second.

"This is Ridge Baneberry."

Bewilderingly, Tug's warm voice grew warmer still. "Hi, Ridge. Y'all aren't going to try and cancel our date tomorrow, are you?" Tug didn't sound worried about it; he was teasing.

"No. You said if I needed anything to give you a call."

"Of course. What do you need?" Tug was instantly serious. It was unexpectedly reassuring to discover that there was someone in the world willing to come to Ridge's aid.

"I was thinking … ." This was probably going to sound rather odd, but Ridge didn't care. It really didn't matter anymore. "Do you think you could bring me a box of chocolates when you come for our session tomorrow? I'll pay, of course."

"Sure. I'll be happy to. What kind do you like?"

"It doesn't matter. Anything. Nice chocolates. In a nice box."

"Nice chocolates in a nice box. I can do that. There's a new sweet shop in town. I'll go there. Anything else?"

Ridge was surprised to realize how much he wanted to tell Tug about the argument with Raleigh. Why he thought Tug would give a damn, let alone be sympathetic to his plight, he had no idea — yet he knew somehow that Tug would be.

And it was ridiculously tempting to solicit that sympathy, that attention.

Disgusted with himself, Ridge said briskly, "No. That's it. Thank you."

"See you tomorrow at ten, Ridge. Have a good e — "

Ridge replaced the handset, firmly cutting off that sociable voice.

○ ○ ○ ○ ○

Ridge woke early the next morning. He always woke early. The nights were torture. He didn't sleep well. Not only was he in pain, he still had nightmares about the accident. Not just about the accident, about waking up in the hospital and finding out he was paralyzed — at least he could move his legs and reassure himself that was no longer true — and about Uncle Beau's death.

Yes, nights were the worst. Though the days weren't great.

But that morning Ridge woke with a renewed sense of purpose. He was almost lighthearted as he went through the laborious process of getting washed and dressed, and then he wheeled himself out of his bedroom and into the creaking elevator that had been built to accommodate his Aunt Mary's wheelchair after her many strokes.

It probably wouldn't be hard to arrange some kind of accident for that gilded cage of a death trap, but since Ridge was the one mostly stuck using the elevator, it would likely backfire. Almost certainly, the way his luck was going.

No, he had a better plan and he would stick to it.

The doors opened on the ground floor and Ridge wheeled himself down the long intersections of cobwebbed halls to the conservatory. He wheeled through the dead lemon and fig trees to the back door which opened on the central courtyard.

It took navigating to get the French doors open, but Ridge managed without knocking any more glass out of the panes than had already been lost through the years.

Then he was on the rough stones of the side courtyard. The bricks were in very bad shape — some missing entirely — and overgrown with grass in places. It took effort to travel across the uneven terrain. Ridge trundled forward, popping the front casters over the rough bricks by leaning back and propelling the chair in short, hard strokes. He picked up speed as he went, careful to avoid doing an actual wheelie or tipping himself onto his back.

The jostling motion jarred his spine considerably, but he ignored the pain, shoving himself forward in determined bursts.

The paving stones smoothed considerably when he reached the pool yard. He rested for a few seconds, gazing down into the green scum of the water. There were old rotting flotation toys rising from the murky water, and the tiles ringing the pool were stained and brown, the grout black and disgusting.

He remembered his parents bringing him to swim in this pool when he'd been a boy. That was before the first car crash. Before everything had changed. The water had sparkled like blue crystal and the tile gleamed. The adults had sat on the ornate white iron patio furniture and drank cocktails and laughed and made bitchy comments to each other while Ridge and his cousin swam and rough-housed, their voices ringing off the weathered stone of the house and courtyard.

Even when Ridge and Raleigh were in college the pool was still kept up, though the grounds had become overgrown and increasingly wild. Now the front courtyard looked more like a meadow and the terraces were littered with broken debris from the disintegrating roof.

It would take a lot of money to put the pool right, Raleigh was correct about that.

Ridge carefully backed his chair from the pool and continued down the courtyard and then down the path toward the garden shed.

The brick was rough and broken here too, and the path was much narrower. He hoped the wheels wouldn't be damaged by the sharper stones, and he had to watch carefully that he didn't tip to the side. It was stressful and tiring, and probably not doing his back any good. But that couldn't be helped.

At last he reached the green shed. He worked the key from the pocket of his jeans, and leaned forward to unlock the door. It swung inward with a screech of hinges. Ridge peered into the gloomy interior. Feeble daylight poked through the dirty windows illuminating cobwebs as thick as veils draped from the ceiling and across shelves stacked with dirty bottles and terracotta pots and assorted tools and watering cans.

Somewhere in this little shop of horrors would be the thing he needed.

If he could get over the threshold.

He threw his weight against the back of the chair while pushing sharply forward on the rear wheels. The chair tipped back alarmingly, the front casters popped over the rim of the threshold, and the chair lurched forward — and down a couple of inches. The floorboards on the other side were partially missing.

But he was in.

In and stuck. Ridge tried to roll forward, tried to pop the casters again... nothing. The left front caster was jammed between the broken slats. The right armrest was wedged between the door frame and the edge of one of the bottom shelves.

"Fuck!"

Well then. Exasperating as that was, he should be able to hang onto the shelves and walk as far as he needed. Ridge gripped both hands on the arm of his wheelchair and pushed to his feet. His legs were heavy and stiff. He had to stretch to reach the nearest shelf, and the pain made him cry out, but he did it. Hanging onto the shelf, he leaned and shuffled and dragged himself to the shelf at the back with its grimy and cobwebbed bottles. The carcasses of bugs in various states of decay fell away as he lifted the bottles one by one. Weed killer, bug killer, rat killer. The contents of many of the bottles had evaporated or congealed, but some of them splashed inside their skull-and-crossbones adorned bottles with the juicy buoyancy of a cocktail shaker.

Arsenic read one faded, handwritten label on a brown bottle with an eye dropper. Ridge shook the bottle and heard the deadly slosh of its contents. Still plenty inside. More than enough for his purposes.

He shoved the small bottle in his pocket and made the slow, miserable trip back to his chair, lowering himself carefully to the padded seat. He'd never been so grateful for its support before. His body was drenched in sweat, his muscles trembling.

Now, of course, he needed to get *out* of the shed. He considered logistics. He was fairly sure he could do a backwards wheelie. His fearlessness in learning to perform wheelies had been his sole claim to fame in rehab.

But the wedged armrest made it impossible to achieve the wheelchair's balance point on its rear wheels. He couldn't roll forward and he couldn't roll in reverse. The only possibility was to tip the chair completely over, but Ridge's spine was fragile enough without going out of his way to hurt himself more. He had learned to fear physical pain, and he was still shaking from his short walk.

It was getting warm in the shed. The weird odor of old chemicals began to rise. The sun flooding through the open door was hot on the back of his head and neck. Ridge's heart began to pound faster as he absorbed the full implications of his predicament.

It was going to be hard to explain what the hell he was doing in the gardening shed. That would be bad enough. He was already aware that even the most rudimentary police investigation would reveal that he had been in the shed. Ridge watched a lot of TV these days, and he knew there were a million ways for your DNA to betray you at a crime scene.

He didn't particularly care about that. His hatred and need for revenge superseded his desire to get away with his crime. He didn't want to be stopped, though, which meant it was vital he not get caught stealing rat poison before he had a chance to use it.

However, as the minutes passed and he grew more warm and more uncomfortable, it dawned on him that being found in the garden shed might not be as bad as not being found.

No one came out here nowadays. There was no one to come out. Even if Raleigh happened to notice he was missing, Raleigh was unlikely to think of looking outdoors. And Ridge could sit here screaming his head off and no one was going to hear him.

Which meant?

Which meant it was not out of the question that he could wait hours without help. Hell, he could wait days. It was not inconceivable that he might die out here and not be discovered for months.

There was a terrible dusty taste in his mouth. Ridge swallowed dryly.

No one was going to help him. If he was going to escape the fate of the withered insects around him, he was going to have to get himself out and then figure some way to retrieve his wheelchair.

He couldn't lift the chair or pull it aside. The only possibility was to get out of it, push it over without hurting himself, and then climb over it. He rested his face in his hands, psyching himself for the effort. At last he braced his hands on the door frame, pulled himself up, swearing at the searing pain burning up and down his back. His legs were as heavy and unwieldy as wooden logs. He moved to the side and then shoved the chair. It took several efforts and he was sobbing with effort by the time he managed it. The chair crashed over onto the bricks.

From there it was relatively simple to step past the chair. He hung onto the side of the shed and walked with dragging steps until he was out of supporting structures. He couldn't walk any distance without something to hang onto, and it was half a mile back to the house.

Maybe if he rested? He already felt better out of the hot, humid box of a shed, away from the poisonous smells and cobwebs. He glanced over at his fallen chariot, gleaming dully in the bright sunlight. He wiped his forehead and then very carefully, hanging tight to the corner of the shed, lowered himself painfully to the dusty bricks.

What time was it? He never wore a watch these days. He glanced up at the sun. Eleven, maybe? He watched black birds circling over the treetops, swooping through the arched second-story windows.

The irrepressible Tug would have come and gone by now.

Ridge felt a flicker of regret for things that could never be. How much simpler it would have been to spend the morning with Tug. Certainly a lot less painful. Maybe even mildly pleasant, if he could get used to all that exhausting optimism.

He closed his eyes, touched the bulge of the small bottle in his pocket. At least he'd done what he set out to do. That was something. Unless he died here before he managed to poison —

"Gosh, here you are!" a voice spoke from on high. "I was starting to get worried about you."

Way too cheerful for God — and anyway, this voice was familiar, and Ridge and God were only nodding acquaintances.

Ridge opened his eyes as Tug knelt beside him. He looked exactly the same as the day before, only today his polo was forest green and his eyes were solemn despite the white smile.

"What happened?" Tug's face was so close to Ridge's that he got a little Binaca blast. There was a faint sheen of perspiration on Tug's forehead and upper lip. His mouth looked soft and pink as he asked his question.

Wait. What was the question?

Luckily Tug wasn't waiting for an answer. He jumped up, went to the shed and lifted Ridge's chair, setting it on its wheels and giving it an experimental push. "Seems okay."

He rolled the chair over to Ridge, and knelt beside him again. "Okay. Put your arms around my neck. I'm going to lift you."

"No, no. You don't have to do that." Ridge nervously edged away. Tried to. He wasn't going far. "Just help me stand."

"I don't want you standing after a fall like that till I've had a chance to check you over." There again was that disconcerting seriousness. But then Tug grinned. "Don't worry, Ridge. I'm very strong. I haven't dropped a patient yet. You're pretty skinny anyways."

Ridge was still protesting as Tug slipped one muscular arm beneath his thighs, wrapped the other around his back and lifted Ridge up as though he weighed no more than a child.

It had been a while since Ridge had been this close to another man, and he was startled at how it felt to be wrapped in warm, strong arms, to be held against a warm, strong body. Tug's peppermint breath gusted against his face and he got a whiff of Tug's aftershave. Something very light and outdoorsy and vaguely pine-scented.

Tug set him in the wheelchair, positioning Ridge's heavy legs so his feet were lined up with the foot rests. Ridge resented the indignity of it, but he was so tired and Tug was quick and careful. "How's that? Better?" Tug bent and fastened the lap belt around Ridge's pelvis.

"I don't use that," Ridge objected.

Tug said serenely, "Y'all are going to use it from now on."

"Who the hell do you think you *are*?"

Tug looked earnest. "Think about it. Isn't it better to put up with the irritation of me bossing you around over the irritation of getting bounced out of this here chair onto your head?"

Ridge snarled, "You underestimate just how irritating you are."

"Ouch." Tug's smile was rueful. "I guess I do." But he didn't remove the belt. Instead he took charge, wheeling Ridge's chair carefully but quickly back to the house.

Short of throwing himself onto his head in the previously described fashion, there wasn't much Ridge could do about it, but there was nothing he detested more than having people push him, shoving him around like a sack of potatoes in a wheelbarrow. In fact, he hated anyone touching his chair at all, moving him out of the way like a piece of fucking furniture.

He sat fuming for a few seconds, but the fact was, he was worn out after the adventures of the morning, and it was sort of a relief to not have to do anything more than sit there and control his temper — that was enough of a challenge, if he was honest.

If he glanced to the right, he could see the tall, black shadow of himself in the chair gliding along with Tug striding behind. He watched their separate silhouettes coalesce with each bounce of the chair's wheels over the uneven ground, watched them sliding across the bricks and baked earth like stick puppets.

It was still unbelievable to him that he was the man in the wheelchair.

"What were you doing out there in that shed?" Tug asked as they rounded the corner to the courtyard and the pool.

Uh oh.

Inspiration struck Ridge. "I'm thinking of taking up gardening," he said glibly. "I know I need some kind of hobby, something to take my mind off this." He nodded at his immobile legs. "I was seeing what there was out there."

"Gardening!" Tug sounded surprised. Probably thinking there could be no more unsuitable hobby for a man in Ridge's condition.

"I have to do something." That was certainly true enough.

"Sure." Tug sounded uncharacteristically absent.

Ridge spotted a large, square, pastel parcel lying on one of the rusted round tables beside the pool. "What's that?" Ridge tilted his head back to see Tug's face. Mostly what he saw was Tug's shirt and shoulders and chin.

Tug looked where Ridge indicated. "Damn." He sounded genuinely chagrined. "Those are your chocolates. I set them down when I was looking for you." He stopped pushing the chair and went to fetch the candy.

Ridge watched him curiously. "Where were you looking for me out here?" It wasn't as though there were any place he could be hiding in the courtyard.

Tug's clean-shaved face turned pink. He looked automatically and inadvertently toward the swimming pool.

Ridge followed his unhappy gaze to the green clouds roiling gently, sinisterly through the deep, dead water. He laughed.

CHAPTER THREE

Sweets to the Sweet read the elegant script on the candy box's black-edged card. The paper was a delicate shade of robin's egg blue. The black ribbon matched the black edging on the card.

"It's probably soup after sitting in that sun," Tug said regretfully.

Probably. Ridge tugged gently on the silky black ribbon. It felt oddly cool running through his fingers.

He was sitting on the edge of his bed. Tug had examined his back and pronounced him unharmed. In fact, despite all that happened that morning, Ridge was feeling startlingly good. Tug had given him another of those brief, gentle massages that seemed unreasonably beneficial, considering the fact that Tug wasn't even trying. Perhaps Tug was blessed with a healing touch. More likely it was coincidence. Either way, Ridge found that he was looking forward to having a real, full body massage from Tug. Hopefully there would be time for that.

Maybe not.

"How did you happen to find me?" Ridge looked up from the candy box.

Tug was putting away his stethoscope. "When you didn't come to the door, I got worried. I didn't see your cousin's car out front."

"You know Raleigh's car?"

Tug looked fleetingly uncomfortable. "Everyone on Black Turtle Island knows the Baneberrys."

The Batty Baneberrys. Oh yes. They all knew their reputation. In later years, Uncle Beau had taken malicious delight in playing up to the role of the eccentric patriarch of an eccentric clan. Of course, it hadn't all been an act. Even Ridge knew they were all a little … different.

He pulled the ribbon and it fell away from the box like a dead snake, its silken coils tickling the top of his left foot. He peeled away the colored paper and lifted the lid of the candy box.

Well hell. Even Raleigh, with his voracious sweet tooth, wouldn't eat this.

The contents looked literally like shit, soft and misshapen, but the smell wafting up was as heady and delectable as walking into a candy store. Chocolate. Who knew there were so many strains and lines to that melody? He could smell vanilla and hazelnut and berry and leather and earth and sunlight … . He opened his eyes and shook his head, trying to clear his senses. He didn't even like chocolate.

"Gosh. That's a real shame. It still smells wonderful." Tug stood next to him, gazing down at the box.

The fragrance of the chocolate filled every corner of the room, evoking remembrance, evoking cinnamon and tobacco and polished wood and crumbled autumn leaves and woodsmoke on a cold day and cobblestones and the scent of rain and the feel of grass beneath his bare feet and sex and the ring of chimes on a soft summer's evening. It was the scent of memory, of everything that was lost to him. Tears stung Ridge's eyes, hung on his eyelashes. He blinked hard.

"It's no good now." He was surprised to realize the muttered words came from him.

"I'm sorry." Tug was contrite. "It's my fault. I should have left it in the house."

Thank God. Something to distract from the terrible pain of the reminder his life was indeed over. Gratefully, Ridge reached for it. "In the house?"

Tug blushed. "When nobody came to the door, I got worried. I looked for an open window and climbed in. When I couldn't find you inside, I started searching the grounds."

Ridge became aware that his mouth was hanging open. "You searched the *entire* house?"

Tug went pinker still. "Well, no. Most of the castle isn't wheelchair accessible."

Most of the castle wasn't accessible, period. The whole north wing teetered close to falling down. Never mind the broken windows and holes in the floor, whole sections of the roof were falling in. Even as boys they'd had strict orders not to roam the north wing. Not that it had stopped them. And the south wing wasn't much better. In fact, it was dangerous as hell poking around anything but the main house.

"I tell you what," Tug was saying. "Why don't we drive into town directly and get you another box?"

Ridge jerked back to the present. "No. You can bring another box tomorrow. Or whenever it is you come again."

"Our next session is the day after tomorrow. But no need to wait. It's a nice day for a drive. You'll love the shop. The guy running it is like someone out of a play. His name is Chance. Very handsome." Tug wiggled his eyebrows.

"No."

"Yeah, it is. Really. It's right there on his apron or his coat thingie. Whatever you call that."

"I mean, no. I'm not going into town."

Ridge was very definite, but Tug simply didn't seem to hear him. "We'll get your chocolates and then we could have lunch afterwards. What's your favorite place to eat?"

Ridge hung onto his patience with an effort. "I don't have time for that today."

"Sure you do. What have you got planned?"

"My plans for the day are not your concern," he said loftily. "Although I assume we're supposed to have a session of some kind." He found he did very much want Tug to give him a real massage.

"I think you've had plenty of exercise for one day." Tug smiled at him. "I think we might could do with a session of another kind. You need to get out of this place for a few hours, that's what I think."

When all else failed, flat out rudeness usually did the trick. Ridge said coldly, "Where do you get the idea that I give a shit what you think?"

Tug's forehead creased in thought. Ridge could practically see the gears turning behind those big blue eyes. "I think you kind of do, don't you?"

Ridge opened his mouth to repudiate such foolishness — only to find that, bewilderingly, it was maybe sort of true. He said instead, "I don't like to go out." It felt like a costly admission.

"I know." Tug's smile grew sympathetic. "And you don't like anyone visiting. But you need to get out and see people again, Ridge. It's not healthy for you sitting in this mausoleum brooding."

"You have no idea what you're talking about."

"Sure, I do. You hate people seeing you in a wheelchair. I know. Everybody knows. Nobody wants to be in a wheelchair. But you *are* in a wheelchair. So what are you going to do? Hide out in this ruin till you really do go nuts and roll yourself into that swamp out there?"

When Ridge got his breath back, he yelled, "Get the fuck out of my house and never come home." What the — ? In disbelief he heard the echo of his words, and corrected hastily and loudly, "*Back*. Never come *back!*"

Tug continued to study him with that infuriating expression of his — affectionate sympathy or sympathetic affection. Where the hell did he get off looking at Ridge like that?

"Don't you worry. I'm not going to do that."

"I am *ordering* you out of my house."

"And you know why I'm not going to do that?"

"Get. Out. Now."

"Because you once did me a great favor. And now it's my turn to help you."

"I don't *need* your help!" Ridge couldn't stop himself from asking, "When did I ever do you a favor?"

Tug sat down on the mattress beside Ridge. He stared at his hands resting on his khaki-clad knees. "Well, you won't remember this. It was back when we were in high school. I was a freshman and you were a senior. This was not long after you ... moved in with your uncle."

Ridge looked away. That had been a difficult time. It had been some better when Raleigh had come to stay.

He'd forgotten that.

Tug was still talking. "Anyways, in addition to being queer as a three dollar bill, I was a pudgy kid who wore coke bottle glasses." He smiled regretfully at some memory. "You know. The kind of kid with a big target on his back all through high school."

Ridge said nothing. Like all the Baneberrys, he had been gifted with good looks and a razor sharp tongue. It was a safe conduct pass through the realm of adolescent interaction. But he wasn't unobservant. He remembered what school had been like for the Tug Gildens.

"Every day, Brad Davis and his goons used to knock me around. Knock my books out of my arms, knock me off my bike, knock my glasses off."

"Assholes," Ridge growled automatically. He had no idea who Brad Davis was. He barely remembered that year. He had been in a daze of misery after the death of his parents. One of the only things that had helped was knowing Raleigh, abandoned by his beautiful, irresponsible mother, was even more miserable.

They had been pretty close back then, for two such very different boys. Rivals, of course — as all the Baneberrys were — but friends too.

"I thought it would never stop," Tug said. "I used to think about... well... ." He gave Ridge a sideways look. "It sounds kind of dramatic, but I used to think about... ending it all."

Ridge didn't know what to say to that. TMI? He cleared his throat.

"But then one day you showed up in school and... ."

This was getting embarrassing. Ridge said, "I don't remember you. I barely remember high school."

Tug nodded, apparently embarrassed too. "I know. But you used to walk past and if your eyes met mine, you'd smile. I guess that doesn't sound like a lot, but it changed something for me because someone like you saw me as a normal person. That you *saw* me."

I don't remember you. It was just a reflex. But Ridge didn't say it.

Tug sucked in a deep breath. "And then one day after Brad tripped me and I fell flat on my face in front of the entire fucking school, I saw you lean over to him and you whispered something in his ear. And everyone with you laughed and kept laughing. Brad turned beet red and looked at me and then he slammed his locker door and he never looked at me or bothered me again."

Thankfully Tug stopped talking then.

Ridge rubbed his forehead. "I don't remember. I'm sorry." He wasn't even sure why he was apologizing. It seemed he had played a role in a life-changing moment in Tug's life, but he had no recollection. It had meant nothing to him. And it was alarming that it felt like it meant something now.

He said, "You're making me uncomfortable."

There was a short, sharp silence. Ridge saw Tug's hands move spasmodically on his knees and then still. Ridge closed his eyes.

Tug said quietly, almost inaudibly, "I'm very sorry. I just wan... ." His voice gave out. Ridge closed his eyes tighter.

No, no, no. It's too late for this. He was not going to feel anything.

Tug got his voice back. He said with unexpected steadiness, "I just wanted you to know that you helped me once and I want to repay that kindness. So if it seems like I'm being — I just don't want you to think this is weird or creepy or anything. I'm not wanting anything from you. You need help now and I can help you."

Ridge opened his eyes and looked at Tug. Tug gazed right back at him. His eyes were blue and direct, fringed by stubby gold eyelashes and nicely shaped eyebrows. His freckles were the color of pale gold, too. He had a very pretty mouth for a man.

Tug repeated softly, "I can help you. Let me."

The shop was new. Or maybe it wasn't. It had been months since Ridge had been in the small town of Horton. Come to think of it, the shop didn't look new. It looked like it had always sat there, perfectly positioned between the green awning of an art gallery and the gingerbread-trimmed porch of a stationery store.

Sweets to the Sweet read the elegant gold and black script across the polished window front.

Tug opened the door, the bell jingled cheerily, and Ridge executed a neat, quick bounce over the threshold, wheeling himself inside.

The rich, Cimmerian smell was almost overpowering. Chocolate, yes, but other scents. Subtle scents. Espresso, marzipan, honey, rum, green apples, toadstools.

Toadstools? Where did that thought come from?

"Wonderful, isn't it?" Tug looked around smiling.

It was certainly nicely laid out. Ridge looked around, bemused. The floor was a pattern of black and red squares, like a game board in hell.

"Well, well, well." The voice was soft and accent-less.

Ridge had thought they were alone but now he spotted the man behind the counter. In fact, he wondered how he'd first missed him.

This could only be the like-a-character-in-a-play Chance. He was tall and slender with a pale face framed by long, dark hair. His eyes were what Ridge noticed most. They were heavy-lidded and of an indeterminate color. They glittered in the flickering sunshine as he studied Ridge with unconcealed curiosity.

"Back again," Tug said. "I left the box I bought this morning out in the sun."

"How careless." Chance continued to eye Ridge. "That could be an expensive mistake."

Generally, the wheelchair acted like a cloak of invisibility. This unstinting appraisal was making Ridge uneasy.

"But this is better. You can pick exactly what you like." Tug moved to the glass cases and their temptingly arranged trays of confections.

"Yes, this is better," Chance agreed.

"Do I know you?" Ridge asked.

"You don't remember? I'm wounded." Chance put a hand to his heart in a theatrical gesture. His eyes laughed wickedly at Ridge.

Ridge wheeled forward, but all at once he lost his nerve and guided the chair next to Tug. He looked into the case of beautiful candies as though that had been his intention the whole time.

"What do you like?" Tug asked. His hand rested absently on the back of the wheelchair as though unconsciously picking up Ridge's unease.

"I don't. I don't like chocolate."

Tug looked puzzled, and no wonder. "Oh, I thought ... ."

"I wanted — want — the chocolate for a gift."

"Oh."

"For that certain special someone," Chance supplied.

Ridge turned to him. Was he imagining that Chance seemed to know something ... something he couldn't possibly know?

Chance met his gaze. His elegant eyebrows shot up in inquiry.

No. Chance was simply one of those smartasses who always had to put his two cents in.

"How can you not like chocolate?" Tug sounded interested, not critical.

"It does seem rather sinister, doesn't it?" Chance remarked.

Tug chuckled.

It came suddenly to Ridge that Tug was a very relaxing person to be around, that life with someone like Tug would be ... .

Impossible now.

"Just pick something," Ridge said. "I don't care."

"Have you ever tried white chocolate?"

"I don't like sweets."

Tug did a double take. "*No* sweets? None? Nothing?"

"No." Ridge wasn't even sure if that was true, but nothing came to him, and he wanted out of the shop and the candy case that was beginning to smell like damp, dark earth.

"You pick," Chance advised Tug. "Maybe Ridge will share with you."

"No, I won't." Ridge glared at Chance. What the hell was he suggesting? Ridge wouldn't harm Tug. Wouldn't harm anyone — except the person who had harmed him.

"That's okay. I can buy my own candy." Tug reached for his wallet. "In fact, I want to buy yours, too. It's my fault the first box was spoiled."

Ridge waved him off like the crotchety invalid he would no doubt become if he didn't — never mind that. Chance had used his name. Chance had called him *Ridge.*

How could he possibly know his name? Had Tug called him by his name? Or perhaps he had referred to Ridge when he bought the first box that morning?

"Something with almonds, I think," Chance said thoughtfully. "That's right, isn't it? Almonds? Almond bark? Almond clusters? I know! I have some lovely almond toffee." His face fell. "But no. No, you'd prefer something with a cream filling, I imagine."

Ridge couldn't seem to tear his gaze from Chance's face: that solicitous smile beneath those maliciously dancing eyes.

"Oh I know the *exact* thing. Almond chocolate balls."

Ridge couldn't seem to get the breath to answer.

"Sounds delicious," Tug said on his behalf.

"It's fine," Ridge said faintly. "Just throw them in a box."

"*Throw* my beautiful handcrafted work in a box?" Chance sounded shocked. He reached over the counter and handed Ridge a perfectly wrapped box. "There you go. One pound of almond chocolate balls." He named an outrageous figure and Ridge fumbled his wallet open.

Chance delicately snatched the bills from Ridge's not quite steady hand. He smiled widely. "Guaranteed to take care of that special certain someone's sweet tooth. Or your money back."

As Ridge clumsily backed his wheelchair, narrowly avoiding a stand of prettily wrapped boxes, Chance turned to Tug and mimed a sad face. "Better luck next time, Thomas!"

○ ○ ○ ○ ○

"If you're too tired, we can do lunch another time."

Tug was looking at him with concern as they sat in the car beneath the shady pecan trees that lined the street.

Ridge shook off his preoccupation. He wiped his damp forehead. "No. That's fine. Maybe I'll feel better if I eat something." Come to think of it, he'd had nothing to eat all day. No wonder he was feeling lightheaded.

"What do you like?" Tug asked.

"Anything is fine."

"No. What do you *like*, Ridge?"

Ridge glanced over and saw Tug was serious, that it mattered to him that Ridge chose something he would enjoy, that Tug would enjoy it more if Ridge was happy. *Why?* Why did it matter so much to Tug? All right, once upon a time Ridge had been kind to him, but that hardly explained this dark-eyed intensity that Ridge should be happy. But there it was. He could see it in Tug's gaze.

It made him want to cry.

"What's wrong?" Tug's brows drew together. "Is this too much for you?"

Yes.

And it's too late for me.

Ridge shook his head. "Believe it or not, I'm not that hard to please. Burgers are fine. In fact, I love burgers and fries."

"Me too." Tug was instantly all smiles again. "I know the perfect place." He put the car into gear.

In a few minutes they were seated in Mary Moo's at a nice table overlooking the ocean.

Ridge had been dreading the complications of dining in public, but there was nothing to it. Tug helped him out of the car and into his wheelchair, keeping a light though unnecessary hand on the back of the chair as Ridge rolled up the handicapped ramp leading to the front doors of the restaurant. Inside the restaurant, the waiter removed the extra chair from their table and Ridge rolled his chair into place. Nobody was looking at them, nobody was thinking anything. Everyone but the wait-staff was sitting down, anyway.

Ridge stopped sweating and began to relax — although his heart jumped uncomfortably every time his gaze fell on the blue-wrapped box of candy sitting on the table. Tug had insisted on bringing it in for fear it would melt in the car.

They ordered burgers, cokes and fries — onion rings for Tug — and talked casually about food and the music they liked and the movies they'd seen, and their work. It was so normal, it felt surreal. It was as though the accident had never happened at all. As though it were an ordinary day and they were two guys having a nice lunch and getting to know each other.

"What kind of greeting cards do you design?" Tug picked up an onion ring. Ridge smiled inwardly at the thought of Tug having to pull double duty with the mouth spray. He wondered how Tug's mouth tasted after onion rings and how it tasted after Binaca.

"What do you mean?"

The dimples appeared briefly, vanished in a wry smile. "Are they the funny, sarcastic kind?"

"No," Ridge admitted. "They're not."

For some reason that seemed to relieve Tug. He smiled. "And they sell well?"

"They used to. I haven't worked much … lately."

"Sure." Tug seemed to recollect himself. "Did you want an onion ring?"

Ridge shook his head. "Is your first name really Thomas?"

"Yeah, it is." Tug's expression changed. "That was weird, wasn't it? Chance knew my name."

"Did you use a credit card this morning to pay for the candy?"

"No. Cash."

"He knew my name too."

Tug's eyes widened. "Wow. Of course, everyone knows the Baneberrys."

Ridge nodded and gazed out the picture window at the waves creaming around the dark wooden posts of the pier.

"Is it true … ?" Tug's diffident voice stopped.

Ridge looked at him in inquiry.

"Is it true the castle was supposed to be left to you?"

God only knew what stories were circulating. Ridge nodded. It wasn't going to stop there, though, he already knew that. And anyway, what did it matter? Why not tell Tug? Someone might as well know the truth.

"Supposed to, yeah. You have to understand. From the time the castle was built, there was always competition for who was going to inherit next. Uncle Beau was the youngest of his brothers, but his eldest brother died in the war and the second brother was disinherited for marrying beneath his station. Of course Uncle

Beau didn't marry and didn't have children, so from as far back as I can remember there was competing and jockeying and positioning among the family who hoped to inherit. Even our names — I was named for Uncle Beau's brother. Raleigh was named for Grandfather Baneberry." Their parents had sought any and every advantage in the war of succession.

"It must've cost a fortune to keep up that place."

Ridge nodded absently. "When my parents were killed, I went to live with Uncle Beau and he made me his heir. Then a few months later, Raleigh's mother dumped him off before she split for Tibet never to be heard from again."

"*Tibet*?"

"Yep. Uncle Beau used to threaten to disinherit me for Raleigh and vice versa whenever we irritated him, but it wasn't until I came out that he really did it."

Tug looked shocked. What world did he live in? "Your uncle disinherited you for being gay?"

Ridge nodded. "I didn't care. I was living with a guy — " He suddenly pictured Doug seeing him as he was now, confined to a wheelchair, and he knew Doug would stop thinking his heart was broken and start believing he'd had a lucky escape. Ridge no longer fit Doug's image of a romantic partner. Doug would be sorry for Ridge, but he wouldn't want any part of a relationship where he had to help take care of his disabled lover. Ridge probably would have felt the same way once. He cleared his throat. "It doesn't matter. It fell through, and Uncle Beau wasn't in good health and he asked me to move home, so I did. And Raleigh, of course, never left."

Tug looked disapproving but only ate another onion ring.

"Anyway, Uncle Beau had mellowed a lot, and he was planning to change his will back, but he died before he had the chance."

It sounded so undramatic phrased like that. Like it could have happened to anyone. Hardly even grounds for revenge.

Tug nearly choked on his onion ring. He drank hastily from his coke. "So it's true Raleigh tried to kill you?

CHAPTER FOUR

For what felt like a long time Ridge couldn't think of any answer to that. He said finally, "Is that what folks say?"

Tug nodded unhappily, "They say he deliberately drove your side of the car into the tractor."

Well, what did you know? Here was his defense plea all laid out for him. No wonder Raleigh looked so hagridden these days. It couldn't happen to a nicer guy.

And yet … .

And yet it wasn't true. Raleigh was guilty of a lot of things, but not attempted murder.

"No." Ridge said slowly, "That's not the way it happened. He'd been drinking, as usual, and he was … ."

Tug got busy eating the remains of his burger. "Did you want another coke?" he asked thickly, keeping his eyes on his plate.

"He'd been drinking," Ridge repeated, remembering. "He was upset and I thought I should talk to him. We weren't arguing, exactly, but we weren't … ." He shook his head. It was strange that he could recollect this. Recollect right up to the point of seeing the tractor in the circle of the headlights but nothing after that. That was probably a mercy.

"He kept looking away from the road to talk to me and there was a branch in the highway. When he saw it, he swerved and lost control of the car."

And the rest, as they say, was history.

"I'm sorry, Ridge." Tug's sincere voice snapped Ridge out of his preoccupation.

He stared at Tug, but he wasn't seeing Tug. He was seeing the procession of terrible events that had followed the lights going black. And now Uncle Beau was dead and the castle was destined for the auction block and Ridge was sitting in a wheelchair he would be using for the rest of his life.

He waited for the anger to rush in and wash away the grief and loss, but he just felt strangely empty. Empty and tired.

He was startled to hear his own quiet admission. "Raleigh wants me to go into some kind of assisted living place."

The effect on Tug was instantaneous. His eyes darkened, his face flushed red. "Why the hell should you?" Ridge realized that this was Tug angry. He had a feeling it was a side of Tug most people never saw.

"Because he wants to sell the castle and I can't take care of myself."

"Can't — ?" Tug spluttered. "Sure you can! People in a lot worse shape than you take care of themselves. I see it all the time. Only reason you can't take care of yourself now is you're living in Gargamel's Castle."

What in creation was Gargamel's Castle? Ridge opened his mouth, but Tug was still repudiating the idea of assisted living with reassuring force. "You got a mighty strong will to get yourself out to that shed the way you did this morning. You could live anywhere you like."

"Anywhere I could afford."

"Well, sure." Tug took a deep breath as though he knew his next words would not be popular. "The fact is, you shouldn't be living in that ruin anyway. It's not a healing environment."

Ridge said shortly, "It's my home."

"Heck, your cousin shouldn't be living there. Best thing that could happen to either of you is that they raze that place to the ground and salt the earth."

"You don't know what you're talking about. The castle isn't just our home, it's our legacy." But Ridge said it without heat. He found he really didn't want to argue with Tug.

And Tug must not have wanted to argue either, because after a stern-eyed moment or two he pulled a face and said, "Sorry. I kinda get carried away sometimes. You want dessert?"

Ridge didn't particularly want dessert, but he realized he didn't want this lunch to end. He didn't want this day with Tug to end. Maybe Baneberry Castle was his home and his legacy, but right now he had no desire to return to it.

"Maybe. Maybe we can share something?" Tug brightened, opened his mouth, and Ridge headed him off. "You pick."

The next thing Ridge knew a pretty glass dish filled with vanilla ice cream and topped with caramel and pecans was placed between them, and he was being handed a spoon.

He shuddered inwardly, but Tug was smiling so endearingly, his blue eyes tilting, freckled nose wrinkling as he waited for Ridge to take the first bite.

Ridge smiled weakly, dipped his spoon into the golden syrup and nuts, and took a brave mouthful. It melted all across his tongue, honey-sweet and nutty and not so bad at all. Not once you got used to it.

"Good?"

Ridge shrugged.

Tug's smile widened. His spoon clinked companionably against Ridge's as he took a bite. "Gosh, that *is* good."

Ridge tried to remember the last time he'd shared a dessert with anyone. Hell, he couldn't even remember the last time he'd had dessert, let alone shared it. A day ago he couldn't have imagined sitting here in the golden sunlight watching the seagulls soaring over the ocean and listening to —

He realized that Tug was speaking to him, repeating something he'd already said.

"What's that?"

"When we finish up here, would you like to come back to my place?"

"Why?"

"So you could rest up before I drive you back."

It was a simple statement, but Ridge couldn't seem to figure it out. He stared at Tug, trying to make sense of it, and Tug blushed as he was wont to do, and said, "I want you to see my place."

Ridge considered this new information. "Are you taking me back to your place as my physical therapist or as … what?"

"As what," Tug replied promptly.

"Ah. But what is what?"

"What do you want it to be?"

"What happened to that whole repaying kindness with kindness?"

"That still stands. But." Tug's smile was lopsided. "It doesn't have to *only* be that. Unless that's what you want. In which case that's what it is. I give you my word."

This was a horrible mistake. He was going to drag Tug, whose only crime was a soft heart and a lingering, rusty crush on someone who didn't even exist anymore, into the train wreck of his life. If Ridge had any kindness left in him, he would stop this before it went any further.

"I guess it wouldn't hurt to take a quick look," Ridge said slowly.

○ ○ ○ ○ ○

The house was sublimely ordinary. A large, rambling, glass-front beach cottage five houses from the ocean. Ridge was strangely relieved to see that it was completely unsuitable for a disabled person — starting with the long, shallow steps leading to the front door. The halls were too narrow for his chair, the throw rugs caught on the wheels, the kitchen cupboards were too tall and the fixtures in the bathroom too low.

Plainly Tug did not bring his patients here.

That was the good news. The bad news was that, equally plainly, coming here had been a mistake. Ridge couldn't maneuver his wheelchair, and he hated feeling helpless again after an entire afternoon of feeling almost normal.

"It's nice," he said flatly after Tug had unhooked the fourth throw rug to get caught on the chair. "It must be great having the beach so close."

Tug heard the words, not the tone, and looked pleased. "It is. Would you like a drink? I practically have a full bar."

Of course he did. He had everything a boy could want. Including a car that Raleigh would envy.

"Not really." Belatedly, Ridge was taking in all Tug's toys and gadgets — from the top-of-the-line home entertainment system to the five-quart electric wok in the kitchen. It dawned on him that Tug must earn one hell of a lot of money, and that explained why he wasn't particularly — properly? — impressed by the Baneberrys or their castle.

Why that should bother him so much, Ridge wasn't sure, but it did. It was as though he found himself suddenly without currency in the transaction of this tentative relationship. What did he bring to the table? A kind gesture twenty years ago? No.

No.

"Would you like to sit on the deck? The view of the ocean is spectacular." Tug didn't even sound like himself anymore. He sounded like someone trying out for a part in a commercial.

"I don't think so. I'm more tired than I thought."

"Did you want to lie down for a while?"

"No." Ridge hardened his heart as Tug's face fell. Why should this be difficult when he'd been plenty rude to Tug at the start of their acquaintanceship? "If you don't mind, I think I need to go home."

"Sure. Of course. I shoulda thought." Ridge had to look away. Tug's disappointment was painful to watch. Why did it matter so much to him?

Why did it matter to Ridge?

The drive back to the castle was quick and quiet. Ridge could see Tug was trying to work out where he had gone wrong, and Ridge was trying to think of a way to let Tug know that he should not hold himself accountable for anything that happened once Ridge left his company.

But nothing occurred to him, or apparently to Tug either, and they reached the overgrown circular courtyard of the castle. Raleigh's Mazda was parked as close to the front door as he could get without driving over the fountain.

Ridge waited, watching Tug lug his wheelchair out, and trying not to care that Tug looked like his puppy had died.

Tug came around and opened Ridge's door and bent down so that Ridge could hook an arm around his broad shoulders. Tug half lifted him out — they already had this down to a science — but instead of settling Ridge in the chair, he held him tight.

After a moment, Ridge patted him on his back, kindly — because this was starting to get weird again.

Tug hugged him tighter, and then let go and helped Ridge into his chair.

"I've got it from here," Ridge assured him, but Tug took charge of the chair anyway, pushing Ridge carefully over the weeds and paving stones all the way to the front steps, which, of course, Ridge couldn't get up without his help, so it was a good thing one of them was thinking clearly.

"I'll see you Thursday, then." Tug gazed intently into Ridge's eyes and Ridge wondered uncomfortably if Tug somehow suspected what Ridge was planning, and that's what all those questions at lunch had been about.

"Er, yes."

Tug nodded reluctantly. He started back to his car. Ridge managed to open the door without knocking himself down the steps again.

Tug stopped walking. He turned back to the house. "Ridge — " *No. No. No.* Ridge started to close the door but Tug finished, "You forgot your candy."

Ridge froze.

Fate. That had to be Fate, right?

He waited as Tug leaned in the car and lifted out the blue parcel. Tug loped back to the house and ran lightly up the steps. He handed the candy box to Ridge.

Ridge said mechanically, "Thank you."

"Let me stay."

Ridge looked up. "What?"

Tug's face was set in determined lines. "I want to stay with you tonight."

Ridge shook his head. "That's just … ." Just what? Crazy? More crazy than what Ridge was planning?

Tug squatted down so that they were nearly on level. "Let me stay. I don't know why it went wrong a little while ago, but I know there's something here. There's something between us. You feel it too, Ridge."

"No, I don't. I don't feel anything."

They both listened to the words reverberating off the silvered mirrors and cracked marble.

Tug said quietly, "Then let me help you feel something."

He leaned forward to cover Ridge's mouth with his own in a warm, insistent kiss. Ridge tried to draw back but already his body was betraying him, rational thought fleeing before the feeling, so much feeling … the texture of Tug's lips on his own, Tug's scent filling his nostrils, Tug's warm hands on his shoulders, steadying and caressing at once.

Ridge heard himself give a soft, disbelieving sound. Tug's breath was filling his nostrils, the moisture of Tug's mouth mingled with his own. It was overwhelming, amazing — like a very first kiss — only very much better than Ridge's real very first kiss.

○ ○ ○ ○ ○

Tug helped him undress. It was a lengthy process. Not because Ridge was clumsy and slow, although of course he was, but because Tug insisted on stopping to linger over every newly revealed bare inch of skin with hot kisses and delicate nips. Ridge's collarbone, his shoulder, the crook of his elbow, his palm. By the end of it, Ridge was gasping for breath, his heart pounding in a mix of excitement and alarm.

He was very much afraid he was out of his league, that he'd have been out of his league before the accident, let alone now.

"Wait," he got out desperately, and Tug stopped at once.

"What's the trouble?" Tug crouched on the mattress beside him, beautifully unselfconsciousness in his nudity.

Ridge looked at him wordlessly.

"You haven't done this since the accident?"

Ridge nodded.

"We'll go slowly," Tug promised.

"It's probably not going to be what you want."

"What is it you think I want? Besides you?"

Ridge said carefully, "I'm not even sure if I can."

"Oh. Well, we won't know till we try, right?" Tug's blue eyes considered Ridge, waiting for Ridge to say something, but Ridge had no idea what to say to that. "I just want to be with you, Ridge. We can just hold each other if you like."

"That's not going to be enough for you."

Tug said softly, "Let me love you. I'll make it nice for you, I promise."

Hesitantly, Ridge nodded.

"Lie back." Tug slipped his arm behind Ridge's shoulders, helping him lean back. "Relax."

Ridge was trying, but it wasn't easy. He kept anticipating problems, but they didn't happen. Tug's strength was there for him to lean on.

The sheet felt cool and caressing against his bare skin. "I — I can't move a lot. My legs — "

"I know, honey." Tug bent over him and kissed Ridge's belly, then lower. His five o'clock shadow felt like rough velvet on Ridge's flushed skin.

Ridge moaned. Tug smiled against him, then rolled back on his heels, resting his hand on Ridge's cock, which sprang instantly to life as if it had only been waiting for the call to action.

"Looks to me like the equipment's still operational."

Ridge tried to lift himself, but Tug whispered, "Just lie still. Let me do it."

Ridge swallowed hard. Nodded.

"Does it hurt anywhere? I won't put any weight on you, so don't worry about that."

Ridge shook his head. "No, it's okay right now." He was startled to realize that was true. All day the pain had been at a manageable level. So manageable, in fact, he'd largely forgotten about it.

Tug's gaze held his. His eyes looked soft and shadowy as he stretched out beside Ridge. "You're beautiful, Ridge. You know that?"

"Yeah, ri — " Tug's kiss cut off his derision. Just a brush of his lips against Ridge's. He closed his eyes and Tug kissed his eyelids. It felt like a lifetime since anyone had kissed him; certainly since anyone had kissed him in such a teasing, cherishing way. Ridge stroked Tug's shoulders, feeling the muscles move beneath his palms. Tug feathered tiny kisses over his eyelashes, the bridge of his nose, his temples. Ridge smiled and Tug kissed the corner of his mouth.

"How's that?"

Ridge opened his eyes to find Tug contemplating him. He nodded, too moved for words. He had given up on the very idea of this, convinced no one would want him now, and here was Tug showering him with kisses and endearments.

"Am I going too fast for you?"

Ridge shook his head. Tug smiled, his eyes seemed alight with pleasure.

Very, very gently he put his arms around Ridge. Ridge clasped him back cautiously, prepared for the slice of pain, but despite a twinge or two, he was all right. Tug reached around, shifting the pillows and bedding so that Ridge's back was bolstered. His cock pressed into Ridge's belly, and Ridge's cock thrust blindly against his muscular thigh. Tug rubbed himself against Ridge, his crotch grinding against

Ridge's. Ridge tensed, ready for pain, but the pain didn't come, and Tug didn't take it any further. He seemed content just holding and touching and kissing.

Ridge kissed him back. He'd forgotten how wonderful kissing was. Even so, it was difficult not to be self-conscious. He hated his body now. Hated anyone to see him naked. He was not only naked, but every inch of him was being fondled, caressed and massaged.

"Am I hurting you?" Tug whispered.

"No."

After a very long time, a foreplay that lasted longer than any entire sexual encounter Ridge could remember in his life, he felt Tug's hand close around his cock.

He opened his eyes. Tug's gaze was trained on his face. "May I?"

"I ... ."

His hand slid up and down Ridge's penis, slowly, rhythmically. "How's that?"

"Feels good."

"Slower?"

Ridge shook his head. Tug's grip tightened and Ridge felt his face quiver with pleasure.

"Better?"

Ridge whispered, "Yes." It was so good. He'd forgotten how good. Just the right amount of pressure, just the right pace. Once he would have come right away, but now his body reacted so slowly. All he could do was sigh, moving restlessly against the pillows propping him. It was almost too good to bear, this slow, intensified love play. His hands tangled weakly in the bed clothes. His legs shook a little.

Tug reached with his free hand and lightly stroked Ridge's thighs, and it helped. Tug really did seem to have a healing touch.

Ridge thought for sure Tug would grow bored with pumping his impotent stick, but when Ridge glanced at him through his lashes Tug was smiling quietly, watching him.

At last, to Ridge's delight, something began to stir inside him and he realized he was about to come. He gasped as his muscles locked. It hurt some but not so much as to get in the way. And then Tug let go of him. Ridge barely had time to register the shock of disappointment before Tug took the head of his cock into the wet warmth of his mouth.

It was incredible — the best thing Ridge had ever felt in his life — as Tug began to suck him.

"Oh god," Ridge choked. "Don't stop."

Tug sucked harder and Ridge began to come. Hard. His body convulsed in pleasure, his heart pulsed with waves of delighted physical sensation that rippled from his fingers to his numb toes. He was blind to everything around him, whimpering in a kind of ecstatic trance as he rode it out.

When he surfaced again, Ridge's first amazed thought was that he'd had no idea when he woke up that morning what an incredible day it was going to be.

In fact … .

He turned his head on the pillow and Tug was studying him with a funny, sweet smile. "Not so bad, I guess?"

Ridge laughed unsteadily. "Could have been worse."

Tug chuckled. "Flattery is going to get you everywhere."

"Yeah. Well. I thought I might be impotent."

Tug snorted, leaned over Ridge and kissed him. Ridge could taste himself on Tug's lips. Another erotic frisson shivered through his body. His libido was back with a vengeance.

Something changed in Tug's face. He kissed Ridge again very slowly and tenderly and brushed his hair back from his forehead.

"Everything's okay now. Close your eyes and rest, Ridge."

Ridge *was* tired, but for the first time in a very long while someone else's satisfaction — happiness — meant even more than his own. "That would be just plain bad manners."

"How you figure that? Were y'all planning for us to play Scrabble all night?"

"No. But what about you?"

Tug's mouth twitched. "I came watching you."

Ridge's mouth parted in amazement as Tug knelt, showing him the shining wet stickiness on his taut belly and thighs. "Wow."

"Wow is right." Tug said with touching smugness, "And it's only going to get better for us."

Ridge shook his head. "You're crazy." He reached up and gently fingered the soft fair hair falling over Tug's forehead.

"Well? That makes me a perfect match for one of the Batty Baneberrys. Right?"

Ridge was smiling. He'd forgotten what contentment felt like. "Maybe."

Tug stretched out beside him again, slipping an arm around Ridge's waist. "Do you believe in Fate?"

"I don't know. I don't think so."

"I do." Tug glanced at the box of chocolates sitting on the floor. He said levelly, "I guess you won't be needing those now."

Ridge stilled. "What does that mean?"

"I know what you were planning, Ridge."

"You … do?"

Tug nodded. "I know you were thinking there wasn't a lot to live for, but — "

"You thought I was planning to kill *myself*?"

Tug nodded.

Ridge's mouth twitched, but he managed not to laugh. After all, Tug wasn't so far wrong, really.

"I'm not dumb. The day I arrived, I saw you trying to hide that old book on poisons." Tug's voice was soft, his face solemn. "Then you half killed yourself to get into that gardening shed, and I don't think it's 'cause you decided you want to grow African violets. And *then* you wanted almond-flavored candy."

Ridge said feebly, "I didn't care about the flavor."

"I watch TV. I know arsenic tastes like burnt almonds."

Ridge didn't move a muscle.

"I know this is hard on you, honey. Nobody knows better what you're dealing with. But it's going to get better. I swear to you. You'll get stronger and we'll find ways to manage the pain. Things seem bleak n — "

"Tell you the truth," Ridge interrupted gently, "they don't seem so bleak now."

Tug's serious gaze held his, and then Tug's face broke into one of those blinding smiles. "No?"

Ridge shook his head, his own smile self-mocking. "Not at all."

○ ○ ○ ○ ○

Tug was still sleeping when Ridge woke, one arm draped in possession or protection or maybe both over Ridge's waist. His breath was warm and sweet against Ridge's face.

Ridge moved experimentally, and Tug opened his eyes and smiled sleepily at him. "I had the best dream."

Ridge laughed, surrendering to Tug's kiss. He'd had good dreams too. He'd been dreaming that he and Tug were swimming, swimming in crystal blue water beneath crystal blue skies. Ridge had felt strong and confident as he cut through the water in powerful strokes with Tug right beside him, urging him on. Now, awake, he felt relaxed and oddly clear, as though a fever had broken.

He moved carefully and discovered the miracle only went so far. His back was stiff and painful and his legs heavy and hard to move, but somehow that didn't seem to be the most important thing that morning.

Tug watched him rise and go through the slow-motion drill of getting dressed and getting into his wheelchair. To Ridge's relief, Tug didn't jump up and try to do everything for him.

"Where you off to?"

"To see if there's anything for breakfast."

"Can you cook?"

"I can just about boil an egg and make toast."

"We could eat chocolate," Tug said hopefully.

"No." Ridge rolled a couple of inches forward, stretched, and picked up the box of chocolates. "We couldn't. I'll be back."

"I'll be waiting."

Ridge wheeled himself down the long, drafty hall, wheeled into the elevator and rode it down to the ground floor.

He found Raleigh in the kitchen hunching over the table, drinking coffee. He stared at Ridge as Ridge propelled the wheelchair into the kitchen. As usual his eyes averted from the sight of Ridge's powerless legs.

"You're up early," Ridge said.

"Did you bring someone here last night?"

"I did. Yeah."

"Who?"

"You don't know him."

"Knowing how Uncle Beau felt about that?"

Ridge put the box of chocolates on the table.

After a frowning moment, Raleigh's stare dropped to the blue box. "What are those?"

"These are for you. Call them a going away present."

Raleigh curled his lip. "Are they poisoned?"

He was kidding, but even so he was clearly surprised to see Ridge laugh.

"Not this time," Ridge said. "Anyway, you're not the one going away. I am."

"You're *going?*" Raleigh looked shocked. He stared at the chocolates and back at Ridge. "Where are you going? Where could you go?"

"Do you care? Aren't you just glad I *am* going?"

He was startled when Raleigh's face twisted. He cried, "What do you want from me, Ridge? What *is* it you *want?*" Raleigh half rose and shoved the box of candy back toward Ridge. "Haven't I suffered enough?"

In the silence that followed his words, Ridge could hear the raucous cawing of the crows in the north tower.

It dawned on him that there were all kinds of ways to be crippled. It wasn't an original thought, but it was new to Ridge. He was the one sitting in the wheelchair but somehow, suddenly he was the one with all the options.

"I don't know. Maybe you have." This might be the last time they spoke with any real honesty. He needed to try and find the words that might make a difference to Raleigh. Ridge took a breath. "Listen, I can't say I'm grateful for what happened, but in a way I wouldn't have figured on, I got something back. Something I didn't even know I'd lost. So for that, thank you."

Raleigh's eyes started from his head. "You're *thanking* me?"

"That's probably pushing it." Ridge could hear footsteps coming down the hallway. Tug. His heart lightened. He backed the chair and turned it toward the open doorway. "But Uncle Beau used to say people need love the most when they deserve it the least. I hope you get more than you deserve, Raleigh. I hope we both do."

ABOUT THE AUTHOR

A distinct voice in gay fiction, multi-award-winning author JOSH LANYON has been writing gay mystery, adventure and romance for over a decade. In addition to numerous short stories, novellas, and novels, Josh is the author of the critically acclaimed Adrien English series, including *The Hell You Say*, winner of the 2006 USABookNews award for GLBT Fiction. Josh is an Eppie Award winner and a three-time Lambda Literary Award finalist.

Follow Josh on Twitter, Facebook, and Goodreads.
Find other Josh Lanyon titles at www.joshlanyon.com.